Memory's Bride

Memory's Bride

The Burton Brides: Book 1

by Decca Price

KITTATINNY PRESS

To Betty

— we'll always have Longtown (and Clodock, and Lower Bache)!

Chapter 1

"YOU STUPID GIRL!" Claire cried out. "How could you?"

"I didna mean to, Miss, I didna!"

The young maid—she couldn't have been more than 14—shrank into the angle by the fireplace and began to wail.

That was how Miss Simms found them when she hastened into the room—mistress and maid both sobbing, the small girl cowering against the wall, the young woman crouched on the floor, salvaging bits of china from the Axminster carpet.

Ignoring the maid, Beatrice Simms placed her hand gently on Claire's shoulder.

"Claire! What's wrong?" she asked softly.

Claire lifted brimming blue eyes to the older woman's face. A tear traced her cheek as she raised an outstretched palm.

"His paw, his poor little paw! She's broken him, Simmie!"

She held bits of a small china dog that had stood at the back of her dressing room mantel for the better part of two years, a humble ornament lost among the fine porcelain objects that cluttered all the young ladies' rooms at Thurn Hall.

Turning to the sniffling maid, Miss Simms said, "Go downstairs, Parsons, and tell Cook I said you were to have a cup of tea. I'll come and speak to you later."

She pulled a plain handkerchief from her pocket and handed

it to Claire.

"Stand up, Claire. This is no time for nonsense. Accidents happen." Then, when the door closed behind the maid, she said more gently, "Come, dear, let me see it. Perhaps it can be mended."

Claire stood, handed the broken figurine to Miss Simms and went to the window behind them. Leaning her forehead against the glass, she sighed.

"What's the use, Simmie? It's just a trifle. Wrap it in some tissue and throw it away. I shouldn't cling to what might have been. Mr. Carter is dead, so Papa's won after all." She turned. "Give me a hug, and after I've composed myself, I'll find Parsons and ask her pardon."

"I hate to see you unhappy, Claire. But you must at least own that your father only wanted what's best for you. A self-made man, with no family or station to speak of..."

"Stop, Simmie. You know Mr. Carter was the best man in all the world to me and I don't care that he earned his fortune with a pen. Why is it that men who claim to respect hard work, discipline and brains scorn the ones who profit by it?"

Simmie had nothing to say on this point. Instead, she stroked Claire's shoulder. "Are you sure you don't want to keep this, my dear?"

"Yes, Simmie. Throw it away—no, give it to me. I should do it."

Claire rummaged through a drawer in the heavy mahogany dressing table beside the window and produced a bunch of tissue paper. Taking the china fragments from Miss Simms, she carefully wrapped them and placed the bundle in the wastebasket beside the dresser.

"Thank you, Simmie," she said, her voice steady again. "You've always been the best friend I could have. Your advice is good, even though I don't always like it. Not many girls are that lucky in their governesses—or their friends."

"Then I'll give you a bit more. Perhaps a visit to your Aunt Manwaring in town can be arranged. You could bid farewell to these 'what ifs' in peace, for no one would expect you to accept social engagements there, or not many, since she does not go out much."

Claire groaned.

"Aunt Maud—am I that desperate? She'll expect me to read her a sermon every night before bed, forgo sugar in my tea and dance attendance on her smelly pug—though, I admit, the last time I was banished to Aunt Maud's care, at least Napoleon's constitutionals in the garden took me out of the house twice a day. Still, even Perdition would be preferable to staying here."

"Claire—such language!"

"Oh, Simmie," Claire said irritably. Her short train twirled about her ankles as she began to pace. "I've been proper all my life and look where it's gotten me. I did everything right, yet life is passing me by. I went to the right parties, I wore the right clothes, I acquired the right 'accomplishments.' I said the right things— which meant saying nothing most of the time. Then I fell in love with a wonderful man who loved me. But that's when everything went wrong."

Claire stopped abruptly to face her friend.

"I've been lectured and preached at all my life about duty, Simmie—oh, don't look at me that way. You were just as bad as they were when it came to that. Tell me, what was my duty then, when Josiah proposed to me? I loved him, but I love my family, too."

Miss Simms said nothing.

"Tell me, Simmie. What choice did I have?"

"We always have choices," Miss Simms said, hoping she didn't sound like she was lecturing. "Letting someone else decide for us is a choice."

"Are you saying I should have defied Papa? What of the scandal, my sisters? And Mama would have been so hurt!"

"That was a choice, too, dear heart." Simmie paused. "They say our choices show us who we are, but I think accepting the consequences of our choices is the real test of character."

Claire reached out and took Simmie's hand. "You are so right. What's done is done, and regrets only make it worse. Send a footman down to the post office and wire my aunt that I am coming. At least I'll be able to mourn in peace there."

No sooner had the door latch clicked behind Miss Simms than Claire rescued the wad of tissue.

Revealing the small china spaniel, now missing a paw and part of an ear, she placed a kiss on its brown and white head.

It was the only present Josiah had ever given her. Claire knew the trinket was past repair, but a damaged remembrance was better than nothing at all.

To her dismay, Claire did not find Parsons in Thurn Hall's vast basement kitchen.

"To be sure, Miss, that girl's taken such a turn, I durst not trust her with the washin' up," Cook said brusquely. "I sent her to bed, she was that trembly. Jenkins will take her up a bit o' something after we've lunched."

Seeing Claire's stricken face, she hastened to add, "Don't be troublin' yourself with that 'un, Miss. She's been actin' like there's a ghost round every corner since she came to the hall. If she doesn't soon put her mind to bein' in service, she'll be back to the farm in no time. And won't my sister be put out at that, no doubt blamin' me. I told her—"

"I'm sorry, Cook," Claire cut in. "This is all my fault and I want to put it right. Being away from home so young must be dreadful. Is that tray for her? Let me take it up. I'm sure I don't want to create more bother for you."

"Well, if you must, Miss, it's not my place to stop you. But don't go spoilin' that girl. She needs to stop mopin' and get on with it."

Claire considered Cook's matter-of-fact statement as she gingerly navigated the back stairs to the servants' floor high under the eaves, balancing a tray laden with thick-cut bread, butter, a plain brown pot of tea and the jam tart she purloined from the platter destined for her family's own luncheon two hours hence.

"Get on with it."

Good advice for anyone, but how?

By her mother's lights, she lost her best chance for a good marriage by wasting her only season. The Burtons were comfortable but not rich. Each of the three Burton sisters could expect one season each, and Claire had had hers with no acceptable result.

She had been an awkward debutante, tall and angular. The close-cut dresses in fashion now suited Claire's considerably more womanly form better than the overly fussy puffed-out gowns and hoop skirts that had been in vogue when she was 18. The straight fall of the soft fabric on the front of her dress today accentuated her lithe body when she moved, and the elegant bustle added a subtle allure to her stride.

Coiffures had simplified with the change in couture, again to Claire's advantage. Sausage curls and ribbon cascades gave her the look of a tall poodle, while the chignon she now favored accentuated a slim neck and classic profile. Assiduous rinsings with a concoction of chamomile tea and lemon kept the red in her golden hair at bay.

But her failings went beyond appearance. She ignored Mama's advice on which men to flirt with and, truth be told, she refused to be tutored in flirting

Flirting wasn't the only skill Claire lacked, of course. Earning her living was out of the question, for reasons practical and social. Mama still hoped that by chaperoning the younger girls, Claire might catch the attention of a suitable widower, but at 26, her chances were fading.

More likely was a future at home with Mama and Papa, cosseting them in their old age, acting the favorite aunt to a multitude of nieces and nephews and settling into a round of family visits and the family's one annual trek to the seaside—too purposeful to be called a holiday—for one's health.

Josiah Carter had awakened her to a vision of sunny Italian landscapes, sparkling London salons, gay Parisian adventures and long, intimate evenings devoted to discussions of art and philosophy—never to be, her father had made plain.

Josiah said he would come back for her. She knew from reading the Fortnightly Review that he had gone to the States within days of his confrontation with her father two years ago. But he had returned weeks ago without a word. This, too, she knew only from reading the papers: "Lately returned from America, that celebrated novelist Josiah Carter, on the White Star RMS Oceanic." How like him, she thought in her giddy joy, to return to her on one of the fastest ships at sea.

But he sent no word to her. Perhaps he had forgotten her. Perhaps he had found someone else, while she waited patiently, unable to give or receive a word of reassurance under her family's sharp eyes. As she well knew, women flocked to his celebrity and then lingered to bask in the warmth of his smile.

Claire never questioned what he saw in her, out of all those women. She had been too happy.

And then came the black-bordered announcements in those same papers—a fall from a horse on a deserted country lane near his home.

"Get on with it."

Cook made it sound so easy. Claire suppressed an impulse to crash the tray against the wall and drown out her thoughts in the clatter of crockery against plaster and wood. But in this house ruled by the twin rods of propriety and duty, to show any strong feeling, whether grief or joy, was unacceptable. Tears were shed in private and quickly dried lest anyone should suspect. In fact, she had shed very few tears over Josiah, which pained her almost more than news of his death.

She carefully set the tray down in the dim, narrow hallway outside the cramped room Parsons shared with another maid, took as deep a breath as she could manage in her tight stays and rapped tentatively.

"Parsons? It's Miss Burton. I've brought you something to eat—and I wanted to say I was sorry for shouting at you. It was very wrong of me."

The door opened a crack, then swung wider.

"Oh, miss. You ought never to be apologizin' to me. Whatever will my aunt—I mean, Cook—say? She'll be that angry with me!"

"Never mind that, Parsons. If you must, the apology is as much for me as for you. A silly piece of china is nothing to get angry over. Accidents happen, and it's a poor person who can't accept that life is full of mishaps. May I come in?

Parsons stood back and made no attempt to hide her curiosity about what lay under the white linen cloth covering the tray.

The girl was so thin her dark brown eyes overwhelmed her pale face. She promised to be pretty someday, if she could get rid of the perpetual anxiety that marred her features.

"I hope you don't mind," Claire said as she set the tray on the deal dresser and removed the cloth. "I brought a second cup. Cook tells me you are from the country near Hereford and I would so like to hear about that. Someone very dear to me told me it is beautiful. He promised to take me there someday."

"Yes, Miss." Parsons bobbed quickly, then seeing Claire settle onto the one plain chair in the room, she perched on the edge of the narrow bed. "Yes! Oh, the hills is so beautiful—not like here. Surrey is kind o' flat like, Miss. Oh, sorry, Miss. It's not that it's not nice here..."

"That's all right, Parsons. Tell me the way you see it, not how you think I want to see it. I'm not likely to, after all, since Mama and Papa are not fond of traveling. Tell me all about it."

The time passed quickly, as in a rapture Annie Parsons talked about the land her family had farmed for generations and her lively brood of brothers, sisters and cousins. It was a rough life, Claire understood, but it seemed to have such freedom.

Her descriptions were so vivid Claire could see the clouds of apple and pear blossom blanketing the valleys in springtime and almost smell the sweet scent on the air.

Annie began speaking lines of poetry and Claire stopped her.

"That is so fine, Annie—where did you learn that?"

"My grand'da used to say that to me as we walked the hills. He was a preacher to folks round about who could'na get out much. I went with him sometimes. Isn't that the Bible, miss?"

"I think not, Annie. It was so lovely, if I brought you paper and pen, could you write it down for me?"

Annie did not blush or hesitate. "Readin' and writin' are not for the likes of me, miss," she said matter of factly. "What for would I need them? Nor could my grand'da and he did much for folks without 'em."

While Claire searched for a reply, Annie raised the subject that had weighed on her mind since the morning.

"Beggin' your pardon, Miss, but that china dog what I broke..."

"Will I be taking it out of your wages? No, Annie. I said it was just a trinket. A gentleman gave it to me because I liked the dog he took for walks in the park when we were in London. It was a darling thing, with long silky ears and big brown eyes—a lot like yours, Annie, your eyes, I mean—bright and affectionate and trusting. The three of us had such lovely strolls before I had to come home to Thurn."

"A pet, like?" Annie asked. "We had workin' dogs on the farm, and cats in the barn, and sometimes Pap would bring the baby lambs into the kitchen by the fire when their mothers wouldn'a have 'em, but there were'na place for pets. Moochers, Pap called 'em.

Claire sighed. "My friend wanted to give me a pup from his

kennel, but my Papa is a bit like yours, Annie. He can't abide animals in the house. He says they're dirty and that God meant them to serve us, not we they."

The pot was empty and Parsons had consumed the last crumb of bread and flake of tart before Claire realized the time. She flew to her room, tidied her hair and stepped into the dining room just as Papa was taking his seat at the head of the long, highly polished table.

"You are late, Miss," Papa growled as she slipped into her seat across from Mama and next to her younger sister, Frances. The youngest Burton daughter, Catherine, was seated to her mother's right. Her married brother, Cameron, lived in town with his wife, the absurdly named Delilah, and their three toddler sons. There was about as much romance in the young Mrs. Burton as in the plate laden with well-cooked roast beef and boiled potatoes sitting at Claire's place.

"Yes, Papa," she murmured, withdrawing her napkin from the silver ring by her plate. "I am sorry, Papa."

"As you should be. You know I detest waiting."

"Yes, Papa."

He applied himself to his soup, and the hour passed none too soon for Claire, consumed as it was with chatter between her sisters about fittings, flowers and gossip.

Claire said little, thinking instead about Annie Parsons, who seemed to be as starved for food as she was for comfort, and her mind wandered to the picture the girl had sketched of a happy home filled with warmth, laughter and a poetry unexpected in such a setting.

It was outrageous that such a girl as Annie should be dragged away from all that made her life worthwhile merely to dust the shelves of spoiled rich girls such as herself. And that the child was illiterate in this day and age—Claire could change that. Josiah Carter had wanted to start a school for country girls like Annie. They had spent hours discussing what it would look like, how Claire would encourage the teacher. If she did it quietly, she could tutor Annie Parsons...

"Claire!" Her father's voice cut into her reverie. "Must I repeat myself?"

"Papa?" She started and saw that her mother and sisters had

risen from the table.

"I said, I will see you in the library a half-hour from hence," Sir Henry said with deliberation. He levered his imposing bulk from the table and loomed over her. "I have a serious matter to discuss with you."

"Serious!" Mama fluttered like a startled peahen. "Whatever can you mean?"

"Nothing you need trouble yourself with, MaryAnn. It involves only Claire."

"Oh, Claire!" her sister Cat exclaimed in a low voice. "What have you done now!" Frances giggled nervously.

"It doesn't concern you, miss," Sir Henry said sternly. "Look to the log in your own eye before fussing over the speck in your sister's."

"Yes, Papa," the two younger girls said in unison as they rustled from the room with their mother.

Claire's stomach clenched. Could he have heard about the incident with Annie Parsons already? Or was it that he knew about her apology? Which would be worse in his eyes, she wondered. She resigned herself to another lecture on Woman's Domestic Duties and how to conduct herself with inferiors.

But she said simply, "Yes, Papa. In an hour."

Chapter 2

CLAIRE WAS SURPRISED to see three men standing by the fireplace—to her father's left was a gray-haired man of medium height in a well-cut dark suit and, to his right, her brother, a tall ruddy-haired man who could have been her twin.

"Cameron, it's good to see you down from London," she said, brushing a fleet kiss across his cheek. "How are Delilah and the boys?"

"They are well, thank you," he replied. "I had some urgent business to discuss with Father and saw no reason to pretend an interest in damp gardens when Mr. Chambers here arrived."

"Ahem, yes," the man Chambers said, eyeing Sir Henry with poorly masked distaste. "I do apologize for the interruption of my appointment, sir, but I trust the lady will find my information worthwhile."

Was that sarcasm the man was using? This was not going to go well. Papa was bristling already, she could see.

"This is my daughter, Miss Burton, sir," Papa barked.

"Miss Burton," the lawyer said, advancing toward her with a bow. "I am very pleased to meet you at last. Mr. Carter told me so much about you, but words failed even that great author when describing your beauty."

"There is no need for false pleasantries with my daughter,"

Papa said. "Please say what you've come to say."

The man was making her Papa uncomfortable, Claire could see, but she found herself at ease with Mr. Chambers' kind manner. He knew Josiah! She sat on the edge of one of the big leather wing chairs ranged before the fireplace, where burning coals failed to keep the chill off the room, and watched as he produced a sheaf of documents from a portfolio case.

"I have here the last will and testament of Mr. Josiah Colby Carter, late of Oak Grove Hall, County of Herefordshire, signed by his own hand on 12 March in the year of our Lord 1873, and duly witnessed. Mr. Carter being deceased on 29 March this year extant, I hereby discharge the duties entrusted to me as executor."

He paused and looked directly at her.

"Ordinarily, Miss Burton, I would read the will line by line to the gathered heirs, but in this case, it hardly seems necessary, since there is only you, and the minor bequests to former servants and charities don't signify. I have a copy that we can review together later, when you are ready, and I would advise you to obtain legal counsel of your own to keep matters above board. I don't hold with executors having absolute power in an estate of this size, though I hope Josiah Carter's faith in me was not misplaced."

Not sure she had heard correctly, Claire scanned the faces of the three men arrayed before her. Mr. Chambers looked grave. Cameron made no effort to conceal his awakened interest. Papa looked like a hound that had just scented a fox.

"What do you mean, Mr. Chambers?" she asked with rising alarm. Papa's expression hinted toward what the lawyer said next.

"It's only this, Miss Burton. You are an extremely wealthy woman. Mr. Carter names you as principal heir to all his estates, holdings, furnishing and chattel, copyrights, the lot. You are both his heir in property and his literary executor. The land and house at Oak Grove alone are valued at about £100,000 pounds and produce about £3,000 a year clear. Investments currently are yielding another £5,000 per annum"

Papa exploded.

"Impossible! She cannot accept. That man was determined to ruin my daughter from the day he met her. If word of this gets out, she won't be able to mingle in decent society. We refuse this insult!"

"You mistake the matter, Sir Henry. You cannot refuse. Miss Burton is the legatee," Chambers explained calmly. "What she chooses to do with her inheritance is up to her. She can sell Oak Grove, lease it, give it away or let it fall into ruin. She may allow the income to accumulate at her bankers untouched for her lifetime or squander it at all at Monte Carlo. But in the end, whatever remains will go to her heirs, whether she lifts a finger to direct its disposal or not. It is hers."

"There must be some way to refuse this," Papa blustered. "There wasn't so much as an engagement announced between them to give this a cover of respectability!"

"Father, think," Cameron interjected. "We're talking thousands and thousands of pounds here. People will gossip about my sister, yes, and there will be a few who snub her. But times have changed. The way we in society live now, her wealth will buy a lot of forgiveness. With this, she may even be able to look as high as a peer for a husband. Nobody flinches at these American girls coming over here and marrying into the best families. At least Claire is an Englishwoman."

"What about her sisters? This will be a terrible reflection on them as well," Sir Henry replied. "Frances is all but engaged to Lady Hapwell's son. This could ruin everything!"

"I'm sure Claire would not be close fisted, Father. You would make provision for them, wouldn't you?" Cameron addressed this last to her but did not wait for her response. "Besides, this money couldn't come at a better time for me."

Claire flinched. Cameron was becoming more like Papa every day.

"There's no question the property will have to be sold. Herefordshire!" Sir Henry spat. "That's practically in Wales. That damnable Carter couldn't even buy an estate in a civilized part of the country. It's not as though it was family land and he had to make the best of it."

"Papa!" Claire was standing now, too.

"Pardon my language, Claire. I ask your pardon as well, Chambers. This is most vexing, but that's no reason I should forget myself."

"That's not what I mean and you know it, Papa. You must stop disparaging Mr. Carter—at least to my face. And what will Mr. Chambers think of us?"

"I think I know what Mr. Chambers should think of us," Cameron said with a snort. "I'm sure men in Mr. Chambers' line see all sorts of families at their best."

"I am not paid to have opinions about my clients," Chambers replied. "I am paid to advise them to the best of my ability—and my advice to you, though you are not my clients, is to stop bullying Miss Burton. She is of age, and I heartily hope that she will follow her own dictates in this matter, as Josiah Carter desired. He wished to make her independent." He stopped short of saying "of you," but the unspoken words hung in the air.

"Mr. Chambers," Claire said to him, "why did he do this? He must have known how this would look to the outside world and that it would anger my father terribly."

"Josiah had great faith in you, Miss Burton. I have handled his legal affairs for a decade. Before he left for America, he wanted to be sure his legacy would be in the hands of one who truly loved him, should anything untoward happen to him, so he signed this will in the event he did not return."

"But he did return," Claire said half to herself. "He was coming back to me!"

An awkward silence filled the room.

"What happens next?" Claire asked finally.

"There are some papers to be signed, Miss Burton, and some formalities in the courts. But Mr. Carter has no living relatives and there are no claims on the estate, so I am authorized to advance any reasonable amounts to you, should you require. In essence, you are now mistress of Oak Grove. The house is but ten years old, with many modern conveniences, and well situated with fine views of the Wye Valley. A wire will give the household a day's notice of your arrival whenever you choose.

"And, Sir Henry," he added pointedly. "The Great Western Railroad has offered regular train service to Hereford for some time now. The journey is but four hours from Paddington station."

Sir Henry coughed. "You are correct, sir, that this estate should be looked to sooner rather than later. I am sure my daughter will take my advice and sell. It is too remote, and depending on servants to manage a property in absentia is foolhardy. I shall make arrangements to inspect it with my man of business. Perhaps you would work with him to find a buyer?"

"There would be no problem, there, Sir Henry. The present

Lord Montfort has been anxious to bring the land back into his hands since his late brother sold it to Mr. Carter to raise cash. Of course, it is considerably improved since then, but Lord Montfort can afford a handsome price thanks to his advantageous marriage."

"I don't want to sell, Papa."

"Nobody is asking you, Claire. Neither your mother nor I wish to be tied to a country house we have no desire to visit."

"Listen to Father, Claire," Cameron urged. "Think of the good you could do with the money."

"Pardon me, Cameron, but you seem overly concerned about how I can spend Josiah's money on other people. If you are in difficulties, we can discuss that before Mr. Chambers goes back to London. Mr. Chambers, I may give my brother money now, mayn't I?"

"Yes, Miss Burton. Depending on the amount and the circumstances, you may give, invest—or lend."

Cameron Burton shot Chambers a look.

"You see, Papa?" Claire appealed to her father. "I have no need to sell and I don't want to sell. Josiah loved Oak Grove. He grew up in the neighborhood. He wrote his best books there."

"You haven't even seen the place, girl! Didn't you hear what the man said—the house is 'modern,'—it's shoddy construction, no doubt, and lacking any sense of refined taste."

"I would at least like to see the place before making a judgment. I hope you would accompany me. You said there was paperwork, Mr. Chambers—shall we get to it? I'm sure Papa will allow us to use his desk. If you'll just excuse me a moment..."

Claire rose quickly and went into the entry hall, where Miss Simms was adjusting a large arrangement of dried flowers for the umpteenth time.

"Simmie, I need your help. Have someone send a wire to Aunt Maud. Tell her my visit has been unavoidably delayed and that I'll write to her tonight."

"Are you all right, Claire? You seem a bit feverish. What's happened?"

"I'm fine, Simmie. But the most extraordinary thing has happened. Prepare yourself for a journey to the West Country. We must go to Herefordshire."

Claire swept back into the library, head high and eyes a touch too bright. The documents could have been dealt with more swiftly, had not Papa continually paused to read and exclaim over the contents. With a few pen strokes, his eldest daughter was richer than he had ever hoped to be in his wildest dreams. The Burton family would rise in the world—if Claire remained obedient and if society, as his son stated, would overlook the stain on her reputation. He had no doubts about the former.

With the last paper signed, Claire put down Papa's pen.

"Is that it then?" she asked Mr. Chambers.

"There is one more thing, Miss Burton." He reached into his portfolio and produced a small packet. "Mr. Carter left this, to be opened only by you should this sad day arrive. I believe it is a letter."

Claire accepted the packet with trepidation. Perhaps here was the answer to her question. *Why, Josiah? Why make this strange gift to me?*

She handled the packet almost reverently, then felt a hard lump in one corner. She opened the envelope carefully and shook. A heavy gold ring rolled onto the desk.

She picked it up gingerly and held it to the light.

About a quarter-inch wide, the chased gold band was set in the center with three dark, equally sized amethysts. A motif of intricately carved vines and leaves, encircled above and below by single raised rows of black enamel, encompassed the diameter. The outer circumference of the ring was plain gold.

Without thinking, she slowly slipped the ring onto the third finger of her left hand. Her love had been a dream, Josiah a fantasy lover whose whispered promise lingered like a ghost as the dreary days followed one after the other for the past two years. The weight of the ring on her hand broke the lovely spell.

It fit perfectly.

She broke down and sobbed.

The night found Claire searching her heart and mind in a way that meant no sleep. The sensation of putting herself under a microscope, like one of the butterflies her brother Cameron used to bring into the schoolroom, was uncomfortable. She rose earlier than usual and was already going through her things when Simmie brought in her morning tea, listing for the maid she shared with her sisters what she wanted to have packed for London.

Miss Simms tried to help, but Claire gently rebuffed her.

"I am putting away girlish things, Simmie. I never understood that before—what it means to 'see through a glass darkly,' but now I think I do. I think you do, too."

"Tell me what you mean, dear."

"It's just this. Everyone—even Mama and Papa once—started life believing the world was created just for their enjoyment. We hear every Sunday about the 'vale of tears' we live in, but we all think that means somebody else. Look at Francie and Cat. All they think about is their next party invitation and when Papa will let them buy a new dress."

"Be fair to your sisters, Claire. They're just girls. Cat is barely 16."

"Exactly, Simmie. They are still girls. I am not. It's time I accepted that and got on with making myself useful to others rather than dwelling on my disappointments."

She picked up a lace scarf. "I won't need this at Aunt Maud's, for example. But Francie has always admired it, so I shall give it to her. I'll keep the garnet set Papa gave me for my 21st birthday, but I think Cat would look well in my diamante parure."

"Heavens, Claire! You sound as though you're planning to enter a nunnery!"

"I suppose I do." She picked up a bright cerise morning dress. "This would suit Francie's coloring very well. I can't wear merry things like this anymore."

"Claire! It's true you are no longer a debutante, but you are still young. You have plenty of time to meet a nice gentleman and settle into a home of your own. The queen was 38 when she was blessed with Princess Beatrice. Why, your own mother was 30 when Catherine was born."

"Yes, and she was 20 when I 'blessed' her, as you put it. And now that you mention Queen Victoria, I can think of nothing more noble than her devotion to the late prince consort."

"There are many good reasons why a widow chooses not to remarry, Claire. Her Majesty bore nine children in 17 years. When you marry, you will understand."

"No, Simmie, I shall never marry now. I gave myself heart and soul to Josiah. A woman can love that way only once, and not every woman is as lucky as I have been. The memory of our love will be enough to sustain me."

"And what in your girl's experience has taught you that?"

"Nothing, Simmie." She smiled sadly. "I just know it in my heart. Josiah believed it, too. You've read his novels. Remember, in "Lady Jacinta," where the antiquarian explains why her spirit continues to haunt the abbey ruins? 'Love seeks its own through all time.' Of course, she was in agony because Lord Thomas betrayed her. But Josiah and I, our hearts are connected in truth, Simmie. The ceremonies of men may not have united us on this earth as we wished, but nothing can break the bond between our souls."

"That novel was not one of his best efforts, Claire. 'Lady Jacinta' and her ghostly history were a little too sensational for me. I much prefer "Lord Morden." Mr. Carter's portrait of the girl Mary who marries her scholarly friend from childhood instead of the dashing lord who woos her is much more true to life."

"Is there any romance in you?" Claire asked as she gave Simmie a quick hug to soften the criticism.

Claire's mother displayed a gentleness toward her seldom seen since Claire had left the schoolroom and put up her hair. Whether it was anxiety to see her daughters settled well or a sense that they were becoming rivals as her youth faded, Lady Henry adopted an attitude of criticism toward her female offspring that was in sharp contrast to her fawning indulgence toward her son.

She entered Claire's sitting room that evening without waiting for Claire to respond to her knock.

"I don't like thinking of you brooding here alone," she said without preamble, "though goodness knows, the atmosphere downstairs is less uncomfortable with you up here. Your Papa is very good at putting out of mind anything disagreeable as long as it is out of sight. I'm sure he exaggerates, but you never should speak to him in a way that even hints that you disagree with him. Open defiance is unpardonable in a girl."

"Mama, he insulted Mr. Carter. He as much as said I had disgraced him and the family when I've done no such thing. And I spoke only the truth when I said that if my parents thought Mr. Carter was unsuitable as a husband, you should never have brought us together."

"Don't be blaming your blunder on your Papa and me, young lady. You were raised to know your place—and the place of others. Your sisters understand. If we mingled only with those of our station, society would be a dull affair. Look at your Aunt Maud."

"Because she spends her time with men of the cloth and ladies from the missionary aide societies?" Claire asked blandly.

"Don't be pert. It's unbecoming. It's your obstinacy that vexes your Papa so much. Two years, Claire! You should be married with your first little one at your knee by now. Instead, your sister Frances is likely to go to the altar before you, and that is so wrong!"

"Francie? Has she had a proposal then?"

"I don't like to speak out of turn, but your Papa and I fully expect a call any day now from Mr. Hapwell. He has been most attentive to Frances these past weeks, and to all the family. Even you," she said pointedly. "It can only mean one thing."

"But she can't love him, Mama—does he love her?"

"Claire, how can you be so—well, I won't say stupid, that's too disagreeable. I've raised all of my children to be good, sensible and responsible. You are all these things, yet this fanciful streak in you will be your ruin. All two people need to marry is mutual respect —"

"—and an income."

"Yes, you do see. Mr. Hapwell could have been yours if you'd but lifted a finger, but he quickly saw the lay of the land and moved on to court Frances. With her money and his connections, they will have a good life together."

"If that is all she wants, then I am happy for her and I will tell her so sincerely. But I wanted more, Mama, and I don't regret that I gambled everything and lost."

"I begin to see why your Papa has lost patience with you. 'Lost.' How dramatic. I suppose you've gotten that out of some book, like so many of your notions. And I believed education for girls was a good thing. Good money wasted."

"There is much wisdom in books, Mama. We live but one mortal life on earth, but our great English writers help us to see through the eyes of many others and enable us to look into our own hearts before we are tested by life's adversities."

"Pah! That sounds just like something written in a book."

"But Mama, I loved Mr. Carter and told him so. Men want to be first in a girl's heart, so who would want me now, even if I could forget?"

"Men are more practical than you imagine, Claire. The best marriages are based on practicality, and for many wives, loves does come with time. But love doesn't last without a sound basis in social background, family support and—yes—money."

Claire let that pass.

"You and Papa will excuse me from appearing at dinner?" she asked.

"Of course. With the mood your Papa is in at the moment, it would be best. "

After supping from a tray, Claire went back to her sorting, ignoring the hum outside her chamber as her sisters prepared for another night out on the marriage market.

Francie burst into the room without preamble.

"Claire! It's so dreadful and I'm so sorry you're leaving us! And I never said how sorry we were about Mr. Carter. Cat and I have talked about nothing for days but the latest installment in 'The Rector.' All the girls say it's so thrilling! Now we'll never know the secret!"

"Oh —" she caught herself. "You must be—devastated?" The girl's puzzlement was plain. Claire looked so normal. As always, her hair displayed its usual neatness, her eyes were calm, her apparel tidy.

"Was that Mr. Carter's new serial?" Claire asked quietly. "How ever did you get your hands on it?"

"Oh, you know. Now that Augusta and Lydia Fawn are both married and out of the house, Lady Fawn isn't paying nearly so much attention to the younger girls. Diana got a copy from Lydia Sitwell and once Cecilia was finished with it, she passed it on to me at the Maddoxes' party last Tuesday. You won't tell?" she asked anxiously.

Claire surveyed her sister. Another blond, she was not nearly as fair as Claire but more blooming. Arrayed in a billow of pale green organdy and tulle, with an abundance of pink satin rosettes cascading down her sleeves and the front of her skirt, she looked delicious and happy and innocent.

"No, I won't tell. You look very pretty tonight, Francie. Is this a special occasion?"

Francie blushed. "Mr. Hapwell has written to Papa. I think he will speak to me tonight. Thank goodness he did. Papa was in such a fret this afternoon, Cat and I were afraid he would make us stay in tonight. But he is ever so pleased about this."

"Are you, Francie?"

"Of course. I can't wait to have an establishment of my own and make my own calls without always trailing after Mama. I wish you could be so contented, Claire. Whatever will you do at Aunt Maud's?"

"I shall do good works and endeavor to be content myself." Claire picked up the lace scarf she had set aside for her sister. Wear this tonight, and I hope it brings you luck."

Francie embraced her with thanks and, clutching the scarf, swept out of the room.

Claire looked at her other sister, standing quietly beside Claire's desk, fiddling with the little china dog. Catherine's mind always was elsewhere or in a book, or both. She rarely volunteered what she was thinking unless asked.

"What is it, Cat?"

"I wish you were coming with us tonight, Claire. I wish I were going with you tomorrow. I wish I could help you."

Cat held up the china trinket she had been toying with and her solemn gray eyes searched Claire's face.

"He gave this to you, yes?'

"That's right, Cat."

"I've heard that if you hold something that belonged to someone you really loved, you can connect with them—on the other side. If I came to Herefordshire with you, we could—"

"Oh, Cat, stop. Where do you get these notions?"

"It's been in all the papers, people talking to loved ones who have passed over."

"Papers you're not supposed to be reading, dearest kitten! Besides, if you have been, you know that Mrs. Cook was exposed as a fraud last year."

Cat gently replaced the figurine on the desk.

"I only want to help, Claire. This can't be all there is, when two people love each other, can it?"

Claire pulled her little sister into a close embrace.

"No, my dear. No."

Chapter 3

THE BLOOD-RED RAYS of the setting sun transformed the sea of apple blossom flowing across the valley into a blaze of crimson. As the breeze stirred the trees, the glow flickered and danced like hearth flames under a blacksmith's bellows, petals falling in showers of sparks. Swallows darted in the gathering twilight black as bats, and the whisper of rustling leaves washed up at the rider's feet like surf pounding a distant shore.

In the far distance, a pale ochre house crouched on an island of green, where lawns ran down to the river, a bright line of molten steel shimmering toward the Black Mountains on the horizon.

There were lights on in the rooms, he could see from his vantage point on the ridge above. Wisps of smoke rose from the chimneys into the cool twilight air. So they had come at last. He fought the impulse to spur down the incline, ride hard up to the door and demand admittance.

The big horse stirred beneath him, responding to his rage. The need to bring the restive animal under control concentrated his thoughts and his emotions cooled. Best not to show his hand. Stay aloof and let his man of business do his job.

He watched until darkness enfolded the valley and the fire died away, the full moon transforming the blossom to silvery ash. Turning toward home in the chill of descending night, he gave no more thought to the people in the house. He wanted only what belonged to him. The man who had taken it away was beyond reach, but he was prepared to pay a high price to the living to get it back.

He expected his own house to be dark and empty, but light from the library in the east wing told him otherwise.

He flung the reins to the waiting groom. "See that he's cooled down properly this time or I'll have your post! He's had a hard ride." Then he took the treads of the grand curving stairway in the entrance hall two at a time, paused in his rooms long enough to splash water on his face and dashed back down.

The long journey from the main hall to the east wing gave him time to compose himself, and he showed no signs of hurry when he pushed open the door and strode into the room.

The firelight winked from polished brass, dark wood and cut crystal on the sideboard. Edward Latimer had availed himself of his whiskey, he saw. Latimer knew how to appreciate life's little luxuries when they presented themselves. The man lowered the periodical he had been reading, revealing a stark white clerical collar above a suit of black.

"I told Parker we'd dine in here tonight. I hope you don't mind, Montfort."

Rhys Fitzgordon, Viscount Montfort. He winced as Latimer casually tossed his title at him. He should be used to it by now, but it was bitter nonetheless.

"No," he said curtly. "With my mother and sisters in town, we should seize the opportunity to enjoy ourselves." He poured himself a short portion of whiskey, then carried glass and decanter to a seat beside his friend. "What news?"

"I daresay you've heard that woman of Josiah's is in the neighborhood?"

"I saw the house was occupied. I didn't think she would come herself. After I made my offer, I expected only that someone would hurry out to Herefordshire to take stock and make an exorbitant counter offer. Her refusal is merely a ploy to get a higher price. She scarcely took time to think about it."

"You should go and see her. I'm told she's pleasant to look at."

"That goes without saying, though God knows Joss wasn't always choosy in his women. But I intend to stay out of this affair.

If she realizes how personal it is, she'll turn the screws even harder."

"I was actually thinking that her seeing you would be to your advantage. A grass widow is always ripe for wooing, Montfort. You're a little the worse for wear, but most ladies prefer experience. They like a strapping figure and a glowering air as long as the face behind it is pleasing and the purse is deep. And you've got the title now, to boot. What could be easier?"

"Don't be obscene."

"A woman once fallen, Montfort. The charms that won her this wealth could just as easily be her undoing again. Or would you not mix business with pleasure?"

"Sometimes it's hard to believe you are a man of the cloth, Latimer. You think the worst of everyone."

"Only a realist. My profession requires deep study of human frailty, and the good Lord knows I see enough of it in my meek parishioners. Sometimes I wish one would rise to the level of actual sin. It would be more challenging, professionally speaking."

Latimer reached for the decanter sitting between them and poured himself a generous measure. Neither spoke, as Latimer studied his glass and Montfort stared into the fire.

Then, "I was thinking of paying a call myself tomorrow," Latimer said.

"Whatever for? What would your staid parishioners think?"

"My parishioners will admire my courage in risking moral contamination to save a lost soul. The remainder of the county will once again have their worst suspicions confirmed about the Church of England and their plain preachers will have fresh meat for their sermons next Sunday. Everyone will be satisfied."

Montfort frowned, and his friend continued.

"Besides which, a man with a suitable wife and a handsome income has a fair chance of becoming a bishop. She'd be far from suitable, but I'd be willing to give up the bishopric for the income. And perhaps could skip the ceremony. I'd make her sell you Oak Grove for a fair price."

Latimer grinned as Montfort shifted uneasily in his chair. "The scandal would force me to go to Italy or some other warm locale, of course. And Josiah Carter's papers—his manuscripts, diaries, letters—would secure me for life."

"For God's sake, Edward, be serious."

"I am serious, Montfort. Think of the irony, should I become Josiah's 'authorized' biographer! I want to meet this woman, win her trust." His face grew dark. "I want her to let me see Josiah's papers, Rhys. They may reveal something about Lucy's whereabouts."

Montfort put his glass down so hard droplets of whiskey splashed onto the tabletop. The use of his given name told him Edward Latimer was being serious now.

"Lucy! You think Joss knew where she went? Did he say something to you, Edward? Or are you letting yourself be fooled by his latest ridiculous plot? You know how he could take bits and pieces of truth and twist them into grotesque fantasies."

"'The Rector?' Yes, Josiah was definitely mining the past again for his latest best-seller—a parson arrives at his new living in the company of his beautiful young ward—though Lucy was my half-sister. It had all the usual trappings of his productions. Mysterious hints, dark secrets, melodramatic balderdash. 'Was she his daughter?' 'Was she his paramour?' et cetera."

"You should be grateful he died before he finished it. I may never live down 'Lord Morden.' Some people around here still look at me as though I murdered my wife. And the people who should know better are the worst. Thank God the tenants don't read novels, too!"

"Their wives and daughters do, I can assure you, Montfort. A woman used to be content if her cottage was snug and her husband didn't beat her. Now they complain if they don't have fresh doilies for the tea tray and their men don't surprise them with nosegays every other Tuesday. And the young ones! They all fancy themselves Lady Corisande waiting for their Lothair."

"Lucy wasn't like that."

"No, she wasn't."

The arrival of Parker with their dinner interrupted the silence that intruded like a third, unwelcome presence in the room.

Montfort worked his way through the food mechanically, but Latimer ate his chops, roast potatoes and early asparagus with relish. Finished with that, he poured himself a glass of port and moved on to the warm apple tart with cream, then eyed Montfort's portion.

"Going to let that go to waste?" he asked.

"By all means, Latimer. But if you don't mind, I'll make an early night of it. Stay if you wish. The cigars are in their usual place or Parker can get you anything else."

"I'll just finish this article I was reading. Pleasant dreams—and think about what I said, Montfort. Between us, we can both get what we want. If you are going to do nothing but send letters through your agent, I will strike while the iron is hot."

"Suit yourself."

"And Montfort?"

"Yes." He could barely suppress his disgust.

"It is too bad you didn't take Josiah to court over that book. It was a clear case of libel—unless you're keeping something to yourself. When you won, he would have been forced to sell Oak Grove back to you. Now you won't even have the satisfaction of thrashing him."

"He was my friend, Edward. Our friend—yours and mine and Lucy's. Let's not forget those days."

Despite the quality of Montfort's port, Latimer did not linger. Less than an hour after Montfort had retired, he let himself out a side door into the park and started walking. The rectory was less than a half-mile from Oakley Court and he had made the journey countless times since accepting the living from Montfort's father a decade ago. He knew the grounds as well as his own back garden and the gamekeepers were no longer startled to encounter him rambling the park at night. They nodded to one another, muttered knowingly about the effects of too much book learning and left him alone.

This night, the landscape was bathed in bright moonlight and he had to walk a distance just to escape the dark shadow the massive house cast across the terrace and formal gardens. He had no conscious destination in mind but soon found himself approaching the ancient ruins that once had been the seat of the Montfort clan.

Lucy. She had been gone such a long time now and her name was seldom spoken. She was just 18, and her sudden disappearance two years ago prompted gossip behind his back, he knew. But since everyone in his parish assumed she had run off—quite likely with Josiah Carter—they tiptoed around the subject when he was in the room. She was too pretty for her own good, they whispered, and that's what came of letting a girl run wild without a mother's firm hand to guide her.

But how could he not indulge her after her mother died five years ago, he asked himself for the hundredth time. She was his darling and his pet, and he did his best to protect her from a predatory world. If only she had listened to him!

The tongues had started wagging again when Josiah returned from America a month ago. Lucy was not with him, and it was evident to even the most skeptical after a time that he was looking for her.

Latimer's skin crawled every time he recalled that final confrontation before Josiah died. The man had been out of control, throwing wild accusations. He was fortunate they weren't overheard.

"You were her guardian, Edward!" he had shouted again and again. "She trusted you above anyone and you used that against her!"

It was true he had done his utmost to steer her away from both Josiah and Rhys as she blossomed into womanhood. Was that so wrong? They were flesh and blood like any other men. He knew they wanted her carnally. What man wouldn't? She was so temptingly ripe and with an unconscious come-hither look in her eye. Women were weak, and especially vulnerable at that age.

He wondered again how much Josiah had known about his last argument with Lucy.

Had Josiah truly loved her? Had Rhys? He thought not, since both had moved on to other women when Lucy was denied them—Josiah supposedly engaging himself in London and Rhys entering into his catastrophic marriage with that coal baron's late, intemperate daughter.

He barked out a laugh, startling a deer in the undergrowth close by the ruins. It crashed through the woods and in a moment the night was silent again, leaving Latimer alone with his thoughts.

What a set they were—three highly eligible bachelors, the envy of their respective peers. Manly and well-formed gentlemen of station and accomplishment. Yet here was he with no one to mourn him when he passed on, Josiah with only a whore for an heir, and Montfort so soured on matrimony that a 400-year-old title was apt to lapse with him when he expired.

He sank onto a mossy stone in the shadows, head in his

hands. What could he have done differently? Lucy was wanton, a true daughter of Eve. It was his duty to discipline her, for the sake of her soul if not her chances at earthly happiness.

Like this woman of Josiah's. Whether he had meant what he said to Rhys or not, he was obligated to see her, become acquainted if she was in the neighborhood long enough. Perhaps she was not yet hardened and he could awaken her conscience to salvation. She would need a strong hand then to keep her to the path, and that he could supply.

Rhys was still awake when he saw Latimer's dark form cross the lawn and head into the park. The moon had drained the landscape of color and nuance. All was black, white or gray, the shapes flat and edges sharp. Latimer seemed more a wraith than a man as he flitted out of sight.

Rhys turned away from his bedroom window and moved to pour himself another glass of whiskey, then stopped. He should hate the sight of the stuff now, considering what he knew about predilections for strong drink.

Instead he lighted a lamp, opened the center drawer of the escritoire and rifled through its contents until his hand touched a velveteen case buried at the bottom. He opened it to reveal a photograph.

Two boys stood on either side of a pony, with a little girl in a white pinafore perched in the saddle. They were on the gravel drive before Oakley Court's grand entrance, and Rhys could again feel the sun on his skin as they waited for the photographer to finish his work.

Lucy was so excited she could barely sit still. She had loved his pony so much Rhys had given it to her that day. She named him Caesar. Riding him, she said, made her feel like an empress. She was 8 years old.

Under Lucy's doting care, Caesar had lived to a ripe old age, spending his days grazing and waiting for the apples Lucy brought him every morning and evening. Latimer had been forced to put the animal down not long after Lucy disappeared. Laminitis, he said.

Rhys peered at the photo as if he expected the immobile figures to begin speaking to him. In place of the sepia tints, he saw again the rich auburn color of the ringlets surrounding Lucy's heart-shaped face. Her dark eyes looked straight at the photographer from under thick lashes. She adored the pony, but she worshipped Rhys' older brother, George.

Joss, on Lucy's left, had a protective arm wound around her waist. He was a reedy boy then, with a perpetual dreamy look on his face. He had aspired to be a great poet. When he came down from Oxford and found there was better money to be made by plundering the lives of his friends and acquaintances to churn out serial novels, he had spared only Lucy.

In three strides, Rhys crossed the room and pulled a leather-bound volume from the shelf. Flipping it open, he began to read:

"The first time Julian Corwin laid eyes on Lily Latham, he immediately ached to put brush and color to canvas. He knew in his soul, however, that while his prodigious gifts could capture her physical beauty, her ethereal spirit would elude his art despite his most earnest efforts.

"She was arranging the flowers on the altar of the ancient village church, and the rays of the western sun shone softly through the great chancel window, where the beams cast a halo of heavenly light behind her slender form. In glowing emerald, sapphire and ruby, the craftsman had depicted the Garden of Eden as an apple orchard awaiting the harvest. In contrast to the brazen woman reaching to pluck that first forbidden fruit, Lily's modest manner and grace of figure reminded him of the shy roe deer that grazed under the beeches in the park. Even the serpent that wound its gleaming scales around the trunk of the central tree seemed to turn its head away from her holy purity in shame.

"She spoke, and the angels sang. In that sacred moment, Julian bowed humbly to God and acknowledged that he could never be worthy of her. Only the man as pure as she, who won first her heart and then her hand, could have the right to taste those innocent lips and enter into paradise with her."

The novel itself, "Love's Labours Rewarded," was the last Joss published, its final chapter appearing in "All the Year Round" not long after he set off for America. It was claptrap like all the others, Rhys reckoned, but his treatment of Lucy had been the one true thing Joss ever put down on paper. The language was florid and the plot over the top, to be sure, but Joss had distilled Lucy's goodness and quiet gravity into the saintly Lily.

In the final chapter, Lily's love redeems the wayward Julian. Rhys considered Latimer's supposition about Joss's papers. Lucy had taken all her problems to George as a child. Was it possible, after George died, that she had turned to Joss to share the secrets of her heart?

Rhys returned the volume to its place and picked up the photograph again. He himself stood at Lucy's right, gripping the pony's bridle lest Caesar lunge when George triggered the photographic apparatus. He looked like most second sons, he judged, a little too stiff, not quite important enough to take center stage even if his father were a viscount.

And what had he wanted at that age? He could scarcely remember. Only a short span of time had passed, yet he felt he had lived a lifetime, and not well.

Lucy remained the enigma. He had expected her to want what all girls wanted—a comfortable home, a husband to look up to, a secure place in society. When he offered, she rejected him outright. When he tried to embrace her, she pushed him away and ran. If that weren't humiliating enough, she sent Latimer to say she never wanted to see him again instead of telling him herself.

He snapped the case shut and flung it across the room. It hit the wall with a soft thud and disappeared into the shadows.

With an oath, he seized the decanter and poured himself a full measure. His dearly departed wife, Isabel, had found refuge from him in drink. Perhaps he could as well.

The night brought a melancholy joy to Claire. As the day softened into twilight she saw her father and brother settled in the smoking room of Oak Grove with port, cigars and account books, gave a hasty peck on the cheek to Simmie, who was reading in the drawing room, and threw a warm India shawl around her shoulders before heading outdoors.

With a soft, "Come, Kip!" she left the house and retreated to a sheltered bench on the far edge of the garden behind the house. The red-and-white Welsh Springer trotting at her heels had followed her everywhere since the Burton party arrived at Oak Grove that afternoon.

They had been inside the house long enough to exchange introductions with the principal staff and begin discussing the arrangements for their stay when Kip dashed into view and with a sharp bark leapt onto the front of Claire's burgundy paletot.

"I'm sorry, Miss Burton," Mrs. White, the housekeeper, gasped as Noonan, the butler, hastened to capture the bounding dog. "Mr. Josiah, he spoiled that dog like a baby and so we've always kept him in the house. These dogs can pine so when they're not kennel-raised."

"Think nothing of it," Claire said. "Kip and I are old friends— for this is Kip, who traveled all the way to London and back?" At Mrs. White's nod, Claire sank onto the marble tiles and, putting her hands on either side of the waggling dog's head, she looked into its eyes. "How splendid that Kip remembers me."

"He must have picked out your voice among the others," Mr. Carey, the steward, commented. "These springers are uncommonly savvy animals."

"That dog's seen more of the world than I'm ever like to," Mrs. White commented as she watched the kneeling girl and happy dog with a frown. "Mr. Joss even took him all the way to America and back."

Much to Papa's displeasure, Claire let Kip stay close to her, except when they dined that evening and she handed him over to Mrs. White's care.

Now, as the breeze sighed through the trees, Kip settled at her feet with a grunt, and Claire leaned over to caress his silky ears.

All through the long day she had yearned for solitude. Now she let her thoughts drift as she drank in the perfumed air and caught the far-off shouts of men and the lowing of beasts bringing the work day to a close. The disk of the setting sun flamed above the mountains to the west, and golden light poured around her and through the orchard trees beyond the shrubbery, setting them aglow from within like so many paper lanterns.

The house and everything around her seemed unreal as the sensation stole over her that Josiah was here, watching over her, bringing her strength to continue in her resolve to remain true.

She felt his presence close around her, as enveloping and tangible as the soft cashmere around her shoulders. She shivered inwardly. How she yearned to hear him speak her name once more and feel the touch of his hand on hers!

She twisted the heavy amethyst ring round her finger absently and yielded further to the languor, thinking of the man whose love drew her to this place and now enfolded her.

As the light faded into a dreamy twilight, she drew from her pocket the letter she had read daily since receiving it from Mr. Chambers two weeks ago. She pressed a kiss to the words "To my beloved," written in Josiah's sweeping script on the obverse of the single sheet, then carefully turned it over. It was too dark now to make out the words, but she could have recited it from memory.

The letter was dated March 12, 1873. Mere days before he sailed, Chambers had explained when she asked.

My dearest one,

I write with a full heart as I set out for unknown lands and allow the vast Atlantic to divide us, perhaps forever. While I know not what awaits me in my journey—the perils of a savage sea, hunger and thirst in a wild and untamed land, bloodthirsty natives or, more horrific, the hardened hearts of outlaw men—I sail knowing that your devotion will remain as steady as the North Star I will rely on to guide me home to England.

That you are reading this, however, can mean only that my prudent preparations for the worst have proved necessary. None of my earthly hopes, pinned on seeing you again, shall ever be realized.

Now that you have had some little time to recovered from the first shock of learning my sad fate, I ask you to draw on the love you bear me for the courage to sustain this blow. Dwell not on my loss but turn your thoughts toward the future.

Such is my trust in your devotion that I vouchsafe all that is most precious to me into your hands. I leave in your keeping not just lands or money but the progeny of my mind and talent. I adjure you to love them, protect them, cherish them as you would our own babes, never now to be. Turn that maternal solicitude which is chief among your many virtues toward this task for my sake.

My darling, we will never meet again on this earth, but know that I died with your name in my heart and on my lips. Sad I was, indeed, to leave behind this life, and you, but know I am comforted by the knowledge that our spirits will someday be joined forever in perfect union.

Never have two hearts been so in harmony as ours, and never will there be such again. The angels decreed our love too sacred to be consummated on this side of heaven, but you will always in God's eyes be my dearest wife. I die happy knowing

you will be faithful until we are reunited in Heaven.
Until then, I remain
Your most eternally loving,
Josiah Carter

Claire dropped the letter into her lap and gazed into the distance. The mountains on the horizon stood out in black relief as the setting sun limned them in streaks of red, orange and gold.

Dear Josiah. He expected so much of her, believed her more than capable of fulfilling his sacred trust! "I will," she whispered as she clasped the letter to her heart and stood to return to the house. "I will do all that you ask and more, my love. Stay by me and guide me, and I will not disappoint."

She pulled her shawl closer and summoned the dog. Halfway down the path, she paused to survey this place already forming the center of her world. A flicker of movement on the low ridge beyond the orchard caught her eye. In the twilight she glimpsed a dark mounted figure overlooking the valley. With a thrill, she fancied it was Josiah, but the impression evaporated as quickly as it had come.

She turned and went into the house. It was time. Mrs. White had reluctantly yielded the keys to Oak Grove that afternoon, but Claire cared only about one. Gripping it tightly as the others dangled from the large ring, she turned left after crossing the entrance hall and walked determinedly toward the tower that dominated the south front of the house. Josiah's study. The place he wryly called his "theatre of the mind."

She turned the key in the lock and stepped into darkness. At either end of the room, heavy velvet draperies shrouded the large windows. Opposite her, moonlight shone weakly through a round window in the long wall, casting sickly patches of green, purple and red onto the floor and the dim shapes of furniture.

She sensed the room more than saw it. Josiah had described it to her vividly. Here he would pace through long nights working out dialogue, he explained, and act out thrilling scenes, such as the climactic duel in her favorite novel, "Lady Jacinta."

The tower reached above the attics of the three-story house. The wall before her comprised the principal part of his library, she knew. Handsomely bound books in tooled morocco and gilded calfskin marched in ranks up to the ceiling, filling it entirely except for the leaded-glass window he had commissioned for the room. In the far corner, a narrow iron stair coiled from the floor to a gallery halfway up.

In truncated medieval style, the window depicted Lady Jacinta leaning from the castle tower to greet her lover on the ground below. Golden tresses cascaded over her figure and down the battlements. The first time they met, Josiah said she reminded him of the woman in the window.

She touched her hair now with regret and imagined him caressing it. Alone with her (except for the servants, of course) in the London house Papa had taken for the season, Josiah once had boldly asked her to loose it for him, but she had been too shy. Before she could protest, he claimed a kiss as a forfeit.

Her fingers moved to her tingling lips as she remembered the pressure of his mouth on hers. She knew instinctively that he was more experienced than she in relations between men and women. That was to be expected. Too late, she wished there had been more kisses. She had no idea what happened on a girl's wedding night but she was sure it started with kisses. She shivered.

A cloud passed over the moon and blotted out what little Claire could see. Even Josiah's most vivid descriptions weren't going to help her find a lamp in this blackness, so she stepped back into the bright gaslit hall and locked the door behind her.

After Simmie had helped her prepare for bed, she lay in the dark trying to recapture the sensations she felt in the garden. Her breast ached as she tossed in the big double bed, and the moon set before she fell into uneasy slumber, hoping to dream of Josiah in the place he had loved best.

Instead, she dreamed of the watcher on the hill.

Chapter 4

Miss Simms was buttering her second slice of toast when the tranquility of the morning was interrupted by the Burton men.

"... the cellar alone would fetch a good price," Sir Henry was saying as he strode into the breakfast room. His son followed close behind, carrying a pocket notebook and a pencil. "The man knew his claret. We'll need to get someone out here to assess the stables, though. I had no idea Carter was such a connoisseur of horseflesh. There's more than one there, I've no doubt, we'll be shipping back to Surrey. That little bay mare would be capital for Catherine. I am astonished at how lucrative authorship could be!"

"Begging your pardon, Father, but Mr. Chambers did explain that Carter put a considerable sum into American railways after the war between the states," Cameron said. "He undertook a number of shrewd investments in that line."

"Hmm, yes. If she's not lumbered by the actual property, and with a sharp man to manage the portfolio, Claire may escape censure yet. A peer's not so particular about the source of his income if he merely has to confront his bank balance once a quarter."

He took the cup of tea Miss Simms handed him and waved away the dish of kippers she proffered. "Where is my daughter? Still abed? The journey yesterday was rather tiring, so I won't begrudge her the indulgence this once. We don't require her for our business."

"No, Sir Henry," Miss Simms said, trying to keep her voice matter of fact. "Claire has been out riding the estate with Mr. Carey these two hours."

"She's out alone with the steward?" He turned an alarming shade of red.

"Father, it's not so bad," Cameron said, tucking into a plate full of eggs and country bacon. "Carey will be more likely to let something slip in front of her than to us."

"Too right, my boy, too right. I just hope she remembers Carey is to meet with us in an hour. I don't want to spend more time here than we have to. We have a schedule to keep."

Miss Simms, meanwhile, had been listening to them with dismay as she kept an eye on the French doors that opened onto the long terrace at the back of the house. She soon heard the light tap of boots crossing the stone flags and picked up another delicate Wedgewood cup.

Claire stepped briskly into the room, clad in a close-fitting dark blue riding habit, the springer close behind.

"Sit, Kip," she said firmly, and pointed toward a spot by her feet. The dog flopped down under her chair with a contented sigh.

Sir Henry harrumphed.

Claire removed her hat, set it aside with her crop and gloves and accepted the fragrant tea. Her cheeks were becomingly flushed from the vigorous exercise and she was positively bursting with energy.

"Pardon me for not changing immediately, Papa, but I don't want to waste a moment. There is so much to see, and each thing is more amazing than the last. I had no idea a place could be so enchanting! Did you know Oak Grove has some of the best trout waters in the West running right in front of the house? Mr. Carey says the hunting here also is fine, though the shooting is a bit wanting."

Cameron looked up from his figures. "That shouldn't bother you then, sister, though I was unaware that you had an interest in angling. I never understood how a female who 'couldn't bear' to shoot a partridge has no compunction about chasing a fox over hill and dale behind a pack of baying hounds."

Sir Henry and all his children hunted. It was the one activity outside the drawing room in which he encouraged his daughters. Sport set the true country gentry apart from the upstart newcomers, he averred, and an active horsewoman was apt to eschew the vapors as a wife. He regretted the day his own wife had retired from the field. She became much more peevish and subject to headache, in his view, and his nocturnal visits to her bedchamber subsequently dwindled in frequency.

"It does not signify, except in terms of valuing the property. Make a note of it," Sir Henry told his son. "We won't be coming back for the hunting, and Mr. Hapwell more than hinted that the family can expect an invitation to Perthshire for the grouse this year."

Claire and Miss Simms exchanged a glance.

"Now that affairs are settled between him and Frances," Sir Henry confided, "his family will be wanting to improve our acquaintance. Catherine will stay at home with Simms, of course, and it remains to be seen whether he means to include Claire, under the circumstances, but you and Delilah can as good as count on it."

"Delilah will be pleased, though it will mean an outlay on a new wardrobe we can ill afford at the moment," Cameron responded.

"Oh, Cam," Claire said, feigning lightness. "I will gladly make a present to Delilah of whatever she needs—and Francie, too, Papa—as long as I don't have to go. Two weeks on a grouse moor with Mr. Hapwell and the Grimthorpes would be unbearable. There isn't a book in the place."

"It is a hunting lodge. People go there to hunt. Though that's beside the point," Sir Henry said. "It would be best that you refuse, Claire, even should Lord Grimthorpe be magnanimous enough to invite you. You could certainly plead duties to your aunt Manwaring without giving offense."

"I am very sure I shall be otherwise occupied, Papa." She rose from the table. "Isn't it time we see Mr. Carey? He will be waiting for us in the estate office."

Cameron waited for his father's explosion, but Sir Henry disappointed him.

"You may accompany us, if you wish, but please let me do the talking," Papa said. "By the by, I'd be very interested in knowing what Carey had to say to you on your ride."

"Mr. Carey is most knowledgeable about the home farm and the tenants, Papa. The property produced 80 hogsheads of cider this last season, and most of the apples grown here go into cider-making. With the railway expected to come closer to Oak Grove, Mr. Carter was planning to expand—"

"Claire," Sir Henry interrupted, "We can learn all that from the account books. I am more interested in what Carey may have dropped about problem tenants, poaching, whether the servants are helping themselves in the wine cellar and the like."

"I see." Claire quelled a surge of impatience with her parent. "I was more interested in learning from him which tenants were most in need of repairs to their cottages and who would benefit from improvements to their holdings. Mr. Carter had been discussing a drainage project that would greatly improve the land for growing hops."

"Hops! What concern to any of us are hops?" Sir Henry growled. "But make a note of that, Cameron—good potential for the cultivation of hops. And a branch line coming out this way from the town. Your contacts in the City should be able to flesh out the details."

To Claire's mounting annoyance, everything about Oak Grove met with Sir Henry's approval. From the trim clarence waiting for them at the Hereford station to the aforementioned wine cellar, his approbation grew along with his estimation of the pounds and pence to be realized from his daughter's windfall.

As soon as the equipage had turned from the public road onto Oak Grove's long drive the previous day, his appraising eye efficiently tallied up the verdant pastures, abundant livestock and flourishing fields whizzing by.

Even the house, which hove into view after a half-mile of traveling through neat rows of blossoming apple trees, drew praise, though if Claire were honest with herself, it was disappointingly ugly.

It was a massive square block, three stories high, with a dark slate mansard and a stocky tower rising above the roof line at the far end from their approach. At first, Claire assumed it was built of golden stone, but as she stood before it craning to see the white corbel line running under the eaves, she could see it was stuccoed. Flecks of mica in the slightly gritty surface glinted where the sun hit.

As fine houses go, it was wholly unremarkable except for its bulk. Six tall windows ran the length of both the ground and first floors at equal intervals, while smaller oval windows punctuated the top floor. The cornice and the window frames were plain and white. It was devoid of ornament and proportion.

The tower, Claire knew, was Josiah's library. The house faced west, and from the other side of the drive a smooth lawn sloped gently about 200 feet to the narrow river, which sparkled and played in the sunlight.

Three wide stone steps led from the oval graveled carriage-sweep to the porticoed entrance.

Exploring the interior would take her days. Papa intended to complete his inventory and return to Surrey by the end of the week, though Cameron might stay longer. He was welcome, of course, as long as he did not interfere with her plans.

By arrangement on this second day, Claire met with Simmie about 3 o'clock in the small sitting room off the conservatory to compare impressions. She had exchanged her riding habit for a simple plum day dress trimmed with lace. Delicate cameos adorned her ears and throat.

"Are you getting on with Mrs. White?" she asked her companion. "I am finding her rather distant."

"Yes, though she does run on a bit about the best way to brew small beer. I gather there is quite a competition in these parts on the best recipes. Your conference with Mr. Carey went well?"

"Much better than I expected. The talk was all bushels of this and quarterns of that, though. I want to know about the people here. I had no idea Papa knew so much about farming!"

"Men like Sir Henry and your brother do work hard for what they have, try as they might to give the world a different impression."

Simmie handed Claire an envelope. "This wire arrived a short while ago."

Claire examined it. "You did not read it?"

"No. You left the girl Claire behind in Surrey when we boarded the train yesterday morning. I no longer have the right to pry into your affairs, even as a friend."

Claire tapped the envelope against her palm and searched Simmie's face. "No regrets?"

"No regrets."

Claire tore open the envelope and read. The wire was short, but before she could say anything, Noonan rapped on the door and entered.

The unsmiling butler carried a small salver before him. "A caller, Miss Burton. Are you at home?"

Claire examined the calling card. "Of course. But who is Mr. Edward Latimer, Noonan? I don't know the name."

"He is the rector of this parish, Miss. A most distinguished gentleman and a friend of Mr. Carter's, if I may add."

"Ask Sir Henry and Mr. Burton to join us, Noonan, then show Mr. Latimer in. Oh, and tell Mrs. White we'd like tea."

"Very good, Miss."

Claire never imagined the word "beautiful" could describe a man. But Edward Latimer was so beautiful he took her breath away.

Latimer was taller than she, with the physique of the oarsmen Claire had discreetly admired on occasions at Henley, when the family party cheered Cameron on for Cambridge. He carried himself confidently and there was power in his stride as he crossed the room. His dark suit was understated but of good quality and he wore fine polished boots.

His face, still youthful though she judged his age at about 35, brought to mind an ancient marble statue of Apollo she once glimpsed in the British Museum before a shocked Simmie had hurried her and her sisters on to the next gallery.

His fair hair was thick and wavy. Neatly trimmed side-whiskers framed high cheekbones, a perfectly formed nose and full lips. His teeth were white and even. His eyes—clear and green beneath full lashes—were mesmerizing.

"Miss Burton?" he said in a rich baritone. "I beg you to pardon the intrusion, but I heard you had come into the neighborhood and felt I must call."

His eyes held hers a moment too long and the memory of that statue obtruded again. She broke the contact, only to find herself looking down at his trim waist and hips. She flushed, but to her relief he turned his sea-green gaze toward Sir Henry and Cameron, standing by the fireplace.

"I will not stay if I inconvenience you," he said to them.

"Your call is much appreciated, Mr. Latimer," Claire managed to get out. "May I introduce you to my father, Sir Henry Burton, and my brother, Mr. Cameron Burton."

"Indeed," he said coolly. "The pleasure is mine. I hope you are finding Herefordshire to your liking, sirs."

"And this is my friend, Miss Simms." Claire gestured to the sofa opposite. "We were just about to have tea, if you would like to stay?"

"That is most gracious of you, Miss Burton. Josiah Carter was a valued friend and a great personal loss to me as well as the neighborhood. I am glad for any opportunity to be better acquainted with one so obviously dear to him."

Claire felt tears well suddenly and she turned to dab them away before anyone saw. "Thank you from the bottom of my heart, Mr. Latimer. Perhaps now is not the time"—she darted a look at Papa—"but I would so enjoy the chance to hear your reminiscences and see Oak Grove through your eyes. You must have spent many happy hours here!"

"Well, yes, Claire," Sir Henry butted in. "Perhaps if the rector here isn't too busy with parish affairs, he could spend an hour with you tomorrow while we inspect the tenant farms with Carey. I want to get this business wrapped up and see us all back home again."

Latimer raised an eyebrow. "You are not staying long?"

"Certainly not," Sir Henry replied before Claire could speak. "It's all very fine here, not nearly as uncouth as I expected, but Claire is needed at home. Her sister has just accepted a son of Lord Grimthorpe's daughter. There are all sorts of things with which Lady Henry requires the assistance of her eldest girl."

"Papa." Claire put her cup down carefully. "Mr. Latimer will only be bored by our family affairs when he scarcely knows us."

She leaned forward eagerly.

"Mr. Latimer, it is by no means settled when I will be returning to Surrey," she continued. "I invite you to call again tomorrow or whenever you choose. Except for early in the morning, when I intend to ride, I am most likely to be found about the house and will make time for you."

Latimer took that as his cue to depart. "Thank you for your hospitality, Miss Burton." He stood and clasped her right hand in both of his where she sat, and she looked up only to fall again into those green, green eyes. Her pulse quickened. "I look forward to our next meeting."

"And I, too," she said, startled by the firm pressure he exerted before she could withdraw her hand from his grasp. She watched him with puzzlement as he took his leave of the others and walked out of the room.

The door had no sooner closed behind him than Sir Henry rounded on his daughter. "I demand to know what you are up to, miss. You know we are going back to Surrey by the end of the week."

"It is simple, Papa. You are going. I am not."

"Preposterous! Your Aunt Maud expects you in London next week. You sent your boxes already.

"No, Papa. My luggage was shipped, but Simmie helped me change all the labels. It arrived here this morning while we were with Mr. Carey."

"But, this is absurd!" her father spluttered. "Reason with her, Cameron!"

"It is her property, Father. How do you reason with a girl who has thousands a year clear?"

Nonplussed, Sir Henry changed tack. "Claire, child. Listen to what I am saying. No one knows you here. The neighborhood is bound to be tiresome, assuming anyone will even receive you. These back-country people can be very conservative. You'll do far better under my roof and among our set. On your own, with no man about, your own servants are likely to spite you behind your back! Surely you've noticed how they look at you!"

"Pardon me, Papa, but wasn't that the rector who just paid a call?"

"Don't delude yourself, Claire. The man has a duty to inspect newcomers in his parish. If he takes against you, you won't have a chance at holding your head up."

Claire appealed to her brother. "Cam, you live in London. You said the world is different now. Am I wrong to think I can stay here, as *he* wished, without—" her voice broke—"without shaming my family and my sisters?"

"The world is different, Claire. *In London*. I must agree with Father that your scheme to live here is not sensible. Sell this place and buy a villa in Hampstead or Highgate. Or if you must separate yourself from the family, don't be morbid. Travel, take a villa in Italy for the winter. To stay here will confirm the worst of the gossip that's circulating."

"Gossip!"

"Yes. Delilah says your name is on everyone's lips. It has been most awkward for her. You are nobody, of course, and wouldn't be recognized in the street, but Josiah Carter enjoyed a kind of faddish fame and was known everywhere as a ladies' man. What do you think your life will be like here?"

"Perhaps the people here would be more understanding. His friends would never believe him capable of the sort of infamy you suggest!"

Sir Henry threw his hands up. "Miss Simms. What have you to say?"

"I have decided to stay with Claire, Sir Henry. We intend to live quietly and do what good is possible with the money entrusted to her."

"You are both silly, obstinate fools. You will be the prey of cads and mountebanks. Only the worst scoundrels will accept charity from the hands of one they believe to be soiled."

"Father!" Cameron remonstrated. "You go too far!"

The blood drained from Claire's face. "Is that what you think, Papa? That I am—lost to the society of decent men and women?" She drew the telegram from her pocket and held it out to her brother. "Perhaps this may be no inducement to Papa then, and you will refuse?"

Cameron took the piece of paper and scanned it. "It's from Mr. Chambers. 'All is ready. Arrive first train Friday week.' What does this mean, Claire?"

"The papers are ready for me to sign putting the property in trust for you and your sons."

Cameron crushed the paper in his fist. "You've done more than enough already, getting me out of that Melmotte scrape. I'd've been ruined but for you."

Claire went up to her father, unable now to face her. "Look at me, Papa. You have nothing to fear. I will be 27 next birthday, with marriage looking more unlikely every year, even if I could consider loving another man after Josiah. I will live retired here. You will never have to see me again, or acknowledge me, if that is your wish."

"Claire, I beg you. Don't throw your life away. What am I to tell your mother?"

"Think of it this way, Papa. You will add a fine property to the family without the inconvenience of a disagreeable son-in-law." A sound halfway between a laugh and a hiccup escaped her lips. "I'm not sure you can say that about Francie's match."

Sir Henry inspected Claire as though seeing her for the first time. Clearly, he did not like what he saw. "It shall be as you wish, then," he snapped. "But when you've discovered your mistake, don't expect to come back to Thurn Hall as if none of this had happened. A woman's reputation, once lost, cannot be restored. You act without my blessing and the consequences will be on your head."

"I am sorry for it, Papa, but I wouldn't expect anything less of you," Claire said as her tears welled.

"You will have no contact with your sisters, and do not badger your mother with self-justifications or pleas to petition me for mercy."

He turned to his son. "We leave in the morning. Say your good-byes to your sister now. From henceforth she is no daughter of mine."

After their father stalked from the room, Cameron moved to Claire's side and took both her hands in his. "Please reconsider, Claire. Our father is too harsh, but I cannot agree with this step you're taking and I will have to abide by Father's wishes. You understand?"

"Yes, dear brother. I know you are dependent on him. I will see to it that Mr. Chambers sends you copies of the final papers, and annual reports on the status of the estate. There will be provision for the boys' education when they are older, and if ever you are in need, Mr. Chambers will have standing orders to supply any reasonable requests."

"Claire, I—"

"Go, Cameron. Can't you see Papa is anxious to be off? This is what I want. I loved Josiah and I told him so. My duty is to him now, regardless of what Papa thinks."

"But he's dead, Claire! Surely that ends any obligation. Many widows remarry, after a decent interval, and you were never even a wife. Life goes on! Mark my words, you'll see all this differently in six months, but the damage will be done."

"Is that what a married man likes to think about, Cameron, that if he's run over by a hackney cab, his wife will soon find a replacement for him?"

Cameron dropped her hands impatiently. "Yes, Claire. If, God forbid, something would happen to me, I hope Delilah would remarry. I love her. I wouldn't want her to be alone and unprotected. I would want her to be happy again, especially if she were still young."

Claire dismissed his statement with a gesture of impatience.

"This is different. Delilah would have to think about the boys, what's best for them, not just herself. I have been given a similar trust and will do my best to show Josiah's faith in me was not misplaced."

"You mean the copyrights? Claire, you are being foolish. With the help of Mr. Chambers and Carter's literary friends, you could discharge that obligation from Thurn Hall, Australia or the moon."

"There's more, Cameron, much more," Claire responded with heat. "Josiah had such dreams for this place, for the people here. I shared those dreams with him. I must try to make them happen!"

"Well, good luck to you then, Claire," he sighed. "You've had no education, you've seen next to nothing of the world. You'll soon find you are a lamb among wolves."

Claire offered her brother a grim smile, and Cameron next turned on Miss Simms.

"And you? She has some excuse, but you should know better than to encourage her. I shudder to think what sorts of notions my sisters have picked up from you unbeknownst to our family."

"I—"

"Don't accuse her, Cameron," Claire cut in. "She has been Josiah's chief enemy after my family and she did her best to talk me out of this step." Claire gave her a loving look and her voice softened. "I'm sure she only stays now because she wants to be here to pick up the pieces when I fail. But I won't. I won't."

Sir Henry and his son were gone at first light, and Claire felt relief mingled with guilt. She filled the day with rides about the property with Mr. Carey while Simmie wrestled with Mrs. White over the household management.

In the evening, she and Simmie settled snugly in Claire's upstairs sitting room, which overlooked the lawns and river, and worked on a scheme to open a village school.

When Simmie retired and a hush fell over the house, Claire threw on a warm dressing gown and descended to Josiah's study. After her first chilly nocturnal visit, she thanked the assiduous Noonan for the fire she found blazing in the enormous carved stone fireplace just inside the door, and the small jug of sweet cider simmering on the hob.

"Miss Simms's orders," he said curtly as he glided out of the room, which suddenly felt colder again.

At first it was enough to sit in the vast silent room and steep herself in memory. Their introduction at Mama's at-home. The chance meeting in St. James Park the next morning. The daily walks that followed. Shared glances down the table at dinner parties. Exquisite moments in the rare and always proper waltzes they shared. Encircled in his arms, she forgot the crowded rooms, the buzzing people, the hissing gaslight. Josiah created the world for her, then filled it.

His boyish good looks and animated manner suggested a much younger man. Thick wayward locks were forever falling over his impetuous eyes as he talked, to be flicked aside as his mobile hands helped shape the story pouring forth from his lips. Josiah loved to talk.

And how he made her laugh! At first she thought he mocked her gravity, but she soon welcomed his teasing ways.

Every stolen word, every secret glance returned in perfect detail as she sat before the fire in the heart of his private kingdom. And no wonder, she realized after three nights of this forced reverie. In the six months of happiness before they parted, their moments together numbered in the mere dozens and they were alone just three times.

On the first occasion, he mistook the time and called on Mama when she and the girls were out, finding Claire unchaperoned in the house. She should have sent him away, but the force of her desire to see him crushed all sense of propriety. The intimacy of his looks and touch were almost more than she could bear. Her blood fizzed like Champagne.

On the second occasion, in that same room, he proposed. How thrilling he had been, and so direct. *"Miss Burton, may I claim the right to call you by your Christian name always—and to claim you entirely as my own, body and soul?"* It was like a scene out of one of his novels, and she melted into his arms immediately. She lost all sense of time and place lost in his embrace.

The third occasion came that same hot, oppressive August day, when he strode angrily into the room to deliver Papa's verdict. Angry tears glistened on his chiseled face as he recounted Papa's insults. Papa and a footman cut off his opportunity to say more when they all but threw him out of the house.

There was no living with Papa after that, of course, and a month later, in the Times, she spotted Josiah's name listed among the saloon passengers sailing for New York. For a mad moment, she pictured herself dashing to Liverpool, seeking him on the bustling dock, flinging herself into his arms.

But she had never traveled alone, had no idea what trains went to Liverpool. She settled for a visit to Aunt Maud, to begin the weary months of pretending she was unchanged.

The night's chill crept into the room as the fire died. She drank the last of the cider, which made her oddly sleepy. So much to do, while she sat and dreamed instead. The school, the farm improvements. His papers. Unlocking the mystery of his bequest.

She thought about erecting a monument to Josiah on the grounds. Since news of Josiah's death, Carey said, strangers frequented the churchyard or drove up to stare at Oak Grove's front door. As the weather improved, they picnicked in the woods and Noonan discovered one daring couple spying through the library windows. Directing them to a sanctioned spot to visit might preserve their peace in the house.

Even if no one came, she felt, it was no less than Josiah deserved. He would want it.

A large portrait of Josiah in the style of Holman Hunt hung over the fireplace. Posing the great writer at his desk, the artist caught Josiah in the fever of composition. Against a dark, richly detailed backdrop, Josiah's upturned face glowed, his light grey eyes fixed on the characters of his imagination as they danced in the air like faeries, his pen poised above the parchment where he so deftly captured them.

Claire studied the enraptured face, the expression so unlike the petulant glare that marred her final memory of those beloved features. She frowned and drew closer. Hadn't Josiah's eyes been hazel? She couldn't remember.

Chapter 5

CLAIRE AWOKE SUNDAY unrefreshed. Rain thrummed against the windowpanes, but as she and Miss Simms set out for church, the sun broke through ragged clouds and a stiff breeze ruffled the surface of the puddles.

Claire passed up the fancy matched bays meant for the bright phaeton Josiah kept in his carriage house and opted for an unremarkable cabriolet hitched to a sober brown mare.

Still, she almost wished the journey longer than the fifteen minutes it took them to reach the church. "Honestly, Simmie," she said to her companion as they tooled down Oak Grove's drive behind the deceptively spritely horse, "if Josiah had talked horseflesh to Papa rather than literature, he could have won him over in the end. There isn't a one in his stable Papa wouldn't be proud to own."

St. Michael the Archangel stood just outside the village at the very top of the steep high street. Encircled by the centuries-old churchyard, it commanded a breathtaking vista across undulating ridges and valleys into the misty reaches of Wales.

Behind the Romanesque nave ran the walls of Oakley Court's extensive park. A small gate gave the family access to the church and village. Across the road, the ample rectory, built within the last 50 years, stood in its own handsome garden protected by an iron picket fence.

Claire drove cautiously around a handful of people walking in the road to the far side of the lych gate, where a small boy attended a half-dozen other equipages.

"It's Bobby Tressel, isn't it?" she said to him. "I've seen you about the stables at Oak Grove."

"Yessum," he replied. "I helps out there most days. I'm fixin' to be a coachman."

"Really! You look so young."

He gave her a defiant look from under the brim of his crooked cap. "I won't allus be. I'm 12 come Boxing Day."

"How right you are. My apologies. It's good to be ambitious." She handed him a coin and he took the mare's reins. "I needn't worry with you standing by, then."

They walked back toward the gate, Miss Simms pausing to admire the view and to read the weathered headstones nearest the churchyard wall.

"Shouldn't we go inside, Simmie?" Claire asked over her shoulder.

"But we're so early, Claire! There's scarcely anyone here yet. I daresay Mr. Latimer is still enjoying a last cup of morning coffee at the rectory."

"Yes, I wanted to be early. All I could think about last night was how awful it would be to parade down the aisle to our pew with everyone looking. Particularly as I'm not even sure where the Oak Grove pew is."

"Well, here's Mrs. White coming with the housemaids. They must have taken the footpath across the fields. She can guide us."

Not having seen the housekeeper in her Sunday finery before, Claire couldn't judge whether the woman always decked herself out so elaborately for church, but today she looked formidable in a costume of Paris green.

Her bonnet, which added a foot to her height, was a veritable bower of red and white cabbage roses. In her left hand she carried a reticule large enough to hold a small child and in her right she clutched a prayer book that must have been presented for some special occasion, judging by its size and extravagant gilding. The upstairs maid carried the woman's large black umbrella.

"Oh, Mrs. White. How thoughtless of me!" Claire exclaimed. "I should have told you to take the carriage on a wet day like this."

Mrs. White looked shocked. "And what about them, Miss Burton?" she said with a nod toward the maids coming behind her. "Besides which, it wouldn't be fitting."

"The wagon then," Claire said. "You would all fit in the wagon."

"We'll see, mayhaps," Mrs. White said. "Mr. Carter liked the horses to rest, like, on Sundays. He'd say bad weather on a Sunday was the Lord's way of telling us to take a day of rest—at home. Always enjoyed his little jokes, Mr. Carter did."

Claire forced herself to smile at the older woman. "Yes, yes, he did. Shall we go on? I am counting on you to show me where we sit."

Mrs. White threw her a disapproving look. "It's not for me to lead the way," she said and stood aside.

They paraded like ducklings through the gate—Claire and Miss Simms, then Mrs. White, followed in descending rank (and size) by the upper maid with the footman, the tweeny and the house boy, the scullery maids and the boot boys. So much for avoiding notice, Claire thought wryly. Though next to Mrs. White, she in her charcoal grey merino and ivory lace felt invisible.

The church was strange. The neo-Gothic parish church back home was graceful and light, every line reaching towards the heavens, but this church was low and bulky, rooted in the ground like a tree stump. Built of the local red sandstone, its Romanesque exterior suggested a fortress, fronted as it was by a massive square tower out of proportion to the building that squatted behind it. The principal entrance was a low arched door at the side sheltered by a peaked wooden porch.

Weathered stone carvings of fruits and vines surrounded the plain windows, which were glazed with clear diamond-paned glass. When Claire looked up at the corbels under the eaves, rudely carved faces grinned, scowled and leered back at her.

The interior was blinding as the morning sun bounced off whitewashed walls, unadorned except for elaborate blocks of text here and there colorfully painted into the plaster.

"We're just here," Mrs. White said at Claire's elbow, indicating a long box pew to the left high against the wall. Claire led the way up the shallow steps and they filed in, all chatter at an end. They sat in silence for a quarter hour before the church filled, an organ somewhere out of sight began playing the processional, and everyone rose.

Claire's thoughts turned to Josiah as two small boys in white surplices led the village choir down the center aisle, followed by Mr. Latimer in his vestments.

How many times Josiah must have sat in this very pew, joined his voice with these very people in song and prayer, gazed on these ancient walls!

She touched the old wood, worn smooth by the years and the touch of many hands. Just as he must have done so many times.

Claire peered over the edge of her hymnal to see a stout woman looking at her with open curiosity. They made the briefest of eye contact and Claire's slight nod was returned before the woman turned her attention back to her book.

"Lor', fancy that!" Mrs. White breathed. "She's not one usually to come off her high horse."

Claire endeavored to focus on the service.

As Latimer ascended to the pulpit, Claire glanced around the sanctuary and saw all female eyes, from maid to mistress, were fixed on the rector. Even Simmie wasn't immune. Now, in his element, he radiated authority. The sheeplike expressions reminded her of the women Josiah had attracted in London.

She, too, felt Latimer's magnetic pull. His rich baritone thrilled and compelled. She wondered why he had remained at St. Michael's for so long when men of lesser gifts advanced.

Latimer's subject, though, made Claire uncomfortable. At home in Surrey, sermons tended to be gentle admonitions to care for the poor, trust in God's wisdom and cultivate gratitude for one's place in the world.

For his text, Latimer took up the hypocrisy of the Pharisees, likened to "whited sepulchers, which indeed appear beautiful outward, but are within full of dead men's bones, and of all uncleanness." She shifted uneasily, unaccustomed to thundering rhetoric and dark admonitions to repent. His passion struck her as almost indecent and his subject out of keeping with the joyous post-Easter season. Papa definitely would have deplored the emotional display.

The congregation ate it up, however, and from the back where the villagers sat en masse, a few fervent "Have mercys" were audible. Dead silence filled the church when Latimer concluded, yet the worshipers rose with enthusiasm to sing the choir out with "Onward, Christian soldiers."

Altogether an unsettling morning, Claire mused as she gathered her skirts and led the way out of the pew.

A hand gently took her elbow and she turned to see the thickset woman who had caught her eye earlier. "Step out into the sunlight with me, Miss Burton. I would appreciate a word with you."

They passed under the small porch and onto the path, where small clusters of women halted their chatter and tried not to look obvious as they watched.

"Smile, dear. These biddies need to see that we are, if not old friends, at least acquainted. I am about to vouch for you."

Claire did as she was told and put a bright smile on her face.

"I am Mrs. Hanniman, dear, Miss Milford that was," the older woman said. "Your Aunt Maud and I came out together in ... well, never mind the year. She has charged me with looking out for you. She's told me all about your ridiculous father and none too soon. Why that man can't see that he just made matters worse for you..."

They approached a matron with two girls about the age of Cat and Francie, Claire judged. All three were well dressed and obviously "somebody" in village society.

"Mrs. Talwell, may I introduce you to my good friend's niece, Miss Burton?" Mrs. Hanniman said.

Mrs. Talwell bowed stiffly and indicated more than introduced her daughters, Margaret and Mary Rose.

"Mr. Talwell is the owner of the fine house you no doubt noticed just outside the village," Mrs. Hanniman said. "The decoration in the drawing room is said to be in the style of Mr. Adam. I'm sure you will admire it when you see it, Miss Burton."

"Er, yes," Mrs. Talwell responded. "Perhaps we will see you there. After you are settled in, that is. I warn you, though, we lead a rather retired life."

"And you are most welcome at Oak Grove." Claire responded as though Mrs. Talwell's invitation were genuine. "I and my friend, Miss Simms, intend to be 'at home' on Thursdays."

Simmie smiled, Mrs. Talwell moved on, and a few other ladies offered chill nods when caught staring. When the last of their stiff backs disappeared down the hill, Claire let out a laugh.

"I am quite speechless!! Would you have ever thought, Simmie, that Aunt Maud's managing reach could extend so far??"

Mrs. Hanniman said merely, "Now, you will come back with me for nuncheon. It's not far. Nothing elaborate, mind, since it's the sabbath. A cold collation. The boy can bring your gig along. We must get to know one another better."

"How can I thank you, Mrs. Hanniman? You've taken such a worry away, you can't know."

"Oh, I do know," the woman replied. "I came here as a bride 30 years ago and had a hard time of it then. There's still some who regard me as an incomer. You would have never stood a chance on your own, no matter the circumstances."

Claire looked around for Edward Latimer, hoping for a word or a glance, but the rector had not followed his congregants into the sunshine.

The trio set off. As they passed the boundary of the churchyard, Claire stopped. Simmie put her hand on Claire's elbow. "I know what's on your mind, dear," she said softly.

"It all looks so peaceful, so normal, I barely feel anything," Claire replied softly as she gazed at the worn lichen-covered headstones nearest the road. "These old churchyards have such melancholy charm. But *he* is in there somewhere. I must beg Mr. Latimer to escort me as soon as he is able. I dare not go in there alone."

Then she caught sight of two figures back under the trees, at the farthest reach of the enclosure. They were standing close and absorbed in conversation. One was Edward Latimer. The other was a tall woman in black who was gesticulating angrily.

Before she could get a closer look, Latimer took the woman by the arm and they disappeared behind the church.

No one called as the days passed. Not Mrs. Talwell and her daughters, and not even Edward Latimer, to Claire's keen disappointment. The quiet of Oak Grove was a shock after life at Thurn Hall. The routine making and receiving of calls with Mama had seemed positively tedious until there was no one to share the tea table with each afternoon but Simmie, though they had plenty to talk about.

So when Mr. Chambers' gig rolled up to the front door early Friday afternoon, Claire greeted him eagerly. Her dismay was evident when he plucked only his portfolio of legal papers from the seat as he stepped down to the gravel.

"A visit to the country is always refreshing, Miss Burton, but I must get back to London by the 4 o'clock train," he explained. "That should give us more than enough time to take care of matters without rushing and still have me at home to sit down to dinner with Mrs. C. at 9."

"Oh, I am so sorry you had to come all this way if you cannot bide overnight," Claire said.

"It's no bother. I wanted to see how you were settling in. If you don't mind, I could avail myself of some light refreshment while we dispose of the paperwork, and then we will have some time to chat."

"Of course. Let us go in and begin."

As he whisked the last of the papers back into his portfolio and Claire poured them both another cup of tea, Mr. Chambers sighed with satisfaction.

"Most suitable, I thank you," he said. "And if I may, Miss Burton: Please let me remind you again, should your mind or your circumstances change at any time, it is a simple matter to add codicils to the current document or change your will entirely. In fact, I advise all my clients to review their arrangements at least annually, not something most of them can be induced to do."

"I assure you this arrangement to provide for my brother and nephews meets entirely with the wishes of myself and my family."

"No doubt," the lawyer replied drily. "Always remember, dear girl, I represent your interests entirely and no one else's when it comes to your affairs. If you ever need counsel, I hope you will feel you may turn to me."

Claire murmured her thanks as Chambers continued.

"Now that the real property is taken care of," he said, "you need to think about Josiah Carter's literary property, principally his papers, any unpublished works that may exist and the like. Most of his work was purchased outright by his publishers, so those books won't bring you any money. His papers, diaries and unfinished manuscripts, on the other hand... well that is another matter entirely. Do you follow me?"

"Yes, do go on. Josiah talked a great deal about how publishing worked and I believe I understood most of what he said."

"Good. Now I've consulted with some of his colleagues, including his publishers, and there is great interest in getting a 'life' into the hands of the Josiah's devoted readers as quickly as possible. The publishing concern can recommend an author to produce a biography if you agree and are willing to give access to Josiah's papers."

"I will need to think about that," Claire said slowly as she considered the implications of the proposal. "I've barely had a chance to discover what there may be. I know there are some diaries, perhaps some notebooks, but I would have to review them before letting a stranger see them. I must protect his privacy and will feel an intruder myself, I know. I'm not sure I am ready."

"Well, this idea will keep. The more pressing issue is whether any unpublished work exists. There's 'The Rector' being serialized in the *London Journal*, half finished and the public clamoring for more. It's my understanding Mr. Carter brought the final chapters back with him from the States but never sent them to his publisher."

Chambers took a sip of tea, then shifted uneasily in his chair. "There is one more thing. Lord Montfort's agent wrote again increasing the offer for this property. I assume the answer is still no."

"Of course! Why can't he accept that?"

"The current viscount is known as a man who gets what he wants," Chambers remarked. "If he is in the neighborhood, you would be wise to keep that in mind."

"I don't understand."

"Out here in 'the wilds,' as your father would put it, a peer still rules with an iron fist if he chooses. The family own just about everything around you, including the village itself, and it's said the current viscount exhibits a savage temper when crossed. This land you now own had been part of the Montfort holdings since the 15th century. There was a fine Tudor manor house here until it was pulled down to make way for this house."

"I appreciate your advice, but I don't see what harm his lordship could do me." She rose and offered her hand. "Thank you so much for coming, Mr. Chambers."

Claire's bravado dwindled as she watched the dapper lawyer climb back into his hired gig and drive away. As he disappeared down the drive, she felt her isolation more acutely. Determined not to give in to the megrims, she hurried back into the house, donned a bonnet and light cloak and set out to walk off her mood.

Feeling adventurous, she headed through the garden and into the wood that gave the house its name.

Soft shafts of light filtered down through the vaulting branches of ancient trees, and a bird shot through the hushed space, glimpsed then gone. A winding path of wood chips cushioned her footfalls and kept her skirts from peril as Kip trotted close behind. Careful pruning preserved the appearance of wildness without exposing the nature lover to brambles or leaf stain. Along the fringe, young ferns raised their curled heads and a few late dog violets bloomed.

Claire rounded a curve and stopped in astonishment.

As far as she could see in every direction, bluebells carpeted the wood with vivid color. A faint aroma like honey wafted on the breeze and she caught a low insect hum that heightened the air of enchantment as her senses filled. Bewitched, she drank it in and experienced a surge of bliss.

Movement at the edge of her vision broke the spell. She spun right and caught sight of a dark figure receding into the woods. A second glimpse suggested a woman, shrouded in black, and infused with purpose. Kip saw the gliding figure, too, and quivered before bounding off in pursuit.

"Kip! Heel!" The dog ignored her. Claire hesitated, then followed.

In barely a minute, Claire lost sight of both, but she plunged on through the undergrowth. The wide path had dwindled to a mere track, but crushed vegetation indicated a rough trail and she continued without thought, guided by the ever-fainter sound of Kip crashing through dead brush. The woodland grew dimmer as the high tree canopy blocked the sun. Claire felt chill as shadow blended into shadow and twigs caught at her skirts. She picked up her pace, alive to the deepening silence around her. Kip had vanished, and the woman—had she even been real?—was gone as well.

Alone now and disoriented, Claire emerged panting on the edge of a large meadow. Massive blocks of stone lay scattered among the weeds, and on the far side of the site stood high broken walls of brick and stone.

Claire immediately recognized the famous Montfort Abbey ruins—how could she not? A lithograph of the romantic scene formed the frontispiece of the novel that launched Josiah's fortunes and a larger version—hand tinted—hung over the fireplace in his drawing room. A companion picture on the opposite wall showed the abbey before the Roundheads despoiled it during the English Civil War. The artist of the latter painting showed brave Lady Jacinta Montfort trysting with her fugitive husband in the orchard adjacent to the castle. That part of the scene bit at Claire's heart—the loving Royalist couple gazes at each other in bliss, ignorant of the sorrow soon to befall them at the hands of the Roundhead enemy.

Alert for any sign of the stranger, Claire advanced slowly into the ruins of what once was the sacred heart of the abbey. The large, eyeless windows of the transept at the western end soared high above her, but the entire southern side was rubble. The northern wall retained a few broken mullions, and tall weeds grew where grand doors once guarded the sacred space. The choir, though open to the elements, most resembled its intact state, and with a little effort, Claire imagined how glorious the stone carvings, vast stained glass windows and gilded bosses must have looked before the destroyers fell upon it.

Across what must have been a courtyard two centuries ago, Claire made out low, irregular lines of stone and brick. Eager to explore what she supposed was once the main block of the castle, she hastened toward them seeking Lady Jacinta's tower, the mysterious woman forgotten.

The haphazard path dwindled into a stand of stinging nettles and she ran forward—only to be seized from behind.

She shrieked and, feeling herself released, spun around.

"Mr. Latimer!"

"Miss Burton!" He seemed equally astonished. "I... I thought..."

"Oh, but you frightened me!" Claire gasped with relief before he could finish. "I was closeted with my solicitor all afternoon and just had to get out. And then I thought I saw someone in the woods and followed her here—I wonder if too much time indoors has me seeing phantoms where none exist. You must think me very silly indeed." She offered the rector a sheepish smile. Mr. Latimer did not smile in return.

"She?" he asked pointedly. "You followed a woman? Here?"

"Yes. I suppose she must have been one of those literary 'pilgrims' Mr. Carey has been telling me about. Apparently we are to be plagued with trespassers now the weather is fine."

Latimer frowned. "This is a dangerous place to be trespassing. Take my arm, Miss Burton, and I will show you what I mean."

Claire hesitated. "Perhaps you would just lead the way and I could follow behind?"

"Come then—but slowly, and mind where you step."

She followed as he moved a scant three yards beyond where he had stopped her. He gripped her forearm and drew her forward.

"Carefully, Miss Burton, carefully," he said, his voice gravel in her ear. Then as she stood close by him, he said sharply, "Look down."

She peered over the low, broken wall and gasped. Instead of weedy ground and shattered stones, emptiness yawned. She jerked back, her head spinning.

"The old dungeons," Latimer said. "It's a 30-foot drop in some places. The locals stay away from here, some because they know it's dangerous, more because they believe—or tell their children to believe—the old tales of hauntings here. For a stranger like yourself, curiosity could be deadly."

"That woman! What if she doesn't know?"

"Go home, Miss Burton. I know these ruins well and will take a look around to see if anyone is here. It could be she was on her way to visit a servant friend at Oakley Court and passed on before you arrived." His expression lightened. "Do not worry yourself. I am here."

He escorted her to the edge of the meadow and left her with a courtly half-bow. "I hope to see you again next Sunday," he said.

Halfway across the meadow, she turned to see him watching her and gave a little wave. He remained motionless, like a sentinel. When she entered the woods, she looked back again. Latimer still hadn't moved. She felt a little ashamed, not only caught chasing shadows but by him.

Claire's liking for Oak Grove grew somewhat as she began to grasp the ingenuity Josiah's architect had employed for creature comforts. The house itself might be ugly, but in addition to modern conveniences like cold running water with just the turn of a tap in the dressing rooms, the house was equipped with gas lighting in the public areas of the ground floor. Light was produced, again with just the turn of a valve, thanks to a small coal-powered gas plant out of sight (and smell) of the house.

Tonight, she and Simmie relaxed before a cheerful fire in Simmie's rooms, discussing the mystery woman and Claire's encounter with Edward Latimer. The soft light cast by the paraffin lamps created a sense of safety and intimacy.

Kip, already back at the house when Claire returned, now lounged at the hearth by their feet.

"... but now I reflect on it," Claire said, "she couldn't have been a servant. She was too far away to make out much of her costume, but she had the figure of a lady, with full skirts and a regular hat and veil. In fact, I fancied we saw her Sunday in the churchyard."

"No doubt it was someone from the Great House. One of the young ladies, perhaps," Simmie said. Acknowledging Claire's raised eyebrow, she added, "That's what Mrs. White calls Oakley Court—the Great House. This"—she made a sweeping gesture—"is the New House."

"But why would one of the Montfort ladies be walking through Oak Grove wood? Surely they are too grand." Claire reflected on her behavior and sighed.

"If the Montfort ladies are like their brother, they still regard this as their property. Though it does seem unlikely that a fine lady would be walking unescorted. A better question would be where was she coming from?"

"Visiting a tenant?"

Simmie scoffed. "A Montfort? On foot? Visiting tenants?"

"Are they that awful a family?"

"Well, Mrs. White says..."

Claire laughed at her friend. "I'm beginning to feel jealous, Simmie! You and Mrs. White are becoming thick as thieves! She is still quite cool toward me."

Miss Simms tsked good-naturedly and continued. "Mrs. White says the Montforts are cursed. Blood was spilled to get the land and the land demands blood every generation to hold it."

"Oh, gracious heavens!" Claire scoffed. "That's fantastical."

"We're out in the real country now, remember," Miss Simms admonished. "You'd be surprised how superstitious people still are today. In fact, I've a notion for a project. I want to learn all those local stories and write them down. This is a veritable faeryland, compared to other parts of England. It would be a shame if they were lost."

"You mean write a book? That's a marvelous idea! We'll be quite a pair of scholars, won't we, Simmie? I can see us now, buried in heaps of papers, fingers smudged black, burning the midnight oil. I fancy I see a dab of ink on your nose now."

Miss Simms touched her nose involuntarily, then smiled. "I was thinking of something a little more modest, but who knows?"

Claire leaned forward to pour another cup of tea but the pot was empty, so she sat down on the edge of the small velvet settee to face her friend.

"Simmie, will you be happy here? Be honest."

Miss Simms smiled and patted Claire's hand. "Don't worry yourself, my dear. Life promises to be much more interesting here than under Sir Henry's roof. I don't intend to miss it."

"Speaking of Papa's roof, Simmie, —what do you think of offering Annie Parsons a place here? She is from this county, I learned before we left, and I need a lady's maid. I believe she could learn. I don't require much in that way regardless. But would it be wrong to bring her under this roof?"

"I think it's a capital idea, Claire, but it's for Annie and her family to decide. Write to her aunt. That way, if they say no, Annie will be none the wiser. Now, why don't I help you into your night things and let you retire? I admit to a selfish desire to put my own pen to paper."

"You are a gem, Simmie. What if you become a famous authoress and go off to be feted in London? I shall be quite lost!"

That night Claire entered the library determined to put her reveries aside and work. Mr. Chambers was right. She owed it to Josiah and his legion of admirers to overcome her reluctance to invade his private papers and find any remaining publishable work as quickly as possible.

She lighted the lamp on Josiah's desk and gingerly sat in *his* chair. Where to start? The top of the desk held only the lamp, a fresh blotter, a letter opener, a pen tray and the first two volumes of *L'Île mystérieuse*, the pages mostly uncut still.

The room looked different from here. The fire warmed this

corner, but darkness swallowed the light before it reached very far. She craned her neck, but shadows concealed the gallery and bulky drapes blocked both exterior light and sound. She could have been a hundred feet underground or on the moon, for all the rest of the world mattered. She suddenly felt small and abandoned.

On impulse, she hurried to the far windows and tugged at the heavy velvet panels until a gap opened. Masses of clouds obscured the moon, so all she saw was her own reflection staring back at her —a white-faced woman with pale hair streaming over her shoulders. She jumped even as she realized that she was the ghost in the glass. Chiding herself, she forced herself to go back to the desk. She had never been so fanciful at home.

She slipped her fingertips under the edge of the first right-hand drawer and gave a tentative pull. It opened smoothly, to reveal an array of pen nibs and holders, ink wipers, nubs of sealing wax, a box of safety matches and a broken pocket watch.

She tried the other drawers and found jumbles of papers and what appeared to be letters, some bundled with string or ribbon and others loose. The top left-hand drawer held smoking paraphernalia and more writing accoutrements.

She spent the next hour sifting through the papers, scanning them for Josiah's hand, but they seemed to be nothing more than a collection of circulars, bills and letters from admirers. Weary, she rose, blew out the lamp—and froze.

A flicker of movement to her right, a glimpse of a face at the window before it vanished. This time, she knew it was not her own image she'd seen. Out on the terrace, someone had been watching her.

Heart pounding, Claire schooled her breathing to still her thrumming nerves. She willed herself not to look toward the windows. It could have been anyone—a gamekeeper's lad heading out for night patrol, even Cary, her steward taking a constitutional before retiring.

Eyes fixed on the library door as if she were preparing to send her horse at a particularly difficult jump, she walked out of the room the picture of calm. But restless dreams plagued her sleep, dreams filled with flitting dark forms and the silent featureless figure of a man, watching and waiting.

Chapter 6

ONLY THE RHYTHMIC thud of his horse's hooves on the soft ground penetrated Montfort's reverie. As he cantered down the twisting green tunnel formed by high hedgerows and arching oak boughs, he ignored the intermittent drip of moisture left from the morning's shower until one icy spill plunged down the back of his collar.

"Damn!" he exclaimed, pulling up to adjust the collar of his black melton chesterfield. But the shiver he felt next was caused less by the cold water trickling down his spine than the sound of a pure soprano voice lilting on the air, singing, of all things, "Kathleen, Mavourneen."

> *"...hast thou forgotten this day we must part?*
> *It may be for years, and it may be forever..."*

He urged his mount forward.

> *"... why art thou silent, thou voice of my heart?*
> *It may be for years and it may be forever..."*

Montfort had suffered through a half a hundred renditions of those sentimental verses in a dozen overstuffed drawing rooms, warbled by simpering misses angling for a husband. This invisible singer invested the song with a heartfelt longing that lured him, siren like, to hear more.

He rounded a turn in the lane and encountered a large gray hunter plodding slowly down the grassy center. The singing came from the far side of the horse but he could see no one. The song stopped abruptly in midline.

"Is that you, Bobby?" a light voice asked. Then a woman's face peered round the hunter's withers and he saw that a hand gripped the horse's bridle on that side.

"Oh," she said. "I thought you were my groom. Ridiculous thing—the bit broke as I took Toddy here over a hedge about a mile back. I sent Bobby to bring me another mount so I could continue on to the village."

Lively sky blue eyes looked up from under the brim of a smart ladies' topper. A lock of burnished hair escaped from the snood at the nape of her neck and he noted with approval the way her womanly figure filled her dark fitted habit. Mud splashed her full skirt halfway to the waist. And a very trim waist it was.

He dismounted for a closer look. Just under 17 hands, he decided. Young but no longer a girl. Her clear complexion, freshened by exercise and the cool morning air, was the soft pink and white of unfurling apple blossom.

She was uncommonly pretty, he decided, and her quick smile on greeting him carried no trace of calculation. He caught her cultured London accent immediately, but she lacked the smug look of the self-aware society beauties he knew.

A slow blush crept above her snowy cravat to brighten her cheeks further as he boldly studied her in silence. She stared right back at eye level without flinching, though. Even her delicate earlobes reddened, and he noted with interest the faint throb of her pulse just beneath. There was a fresh ripeness about her that intrigued him.

"You must be new to the neighborhood," he said at last. "Either that, or a fool. No one else would try to jump in these fields at this time of year. As you must have observed, it's rather wet." He stepped forward. "Take these."

Thrusting his reins into her hands, he turned to run his hands over her horse's legs. "He looks sound, but he's too young for a lady to ride securely." He then examined the restive horse's mouth. "He appears unhurt."

"We did not fall, sir, and I did not cut his mouth," Claire said warmly. "Toddy is a capital boy. The bit broke, but I was able to control him. I've been riding since I was four and I never put my mounts at risk."

"My apologies, ma'am. I am told I can be rough about the edges. I was merely concerned for your welfare." He took back the reins. "Allow me to introduce myself. I am Rhys Fitzgordon."

"And I am Miss Claire Bu—aoof!" Toddy gave Claire a mighty shove with his head. She slipped in the muddy cart track and went down on her derriere with a squish.

Montfort stooped, wrapped one arm around her waist and lifted her easily from the ground. Beneath whalebone and petticoats, his experience confirmed, there was a strong lithe body likely worth the trouble of seducing out of its carapace. He liked his women with both curves and muscle.

He pulled her closer, ostensibly to bring her to drier ground but really to gauge her reaction. It was not his habit to despoil virgins. To his dismay, instead of sighing into him, she responded to his embrace like a schoolgirl. With more blushes and stammers, she wiggled out of his grasp and jumped back a good three feet. Right down in the puddle again.

"Miss Claire, be more careful. Let me help you again," he said, lips quirking. This time Montfort extended his arm to the lady. She clasped her hands around his wrist firmly, pulled herself erect and quickly disengaged. She was breathing heavily, he observed, though the exertion was slight.

Claire felt scorched, first by this man's gaze, then the physical contact, even through gloves and clothing. Where his speech was arrogant, his dark eyes were challenging. What flustered her most was the knowingness he did not attempt to hide. "I know you know," those eyes said, and dared her to respond. Know what?

Seated above her, he had stirred only her curiosity. He sat easily on the big black, regarding her intently. A countryman's slouch hat gave him a dashing air in contrast to the meticulously groomed steed and gleaming tack beneath him. Clearly, he was a man of quality, so she relaxed and let herself smile a little at him.

But when he dismounted, her hand tightened convulsively on

Toddy's bridle and her senses sharpened. The dripping trees and lowering sky underscored their isolation in the narrow lane. No one could see them. On the other side of the hedge, a million miles away, a raven squawked, but she heard nothing else over the thrumming pulse in her ears.

He was taller than she, and filled the space they shared. Unlike the pale young men who squired her sisters and friends from picnic to party to ball, he was bronzed from the sun. A thin red scar ran across his left cheek from his brow to the corner of his mouth, giving him a quizzical look. He wore tight buckskin riding breeches that emphasized his powerful thighs and he moved with an assurance that suggested a life in command. She tried to imagine him seated at Mama's tea table and failed.

Time slowed, stopped. She forced herself to stand firm while keen eyes studied her top to bottom. She was acutely aware of the mud on her dress, the tendril of hair creeping round her cheek, the damp seeping into her boots.

At first she thought his eyes were black, but as he came closer, she saw wide pupils surrounded by irises of the deepest brown flecked with gold. He was clean-shaven except for a thick but neatly trimmed moustache and she wondered what other eccentricities formed his character in an age when men of all ages luxuriated in abundant facial hair.

"Are you a fool?" he said in sharp voice.

She drew breath to speak. Then Toddy butted in.

Too shocked after landing in the mud, Claire would have laughed, but Fitzgordon seized her before she could react. Surely no gentleman, even under the guise of helping a lady, would be so—she flailed for a word—so *personal*, regardless of the circumstances.

Before breaking free, she inhaled leather, plain soap and an unfamiliar musky pungency that went straight to her knees. Unsteadied so, she stumbled and fell again.

And experienced his power again as he plucked her from the mire.

She felt gauche under those appraising eyes and tried to think of something to say. The words that came out of her mouth shocked her.

"Do you always inspect the ladies you meet in the same way you examine an injured horse?" she said quietly.

"Don't you, Miss Claire?"

"Pardon?" She didn't quite catch his words.

"Don't all ladies scrutinize each other with the same fervor that men apply to horseflesh and equipage? My sisters maintain that women are the best—and the least forgiving—judges of other women."

"Oh." She bit her lip and tried again. "I only meant to ask if you are always so attuned to your companions as you are today."

"Are we talking horses or ladies now?"

"I think you are determined to misunderstand me," Claire laughed uneasily.

"Pardon me," he said gravely. "I 'inspect,' as you put it, only where I am in the market." Again those dark eyes raked her length.

"I, I see."

"Do you? I think not."

She looked away this time, conscious that she was blushing again.

"That is not a criticism, Miss Claire, but a compliment."

"Oh." Claire tried to steer the conversation into more conventional channels. "You mentioned sisters, Mr. Fitzgordon? Are they still at home?"

"My two sisters much prefer town to the country, as most ladies do." He frowned at her. "They find the hunting there more to their liking than what is on offer here."

"There is no hunting in London, sir," Claire tsked. "As you well know." She couldn't say why she was allowing this man to unsettle her, but he was doing an excellent job of it.

"True," Fitzgordon replied. "If you mean foxes and pheasant. But those animals hold no interest for my sisters."

"Oh." Toddy tugged at Claire's arm and she soothed him with a series of shooshes. Turning back to Fitzgordon, she said, "Your sisters do not actually hunt, then? In the field, I mean?"

"Not in the field, no. But they are experienced trackers, if you take my meaning."

She dropped her gaze "Perhaps we should not be discussing your sisters in this fashion."

"Perhaps not."

He turned his horse to head in Claire's direction.

"I presume the Bobby you expected is Bobby Tressel?" he said.

Claire nodded.

"In that case, we had best begin walking. I saw the young scamp dawdling by the stream as I passed by a half-hour ago. All the Tressels are layabouts. You'll be back to your stable before you see him leading a fresh horse your way."

"How disappointing. I was so anxious to be in the village this morning." She searched his face for signs of displeasure and saw none. "But you were going that way. Please don't let me keep you."

"If you are to believe I am a gentleman," he said, "I should act like one. Just as your purchases can wait a day, so can my business."

He began walking and she matched her step to his.

Piqued by his assumption, she felt an urge to justify herself. "I was going to inspect a building I'm told would make a suitable school," she said, annoyed by the priggish note in her voice.

"A school?"

"Yes. I'm told the peer who owns practically half the county hereabouts can't be bothered to provide more than the basic education for his tenants. It is an appalling lack of responsibility, if you ask me! Promising young people should be given the chance to realize their potential no matter their class, even go to university if they have the ability."

He said nothing and she warmed to her theme. "We live in an age of progress, Mr. Fitzgordon. Yes, it's the law of the land that schools must be provided for children, but no one makes it possible for them to actually go. No one can force their parents or their employers to set aside the time. And this lord seems happy to keep his tenants in ignorance. It is a positively medieval, not to say short-sighted!"

"Perhaps he never had reason to give it any thought. Perhaps he has been away and allows his stewards to do their jobs without interference."

"Then he's criminally negligent besides," she responded hotly.

"And what gives you the right to trespass on his ancestral privilege?" His words were calm but deliberate.

"A great misfortune, Mr. Fitzgordon," Claire replied more temperately. "The death of a great man has given me the power to do much good in the world in his name, and this school was one of his dearest wishes."

"A village school—on my land?" he said in the same clipped tone.

Claire halted abruptly. "Your land? How can it be your land? I thought this was the seat of the Viscounts Montfort."

"At your service, my lady," he said with a sweep of his hat and a mocking bow. "Rhys Fitzgordon, sixth Viscount Montfort. As you so aptly observed, our holdings in the county go back to Henry IV."

"Oh," she breathed. "But you don't look anything like Josiah described you."

"Joss Carter?" He stepped so close now she would have retreated, but Toddy blocked her way. "Just who are you?"

"I'm Claire Burton. I've just taken up residence at Oak Grove."

"Damnation!" Fitzgordon thundered. "You are the woman who refuses to sell me my land? You, you're—"

"I'm what, Lord Mortfort?"

He took a deep breath.

"You are like nothing I pictured," he said more calmly. "I expected Miss Burton to be somewhat more... mature."

Claire tugged at Toddy's bridle and began walking again.

"And what difference does that make, Lord Montfort?" she asked as he kept pace.

"Well, for one thing, I see my agent has been wasting his time. If you will give me the address of your father or the man who heads your family, I will apply to him directly."

"You will still waste your time, my lord. My Papa has already tried and failed. I mean to make this place my home now, despite my family's wishes."

"For God's sake, Miss Burton, tell me why. Why leave friends, family, a life of interesting amusements and pursuits in town, to bury yourself in the country?"

"I already did tell you. I have been given a great trust and mean to fulfill it." She turned her candid sky-blue gaze on him. "It seems more than you do."

Montfort's brow blackened. "This is my home, Miss Burton. My heritage. I have an obligation to my family to see that what was theirs remains theirs. My late brother never would have sold the property to Josiah Carter if he thought it would go out of the family entirely in this way."

"Was there some agreement between them then, when the sale was done?"

"On paper, do you mean? No."

"Then perhaps Mr. Carter thought I would be a better steward than you, Lord Montfort." Claire raised a gloved hand to her brow and peered ahead. "Just as it seems you misjudge your neighbors. I see Bobby bringing me a fresh horse. I will bid you good day."

Montfort seldom found himself at a loss for words. But as he watched that infernal woman's back recede down the lane, he failed to pluck a pithy rejoinder from the welter of thoughts competing for his attention.

The audacity of the woman! *By God, the way her hips sway is fetching.* What the hell had Carter been up to with her? The idea of his proposing a school was laughable. A school! *She must have capital legs under those skirts—see how she springs with ease onto the nag.*

He willed her to look back at him as she settled onto the sidesaddle, her wet skirts clinging to her rump and thighs. *That arse is as plump as a two nestling partridges...* She disappointed him.

Montfort prided himself on discerning what a woman knew. Her eyes usually gave her away. If not, a heightened tension in his presence betrayed the more calculating ones. The uninitiated enjoyed ease in his company through ignorance.

But this one—her veneer of innocence threw off his judgment. He watched until she trotted out of sight and the boy leading the other horse dawdled away across the fields.

The sky darkened and an annoying drizzle began to fall before he mounted and rode in the same direction down the lane. In his mind's eye he saw her flashing blue eyes again, then imagined how they would look clouded by passion. He wanted to redden her lips with savage kisses and watch her flush, this time under his pleasuring hands.

Miss Claire Burton, indeed. Before he was through, she would utter his name in a far different manner than she had that day. By the time he reached home, he had plotted the opening salvos of his campaign.

"What an insufferable man!" Claire blurted before she saw Simmie was not alone in the morning room. "Lord Montfort is everything I heard. Unfeeling, arrogant—"

"Do go on, Miss Burton," Edward Latimer. "You seem to have captured the viscount's character in an instant. But, pray, how did you meet him?"

"To be fair, he did offer to help me," Claire said with less heat. "Toddy's bit broke," she explained to Miss Simms, "and I was walking him back when Lord Montfort came upon me and offered his assistance. I had no idea who he was, of course, and he had the effrontery to conceal his identity."

"Conceal his identity?" Miss Simms was astonished. In her experience, peers tended to flaunt their titles.

"He was dressed more like a country gentleman than a lord, Simmie, and he introduced himself as Mr. Fitzgordon."

"I see," Latimer said. "That's easily explained. Montfort is the second son and came into the title only a few years ago, after the tragic death of his elder brother. He does not carry it easily. When he is not in London, he tends to forget himself."

"You know him well?" Claire asked.

"Yes. I know Montfort about as well as I knew Josiah Carter, dear lady. I'd been down from Oxford scarcely a month when Lord Montfort, that was, presented me with the living here. Joss and Rhys Fitzgordon were only boys then, and they were inseparable in those days. And, thanks to my dear late stepmother, they were also in and out of the rectory like it was their own home."

"But surely, the age difference gave you little in common?" Miss Simms interjected.

"I like to think they saw me as their elder brother," Latimer said, "especially Rhys, since his own brother was so seldom at home. Alas, my influence could not overcome the pernicious influences of Oxford and London. He turned into a wastrel."

His face grew grave. "I do not wish to alarm you, ladies, but do not allow yourselves to be alone with the present lord. It grieves me to say that he once attempted to debauch my young sister."

Claire busied herself at the window to hide her reddening cheeks. The thought of Montfort's hasty embrace fanned unexpected heat in her belly.

"Forgive me," Latimer said behind her, misunderstanding. "This is hardly a fit topic for a lady's ears."

"No, Mr. Latimer," Claire said, turning back to face him. "If it does not pain you, I would like to hear more. I want to be sure I did not misunderstand Lord Montfort's intentions this morning."

"He is sly as a serpent," Latimer said matter of factly. "He approached my sister under the guise of an honorable lover and led her to believe he intended to propose marriage. Fortunately, I saw through his ruse in time and opened her eyes."

"How terrible!" Miss Simms exclaimed.

"Will we have the honor of being introduced to Miss Latimer?" Claire asked.

"I would be most pleased," Latimer responded, "but my sister has left the neighborhood."

"Very wise. I understand," Miss Simms murmured. She failed to notice Latimer's clenched fists, but Claire did not. *Poor man,* she thought, *to love somebody so and to see her hurt by a person you trusted!*

"Mr. Latimer," she said, "if it's not asking you to repeat gossip, what happened to Lord Montfort's brother? You mentioned a tragedy."

"Drink," Latimer said. "If it isn't gambling or other vices, the Montforts give themselves over to drink. The brothers were imbibing one night in the cider house at Oakley Court and one of them apparently knocked over a lamp. Flames engulfed the building before Rhys could summon help."

Miss Simms and Claire both gasped. "That's horrible!" Claire cried. "To see your brother die before your very eyes!"

Latimer hesitated, then said in a low voice, "Rhys escaped without serious injury, though he bears a scar from that night. It is but a tiny mark for a man who claims to have barely survived an inferno."

"I saw it," Claire remarked.

She blanched at Miss Simms's next words. "Do you mean to say Lord Montfort was responsible for his brother's death?"

"Perhaps not in the eyes of the law," Latimer replied, "but his conscience can tell him whether he is guilty in the eyes of God."

Latimer stepped closer to Claire, took his hands in hers and gazed down, searching her face. "Do not be agitated, my dear. I most sincerely beg your pardon. I would wish to keep this unpleasantness from a lady, but sometimes it is better if the lamb knows the nature of the wolf."

Claire looked up into his intense green eyes. "Your concern is most appreciated," she said softly, allowing her hands to remain a moment too long.

Her heart beat a little faster. This man could never match her Josiah, but he embodied solicitude that she found both comforting and flattering.

Miss Simms dropped a book with a loud thud and attempted to look startled. "Claire," she said, "perhaps Mr. Latimer would like a turn in the garden. It looks like the rain has stopped."

Latimer looked pleased. "You wish is my command, Miss Burton."

No sooner had they stepped off the terrace and onto the gravel path than Latimer offered his arm and Claire accepted, striking the correct balance between formality and friendliness. But when Latimer tucked her hand more securely into the crook of his elbow, she did not resist. He was as solid as oak, and she felt security in his closeness.

At her touch, gratification surged through him like the heat of Montfort's fine whiskey, radiating from his solar plexus and settling finally in his nether regions. No painted Jezebel, as he half feared, Miss Burton affected an outward modesty that enticed. Her smooth face bore no traces of past calumny. Alert to the slightest hint of art in her manner, he detected none.

He noted that her sober dress conveyed wealth without going in for display. She again wore some dull purple color and a minimum of ornament. Spotless gray gloves concealed her hands, but to his annoyance, no bonnet covered her abundant tresses, suggesting she felt a little too casual in the presence of men. Their short acquaintance hardly warranted such informality. In the sunlight, he noted, there was an unmistakable reddish hue to her hair.

He frowned and confined himself to small talk until their stroll brought them to an octagonal summer house hidden in the shrubbery, out of sight and hearing of the main house. He steered her toward it, half hoping she would decently refuse.

"Miss Burton, I hope you will not think me too forward if I make a comment? No? Then let us go in where it is sheltered. I have wanted to speak with you on a serious matter since we met."

Claire assented, giving him only half her attention, he noted.

"Mr. Carter loved this place," she exclaimed as she stepped up onto the small porch and preceded him into the cool dimness. Her delight struck him as unseemly.

The young leaves of climbing roses clinging round the windows gave the interior light a green cast, as though the room were under water. Between the windows, panels in the French style displayed exotic birds and fish limned in gold paint. Bamboo furniture amply strewn with soft cushions invited relaxation, but Claire went directly to an ornate table on the far side of the room.

She ran her fingers lovingly across the smooth surface. "He talked so often about the hours he spent here."

"You were very fond of Josiah," Latimer said, watching her closely. The face she turned toward him seemed innocent.

"I loved him with all my heart," she said.

"That is not quite what I am getting at," he said, dropping his voice. He opened his arms toward her in appeal. "I hope to be your friend, Miss Burton, but I also have a duty to my parish."

She moved behind the desk and, with her back to him, began to toy with the antimacassar on the tall desk chair.

Pleased at her unease, he continued more firmly. "My friendship, you understand, can make all the difference in whether you are accepted here. I am respected, people look to me as an example. If they know I call on you, they will call. If I find I must shun you…"

"Friendship requires honesty, or it is a dead thing," she said, turning to face him again. Her set mouth and rigid posture belied her calm voice.

"I am glad you see it that way." He chose his words carefully now, anxious to project sympathy as well as authority. "Love, or what young ladies think is love, can lead them to make dreadful mistakes, mistakes that can never be undone, mistakes that ruin their happiness and the happiness of their families…"

"You are thinking of your sister?"

"You do see what I mean." He shifted his stance, clenching his hands at his sides. "This is most awkward, believe me, but I must ask." He moistened his lips. "Miss Burton, you were not too fond of Josiah Carter?"

Pride and indignation mingled in her expression.

"Are you asking whether I am all a lady should be, Mr. Latimer?

The rector's cheeks flamed. He did not like the challenging tone of her voice.

"Do not distress yourself, sir," she said stiffly. "My father and brother warned me of such suspicions if I ignored their advice. As long as my conscience is clear, I cannot let the opinion of others keep me from fulfilling the trust Mr. Carter put in me. But my own Papa, it grieves me to say, used such shocking language to me, I will never forget it."

She was crying now. Latimer fumbled through the pockets of his coat, produced a fine linen handkerchief and thrust it toward her.

"Thank you, Mr. Latimer." He watched as she quickly dried her tears. "Please pardon my ridiculous display. I didn't realize how difficult this would be. I pretend I am not lonely for Miss Simms's sake, but I fear she is lonely, too, because of me."

Seeing his advantage, he seized it. "I could assist you, if you will let me."

"Do you really think you can alter your congregation's opinion of me??"

"I can also help you put Josiah's papers in order. I have the advantage of knowing him since he was a boy, which makes me peculiarly suited to sorting the wheat from the chaff, as it were."

"Mr. Carter's solicitor says that Josiah's readers are clamoring for a biography. He suggests I hire an author as soon as possible to begin the work."

"And you told him what in response?"

"That under no circumstances could I allow anyone to read Mr. Carter's private papers before I've reviewed them myself." She offered the rector an apologetic smile. "And for the same reasons, I must respectfully decline your offer to help catalogue them.

"Miss Burton, that is most unwise. Even the most upright gentleman harbors thoughts and engages in experiences that no lady should wish to expose herself to. I do not say this task is fit for a stranger, but I assure you, you are not prepared for what you may find."

Claire softened under his impassioned gaze.

"Forgive me, Mr. Latimer. You are so unlike the clergymen I

knew as a girl, I forget myself. Of course you view matters differently. Since we do not see eye to eye on this, may we talk of something else? There is so much I want to learn about my new home."

"One question first, if I may?" He continued at her nod. "When do you intend to begin? And may I help you to catalogue Josiah's papers as you review them?"

"That is two questions, Mr. Latimer," she said with a smile. "I've already begun and work a little every night before retiring, when the house is quiet. At the moment, I'm merely ascertaining the size of the task and hoping to find a manuscript Josiah's publisher believes he left behind."

She missed his scowl as she dipped to gather her skirts and stepped toward the door.

He grabbed her arm before he could stop himself. She halted in mild surprise and he let her go. He expected a reprimand, but her next words shocked him.

"Poor Mr. Latimer!" she said with warmth. "You loved Josiah, too. How selfish I must seem when all you want is what I want—to honor his memory and preserve it for posterity."

He walked her back to the house in silence and left her on the terrace. As he turned toward the stables to collect his mount, she touched him lightly on the arm. Again he felt her power to bid him.

"Please don't be angry with me," she said earnestly, her beguiling eyes seeking his. "I want to be so sure of doing the right thing, the way Josiah wished. I will reconsider your request and give you my answer in a few days."

As Claire watched him walk away, she marveled again at how beautiful a man could be in face, form and conduct. Josiah had been a small man, more a jester than a judge of men. And though some of Latimer's words carried a sting, he spoke with the perfect frankness and meant only kindness. And his life must be lonely, too. A man of his stature would know deference but little true companionship. The losses of his friend Montfort, his sister, then Josiah surely must be hard to bear.

His offer tempted her. Claire was also lonely, and Latimer's words about Josiah's papers awakened a possibility she hadn't considered. What if she did not like what she was about to learn of her beloved's private life? Would it not be better to have someone steady to lean on, to share in the joys and sorrows as they worked on common goals?

Noonan's approach broke her reverie.

"A message from the Great House, miss," he said as she took the envelope from the extended salver. She glanced at the crest, then tore it open.

"Miss Burton,

The building my steward tells me you wish to make into a school is entirely unfit. However, if you or your designee would deign to meet me at 11 o'clock tomorrow at The Dragon Inn, I can show you a place nearby that would better suit your requirements. If this is inconvenient, please name another time. I am, at your pleasure,

"Montfort."

"The man is waiting, miss."

She hesitated, thinking of her recent encounter with distaste, then remembered her duty. The building she had seen was dark and smelled as though it had once been a pig sty, not a place to entice children or satisfy any teacher she might be able to hire.

"Tell him my answer is yes."

Chapter 7

THE VILLAGE OF Abbot Pyon, with its sweeping views across the valley to the Black Mountains of Wales, had been a gathering place for millennia. The area's earliest inhabitants had planted a sacred oak grove where the stout Christian church now stood, and there they had worshipped the triple goddess with feasting and sacrifice.

Victoria's subjects remembered neither the sacred grove nor the rugged plinths raised to mark the grove's perimeter. Those stones had vanished into the very fabric of the village, taken by stout builders for lintels, thresholds and hearths as the community grew. Its people believed themselves good Christians, yet at the vernal equinox, housewives still swept the dust of winter into the street with brooms made of hazel boughs, and at Yuletide logs of applewood burned brightly in their grates. Priests still blessed the orchards each winter and presided over the harvest festival with unseemly gusto. Country lads and lasses danced to near-exhaustion, then disappeared into the fields, oblivious to the origins of the ancient rites that once sanctified their couplings.

The power of the place ran deep and had already touched Claire, though she was barely aware of the spell it cast. It was a hard man or woman who breathed the air of Herefordshire for long without feeling it awaken their desires.

Her hair tucked up primly beneath her city topper, she guided the quick-stepping Toddy from the main road up the High Street lined with low two-story black-and-white buildings flanking the street, so different from the upright brick structures of Surrey.

Finding her destination was easy—the High Street was a long straight road scarcely broad enough on market days for stalls, shoppers and livestock. On ordinary days like this one, she saw only a few housewives or servants tending to the morning's errands. She recognized faces from Sunday mornings, but no one returned her tentative nods of greeting.

She slowed Toddy to a walk as houses gave way to shops—a chandler, a butcher, a tack maker, a mercer and a chemist comprised the whole of Abbot Pyon's mercantile offerings—and then the inn, where she was to meet Montfort.

Handing Toddy off to a lad in the yard, she looked in vain for a ladies' entrance, then gripping her riding crop more tightly, she took a deep breath and pushed open the main door to the single public room.

The interior was dim and cool, the windows the only source of light. The broad stone fireplace that filled most of the wall to Claire's left was dark, but the pungent aroma of wood smoke hung in the air. An array of bright brass candlesticks stood on the low rough-hewn mantle and above it hung a picture so begrimed with soot the lack of light made no difference. Claire assumed it depicted a hunting scene since there were daubs of dull red in the middle ground above longer horizontal brownish daubs and smaller white dabs in the foreground that could have been hounds.

A girl hanging tankards on hooks over the bar to Claire's right paused from her work and called over. "Help you, miss? You lost?"

Her eyes adjusting to the low light, Claire stepped quickly toward her and said as loudly as she dared, "I'm meeting Lord Montfort, but I seem to be early."

"Nay, he ain't been by yet. Fancy a cider?"

"No. Thank you." Claire chose a seat in a nook formed by the wide stone fireplace and the wall. She could see the door she had used to enter and the main door to the street off to her left, but no one entering would immediately spy her. To her right, a twisting staircase crossed by heavy beams and with trends worn crooked by time ran up to a second floor. Doors slammed and footsteps bustled overhead.

Despite the empty public room, The Dragon appeared to be a

thriving business. The wide floorboards gleamed and the windowpanes sparkled. In the yard, horses were being hitched and a dray delivered sacks of flour.

The side door to the yard flew open and a boy tumbled in, his arm locked around the neck of a smaller lad, both of them laughing. Behind them, a man strode in accompanied by a somewhat weary-looking woman Claire guessed to be his wife.

"I'll keep an eye on these rapscallions and settle the bill while you run up," the man said. As the woman began to ascend, the boys flew round her skirts and dashed ahead of her.

"Cecil! Humphrey—" the man shouted.

He was drowned out by the crash of crockery and silverware on the stairs and the shout of the servant who had been carrying them down on a tray.

Soon quiet descended again on the empty room, except for the muttering of the chambermaid, on her knees picking up shards of crockery. The girl from behind the bar swabbed away with a mop at grilled tomatoes, congealed eggs and a puddle of dark tea.

Claire refrained from looking at the watch pinned to her jacket, though a careful observer would have noted the boot tapping under the edge of her skirt. She glanced idly at a week-old copy of the Hereford Times lying on the table next to her and pretended not to listen to the maids' conversation.

"Lor,' she didn't eat much, did she, Sally? And her wantin' to be served so early," the girl from the bar said.

"She weren't there," Sally muttered.

"Whatya mean, she weren't there?"

"I mean she weren't there when I took her tray up." The girl's tone sharpened Claire's attention. "Scarce sunrise and her bed not slept in." Sally lurched to her feet, clutched an apron-full of pottery fragments to her chest and dumped them into a basket with a clatter.

"Mr. Williams'll be hoppin' mad if she skipped out on the bill," Jane replied. "That'll be the third one this month and he'll start making one of us sleep down here nights."

"Nah," Sally said. "Her things're still in the room and she warn't packed nor nothin'. She's an odd duck, though—coming and going at all hours and never talkin' to no one. That one was up to somethin', mark my words."

"Shhh!" Sally nodded her head toward Claire, who quickly ducked her head back to the newspaper. The girls gathered up their things and went through to the back room, leaving Claire alone again. The girl called Jane came back a few minutes later and Claire called out to her.

"Excuse me, but I think I would like a glass of cider after all, unless it's not too early for a cup of tea."

"Cider it is, miss. It's from me dad's own press and you'll not taste nothin' finer," Jane said with pride. "A glass mornin' and evenin' will keep you in long life and health, he says."

"I'm sure it's wonderful," Claire said a moment later as she gazed down into the pint of murky brown liquid Jane put in front of her. It looked more like soup than the clear amber cider her mother sometimes served at garden parties.

She took a tentative sip. Rich cool liquid slipped past her tongue and down her throat, where it left a surprising burn. She tried again and found it more pleasant this time, earthy, tangy and unexpectedly fizzy. A full swallow and the cider went down more smoothly.

By the time the main door of the public room banged open and Montfort strode into the room, Claire had nearly finished the tankard and felt quite content with the world.

Montfort reached the center of the room before he noticed Claire off to the side by the wall. She greeted him with a cool nod and his eyes followed her ramrod straight figure as she rose and made her way toward Jane, now polishing the taps, to pay her bill. Good. She was annoyed with him for being late—like kindling waiting for the match to light it, he hoped.

He was confident he could seduce her with sweet talk and proper drawing-room flirtation, but those sorts of conquests take time. He wanted to play a faster game with her, and any sort of passion once aroused could open the way into a woman's bed, he had found, especially one who had once tasted the pleasures offered there. Women were schooled from the cradle to conceal their yearnings, but the heat of anger often melted the barriers of resistance. He had once heard of a couple drawn into a feverish union by their battling opinions of Lord Melbourne. The randy former prime minister no doubt would have approved.

Task completed, she turned to him.

"Thank you for taking time out of your busy morning, Lord Montfort," she said, "and for overlooking my rude comments to you yesterday. Will we be riding or is the site close enough to walk?"

"We can walk. It is scarcely around the corner. After you, Miss Burton."

His eyes seemed to glitter in the dim light and she noted again his unconventional dress, the soft hat—which he hadn't removed—the open sweeping coat that brushed the insteps of his riding boots and added to an impression of restless energy that reached out and caressed her the way heat from a fire warmed the skin as you approached the flames.

She gave him a wide berth as she moved toward the door but hadn't gotten more than a few steps when she tripped. Claire's cheeks burned in earnest now.

He caught her arm and suppressed a smile as she steadied herself. Then he noticed her slightly unfocused eyes.

"Janey," he called over his shoulder. "Have you been serving Miss Burton here your da's scrumpy?" The girl giggled in response.

"Lor, milord! She were thirsty and there's nothin' better on a fine day. Fort'fyin' da' says, you know."

"Yes, and your da gets drunk as a lord on it every year at the harvest fete, Janey. Miss Burton is a city lady and you should have warned her."

Jane immediately looked contrite. "I'm sorry, milord. No harm intended, I'm sure."

Claire jerked her arm out of Montfort's grasp.

"Don't be silly," she snapped. "I'm perfectly fine. This old floor is uneven in places. Don't make Jane feel bad when she didn't do anything wrong. Her father's cider is very good. I'll have to check with my housekeeper to see if we buy from him."

"It's also as strong as vintage port, Miss Burton, and I'll wager you had a full pint of it. I didn't know the young ladies of Surrey were accustomed to strong drink in the morning—or any time of the day, for that matter. Perhaps I should spend more time in suburbium when I'm next visiting town."

"Please, Lord Montfort. Don't tease." Then she surprised him. "Clearly, I imbibed too much too quickly," she said, looking down at the floor. "I didn't understand about the cider. And I am most embarrassed now. Don't make it worse. It means a great deal to me to be able to work with you since that may get my school opened quickly. If you don't respect me, and all through my own fault, I know my task will be that much more difficult because of who you are."

Montfort reached a gloved hand under her chin and turned her head up and around so he could look into her face. Tears brimmed in those bewitching blue eyes. He dropped his hand abruptly and stepped back a pace. So much for trying to infuriate her.

"Consider it forgotten, Miss Burton," he said in his best drawing room voice. "But do mind your step. The floor is treacherous in spots and we'll be covering some fairly rough ground before we're done. Let's bring the horses with us. You should be able to ride by the time you are ready to go home."

They walked no more than half a mile, but Claire's head throbbed every step of the way. While Montfort tied their horses to a dilapidated fence on the verge of the dusty lane, she pretended to study the vine-shrouded cottage he indicated and steadied herself on a gatepost that no longer supported a gate. That was just visible in the long grass between the road and the front door. Someone had scythed a path just wide enough for them to walk through the overgrown front garden single file and left the long cuttings where they fell.

The sickly sweet smell of dead vegetation fermenting in the sun made Claire's stomach heave. Feeling dizzy, she fixed her gaze on the roof slates above the door as though she were considering their soundness. Then, slowly, she took in the chimney, the door lintel, the window.

Montfort waited, switching his short riding whip against his leg. She wished he would stop. She wished he would go away and leave her there to collect her wits. More than anything, she wanted to lean against him, close her eyes and lose herself in his arms.

Her eyes drifted shut, then flew open abruptly.

"I'd like to see the inside, if you please," she said a little too loudly, her mouth dry. "Do you have a key?"

He snorted in a most ungentlemanly way. "Even if it were locked, I could easily force the door, the condition this place is in."

"But the owner—"

"Never mind the owner. I'm Viscount Montfort, if you recall."

The door yielded to a kick from Montfort's boot heel to reveal a single, musty room. The added sunlight that poured in when Montfort pulled back the shutters on the lone window by the entrance fell on little more than dust, cobwebs and old straw. An overturned stool lay on the flagstone floor by the hearth.

An insect buzzed in the rafters. The sound rang in Claire's ears, as did the sharp clack of her boots on the stones.

For furnishings, only a few benches and tables were needed. Edward Latimer could tell her how many children to plan for. The thought of Latimer set her stomach fluttering again as she pictured how he would react to her current state—inebriated and alone with the very man he had warned her about only yesterday. He would never call again, and no one in the village would have anything to do with her if the rector abandoned her. The school would fail. She needed to leave. Now.

"This cottage will do very well for a school. It's a thousand times better than the place I looked at yesterday," she said to Montfort, who was watching her closely, as though he expected her to trip again. "You must put me in touch with the owner."

"That would be myself, Miss Burton. The Montforts own nearly every place around Oakley Court and the land under the ones we don't. Except for your precious Joss's Oak Grove, of course." His bitterness was palpable.

"Joss? Oh, you mean Mr. Carter. Josiah."

"He was Joss to everyone in Herefordshire, even after he became the grand man of letters. He could fool London, but he couldn't fool us. We knew him too well.

"Didn't you like him, Lord Montfort? You sound angry."

"I don't like to talk about him. We were as close as brothers once. But even brothers can fall out. I'm sorry he's dead, but those damn books of his—"

"Lord Montfort!"

"I beg your pardon, Miss Burton. But it's the truth. Joss's novels may have enthralled thousands of readers, but they drove a wedge between him and nearly everyone in this place. What he wrote hurt too many people, people who would have been glad to celebrate his successes, but for the fact that they paid a very real human price for his literary laurels."

"Jealous," Claire sputtered. "He said people were jealous

because his novels made him rich and he began life with little but his education." She started for the door but Montfort slammed it shut and barred her way before she had taken more than two steps.

"Tell yourself that if you like. I'm sure he did," Montfort snapped. He flipped the stool over and all but shoved her onto it. "Choose one, Miss Burton," he challenged, bending close to her face. "I demand to know your favorite among your beloved's esteemed works."

"'Lady Jacinta,' I suppose," Claire said, as she steadied herself on the shaky low stool. "Josiah made history so brilliantly alive in that one!"

"History?" Montfort laughed. "I think not. But at least you didn't choose 'Lord Merdon.'"

"Papa wouldn't allow us to read that one," Claire admitted. "He said 'Lord Merdon' was sensational."

"I congratulate your Papa on his good judgment. But let's examine your heroine, shall we? Lady Jacinta was an ancestress of mine. She nearly cost the family their lands and the earl his head during the Civil War."

"But she saved everything!" Claire protested. "She sacrificed herself so that her husband could put down the rebellion and return this region to King Charles!"

She tried to rise, but Montfort placed his hands on her shoulders and firmly pressed her down. Despite his supple leather gloves and her serge riding jacket, the physical contact sent a jolt down her spine as though he had touched her bare skin.

"It is a romantic tale, isn't it? But Joss's version is a pretty lie at best. Would you like to know the truth, Miss Burton? Would it please you to know that Jacinta cared only for herself and her own pleasure? She was no better than a harlot, really, with her scarlet lips and long golden hair. She took several men into her bed while the earl, her husband and rightful lord, was away fighting for the king, and she didn't care which side her lovers supported as long as it was the winning one at the time. In fact, the abbey changed hands at several points during the course of the war, and so did your precious Jacinta. She offered her body to whomever was on top, so to speak."

He brought his face closer to hers and her lips tingled as his warm breath touched them. "And oh, the climax of Joss's story is the worst lie of all. In Joss's version, Lady Jacinta rushes from the abbey in the dead of night to warn her husband of an imminent rebel offensive. But in reality, it was the old earl who flew home to Montfort Abbey by moonlight. He intended to confront his wife about her rumored betrayals and instead, he ended up surprising Jacinta in flagrante with one of her paramours. What happened after that is not fit for the ears of gently bred ladies, Miss Burton—are you certain you want to hear how the tale really ends?"

Claire couldn't help herself. A distant part of her knew she was supposed to be shocked, but Montfort's passion was galvanic. She felt Jacinta's fear in her bones. Her pulse raced.

"Yes," she said, meeting the dark eyes inches from hers. "Finish it."

As many times as she replayed what happened next, she could never decide the sequence of things. But which of them made the first move was irrelevant. Their lips met, hesitantly for an instant and then, as though he intended to devour her, Montfort clutched her in his powerful arms and pulled her off the stool. Had she been less tall, he would have lifted her from the ground entirely, no more mindful of her weight than if she were a feather.

His mouth covered hers with firm insistent pressure, urging her to respond. Her hands were trapped against his chest, so she grasped his lapels and clung to him to keep from toppling backward. That pulled him closer and, as her lips involuntarily parted, he slipped his tongue into her mouth and explored its tenderest parts. The sensation was altogether alarming and thrilling, heightened by his musky scent and the bristled contact of his moustache against her petal-soft skin. Like a newborn kitten, she blindly moved her lips against his.

Heat shot directly down through her midsection and her knees melted. She felt herself open in places she never knew existed.

Then, as abruptly as it started, it was over.

"Finish it? Odd you should use those words," Montfort said, thrusting her back and pacing away as though nothing had happened. Her head swam, the buzzing grew louder in her ears and she panted for breath, but he looked as though he had done nothing more than help her up from the stool.

Gracelessly, she groped behind her and half fell to the stool.

"Family history has it those were the words Jacinta spoke

before her husband finally ran her through with his rapier," he said. "He forced her to watch as he killed and mutilated her lover, and then dragged Jacinta back to her chamber by that magnificent hair, dispatched her and propped her body in the turret window with her hair cascading down the wall."

Claire gasped.

"Yes, that part was true," he continued. "She flaunted that famous hair at her window to signal her lovers. This time it was the Roundheads' undoing, because the earl had informed his own troops that a view of his lady's mane from the parapet was the signal to attack.

"Fools who venture into the ruins today swear they know which stones fell from beneath the window when the Roundheads destroyed the tower during the siege, because they're stained with Jacinta's blood.

"That's horrible," Claire exclaimed. "I'll never be able to look at the window in the library again. You've ruined a beautiful story forever!"

"No wonder you loved Joss Carter. Do you also prefer whitewash to the truth?"

"No, no," Claire responded. "But surely you must admit some artistic license? Josiah wasn't actually writing history..."

"Artistic license," he sneered. "I'm doing you a favor, Miss Burton. When you look at that lovely window in 'your' library now, you can consider it a warning to traitors and adulterers. Lady Jacinta was not sacrificing herself to warn her husband of an impending attack—that was Joss's nonsense. The real story is about two angry people who hated and deceived each other.'"

"Is the world so ugly, then? Is there no room for beauty, romance, hope?"

"Not if it is purchased by sacrificing the truth."

"But surely art is meant to uplift us, to show us what we can be, and not force us to grovel in our baser natures?"

"Is it base to be human, Miss Burton?"

Claire huffed out a mirthless chuckle and gestured to Rhys's large signet ring, deeply incised with the figure of a dragon. "You are fierce on every subject, aren't you? So much that I think I begin to understand the Montfort family motto—if that's not one of Josiah's fictions, too. She grasped his hand and reads the words in Latin inscribed around the sigil.

'Trifle not with the dragon,'" Claire parsed slowly. "Do I translate that correctly?"

"Very good. You are a scholar, then?"

"You give me too much credit," Claire said stiffly as she dropped his hand. "I often sewed in the room my brother and his tutor used before Cam went to university. I liked to listen to the stories of antiquity they studied together."

"And what does your learned brother think of this madness of yours, Miss Burton?"

"Madness!" she retorted. "Yes, I suppose it is. But I hope you will not judge me too harshly for it."

"I don't quite know how to judge you, Miss Burton, nor frankly, should you care. My opinion is not worth the bother, I assure you. But let us return to the purpose at hand. I'll send my steward over tomorrow with a lease, if you wish." He shoved open the cottage door and left her to follow or not as she wished.

Montfort squinted in the bright sun, his thoughts addled. That kiss! He had kissed more women than he cared to count, and in more productive ways. But Claire's kiss—the only word he could apply to it was "sweet."

It warmed the center of his being like the cider that had so obviously thrown her off kilter.

But *she* had kissed *him.* It was like the mouse turning on the cat. He said he didn't know what to think of her. That she baffled him would be closer to the mark. She was clever, he'd give her that. If she had fallen to Joss's wiles, he'd wager it had been once only and she hadn't enjoyed it. Her Sunday-school guilt would have seen to that. No wonder she wanted to bury herself in the wilds of Herefordshire. She probably did daily penance or, worse, told herself it never happened.

But an affair with Claire Burton began to offer charms beyond the tangible. Yes, he'd get his land back, but how satisfying it would be to see her blossom as a woman under his hands, to find joy in their coupling. She seemed imminently teachable and more willing to learn than she realized.

But that kiss—he'd been kissed like that once before. Honestly. Fervently. With no thought beyond the moment. No calculation. Before Lucy spurned him, she had kissed him like that. But Montfort sensed a generosity in Claire that Lucy lacked.

If Lucy was a cool draught of water for a thirsty man, Claire was a bountiful spring waiting to be tapped.

Minutes passed. He ran his tongue over his lips, recalling the taste of Claire's lips. Her perfume—lily of the valley?—lingered in his nostrils. He straightened his lapels, stared at the ground, adjusted his trousers. If she had noticed the quickening activity there during their embrace she had given no sign. Finally, he planted himself akimbo by the gate and stared up into the sky, braced for her reproach.

A lark soared amid trailing veils of cirrus, the liquid notes of its song falling to the earth below like crystal shards. Then she stood by his elbow and spoke.

"Lord Montfort," she said, her light voice mingling with the clear trills of the bird. "Where is my horse?"

He started and looked toward the road. His bay hunter, still tied to the dilapidated fence, pawed the dirt restively. Claire's horse was gone.

"He can't be far," Montfort said. "We were inside for only a few moments."

She looked dazed. The scrumpy must still be at work.

"The question is, which way! Did he wander down the lane or was he tempted afield by all this," she said, taking in the cottage and its overgrown surroundings with a sweep of her arm and nearly overbalancing.

"He most likely headed for water—there's a stream behind the cottage. Wait here and I'll see. You'll have the devil of a time in that dress." Montfort headed off to the left of the cottage, and to his mild annoyance, she rustled after him.

"I'll keep close and you can tramp down the grass as you go," she told him. "A horse on his own in full tack could hurt himself. You could startle him. He knows me," she blurted in snatches between awkward lunges.

They found the big gray, none the worse for wear, grazing placidly under a large apple tree close to a broad beck rippling behind the cottage. Catching Toddy's bridle, Claire murmured soothing words to the wayward horse.

Watching her, Montfort felt like an intruder. The woman and the attentive animal seemed to understand each other intuitively, and he could have been on the other side of the moon for all he mattered. The solitary tree, free of the orchardist's pruners over many years, had grown tall and broad and he could hear small birds murmuring high in its mazy branches. Their chatter blended with the song of the beck beyond. The cool air smelled fresh and green.

He forgot himself and his plots and perplexities, simply to drink in the bright clarity of the moment. The dappled light falling through the shifting leaves showered everything beneath it with shimmering gold and rippled across a carpet of fallen blossoms gleaming like pearl around her feet. Free of modern attire, she could have been some ancient spirit of the land, equally prepared to grant a boon or name a curse, depending on whether she took offense at being spied upon.

His mood lasted only a moment. When the light breeze touched his face, it roused him.

"What do you say to bewitch him, Miss Burton?" he asked.

"Oh, nothing really," she replied, turning her head to address him as she continued to stroke Toddy's sleek neck. "I merely tell him he is a handsome boy and that back at the stable, apples are waiting for him—which he won't get here this time of year."

"Indeed. The eternal Eve," he said, sketching a curt bow.

"You tease me again, Lord Montfort," she said with a frown as he came closer.

"I assure you, no. Apples cure any number of the things that ail, as every Herefordshire goodwife will tell you. The serpent did mankind a good turn when it comes to apples." He leaned against the rough trunk of the old tree. "Besides, I have the greatest respect for good horsemanship. I want to know your secret."

She pressed her forehead against Toddy's neck and he didn't catch her answer.

"If you will wait there, Miss Burton, I'll fetch my mount and show you a way back over the fields that will save you time. We can go along the bank as far as the churchyard—there's a footbridge that can carry the horses if your Toddy is not skittish about such things."

"As you wish," was all she said.

Her head drooped like a thirsty flower on its stalk, he noticed—then scoffed at himself. He was becoming a poet, and a bad one at that. But observing her evident weariness prompted him to consider whether they should just go back to the inn, where she could retire to a private room and refresh herself. Too bad she was flushed and dreamy-eyed still. She would become the talk of the village if anyone noticed her state, and she would reach home more quickly his way. He decided to chance it.

Soon he was offering his cupped hands to help her mount Toddy—and marveling at how such a buxom woman could fly into the saddle with so little effort despite her tipsy condition. She did it so nimbly she cheated him of the glimpse of ankle or calf a more artful woman would have guaranteed.

"Lead on, my lord,'" she said with a funny little salute.

Montfort laughed, and retorted. "I trust you've learned your lesson about the local scrumpy."

She muttered something that sounded like, "... not that." He couldn't be sure and wouldn't ask. They rode on in silence along the bubbling stream and the thought occurred to him that Claire Burton could be pleasant company. She knew when not to chatter, and when she did speak, she put some thought into her words. But he wished now for conversation, to better gauge what she was thinking.

His mind drifted back to their first meeting and the song she sang. He'd never known a girl of her class to be so buoyant. Then a suspicion hit him like a punch in the stomach. Again he asked himself, what was her game?

"Miss Burton," he asked after considering his words carefully. "Why did you never marry Joss? You say you loved him and he must have loved you, to drop you into so much bounty. That is to say, he cared enough to provide for you in the event of his demise before the happy day."

"It's simple enough," she replied somberly. "My father forbad the marriage. The day Josiah sought my hand, Papa had him thrown out of the house."

Sure there was more, he waited.

"I learned that Josiah left shortly afterward for America. But I knew he would come back for me and so I decided my best course was patience. My father and mother love me—they couldn't have wanted to see me suffer forever. They would have relented eventually, I was sure."

"Pardon my assumption, Miss Burton, but you are of age. Why not just go with him? Joss had more than enough income to support ten wives."

"Lord Montfort! I said my parents loved me. I love them as

well. I owed them a duty."

"Besides," she added more softly, "Josiah never even suggested it. He cared too much about my reputation."

Montfort coughed to cover the laugh that nearly burst from throat. He'd shattered one illusion for her today already, it wouldn't serve him to pile on if he expected to deepen their acquaintance. She genuinely believed in Joss Carter's decency, but he had no reason to believe love had transformed the man. That sort of thing happened only in cheap novels of the sort Joss wrote.

Their horses approached the footbridge at a slow walk, both riders lost in thought, when without warning, Toddy reared and shied, nearly pitching Claire off his back. Montfort leapt to the ground and seized the plunging horse's reins. Claire struggled to hold her seat.

Montfort managed to turn the horse back toward the way they had come, so that whatever spooked him was behind him.

Between them they calmed Toddy and Claire dismounted unhurt. Montfort's horse stood nearby, quiet but tense, the whites of his eyes showing.

"It can't be the bridge," Claire said. "Toddy's not bothered by things like that—he's excellent in the field, and your horse is upset, too. He's done this before, though."

"What set him off then?"

"There was a dead lamb in a field and we came too close before I noticed it."

"Wait here." Montfort handed the reins back to Claire and she watched anxiously as he walked slowly along the stream bank toward the bridge, examining the ground.

Just before the churchyard, he halted and knelt. Standing on tiptoe, Claire just made out something large, black and shapeless lying in the grass on the bank, as though someone had thrown a dark sack there. Then she saw Montfort running toward a man in the churchyard. She longed to follow but couldn't leave the horses.

The man rushed from the churchyard toward the road and Montfort returned to the bank, removed his long coat and spread it over the object there.

He hastened back to Claire, where she stood, anxious and pale. "Go back the way we came," he commanded.

"What's wrong? What is it?"

"There's a woman—"

"Let me go to her," Claire cut in. "If she's injured, I can at least comfort her until help arrives."

"You can't help her," Montfort snapped. "No one can. She's dead."

Chapter 8

Montfort had acted swiftly, dispatching the sexton in the churchyard to the rectory across the way with multiple instructions. He and Claire made their way back around the cottage to the road—both shocked into silence by his discovery—and he stayed with her until the gig he summoned from the inn appeared.

"Forgive me for not seeing you home myself," he said after handing her in and instructing the driver.

She leaned back on the seat and closed her eyes, grateful to be at rest at last and free to surrender to the sensations churning inside her. As the gig rolled out of sight, Toddy tied securely behind, Montfort loped back to the place where the body lay, now shrouded by one of Edward Latimer's fine linen bed sheets, commandeered from his housekeeper. His coat, damp and smudged, hung over a bridge rail, placed there by the parish constable, who had been snatched from his midday meal.

Three tedious hours passed before the coroner arrived from Hereford, and a small crowd of onlookers gathered along the churchyard wall in the meantime. It was all young Frank Reid could do to keep them away, despite his official capacity, until Montfort stepped in and they scattered like sheep.

It took two stout draymen from the inn to place the woman's

body on a plank and carry it back to the inn after the coroner finished a cursory in situ examination. By that time, Abbot Pyon buzzed and nearly every inhabitant found it necessary to have business near the Dragon.

The coroner followed the corpse into a back room given over to him for the duration, and after he assured Montfort he needed him no longer, Montfort strode over to the rectory.

Latimer rang for the maid when he appeared in the rector's study.

"Ale and sandwiches? They're ready—Nellie just has to carry them in. Have some refreshment, then tell me the news. They say a woman staying at the Dragon was found dead near my church. By you."

"Yes, one of the girls at The Dragon recognized her gown," Montfort said between bites of roast beef and brown bread. He hadn't eaten since breakfast. "She gave her name there as Mary Collins, but no one knows for sure where she came from."

"A common enough name, and likely not her own," Latimer observed. "Some unfortunate girl, then, lost to her family and destitute. It's a pity she chose to destroy herself here..."

"Destroyed? Someone murdered the woman! I saw the marks around her throat! Some brute throttled the life out of her. And she must have fought back. Her hands were those of a lady, but they were cut and scraped as though she had clung to something rough or been dragged.

"If there was misfortune," he added, "it must have been recent. Her gown was good-quality stuff, as were her boots, far too fine for the outdoors."

"Her clothing was torn?" Latimer asked.

"As to whether she'd been interfered with, that's impossible to determine," Montfort said, catching his meaning instantly. "The damage to her clothing could just as easily come from catching on stones or branches in the water. The coroner deduced she fell or was thrown into the beck upstream from the village, though it's impossible to say exactly where, or when. Davies says it couldn't have been more than a day or two."

"Whatever led him to conclude that? Has he taken to speaking with spirits?" Latimer scoffed.

"Her body was not much altered, hence the time. And there were leaves entangled in her clothing. I recognized them as *rhododendron fortunei*—the only plantation hereabouts is in my park, near the beck."

"You are quite the detective, Montfort. But I advise you to leave the matter to the coroner. You don't need more scandal. The first thing you know, people will be saying you knew this woman," Latimer said. "Let the coroner's jury decide whether her death was an accident or not and where—though I suppose what you say puts paid to the possibility of either misadventure or suicide."

He cast a sheaf of papers aside.

"I shall have to rewrite my sermon for Sunday. This is a fearsome business and the parish will expect some topicality. 'All flesh is grass,' hardly seems suited. Perhaps Galatians will loosen someone's tongue."

"Be careful, Latimer, we don't want to turn this into a witch hunt. Surely the man who did this is long gone."

"Do you suppose some thug saw this Mary Collins in Hereford, followed her here and accosted her?"

"Why do you say Hereford, Latimer? She could have come as easily from half-a-dozen other places. Bristol. Or Cardiff."

"I thought I heard someone say Hereford at the Dragon. I made my way over there earlier today to see if I could be of use."

"And?"

"It was evident you had everything in hand, so I returned home to my labors."

"Sally White says she took breakfast up to the woman before 6 this morning and her bed hadn't been slept in. That's one of the points the coroner's jury will try to establish—the last time anyone saw her. That shouldn't be difficult, since she was a stranger. There wouldn't have been anywhere she could have gone without being noticed."

"Perhaps she visited friends in the neighborhood?"

"That's just it—too many perhapses."

"You—the authorities—searched through her belongings for anything that would lead to her home or her business here?"

"Davies had Frank Reid seal up her room until the inquest. He hopes to convene that the day after tomorrow." Montfort finished the last bite of his sandwich. "There's another thing that's troubling—she hadn't been robbed. She wore a number of rings and the usual adornments you expect to see on a woman from a comfortable home. She carried a fine ladies' pocket watch and several sovereigns in a purse in her pocket."

"Perhaps the villain never intended to kill her and lost his nerve when he saw what he'd done?"

"Another 'perhaps.' Frankly, I prefer to think some personal quarrel is behind this. Otherwise, no one will rest easy even after this is resolved. We're supposed to be out of the age of highwaymen and footpads."

Latimer grunted. "The death of this unfortunate will be a seven-days wonder in the village, no doubt, but you and I have more important things to discuss. You were with Miss Burton today."

"Is that a question?"

"No, it is an observation. You met her at The Dragon, walked with her to the old Watkins place, went in and shut the door—shocking behavior, Rhys!—and then took her behind the cottage, again where you were out of view of decent people for rather too long." He grinned. "As pastor of this parish and your spiritual counselor, what am I supposed to think of such behavior?"

"There's nothing to think, Edward. She wants to start a school for older students worth educating, and see to it they can afford to attend. It's actually not a bad idea, though I'm surprised Joss thought of it as she claims, and I have a place suitable for the scheme. And we weren't together that long."

"You must be losing your touch. Or was today just your opening gambit? Do tell, Rhys. What's the wench like? I want all the details. Did you buss her? Nibble on one of those delicate earlobes? Did she let you slip your hand up a silky thigh under her skirts when no one as looking?"

Montfort reddened.

"I see," Latimer laughed. "The lady demurred. Clever girl! Perhaps she knows you too well already, thanks to Joss, and is on her guard. Or perhaps she fancies me better."

"You!"

"Oh yes. I visited the bower of Miss Burton and her dull companion yesterday. We strolled in the garden and enjoyed a charming interlude in her summerhouse—though I refrained from revealing all its history. She cherishes it already as the place Joss did 'his best work.' If she only knew."

"Go on," Montfort growled.

"Only this. Miss Burton has agreed to let me assist her in organizing Joss's papers. I'll be spending hours with her every day while you are out studying leaves, chasing murderers and whatnot. That's just the opportunity I need to convince the lady I am the protector she needs."

"Suit yourself, Edward, but from what I've seen of Claire Burton so far, she has a mind of her own." He rose. "It's been a long day. Thanks for the food."

Latimer walked with Montfort to the study door but stopped him from leaving, his arm across the oaken frame.

"I am in deadly earnest, Rhys," he said, looking him straight in the face. "Claire Burton may not be every man's first choice for a wife, all things considered, but I would marry her under the right circumstances. I am the kind of husband she needs. She's flighty, but no worse than any other woman without a man to rule her. She's refined, respectful, eager to be led." He lowered his arm.

"And what can you offer her, Rhys? Think what you've done. You're not fit to take another bride. I am willing to redeem her now, but I won't take up your leavings if you can't control yourself. What you really want is Oak Grove. I can promise you'll have it. Don't cock this up for both of us."

By the time the gig pulled up to the front door of Oak Grove, Claire's headache had subsided to a dull steady pain behind the eyes. Quiet greeted her in the front hall and she realized the time was scarcely two o'clock. Everyone, servants and Simmie alike, would be at the back of the house, taking a respite at their midday meal. On a fine day like this, Simmie was apt to be on the terrace.

She sent the servant hovering nearby to deal with Toddy and threw her hat and crop on a side table. She was headed for the broad staircase when Simmie emerged from the dining room to the left of the hall and intercepted her.

"Claire, dear! I'm so glad you're back," she said. "Mrs. Hanniman called. We're just in here. Do join us. She is most interested in the school and has such a good idea."

Then Simmie noticed the strain on Claire's face. "What's wrong? Was that Lord Montfort so very awful, then?"

"Oh no, Simmie." She hesitated. "Something terrible happened in the village, and I'd like nothing better right now than to lie down and be cossetted like I was back in the nursery at

Thurn."

"I'll make your apologies to Mrs. Hanniman then and look in on you in a bit."

"No, no, Simmie. I won't be self-indulgent. Let me make myself presentable and I'll just step in for a few moments. A splash of cool water on my face may be all I need. If not, I'll excuse myself. It will be wonderful to have another ally for the school and I don't want her to think we're not grateful for her interest. And Lord knows, she's the only woman in the village willing to be civil to me."

Eleanor Hanniman rose from the table as Claire entered and bustled forward.

"How did your visit to the Watkins cottage go? I assume that's the place Lord Montfort suggested for the school. There no better option in my view."

"Goodness," Claire said with the briefest of smiles. "If I had known your interest was so great, I could have let you deal with the viscount."

"He's not so bad, really. Just a bit wild in his youth," Mrs. Hanniman replied, as she reseated herself on one side of the long table and accepted another helping of salad greens from Simmie. They were dining casually while the servants ate.

"But I understand there was some real scandal," Claire said in spite of herself. "His brother?"

"Poor George. Such a tragedy!" the plump little woman replied, crumbling a roll. "Such a handsome lad, he was. And so kind. But not very bright and he could never hold his liquor, my husband always said. William—my late husband—dined frequently at the house in the fifth viscount's time and watched both boys grow into strapping young men. It was a different world then, you know. The country families and the aristocracy mingled on much more familiar terms than they do now."

"Would you like some soup, Claire?" Simmie interjected. She nodded and Simmie filled her bowl with a fragrant broth as Hanniman rambled on.

"It was fortunate George and Rhys both weren't killed in that fire," she was saying. "The building went up in an instant and it was late. The servants had retired and both boys were the worse for wear, if you take my meaning. No, you'd be thinking of his wife, no doubt, Miss Burton."

"Whose wife?" she said between sips of an excellent asparagus soup.

"Why, Lady Montfort. Isabel. The one they say he murdered!"

Simmie's cup hit the saucer with a crash. "He murdered his wife?" she said in astonishment.

"Well, the official story is that she fell down the staircase, befuddled by the laudanum her doctor ordered to help her sleep. But everybody knew within a month of them returning from their honeymoon abroad that the marriage was a disaster. It wasn't a love match, naturally," she confided, leaning across the table toward them. "It was even said she was unfaithful to him with some count in Rome, which is why they returned after only a few months."

"Gracious, Mrs. Hanniman!" Claire exclaimed, blushing. "You take my breath away. How could you possibly know all these things?"

"Servants talk," she replied. "You must know that! And in a place like Abbot Pyon, they're all related. My Bessie—a wonderful cook, my dear, I hope you and Miss Simms will dine with me soon. I can invite a few close friends and we could have such a lovely time. Do either of you play pique?"

"Your cook?" Simmie urged. To Claire's embarrassment, they both were much too interested in their voluble guest's information to turn the subject, as they knew they should. Her mother would have skillfully elided the conversation toward gardening or Mrs. Hanniman's dressmaker.

"Oh, yes, my cook. She's been with me for ages and makes such a soufflé, you can't imagine. Her daughter Susan is in service with the Montforts. She even traveled to London one season to wait on Lady Adelaide Montfort, who married Sir Harold Saxton the following spring."

Simmie and Claire waited expectantly.

"Isabel Brown was the daughter of a coal magnate in Yorkshire. Her father was frightfully rich and brought her to London for the most extravagant season you could imagine. He sent her to the best finishing school in Switzerland, intending all along to buy his future grandchildren the best title he could afford. That turned out to be Rhys Fitzgordon. It would have been his brother, no doubt, if the father could have managed it, but George was besotted with Lucy Latimer and, as I said, he wasn't very practical. Who was Lucy but just the rector's half-sister, with maybe £500 to look forward to?

"Well, you know, my dear Claire," she rattled on. "The Montforts needed money badly. You wouldn't be here today otherwise. Rhys thought he knew the terms of the bargain, but if you ask me, she was thoroughly bad right from the start. European education!"

She paused for a sip of water. "He couldn't have mistreated her that badly that she'd run off the rails within a month. That's my opinion. Wicked to the bone, she must have been. Common."

"Would you like some of Mrs. White's apple tart, Mrs. Hanniman?" Simmie asked when their guest paused for breath. "Claire?" Simmie passed the dish around. "Cream?"

They ate quietly for only a few moments when Mrs. Hanniman appeared to catch her second wind.

"Well," she said. "Even my Bessie can't produce a crust like that. There were no other family at Oakley Court when Isabel died, and most of the staff were in London with the dowager and her two unmarried daughters—and goodness knows how those two could have hoped to find a match without Rhys! Again, it was late, and all the servants who were there had retired. They found her at the foot of the stairs in the morning when the maids started round to light the fires. Stone cold. She broke her neck. When his valet went to wake him, Rhys was dead drunk."

Wordlessly, Simmie refilled their teacups and exchanged a glance with Claire. Mrs. Hanniman continued like a wind-up doll that was far from running down.

"The funeral was grand, no expense spared. Your Mr. Carter was there, Miss Burton. He and Rhys were such good friends. But then 'Lord Morden' came out and that's when the trouble started."

"Claire hasn't read the novel, Mrs. Hanniman," Simmie managed to interject.

"You have, Miss Simms?" Simmie nodded. "You know, then."

"I don't," Claire put in with a touch of impatience. "I do know Lord Montfort hates the book, though."

"Of course he does. Everyone in the neighborhood knows 'Morden' is Montfort to the life, right down to the scar on his face. And Morden murdered his wife, Lady Iolathe, by drugging her and throwing her down the stairs of the ducal mansion. It was common knowledge that Rhys and Isabel had a raging argument the day she died. People put two and two together."

"Oh," was all Claire could manage in response. "That's—that's appalling."

"Appalling, yes. Rhys can protest his innocence from now until doomsday, but you can't deny that within the space of a year, Rhys Fitzgordon lost a spendthrift brother and a disagreeable wife, only to gain a peerage and an enormous fortune. Poor boy! It didn't help that he put off his mourning for Isabel after just three months."

She stopped and looked at Simmie and Claire in turn, her eyes wide.

"Dear me, have I been dominating the conversation? And I didn't even get to what I wanted to tell you about your school. The Watkins cottage—is it arranged?"

"Yes," Claire said, "or it will be in a day or two. If we can find a teacher, I hope to have the school open in month. I plan to ask Mr. Latimer to advise on pupils and curriculum, and Mr. Carey has been educating me on wages so I can plan a scale of fair stipends—"

"Well, I beg your leave to recommend a teacher before you consult him on that head," Mrs. Hanniman said eagerly. "I know just the young woman. Evangelina Gilbert is genteel, accomplished and something of a scholar. Her father was a bookish man, quite the antiquarian in these parts, and she often assisted him in his later years. When the poor man died last winter, he left Lina and her mother nearly penniless. If you give her charge of the school, you'll be doing a deed of Christian charity in a way that will allow her to hold her head up again."

Claire was intrigued. "But can she teach, Mrs. Hanniman?"

"Talk to Mr. Latimer," the little woman suggested. "He can examine her and I'm sure you'll find that she suits. Now I must be off. Thank you for a most lovely afternoon. Don't forget you're coming to dine at Wisteria Lodge soon!"

"I didn't see your carriage when I came in," Claire replied. "How will you get home?"

"My dear! I'll walk across the fields between Oak Grove and Oakley Court. It's much shorter than going by the main road and the path comes out near St. Michael's. From there, it's practically a hop and a skip and I'm home. It shouldn't take me more than three-quarters of an hour."

"No, you can't do that. Not after…" Claire said more forcefully than she intended. "Please, let me have the gig brought around. I insist. It's warm today."

Not one to be asked twice, Eleanor Hanniman acquiesced, and the two ladies of Oak Grove soon were alone to contemplate the titillating information she left in her wake.

Simmie turned to Claire before the gig disappeared from view. "Let me help you to your room. You can tell me what happened later if you aren't up to talking now."

Claire sighed "Feel up to it? I may never feel up to talking again! Mrs. Hanniman seems like a good woman, but my heavens. Can you imagine her and Aunt Maud together?"

"Perhaps that's why your aunt is a woman of so few words," Simmie said with a straight face—before allowing a smile to creep across it.

The two went inside and climbed the stairs with their arms around each other's waists, Claire leaning her head on the older woman's shoulder. This is what she had been longing for since the morning, Claire thought. To lean on a dependable friend.

By the time they reached Claire's room, Simmie knew nearly everything: the inn, Montfort's lateness, the school, the grisly discovery. The only item Claire omitted was the kiss.

"And I pledge to you," Claire added as she sank onto the chaise in her room, "I will never consume scrumpy on an empty stomach again, nor in that quantity, nor that quickly."

"So you've had a lesson today?"

"Ummm," was all Claire said, lying back with her arms above her head. She thought about the way she felt in Montfort's arms. "Yes, a lesson." Unconsciously, she began twisting the heavy amethyst ring that never left her finger.

Claire slept well past nightfall. Simmie brought her a supper tray, then later removed it after the food, untouched, had gone cold. Whatever dreams soothed or troubled Claire vanished without a trace when she awoke. The musical clock on the mantel chimed nine times as she splashed cool water on her face. Refreshed but still unable to contemplate food, she changed into her warm woolen wrapper and descended to Josiah's library.

The fire burned brightly and eerie shadows flicked on the walls. Claire glanced up at the "Jacinta" window, but with no moon tonight, the round space was a black void. Just as well, she thought, her mood flat.

Claire made straight for the section where Josiah's own works were shelved in order of publication. The volumes in this special edition were beautiful, hand-tooled red calfskin embossed in gold with an extravagantly curlicued "JFC" monogram on each cover and gilt-tipped pages.

She located "Lord Morden" quickly and pulled it from the shelf. She opened the heavy volume to the frontispiece and carefully turned the thick octavos past the title page to the dedication:

> *"To the friends of my youth and those better days—*
> *Waters on a starry night*
> *Are beautiful and fair;*
> *The sunshine is a glorious birth;*
> *But yet I know, where'er I go,*
> *That there hath past away a glory from the earth.*

Wordsworth. That must have stung Montfort when he read it, she mused. She turned a few more pages, holding the edges gently between her fingertips. Edward Latimer would be coming any day now and if they were to begin well together, she reminded herself, she needed to make headway on the promised inventory of Josiah's papers and journals. Setting the novel aside, she scanned the shelves.

Two levels higher, but still within reach, was an equally impressive set of volumes bound in dark green leather. Reaching on tiptoe, she pulled one from the middle of the range down to her. Her heart began to pound when she opened it to the words, written in firm masculine script: "Journal of Josiah Fitzgordon Carter, 1868-69."

Setting it down next to the novel on the shelf, she pulled a library stool closer and climbed up. There were more than a dozen of the green books neatly ranged there—the first, she found, dated 1860-62 and the last, 1875.

Grasping the first volume in her right hand and her skirts in her left, she climbed down. Curling up in the wing chair by the fireside, she began to read.

"1 January 1860

"Now that I am to be the toast of literary London, it seems fitting that I record my comings and my goings, my most profound thoughts, the trials and triumphs of my love play with my darling, daring Muse. Hence I commence: Slept late, dined with Higby and Morris at their club (to which they promise to propose me, though I'm not entirely certain now I should be satisfied with an establishment as quotidian as the Beargarden, with the Athenaeum and its august company within my grasp.) Much talk, many cigars, adequate port in copious amounts. They went on about 2 to a gambling den they favor, but I, the earnest artist, must keep my head clear, since the next number of "Love's Labors Rewarded" is expected in M.'s hands next Tuesday and I've scarce begun it. And so to bed"

Claire closed the book over her finger to hold her place. How thrilling to see into Josiah's thoughts at the dawn of what would prove, as he suspected, so successful a career! How like him to turn aside temptation to labor at his art. But she should be taking notes. Discovering the identity of "M"—that would be easy enough. But Higby and Morris? Perhaps Mr. Latimer would know. Or Lord Montfort. They struck her as rather wild companions for the serious Josiah—unless, of course, he had used the opportunity to study society's darker side for his art's sake.

She rifled through the desk drawers until she located blank sheets and a pen with a serviceable nib. Drawing her robe more tightly against the chill, she resigned herself to working at Josiah's broad desk away from the fire. But the inkwell was dry.

With relief, she resumed reading in the big chair, where the renewed warmth and the turmoil of the day overcame her. Her thoughts drifted, and the heavy volume slipped from her fingers onto her lap. Staring into the dancing flames, she tried to summon Josiah's presence as she had experienced it that first night in the garden and failed.

Finally, unable to stop herself, she crept to the place where the diaries were shelved, climbed up slowly and retrieved the one from *her* year, the year she bound her heart to his. Feeling almost guilty, she opened it and turned the pages until she came to the day they met.

There was nothing.

Paging forward, she saw that Josiah had skipped over numerous days in that time so momentous to her yet, apparently, of so little consequence to him. Then she found it, the first mention of her name.

4 June 1873

Dined at Sir Henry Burton's home. What an ass! But the good bart. is a type of his class, solid, true blue, the backbone of the nation. He will make a good study—a "life among the gentry" to follow my sketches of the provinces perhaps? That Miss Burton was there, quiet as ever, though she couldn't take her eyes off me, of course. Quite nice eyes.

Claire was baffled. By the time Josiah had dined at the Burtons' house in town, she and Josiah had met more than a dozen times at various social events and in Regent's Park, where she got to know Kip as well. She began flipping forward, skimming the pages for her name. *"Danced with Miss Burton again." "Called at the Burtons." "Saw Miss Burton at the opera."* All this time she had been dreaming of him, she had been merely a footnote to his days?

Then she slowed to read,

10 August 1873

That poltroon Burton threw me bodily out of the house. I blustered and swore at him but can scarce find the words now to capture the outrage in my heart. My Claire would be the perfect wife for me—amid the cackling geese that pass for the haute monde today, hers is the only voice speaking sense. And she truly loves me! I know not what to do. I shan't get near her again—her dear Papa will see to that. And she is too dutiful to sink to a clandestine affair, though that would force the D.P.'s hand once he knew. But I tried to mount that citadel and failed. Claire is a "good" girl, more's the pity. How Montfort and Latimer would laugh—that Josiah Carter in the end would be captured by an honorable woman. And know it! Well, there it is. Forster's been wanting me to do another "foreign" book—perhaps the ladies of the Punjab or Siam will bring me succor. Or shall I take the advice of that American chap and "Go West?"

The remainder of the volume was nothing but blank pages.

Chapter 9

SIMMIE CAME TO the door of Claire's sitting room and left twice over the course of the morning. The third time she entered without knocking, bearing a tray with tea, butter, toast and a pot of Mrs. White's strawberry preserves. Kip looked up from his place under Claire's desk and eyed it hopefully before dropping his head back to his paws with a snuffle.

Claire, seated at the desk, reluctantly closed the journal and laid down her pen. A full week had passed before she could bring herself to return to Josiah's journals. But she had her duty to him and, perplexed as she was, she was determined to fulfill it. With every page, she hoped to find the key to understanding him.

"I don't know when Josiah had time to write!" she said to Simmie. "It seems like every night he was dining with friends, playing cards at a club or visiting the theatre. Honestly, if it weren't so long ago, I'd be jealous. I'm afraid I am jealous. At least once a week he'd meet a Miss Laycock at the theatre and take her to supper afterwards. Listen." She carefully leafed through a few pages and began to read.

"Jolly good day's work—won't Forster be pleased to have two chapters together this time." He's working on 'Jared Cooper - or the Lost Inheritance'," Claire interjected. *"And won't I be pleased*

to have the ready in consequence! A few hands at the club and then Pembrook and I will head for Haymarket, never mind what's on. I'm sure to get my money's worth with my Dolly tonight since I can pay so well and we'll be sure to tip the velvet before dawn's rosy fingers—"

Claire broke off, Simmie looked so peculiar.

"Miss Laycock?" she said sharply. "Miss Dolly Laycock?"

"Why, do you know her, Simmie? How extraordinary that would be!"

"May I see that?" Simmie asked, extending her hand. Reluctantly, Claire gave her the journal, still open at the passage she had been reading. Simmie read the entry to herself, then flipped at random through the volume, paused to read other entries here and there.

"No," she said slowly after a few minutes. Claire saw that her friend's face was quite red.

"But you have heard things?" Claire prompted.

"No," Simmie said. "That is to say... Claire, does Mr. Carter write much about their meetings other than they went to the theatre and supper?"

"Well, he does comment on her ankles, and on her complexion" Claire admitted. "A gentleman would do that, wouldn't he, if he admired a lady? It is a private diary, after all. He would write things he couldn't say to her? He says she has very trim ankles—in fact, he underlines that more than once—and skin—he uses the word 'skin,' which is so odd for the circumstances—'as silky as an angel's cheek.' He... he was very fond of kissing her."

Simmie put the journal on the desk and grasped Claire's hand in hers. "Claire," she said, then stopped. "Dear heart, 'Dolly Laycock'—that's a casual term men use for a certain kind of woman. A woman who sells her body to men for their pleasure."

Claire stared at her.

"But Josiah wasn't like that," she said at last. "He was a gentleman."

"Men live different lives than women do, Claire. Some do things that make no sense to us and things that, if we knew, would break our hearts nine times out of ten."

"It all makes sense then—the money, the night out." Claire wrinkled her mouth, and Simmie feared her friend would burst into tears.

Giving her a moment to compose herself, she poured Claire a cup of tea. "Leave it, dear. What harm was done is long in the past."

Claire looked thoughtful. "Harm," she said. "Yes. Those poor women—how sad their lives must have been."

"Life for women of a certain class can be very hard." Simmie replied. She handed Claire several envelopes. "The boy brought these from the village ages ago. There's a letter from your aunt and I think a note from Mr. Latimer. I can go if you wish."

"No, stay, Simmie. Aunt Manwaring is sure to have news from home and we can read her letter together. Mr. Latimer's note will be about our work together, but I'd rather not think about that right now."

As Claire surmised, her aunt intended to keep Claire and her family connected, despite her father's obstinance. As she noted wryly in her letter, her suddenly frequent visits to Thurn Hall obviously discomfited them, despite their efforts to appear pleased.

"Your Papa," she wrote to Claire, *"takes great pains to discuss the weather, which I find tedious, and what he imagines to be my interest in London society, which he would just as soon ignore as well as I. Pleased as he is by dear Frances's engagement, your mother is wearing him out over the expense of the trousseau and talk of Catherine's season—two years away!—for which she now has great hopes, since as Mrs. Hapwell, Frances will be able to give her sister entree to a more eligible class of suitor. Of course, as a mere nephew, Henry Hapwell is not so much as an 'honorable,' but Frances is quite pleased with her achievement."*

Claire handed the page over to Simmie. "How I wish I could be there!" she sighed before she continued reading. "Even though Mama is sure to be driving Papa mad. Francie, silly as she likes to appear, will be all business and counting up every handkerchief and chemise to ensure she goes to her new home with the correct numbers of things. And Cat! Poor Cat—she'll be chafing soon under Mama's basilisk eye, with both Francie and me gone."

"The wedding is to be soon, then?"

"Yes. Aunt says they've fixed on January. They'll be married from Lord Grimthorpe's townhouse in London and—oh, listen to this! *'Mr. Hapwell learned yesterday he's to be a secretary on Lord Augustus Loftus's staff and posted to the diplomatic mission in St. Petersburg. It's all on the qui vive at the moment, but he and Frances expect to travel out in the spring after the wedding.'*

"I wonder what Francie thinks—to be so far from home and among strangers as a young bride. She'll have much to learn and no one to guide her."

"She'll have Mr. Hapwell," Claire chided.

"Yes," Simmie said absently. "That will scarcely be enough, poor girl."

Claire looked puzzled. "All Francie will have to worry about is calls and clothes, and she has excellent manners and taste. It's not like she'll be running a household, as she would here in England."

"There is much more to marriage than that," Simmie commented, "and much is learned after the fact. If a girl isn't prepared properly by her Mama, life can be quite difficult those first months."

"I'm sure Mama will do everything she can for Francie," Claire replied. "Let's see what else has come in the post. I don't recognize the handwriting on this one."

Using her sharp paperknife, Claire carefully slit the sides of a flimsy penny lettersheet and opened it. "Oh, how wonderful! Cook writes to say that Annie would be pleased to accept the position here and awaits my direction on when she should come. Right away, I'd say, wouldn't you?"

"For your Mama's sake, you should let her give proper notice," Simmie responded. "I can serve as your maid a while longer."

"Very well, in a month then. I'll write to Cook and send her enough for Annie's fare and a little pocket money—that is, an advance on her first quarter's wages," she amended. Setting the penciled note aside, she reluctantly turned her attention to the remaining letter.

"It is from Mr. Latimer. Even his hand is beautiful," she remarked, showing Simmie the bold, flowing script on the heavy cream envelope. Claire extracted from it a short note.

"Dear Miss Burton,

I hope this finds you well—I understand you suffered a shock recently and it would not be unexpected that you feel repercussions for some time to come. I had purposed looking in on you this afternoon but will postpone my visit until you name a day and time. It is my opinion that to accomplish the solemn and scholarly task before us in as timely a fashion as the publishing world seems to expect, we set ourselves a regular schedule for our labors, when you are up to it. This I would like to discuss with you and also, I must confess, it would set my mind at ease to see for myself that you suffered no ill effects from your lamentable experience. Until then, believe me to be faithfully yours,

E. Latimer

"Mr. Latimer is right, Simmie. He says we should get down to work and apply ourselves in a regular way. I mustn't be miss-ish because I learn Josiah wasn't perfect." She got up and took a stab at tidying her hair in the mirror that hung above the washstand in the corner. Since she had left off the chamomile rinses, the red tinge was becoming unmistakable.

"I'll invite him to tea tomorrow and we can begin. Meantime, should you like to go for a ride? You haven't seen much of the country yet and I could do with some air."

Though she knew how to ride, Beatrice Simms was no horsewoman, but she was game. Claire ordered a quiet cob—kept in Oak Grove's stable for no reason she could discern, for next to Toddy and the other saddle horses, this horse was runtish and stolid—to be saddled and brought forth for Simmie's inspection.

"He seems an absolute pet and just right for you," Claire said encouragingly as Simmie eyed the little roan, which gazed placidly into the distance. "He's bigger than the ponies you're used to at Thurn, but you are a country woman now and should ride a proper horse. He's called Pippin, like the apple."

"I'm not sure he's what you'd call a 'proper' horse," Simmie replied, comparing him to Claire's imposing hunter, "but he'll do for the likes of me."

"Just wait," Claire teased. "If we ride every day, you'll soon be scouring the stable for a better mount. We'll have you riding to hounds by autumn."

With the help of Bobby Tressel, who always seemed to be about when wanted, Simmie settled into the saddle and looked at

Claire expectantly.

Using the mounting block in the stable courtyard, Claire swung up onto Toddy's back and adjusted her habit. Sitting higher than her friend, Claire looked back to see that Simmie was ready, then urged her horse forward. Pippin followed with more enthusiasm than she expected.

Soon Simmie did relax, and they began to enjoy themselves. All around them under the warm May sun lay rich brown fields striped with bright green where tender spears of corn reached skyward. The lanes were scarcely more than a cart's width, with soft grassy verges should a traveler need to step aside to allow one to pass. Billows of white hawthorn blanketed the hedgerows on either side like late spring snow, while a few early dog roses spangled them with pale pink and gold. Both women found exhilarating the smell of the moist earth mingled with the heavy scent of hawthorn.

Plowed fields gave way to pasture as the lane climbed, and through gaps in the hedge they caught glimpses of small white-faced sheep grazing on the lush vegetation.

"Just look," Simmie said happily. "It's such a picture I wish I had my paints with me, though I couldn't do it justice. The sheep look like clouds come down to earth and the hawthorn looks for all the world like wool tufts caught on the brambles."

"Or the sheep grew wings and flew into the sky!" Claire laughed.

At the top of the hill, their way grew unexpectedly wide and straight. As one, the two women urged their mounts to a canter and thundered down the lane, Claire leading the way, until they plunged into a shadowy woodland dell and pulled up.

"Don't you feel it?" Claire exclaimed. "This land a living thing, just like the sheep and the grass and the people. Just breathing in the air makes me feel—I don't know, Simmie. Like I've just been born!"

Indeed, her blood was singing as she drank in deep drafts of the cooler air under the trees. Her corset pressed uncomfortably on her rib cage, though, and she suddenly felt feverish in a way that had nothing to do with the exertion. Her skin tingled and the soft linen of the chemise under her fitted jacket rasped across the flesh of her breasts like rough wool. The heat flooded through her nether regions and involuntarily she closed her eyes, clenching her thighs tightly until the sensation climaxed and died away, leaving her lightheaded and spent.

She shuddered, moistened her dry lips and glanced at Simmie as Toddy's muscles rippled beneath her. It was like being drunk again, only this time her senses were sharpened. Every leaf, every stone, every sound was magnified, her every fiber vibrating with the hum of life around her.

Surely Simmie would notice—but Simmie was trying to retie her stock with one hand while holding onto Pippin's reins with the other. She gave up and nudged the cob toward Claire.

"Where does this track go?" she asked while Claire adjusted her neck cloth for her.

"We've just left the home farm," Claire said. "A few minutes ahead, the lane forks and we can ride down to Abbot Pyon, if you'd like, or we could just go back. Up leads into the park. I want to show you something first, though, if you feel up to it."

Simmie smiled again. "I didn't know how much I needed to get out of the house. Show me and then let's go into the village. There are a couple of trifles I've been wanting and—I don't suppose Abbot Pyon supports a tea room, but perhaps we could just call a moment on Mrs. Hanniman. "

They trotted on for another half mile and took a turning to the right that led them still higher, until they came out above the hedgerows. There, valleys and ridges spread in undulating ranks east and west, a patchwork of greens, browns, blacks and ochres until they merged on the horizon into layers of misty blues and white. Here and there the women could pick out a cluster of dwellings or a cultivated spot that indicated a farmstead. In the far distance, a train the size of a child's toy in their view trailed a white veil of steam as it inched its way across the land.

"This must be how the angels view the earth," Simmie breathed in delight. "What a wonderful country this is!"

"Yes," Claire agreed. "Take away the signs of human habitation and you can imagine what Eden must have been like, it's so pure and lovely. Up here I begin to see how men and women can become obsessed with a place."

Simmie looked at her curiously. "You don't mean you are beginning to sympathize with Lord Montfort?"

"Sympathize? No," she replied. "But I see why losing even a part of it would be like losing a part of himself."

They entered Abbot Pyon from the road that led past the church and rectory, and as St. Michael's came into view, Claire halted.

"Simmie," she asked. "Would you mind terribly if I stopped here and left you to do your errands alone? It's time I went in there," she said, indicating the churchyard with a nod. "I half think I'm avoiding Josiah's grave on purpose, as though not seeing it will mean he's still alive somewhere."

"Are you sure? You didn't want to be alone before."

"I need to be alone. You take your time and I'll be waiting at the lych gate when you return. The cottage for the school is just down the road and we can go by before riding back to Oak Grove."

"Very well, then," Simmie said reluctantly. "I shan't be long."

Claire waited until Simmie was out of sight before dismounting and tying Toddy to the rail beside the gate. Taking a deep breath, she walked through into the churchyard and past the weathered headstones nearer the road toward the newer ones, farther back near the rear of the church. A few newer graves were neatly tended, but most of the churchyard was a riot of flowering grasses and daisies. Here and there, the dried heads of daffodils rustled in the breeze.

Josiah's plot lay under a tall willow whose branches had been clipped back on one side to clear the way for funeral parties, visitors and headstones. On the other side, the trees' graceful wands brushed the thick turf and trailed in the beck where the water rippled gently before tumbling down over the stones toward the footbridge where Montfort had made his ugly discovery.

A simple slate stone no taller or showier than any other in that quiet corner marked the grave she sought. Young grass covered the low mound of earth, and near the edge, small clumps of dark purple violets clung to the flinty disturbed clay. Resting against the stone was a withered bouquet of wild flowers.

Only a name and two dates were incised into the slate: Josiah Fitzgordon Carter, 1840-1875.

Blinded by tears, Claire bowed her head and tried to pray, but no words came.

A cloud slid over the sun and she shivered as the warmth of the day suddenly withdrew. Her spirits plummeted and she questioned the wisdom of the course she had chosen, unable to force the doubt away. She missed her sisters' gaiety, just as she missed her Mama's vigilant though often tedious care and even

Papa's blustering. Life at Thurn Hall was certain, and with predictability came security.

At this moment, while Cat stayed at home to practice her piano or sketch, Mama and Francie would be making calls. Had she listened to her parents, Claire would be sitting with them in a neighbor's drawing room, balancing a delicate porcelain cup and plate and listening politely to the older women discuss Francie's bright future. Francie's new status, she realized, could help not only Cat but herself, should she choose to live by society's rules.

Instead, she stood here, alone, an unwelcome stranger in a country village, learning to run a complicated estate and endeavoring to be "literary," tutored by two men she barely knew—one of whom openly disapproved of her efforts, while the other revealed a side of her she could barely acknowledge to herself. She wondered whether she would complete either apprenticeship with credit. She no longer had to worry about the tedium of social niceties, since that odd Mrs. Hanniman was the only woman in the county willing to call at Oak Grove.

In Surrey, her place in the world had been as fixed as the stars. In Herefordshire, she feared to contemplate the slippery path she walked. Once again she asked herself whether she had done right in allowing Beatrice Simms to share her exile.

Exile. The word stabbed her heart like cold steel. In reaching for freedom, is that what she had done to them?

The chill breeze strengthened and the dry stalks of the flowers rasped against the dark stone at her feet.

Spying a scrap of paper attached to the sodden ribbon that bound the stems together, Claire stooped to pick the bundle up. The ink had run but she made out the words, "... my devotion is as steady as the North Star..." and what remained of a name, "...all.." or "...oll..." or maybe even "...dl..."

Immediately her thoughts flew to Josiah's letter, the one Mr. Chambers has given her that day in Papa's study. "... *your devotion will remain as steady as the North Star I will rely on to guide me home to England,*" he had written. Had he, then, been quoting from some poet or his own works? If the latter, the words came from one of the novels she had yet to read, for she had the others almost by heart. A tribute from an avid reader?

"What are you doing here, Miss Burton!"

Claire dropped the dead flowers with a start and spun to see

Edward Latimer all but running toward her. He reached her in another two strides, grasped her elbow roughly and demanded again, "What are you doing here?"

"Miss Simms had some errands in the village. I—"

"The two of you are out riding alone? Are you mad?"

"I ride most days," Claire said, gently pulling out of his grip. "I enjoy exploring my new home and the air is so bracing." He resisted an instant, then released her.

"Pardon me," Latimer said curtly. "Apart from the fact I don't like to see ladies unescorted at any time—what if your horse should take a tumble or some insolent bounder insult you? But to be out and alone is more than even a man should do just now, after that poor woman's murder."

Claire thought she misheard him at first. "Murder?"

"Didn't you know?" Latimer said harshly. "There's no question that unfortunate soul Montfort lays claim to discovering met with foul play. So you see, no one is safe until the miscreant is apprehended and brought to justice. He and the police believe some gypsy ruffian is to blame. It's even possible she was with a gang and fell out with her henchmen. There have been a number of burglaries... are you quite well, Miss Burton?"

"I'm sorry," Claire whispered. "I just need to sit down. This is so shocking!"

"Let me help you to the rectory," he said, taking her arm again. "I will send my boy into the village to find your companion."

This time Claire did not resist. As the first drops of rain began to fall, she leaned against his strong shoulder and let him help her to the house across the road. She waited quietly as he unlatched the iron gate and let him lead her up the front steps into the house.

She sank with relief into a deep chair in the front drawing room and marveled as Latimer himself saw to it she had hot tea, soft cushions and other little comforts, even adjusting the blind so she could see the road and watch for Simmie's arrival. It was a soft side of him she never suspected.

An hour later, after Simmie was refreshed and the shower had passed, he insisted on riding back to Oak Grove with them. Before he left them there, he had arranged to return next morning to begin work on Josiah's papers. And he had Claire's promise not to go riding unless Carey, a stout lad from the stables or he himself accompanied her.

When darkness fell over Oak Grove and its fields and orchards, Simmie retired to her room to open the blank book she had purchased that afternoon to begin transcribing the first folk tales she had gathered through talking with the servants. Claire, more weary than she wanted to admit, again found herself in the library. The inkwell on the broad desk was full, pen holders with new, sharp nibs lay on the desk tray, and she settled into Josiah's leather-padded swivel chair determined to work for several hours before allowing herself to sleep.

Her plan was to keep a running list of names, places and other references so that Mr. Latimer or others could research them while she went back and performed the more exacting task of redaction. Her expurgated version of Josiah's journals would be the foundation of the official biographer's work. Already, she feared, more would be left out of her transcription than not.

For more than an hour, the only sounds in the room were the scratch of Claire's pen, the hiss of the lamp and the crackle of the fire.

The deeper she read into Josiah's bachelor life in London, the greater her sense grew that her idol had feet of clay. He was intemperate, fond of gambling, careless with money, frequently in debt. She told herself that these early journals portrayed the unformed character of a callow youth, that maturity and sobriety had come with age. She told herself his more recent journals would return to her the Josiah she loved, but seeds of doubt had taken root in her heart.

His experiences also provided rich material for his works, so she couldn't regret them entirely. How else could he see so keenly into the secret corners of the human heart to create his characters?

Still, she couldn't suppress a wish that he had been an observer of life's darker side rather than a participant. For she read the passages concerning his female companions more closely after her conversation with Simmie—it was obvious to her now that many "Miss Laycocks" filled a spot on Josiah's social calendar, for "Dolly" had every color of eye and hair known and unknown to nature.

The picture forming in her mind of Josiah's reputation as a man about town gave her new perspective on Papa as well. If this is the Josiah he knew—but why would Papa invite him into their home, if that were the case? Besides, Josiah surely had sown his wild oats, as young men were wont to do, well before he crossed the Burtons' threshold.

She could hear Papa as clearly as though he were standing at her elbow, though: *"A reputation once lost..."* Oh, why couldn't fathers explain their reasons to their wives and daughters instead of expecting blind obedience! How could truth sully their purity?

Claire caught herself nodding off and stood to take a turn around the room to clear her head. Stifling a yawning, she banked the fire, extinguished the lamp and went up to bed.

But she couldn't sleep. She brushed her long hair until it flashed red and gold as the firelight. She picked up "Lord Morden," but the florid language and exaggerated characters exasperated her as Josiah's writing never had before. She darkened the room and tried an old childhood trick of reciting poems she had memorized until she dozed off. She finally gave up and let her thoughts go where they insisted.

She couldn't stop thinking of Josiah and how she had pictured their life together: She, tiptoeing into his quiet study of an evening, bearing tea or ready to mix his hot water and whiskey as he penned his latest serial. He, ensconced in his armchair before the fire, reading aloud while she darned a sock or sewed a tiny garment. Somewhere in her vision, rosy-cheeked children crowded at his knee, begging for a tale or just eager to climb on The Great Man's lap while she beamed on the cozy gathering. There was even a place for Kip, content on the hearth rug.

Finally, he and she, climbing the stairs hand in hand at the end of the day and parting with a kiss before retiring to their rooms. That thrilling moment when he looked into her eyes and murmured, "I don't know how I managed before I met you!"

Reconciling that with the chaotic scenes that now crowded her brain seemed impossible. Josiah, surrounded by a whirl of color, light and wild music, punctuated with the loud laughter of men, the hissing of gaslight and the high tinkle of women's voices. Josiah, dancing until dawn with ladies who put nature to shame with their bright dresses, rouged lips and sparkling paste jewels.

So much for the image she had cherished of Josiah, laboring in cold bachelor lodgings with only a kindly landlady to see to his needs. For that matter, she told herself harshly, she had never darned a sock in her life. Nor had she ever danced until dawn, not even during her miserable season.

She permitted a traitorous question: Would life as Mrs. Josiah Carter have meant nights alone waiting for her husband to come home from who knows where? And if she could doubt Josiah so easily, had she ever truly loved him?

She threw the bedclothes back. Lighting an oil lamp and pouring herself a glass of water, she sat at her dressing table in her light muslin nightdress. The night was too warm for a dressing gown. She toyed with her comb and brush and rearranged the various toiletries in tidy ranks on the tabletop. She sipped the water. Thinking that brushing her hair again would soothe her into sleep, she took up her brush again and paused, looking at the soft boars' hair bristles.

Josiah. So much kissing in his life. It was clear from his journal that he relished kissing. He positively reveled in it. The few kisses she shared with him had been pleasant and seemed to please him, though he was always asking for more. Once, she thought he would devour her, given the chance—which he wasn't, since Mama and Francie returned early from their calls. What was she missing?

Simmie must be right, as she so often was, Claire mused, though her experience as a governess couldn't be much broader than the girls she taught. Men and women think differently, want different things from life, find satisfaction from each other in different ways.

Claire looked at the brush still in her hand. Involuntarily, she softly drew it across her lips—and shivered in wonder. Instantly, she was back in the dusty cottage with Montfort, crushed against his chest, his lips pressed to hers.

All of the suppressed sensations and disordered thoughts of that wild moment flooded back. The darkness of his presence, his musky scent, the prickle of his short moustache grazing her lips and earlobes, the pressure of his hungry mouth. Her desire to press her body ever harder against his until she lost herself in his embrace.

She drew the brush across her lips again. It tickled but there was something more, stirring deep inside her. She pressed the brush to her lips harder, closed her eyes, leaned her head back, parted her lips slightly. Her nipples hardened and she dropped the brush as though it burned her fingertips.

Picking it up, she stood and after a moment's hesitation, she closed her eyes again and drew the brush lightly down her bare throat and across her bosom, just above the swell of her breasts. She experienced again the heat efflorescing at her center, secret channels flowing as if thawed by a late winter sun. The throb of her pulse pounding in her ears blotted out the sound of her sigh.

But now it was Latimer she imagined kissing, with her fingers entwined in his luxuriant flaxen hair. She felt his thick moustache and sideburns caress her lips and face as she slipped the brush under the top of her nightgown and circled her breasts slowly at first, then faster. His strong arms enfolded her, and she felt a tightening between her legs. Moaning slightly, she withdrew her hand and moved to the chaise longue. Reclining against its firm cushions, she gingerly skimmed the brush over the sensitive flesh of her inner thighs and the ache just above intensified.

She stopped abruptly and slumped against the back of the chaise, horrified. That last time alone with Josiah, in Mama's drawing room, he had kissed her and kissed her, gently pressing her back onto the sofa until she was pinned. His weight pressed down so that she could hardly protest as his hand crept up her leg under her dress. He had managed to shove her skirts aside enough to insert his knee between her legs and flop himself in the space created when he eased them apart. His grip on her thighs, she discovered as she undressed for bed that night, had left small bruises.

A part of her wanted to giggle at how ridiculous she must look, one leg sprawling to the floor and the other bent awkwardly with her foot on the sofa by his chest, but what she really felt was blind panic as Josiah kept repeating, "I must have you, Claire, I must!" and bumping his crotch against hers.

Fortunately, she heard Mama's carriage on the drive and found the strength to thrust him off her before they were discovered. By the time Mama walked into the room, Josiah was examining a picture book left out for visitors and she had fled to her room. She had scarcely thought about that day since, but now it was Latimer's voice breathing in her ear. They were in the summer house and she sank into the deep cushions beneath him...

Claire shot to her feet and flung the hairbrush on the dressing table as though the glass and metal burned her fingers.

She had just splashed some cold water on her face and returned to bed when she heard footsteps hurrying through the hall toward her bedroom. Someone pounded on the door and threw it open. Simmie rushed in, her hair down over her shoulders and still fastening her dressing gown.

"Hurry, Claire!" she said "The house is on fire!"

Chapter 10

"CONSTABLE REID HAS arrived, miss," Noonan announced to the sooty group gathered in the vast basement kitchen after a harrowing night. "Dr. Bevans is with him."

Mrs. White was handing out mugs of hot coffee to the half-dozen men crowding the space near the fireplace, while Simmie passed round a plate of thick ham sandwiches. The men's teeth gleamed white in their dirty faces as they joked among themselves. They looked more like coal miners than men who normally worked the surface of the land.

One man, his hands held out awkwardly from his body, sat apart as a girl brought a mug to his lips and coaxed him to drink. Wet streaks tracked down the grime on his twisted face, though he made barely a sound.

Claire, hollow eyed, her dressing gown smudged with black around the hem and on the sleeves, rose and threw a shawl over her shoulders. Gesturing to Matthew Carey to follow her, she stopped briefly at Simmie's elbow. "Send some coffee and sandwiches up to the morning room," she whispered. "I'm sure that poor young man didn't have time for a morsel before we roused him. Dr. Bevans will appreciate something stronger than tea before he leaves as well. It's barely daylight."

Noonan's back seemed stiffer than usual, she observed, as she followed him up the narrow steps and the trio proceeded through the green baize door into the broad front hall.

Watery gray light filtered through the lunette over the front door and the acrid smell of burned wood and fabric hung heavy on the air. It was worst in the hall and on the stairway to the first floor, because the high open space acted as a chimney when the big double library doors had been flung open and the smoke billowed out. It stung her eyes and irritated her nostrils.

"Thank you for coming so quickly, constable," Claire said to the thin young man introduced to her as Reid. In his dark navy tunic, buttoned high under his chin, he looked to her to be about Cat's age, but she pasted an expression of confidence on her face.

Turning to the older man standing a little apart from Reid, she said, "I thank you as well, doctor. I am Claire Burton. The injured man, Harry Tressel, is in the kitchen, but if you'd prefer, I can have him brought to you somewhere more private. I'm afraid he's hurt his hands rather badly, but he is quite the hero of the hour, since he raised the alarm and saved us all."

"Miss Burton," the doctor said with a nod, eyeing her dishabille. "A quiet place where I can work would be best, of course."

"Noonan, please show Dr. Bevans up to the lavatory off the corner bedroom. You there!" she said to a lad lingering by the doorway. "Go down to the kitchen and tell Mrs. White that Harry is to be brought upstairs. Then tell her I said you were to have a good breakfast."

"Yes, mum," the excited lad bleated as he dipped his head and darted past her.

"Who is that boy?" Claire asked Carey as the lad pushed hard through the swinging door with both hands and clattered down the steps.

"That's another Tressel, Miss Burton," the steward answered with the briefest of grins. "That's Ned, the liveliest of the bunch. He never sits still."

"You will have to help me find some suitable way to thank Mrs. Tressel for her remarkable sons, Mr. Carey. She should be proud of two of them today."

"Just be sure you don't enquire too closely into what Harry was doing away from his bed in the middle of the night." Carey lowered his voice so Reid could not overhear. "He may have been out courting a sweetheart, but he's just as likely to have been engaging in a little poaching over around the Great House. The Montforts can be pretty stiff about that sort of thing."

"I see—that is to say, I won't see," Claire replied, a finger to her lips. "Mr. Reid!" she called over to the constable, who stood helmet under arm, peering toward the now-closed library doors tense as a bird dog. "Come with us, please."

Carey grasped the heavy knob of the right-hand door and pulled it open, allowing Claire and the constable to pass through before entering himself and closing the door behind him. An offensive smog of odors struck them and Reid sneezed apologetically.

Pale light flooded the room from the far end where the tall windows gave onto the garden. Most of the glazing was gone, however, and many of the wooden mullions were broken out as well. Shards of glass crunched under Reid's boots when he moved closer to inspect the damage. The remains of the heavy velvet drapes lay in sodden pools on the terrace, and the grass beyond was littered with wet, charred books, bits of paper and pieces of smashed furniture. A swift shower had soaked everything only an hour before and a damp chill permeated the room.

On the two long walls, Jacinta combed her golden hair, blind to the disarray below, and opposite her, Josiah continued to dream, though soot and pale patches of color cast by the medieval-style rosette gave his face a ghastly mottled appearance.

After the danger to the house had passed and the household had assembled in the kitchen, Harry Tressel gave his account, through clenched teeth, as best he could. A bright glow from the direction of the house had caught his eye as he walked through the wood. Running closer, he saw a sheet of flame climbing the closed library drapes. With no means of extinguishing the fire, he roused the house and then rushed into the library from the hall. He threw chairs through the windows, pulled down the drapes and dragged them outside. That was how he burned his hands. As other members of the household scrambled to assist, they took his lead and seized everything portable they could put their hands to and flung them onto the lawn.

Unfortunately, Claire saw now, that meant quite a few things now damaged beyond repair had never been in danger. But in the circumstances, she was not about to fault anyone for an overly enthusiastic reaction. Harry's quick thinking prevented the fire from spreading and the significant damage was confined to the window area.

The entire library could have gone up. As it was, she had lost several dozen books, some chairs, a few ornaments. The window could be repaired, new drapes ordered in Hereford or London, the books and furniture replaced.

Claire remained near the door, watching Carey and Constable Reid as they picked through the debris here and there and conversed sporadically. Then glass crunched again as they climbed back through the window.

Reid looked uncomfortable. "Begging your pardon," he said to her, "but what is it you were wanting me to do?"

"Can't you smell it, man?" Carey burst out. "This place reeks of kerosene."

"That's right, sir. A lamp was left burning, I figures, and somehow it fell over and, well, we know what happened then. A flame close to hangings like those draperies you had there is just asking for trouble. Right fortunate young Harry happened along when he did."

"Constable, there must have been quarts of it. Miss Burton, tell the constable how many lamps are kept in the library."

"One. On the desk here." Claire indicated the double-globed lamp still standing on the corner of Josiah's desk. "This floor of the house has gas for the wall lamps, but this is better for close reading and writing."

"Are you suggesting this wasn't an accident, Mr. Carey?" Reid looked shocked.

It was Claire who replied. "I extinguished the lamp and raked the fire over hours before Harry Tressel noticed the flames," she said, ticking off two fingers. "The fire seems to have begun in the draperies, which as you can see are several yards from the lamp and the fireplace." A third finger.

"Worse," she said, her voice rising, "Harry Tressel told me that when he first ran into the room, he saw glass on the carpet near the window." The fourth finger. "Inside the room, Constable Reid, *inside* the room."

Reid cottoned on immediately. "Someone broke in and set the fire," he said. "But why?"

"That's why you are here, constable," Carey responded.

"Right oh." Reid drew himself up and placed his helmet back on his head. "I must go to the village immediately and notify my superiors. If you please, sir, if you could lock the library doors and keep people away from the other side until I return. I'll want to talk to Harry Tressel then as well."

"Aren't you going to ask me who would want to do this?" Claire asked.

"Well, miss, I wouldn't think it was personal, like. There've been problems, like, in the neighborhood..."

"Don't say that!" she said sharply, startling him. "I've heard all about the gypsies and such prowling the farms hereabouts. But what common thief would break into a house, set fire to it and not steal anything? Nothing is missing. And Harry Tressel told me something I've asked him not to share with anyone."

She drew a deep breath and spoke with a calm she did not feel.

"When Harry Tressel ran into the library, the gas was full on but the sconces weren't lit. All of them. Thank God he had the presence of mind to close the valves once the drapes were down. How he managed with his injured hands, I'll never know. The whole house would have been blown to bits if the fire had reached them! What mere house breaker would do that?"

As the ashen-faced Constable Reid peddled down the drive on his bicycle, she spied a horseman posting up the drive. She stepped back into the hall intending to run up to her bedchamber only to see Dr. Bevans crossing the hall toward her.

"Young Tressel should be fine, though he will be in some pain for a while," he said. "I've left medicine and instructions with your Miss Simms. If you need anything else, just send for me."

"Won't you stay for some refreshment?" she asked, suddenly conscious of her disheveled appearance. "It should be waiting for you."

"Thank you, no. I have calls to pay this morning and need to stop at home first regardless." On the drive, he stopped to speak to the newcomer and Claire saw then that it was Edward Latimer.

The house appeared to be unscathed, Latimer noted as he mounted the steps, but its lady did not. As she stood in the doorway watching him approach, she looked tired and frightened.

In her ruined bedclothes, she resembled a London drab after a particularly rough night, and the dark circles under her eyes suggested passion and too much wine rather than the ordeal she had just experienced. A smudge of soot on her left cheek added to the impression.

She looked vulnerable and he felt a sudden stab of pity for her. She needed him, he could see, and if he could just persuade her to accept his protection, she need never suffer through her own fault again.

"Mr. Latimer!" she said with genuine pleasure in her voice. "This is far too early for a call, so you must have heard of our near-disaster this morning." She extended a bare hand but he did not take it. "Please, come in. There is plenty of breakfast in the morning room and no one to eat it."

"Miss Burton, I came the moment I heard—the news is all over the village already, of course. But to find you in this way is most distressing!" He half-turned his body away from hers, eyes averted, and waited.

"Oh!" she exclaimed softly. "Oh, I do apologize. Everything this morning has been such a mess. For a moment when you came up the drive, I saw only a friend and forgot your position. I hope you aren't offended."

"No, not offended, Miss Burton. Only concerned that others who see you may not understand. I'm only thinking of you."

That much was true, at any rate, as he turned back to see her retreating toward the stairs. His eyes followed the sway of her uncorsetted body as she crossed the hall and began to climb the broad steps. He stirred and his hands ached to seize the long hair that rippled down her back and press her yielding flesh closer to him. Instead, as she disappeared around the landing and he found his way to the morning room, he imagined what it would be like to command her through right as a husband, to have her sole concern be his comforts and his needs because he took care of all other things.

He had warned Montfort he wouldn't take on damaged goods, but that was more to exercise his influence over the man than because of any serious thought of claiming Claire Burton for himself. It amused him to play on his friend's insecurities and stoke his secret guilts. But now, as he waited for her, the thought struck him that having her as a wife could be a very good thing indeed.

Clearly, she could manage a household. He had arrived at Oak Grove expecting to find cinders, tears and chaos. But here he was, enjoying an excellent coffee and breakfast as though nothing more serious than a chimney fire had occurred.

Carrying his cup to the window, he examined the garden and land beyond with an appraising eye. Joss had built well if not felicitously. The house had all the modern conveniences, the grounds were moderately tasteful and the farms productive. With the parish living and her money, he could afford to install a curate in his drafty residence and take up a more decisive role in county affairs than Montfort ever would recover. The right word in the right ears would quell any whispers about the rector's wife.

Aside from her obvious charms, Claire possessed all the qualities a gentleman desired in a life mate—health, good family, fortune, loyalty, compassion, a loving nature. And he wanted to be loved. The rectory was lonely without Lucy. His heart twisted in his chest.

A little serious wooing could bring him nearly everything he desired, and if he managed it well this morning, they'd soon be together nearly every day. Claire, he presumed, was reaching that time in life where, if she didn't receive an offer, she'd lose all chance of a respectable home and children. Without conjugal relations, besides, as every medical man knew, her health would suffer and her beauty fade more quickly. A marriage would be good for both of them. And whatever Claire had been to Joss Carter, that mistake could be buried just as surely as the man himself.

When Claire returned nearly three-quarters of an hour later, he was sitting near the window with a volume of Arnold's sermons that she had left lying on a table several days before.

She was fully dressed down to an elaborate bustle and overskirt, heavily pleated underskirt and whale-boned bodice. Simple pearl drops trembled at her ears and a pearl brooch pinned together the points of a creamy lace collar. Her hair firmly fastened in a chignon, not a tendril escaped to soften her drawn face. She hoped to erase the impression she had made when he arrived.

Despite her efforts, soap and water couldn't erase the shadows beneath her eyes, though, and she was conscious that the dark gray and maroon ensemble did nothing to brighten her complexion.

She watched him for a moment before speaking. He seemed absorbed in his reading, quite at home in fact, and she wished she didn't have to disturb him. But there was much she needed to discuss with him.

"I am so sorry to have kept you waiting," she said as she rustled softly into the room.

"Not at all." He rose to assist her with her chair and had filled a plate of food for her before she could protest. "I am pleased to see not all your reading consists of popular novels."

"Papa taught us always to start and end the day with something edifying," Claire said without irony. "Poetry and literature were reserved for the evening with the family, though I do admit my sisters and I managed to slip a few hours of pleasure reading into the afternoon if we didn't have callers or other duties to attend to."

"I think I should like your Papa," Latimer said, seating himself next to her at the table.

He offered her the toast rack. "You must eat before you tell me what happened. The shock of being pulled out of a sound sleep by the shouts of your servants must have been terrible!"

"I was awake, fortunately," Claire said, feeling herself flush. "I couldn't sleep."

Dropping her fork to the plate, she turned to him abruptly. "Oh, Mr. Latimer, I don't know what to think. Josiah's journals are so different than I expected. I wanted to talk to you yesterday, but my thoughts are confused and I didn't know what to say."

His brow furrowed. "Different in what way?"

"I... he... well, his life was so, so..."

"Profligate?"

She flushed. Impulsively, she leaned toward him and placed her hand on his where it rested on the table between them. "You were his friend—what was he really like then? Please tell me!"

Deliberately, Latimer turned his hand palm up and clasped hers lightly.

"Josiah Carter was like many young men, my dear," he said. "He had a little too much money, a little too much regard for himself and too little regard for the friends who tried to caution him about the habits he was forming."

Latimer's thick lashes veiled his green eyes and Claire sensed he was uncomfortable. But he twined his fingers with hers and looked up again into her eyes. The contact reassured her as he spoke.

"Not for the world would I distress you, Miss Burton. I'm sure Josiah was perfect in your eyes or you would not have given yourself to him so fully. But no man is perfect." Now both his hands enfolded hers. "I implore you, let me be the one to read these journals and decide what is fit for the public to know."

She gently withdrew her hand. "No. No, I've explained to you why I can't do that."

Latimer jumped to his feet, nearly knocking the chair over in his haste.

Claire stood in alarm. "Please don't be offended! I know you are only trying to help me."

"Yes, I'm displeased," he answered. "But it's not that. Miss Burton, it just occurred to me—the fire in the library—have you fully inspected the damage? Are the journals intact? What about Josiah's other papers?"

"You can rest easy," Claire said with relief. "I've taken most of them to my rooms. It's much more comfortable to work here."

She regarded the cold sausage and eggs on her plate. "I think I'm finished here. Let's go into the drawing room and begin planning our work. I expect the police will be back this afternoon and you must have so many other things to attend to."

"The police!"

As they walked slowly toward the other end of the house, Claire recounted Harry Tressel's story and told Latimer about the broken glass on the floor. For reasons she couldn't explain to herself, she said nothing about kerosene or the gaslights.

She feigned a sneeze to hide her confusion when he suggested they turn the summerhouse into a semi-permanent work area.

"My dear Miss Burton, you've caught a chill!" he exclaimed as he again produced a snowy handkerchief for her use. "I should leave you to get some rest after the terrible events of last night. When you are ready to begin, just send a boy with a note."

Reluctant to see him go, Claire walked to the door with him and halted on the top step. There would be so much to face once she was alone again. But Latimer smiled, and the rare sight burst on her like a ray of sunshine amid the morning's clouds.

He raised her hand in a courtly manner and was about to touch it with his lips when he froze.

"What is he doing here?" he growled.

Claire followed his gaze and saw Mr. Carey and Lord Montfort coming around the corner of the house, accompanied by a man hanging onto the leads of two massive brindled dogs.

"I heard about your trouble," Montfort said, taking the steps in two long strides and ignoring Latimer.

"What are you doing here?" Latimer said to him. The savagery of his address took Claire aback.

"I came to offer Miss Burton my assistance," Montfort said coolly. "And you?"

"I came as soon as I heard to lend her my support. And to persuade her to move into the village until these miscreants are caught."

"What!" Claire exclaimed.

"I don't know why I didn't think of it sooner, Miss Burton," Latimer said to her. "Clearly, it's not safe here and there's plenty of room at the rectory—it's meant for a large family, after all. The presence of my housekeeper and Miss Simms would make everything proper."

Claire's consternation showed.

"Or I could move temporarily to The Dragon for propriety's sake," Latimer added.

"You call that help, Latimer? I've brought help," Montfort said, indicating the dogs, now sitting placidly on the gravel drive. "Mars and Jupiter are two of the best from my kennel. I've just been explaining their training to Carey. Set them loose at night in the grounds and no one will be breaking into this house again."

"They are... enormous," Claire said weakly. Other than Kip, her entire experience with dogs consisted of foxhounds and Aunt Maud's pug. "They seem very dangerous. I must decline—what if they attacked the gamekeeper's lad or one of the children hereabouts?"

"These are disciplined animals, Miss Burton. Tell her, Carey."

"Lord Montfort neglected to mention that one of his kennel men would be with them at night," Carey said. "And their training is most intriguing. With anyone who knows the proper phrase to control them, they are docile as lambs."

"And you know this personally, Carey?" Latimer asked.

"No sir, but Lord Montfort says—"

"He would," Latimer cut in. "Miss Burton, don't let them persuade you into a false sense of security. Come into the village."

"If Miss Burton intends to be a landowner," Montfort cut in, "she needs to learn how to act like one and defend her land. You don't run away."

Latimer stepped closer to Montfort and Claire thrust herself between them, fearing they would come to blows. She was angry and embarrassed.

"Please! Stop!"

Montfort stood his ground while Latimer spun on his heels and stepped back a pace, fists clenched.

"Mr. Latimer, I appreciate your concern. Yours as well, Lord Montfort. Yes, I am uneasy and will be until the police discover who broke into Oak Grove last night. But I cannot go and leave the servants here alone. That would be cowardly." She appealed to Latimer. "Surely you see that?"

"She's right. You know it," Montfort said.

"Please don't be angry with me," Claire said softly, just touching Latimer's sleeve.

"Very well then. But I ask you to discuss this with Miss Simms. You endanger her, too, you know. If you change your mind, just come. I'll be waiting." He stalked over to his horse, untied the reins, mounted and rode away without a backward glance.

"Buck up, Miss Burton," Montfort said. "You're making the right decision. Do you want the dogs or not?"

"Yes. Yes, I do," she said, attempting a smile. "If Mr. Carey trusts them, I will, too."

"No question, ma'am," Carey said. "Lord Montfort and I have taken them over the area to familiarize them. I'll just find them a place in the stable until nightfall."

Claire shivered. "What a horrible day. I wish I could wake up and find this was all a nightmare! Even to see the sun would be an improvement."

In lieu of the reply she expected, she heard the crunch of boots on gravel as Montfort caught up to Carey and the man with the dogs. If he didn't want to come in, that was fine with her.

Chapter 11

MAY'S HEDGE BLOSSOM melted into leafy June, and that spring's lambs and calves, once inseparable from their dams, dozed peacefully in groups under the trees while their mothers grazed placidly on the summer grasses of Herefordshire's rolling hills

Here and there, the broad serrated leaves of hops vines fluttered in the breeze as the curling bines twined up their wirework supports. But on nearly every acre of the county, the apple reigned supreme. On thousands of trees, in the orchards of every farm and small holding, millions of small, bright yellow-green globes clung to their calyxes and swelled a little more each day. Bittersweet, bittersharp, sweet and sharp—when they ripened they would be blended with as much skill by the cider masters as French vintners brought to their grapes. Day by day, Claire learned their names. Cowarne Red and Foxwhelp, Collingtons, Kingston Black and a dozen others, the varieties looked back to a time before memory and each master jealously guarded his favorites.

The nine-day's wonder of the fire at Oak Grove was soon capped by the news that two vagrants had been arrested in Leominster after trying to sell a pair of brass candlesticks stolen from a farm seven miles east of Abbot Pyon. Thinking them made of gold, the thieves accused the pawnbroker of cheating them.

Their quarrel brought the constable, who clapped them into jail to await the next criminal court sessions.

A farmer near to Oak Grove remembered hiring one of them as casual labor the day before the fire, so the pair bore the blame for that as well. Much to everyone's dismay, however, no one contrived a way to pin the murder on them. It was unfortunate, Constable Reid remarked to Jane at the Dragon, but the men had been enjoying the queen's hospitality in Worcester at the critical time after being taken up in a brawl.

The inquest into Mary Collins' death concluded with a verdict of murder by person or persons unknown, her few belongings were packed up and consigned to the sheriff's keeping and the young constable's rounds resumed their daily monotony.

The county soon forgot about those lurid events, however, as it had more interesting matters to consider. The rector was observed riding over to Oak Grove nearly every day, where he closeted himself with the woman from London. Fathers nodded knowingly and their sons craned their necks as they rode down the High Street of Abbot Pyon hoping to catch a glimpse of her. Their mothers clucked with delight over the fresh scandal, while their daughters, alone in their rooms at night, dreamed romantic fantasies of love and redemption.

All were almost grateful to Claire for relieving the dullness, though none would be anything so daring as to call on her.

As for Claire, she discovered first that the hard work of deciphering and studying Josiah's papers suited her. She had a retentive and disciplined mind, and she enjoyed the puzzle-solving aspects of scholarship. The weeks quickly fell into a routine in which she found that the more she did, the more she was capable of doing.

She and Latimer labored in the summerhouse while work progressed on the library and continued there when the glazier and carpenters left, the draper completed his task and she herself shelved the last book with Latimer's help. Sometimes he would stay to luncheon with her and Simmie, but more often Claire would order that food be sent out to them in the summerhouse. There they would eat under the watchful golden eyes of the fantastical birds and beasts that decorated the walls as they continued to parse Josiah's sometimes cryptic commentaries and discuss their progress.

She soon found that the company of Edward Latimer also

suited her. He brought rigor to everything he did and was a painstaking teacher. Gradually he won her over to his argument that not everything Josiah wrote was suitable for her eyes.

Claire turned the letters over to him after one particularly indiscreet passage made it clear they contained matter Claire neither fully understood nor could discuss without embarrassment for both of them.

"I've read this over and over," she said with some exasperation, "and I can make out neither head nor tail. And it is in English, not French as he took to using when he wrote from Paris."

He smiled grimly and took the sheet of writing paper from her.

"It doesn't signify. Clearly, this will go in the box with the other papers we've decided a biographer won't need."

"Of course. Let's go on. The next letters deal with negotiations with his publisher concerning his next novel, which came out as 'Lorinda —Sketches of High Life in the Provinces.' They illuminate what a good head for business Josiah had, I think."

"Miss Burton?"

"Yes?"

"Miss Burton, you've been working so hard and the day is so fine. Why don't we take a turn in the garden? There is a matter I wish to discuss with you."

Claire never would have admitted aloud how she yearned to be out in the open air with him. She could never quite relax in his company, especially in the summer house with its intimate, exotic atmosphere. The closer the work on Josiah's papers brought them, the more she found herself watching Latimer. When he was absent, she could sketch the outline of his profile, she had studied it so closely. When he reached across the desk to hand her a pen or a document, her attention fixed itself on his well-shaped hand and strong tapering fingers and she remembered the day of the fire, when that hand held hers.

She thought she did these things surreptitiously, but Latimer was keenly aware of her interest. He proceeded cautiously, however, hoping that, undisturbed, some genuine feeling toward him might gradually take root.

Spending more time in her company these past weeks, he thought he understood better the reason behind her insistence that she carry out Carter's wishes. Claire was repentant, he surmised, but saw no way to escape the carnal bond forged when Joss had ensnared her. She may not fully understand it, but her woman's nature knew her soul had been forever marked.

But he was confident the worm could be plucked from the bud. Even the Magdalene was redeemed. Their bond would be forged out of her shame and his forgiveness. The world would see a respectable couple and need know nothing more. Any secrets would be dealt with between man and wife behind closed doors.

As Claire adjusted the ribbons of her hat, Latimer waited patiently by the door. Their journey, he decided, would begin in earnest today.

They had no sooner stepped out into the afternoon sunlight than Claire said, "Do you mind walking toward the paddocks? My horse picked up a nail yesterday morning and I want to see how he's doing. He's such a capital animal, I'd hate to lose him so soon before the cubbing starts."

"You enjoy the active life, I've observed."

"I am fortunate," she replied with more seriousness than he expected. "I am equally contented with a book in my hand or out in the fresh air. There's nothing I love more than a good ramble or a run on a fine horse.

"Unless," she added with a smile, "I've an interesting book waiting for me back at the house. So many young ladies of my acquaintance in London seem unable to enjoy either. When they're out, they fuss about the weather and wish to be back indoors. Yet when they're at home, they long to be out and about."

"Life before marriage must be tedious for any young lady," Latimer replied, "especially if she has no purpose in life other than to catch a husband. Too much time fretting about costume and parties—too much time centered on self, that is—can ruin a girl before she knows where she is. And in any case, the choice of a life partner often is best left to the young lady's parents, who have more experience of the world."

From under the downturned brim of his hat, he watched Claire closely.

"Papa believed in fresh air and exercise for all his family," she said rather stiffly, "and this is one point in which he and I always were in complete agreement."

"But surely," Latimer said slowly after appearing to consider her statement, "surely your Papa did not approve of young ladies riding harum-scarum across the countryside. A daily turn about the garden or a moderate callisthenic regimen in the privacy of her boudoir—tailored to a lady's more delicate constitution..."

"You are sadly mistaken in my Papa's outlook, Mr. Latimer. Sir Henry Burton is a gentleman of the old school. The Burtons have held their land for many generations, and sons and daughters both forge ties to that land through the time-honored country pursuits."

She paused, wondering briefly where she had heard similar words before, then continued. "Those pursuits, I'm afraid, include cub hunting and, yes, galloping after the wily Reynard himself. Why, in Papa's view, it's been a sad erosion of country values that he's forced to take a house in town every winter. Indeed, he spends as little time there as decently possible when the females of his family decamp the ancestral home."

They were approaching the stables at a rather brisk pace, Latimer noticed, and Claire was not the least winded despite her fashionable costume. He stopped short, forcing her to turn back to him, skirts rustling. A sudden breeze lifted the light ribbons on her hat, and she raised her right hand to catch at the stray lock of burnished hair that brushed her cheek while she clutched at her skirt with her left.

He had a sudden flash of the Botticelli Venus and lost all taste for further conversation. Their moods were out of step suddenly, and he could barely suppress the urge to seize her and shake her. Today was not the day for wooing, after all.

"I fear we will not agree on this subject, Miss Burton," he said as lightly as possible, "at least not today, and I know I will not be able to compete for your attention once you cross that threshold"— he nodded toward the stable—"in your guise as Epona, the ancient protectress of horses. I will see you tomorrow?"

"Yes. Yes, of course, unless you have more pressing business."

"I'll send a note over if I am unable to come."

Claire stood watching him as he walked away toward the house.

"Mr. Latimer!" she called after him.

He turned.

"Mr. Latimer," she said. "I know I don't say it often enough, but I am grateful. Grateful for your help, grateful for your interest in me—for the interest you are taking in this work for Josiah. I know he would be grateful as well."

The brief, false smile he gave her before moving away again was nothing short of ghastly. Shocked, she ran toward the stables and dashed through the open door to shelter in the dim interior.

Claire sighed and rested her head against the polished oak column supporting the roof where the row of sumptuous box stalls began. She had put her foot in it again, though she was unsure exactly how.

She shouldn't be so self-assertive—so pert—with a man like Edward Latimer. He was an educated, God-fearing man, the rector of the parish, for heaven's sake. And there she was, blithely, nay thoughtlessly, disagreeing with positions on life and correct conduct on which he, rightly, should be the arbiter. Or at least be given some benefit of the doubt, an appearance of thought, before she contradicted him.

Claire's memory flew back to when she was 4 and she was brought into the drawing room to meet an imposing man in black. The family lived in a relatively modest manor then, several miles from Thurn Hall, and all her days there were happy, except for this one.

It was clear from the moment she toddled into the room that every adult deferred to this stranger, and she ducked behind her nursemaid's skirts in alarm. Papa harrumphed, and Mama gasped, as her nurse yanked Claire's clutching hands from her skirts and pushed her forward toward the man, who looked down at her without smiling, as though she were a particularly unattractive type of beetle.

She stared back, fascinated, and she sensed the others in the room beginning to relax. The man was ugly, with a scraggly black beard streaked with gray and bushy side whiskers. There was a misshapen dark mole on the side of his nose that sprouted three black hairs. His teeth were uneven and yellow.

"Sir," Papa said, "if you please, this is our daughter, Claire Elizabeth."

"She looks like a fine child, for a girl," the stranger barked. "I trust, ma'am," he said, looking toward Mama, "that the child you are carrying now will be a boy. We don't want to see Thurn, or the title, go to that scapegrace nephew of mine with the foreign mother! There's no guarantee Henry here will outlive me. We need insurance!"

"Yes, sir," Mama had whispered, looking down at the floor. Claire had never seen her mother so cowed, before or since.

"Come here, child. I want to look at you better," the stranger said to her. She moved closer cautiously. Then, in an abrupt motion, he scooped her up and held her out in the crook of one strong arm while he leaned away and examined her with an eyepiece.

Claire took a deep breath and coughed, but she didn't cry.

The man brought her his awful face closer, one watery eye peering at her through the glass, and that's when it happened. She pushed down on his arm with all her wee might, wiggling and kicking until he half-dropped her onto the floor.

"Mama, Mama!" she called out running toward her red-faced mother. "That awful man *smells*!"

She was banished to the nursery without supper, and later that night, the harried nursemaid explained to her that the stranger was the incumbent baronet, possessor of the grand Thurn Hall and all its riches, and the sole benefactor of her family, which had next to nothing until the old man died. Even the roof over their heads belonged to him.

She never forgot that feeling of guilt and mortification. She wasn't to know that after she was hustled from the room, the old man had laughed heartily and given her abashed mother a guinea "for the lusty little vixen."

She only knew that she had told the truth, and once again, it had been the wrong thing to do. Perhaps it was time to accept who she was rather than hoping time would make any difference in her disposition or conduct, she thought.

She most definitely wasn't like other women now. She had independent means, she was free of family ties and as life stretched out before her, a conventional home with a husband and half-a-dozen children was increasingly unlikely. Nor did she want that, she realized.

She considered again whether it might be wise to go abroad, at least for a while, after she finished cataloging Josiah's papers. She had always wanted to travel.

Perhaps that was the lesson she had failed to heed her whole life: She didn't fit in anywhere and there was no point in denying it.

A horse whickered softly to her right. Claire looked toward the sound and smiled. Everything in the stable shone, and the cool air smelled of saddle soap and expensive horseflesh. She felt at home here.

"Toddy, my friend!" She plucked a palm-sized apple from the barrel near the door and walked over to his box. The horse thrust his big head over the open half-door and snatched it from her greedily. His powerful teeth ground it to pulp in seconds and he nudged at her seeking more.

She opened the box, pushed him aside and stepped in. Running an appraising eye over his gleaming coat, she noted the bandages that swathed his left front hoof.

"The poultices is workin' well, ma'am," a male voice said behind her. "The swellin's down and he should be right as rain in a coup'la weeks."

"Tressel! I'm glad to hear that. I feel responsible."

"Could'a happened to anyone, ma'am.'

"Yes, but it happened while I was riding him. Still, it gives me a chance to get to know some of the other horses. I'll be riding out with Mr. Carey this afternoon to look at that drainage project he's started over by the spinney. Who is in most need of the exercise?"

"Well, ma'am, there's Lanc'lot over there, though he's a bit rough, beggin' your pardon. Don't mean to 'parage your abilities, ma'am. What I meant to say is he's a bit unreliable, like. Mr. Joss kept him around for some of his Lun'un friends what he didn't quite like, so to say."

"Tressel, you astonish me! Who's in that box over there?" Claire say, walking down to the furthest box after casting a skeptical look at the unsteady Lancelot.

"That's Dickon, ma'am. He's a grand'un, got a bold heart but gentle as a lamb under the right hands. We've not quite known what to do with him, since, y'know... it didn't seem right..."

The man suddenly reddened.

"Dickon!" Claire said in genuine astonishment this time. "I assumed he was—gone. He wasn't here when I arrived!"

Tressel twisted his cap as he gazed down at the paving. "We been keepin' him down in the bottom, but we had to move him up here last week because of the diggin'. Mr. Carey was supposed to break it to you, like."

Claire drew in a long, deep breath.

"I will ride Dickon today," she said firmly. "And I'll deal with Mr. Carey. You have nothing to worry about, Tressel."

Claire remained composed until she was out of the stable block and halfway across the lawn. Then she ran across the terrace as fast as she could and flew up the back stairs to her room, angry tears streaming down her face.

Hairpins flew as she wrenched her hat from her head and tossed it aside. She flung herself down on the bed, gulping for air. Carey was about to see a new side of her and it wouldn't be pleasant for either of them. To hide the horse Josiah had been riding when he died—what else was the man, a man she trusted, capable of?

"Carey!" she called peremptorily as Dickon danced beneath her two hours later. "Carey, come out here!"

The steward emerged from the low building that served as the estate office with one arm in his jacket and fumbling to get himself into the other sleeve.

"Miss Burton, forgive me, I must have lost track—" His jaw dropped when he saw the fiery red horse she was riding and her set lips. He settled his jacket on his shoulders, straightened his hat and said calmly, "I see you've discovered Dickon. I can explain."

"Explain what, Mr. Carey?" Claire said sharply. "That you kept a secret from me, that you presumed you would know my wishes in this matter—in any matter—and then have the gall to do the opposite?" She moved the horse a step closer to where he stood and looked down. "Or did you think I wouldn't notice at all what you'd done? Perhaps you and your fellow conspirators were planning to cheat me?"

Carey had remained calm to that point but blanched at the word "cheat."

"No, not that, Miss Burton, I assure you."

"That's easy to say now that I've caught you out." Dickon took her mood and pivoted his hindquarters so that Claire was now glaring at Carey from the horse's opposite side, the stallion's tail swishing imperiously and his head bobbing as she shortened her hold on the reins.

"Miss Burton, please, hear me out," Carey said as he ducked back.

"This had better be good."

"Yes, well..." Carey removed his hat, took out a large kerchief, wiped his brow and carefully replaced his hat.

"Don't stall, I warn you," Claire snapped.

"It's like this, Miss Burton," Carey said at last. "Dickon here is a valuable horse, and I don't mean just that Josiah Carter paid a thousand pounds for him. He's young but he's good stock. Mr. Carter intended to go in for breeding competitive jumpers, and Dickon was to be the foundation stud."

Claire said nothing.

"Besides which," Carey added in a low voice, "Mr. Carter was inordinately fond of Dickon, and there's a number of us who believe that, whatever happened when Mr. Carter died, it wasn't the horse's fault."

Claire resettled herself in the saddle. "What did you expect me to do, Carey? Have him destroyed?"

"We didn't know what to expect, Miss Burton," Carey replied. "Sell him, perhaps, though I didn't rule out your deciding to have him put down. You never asked. There's no telling—"

"There's no telling what an emotional, overwrought woman would do? But maybe if enough time passed, and you hid the horse, you could bring her around?"

Carey coughed. "No, miss," he muttered.

"What did you say? I didn't catch that."

"I said 'No, Miss Burton,'" Carey said more audibly.

"You're a liar, Carey. I should dismiss you on the spot. Goodness knows what else you may be doing behind my back. My father warned me, you know."

"Yes, Miss Burton, you should dismiss me. But I'd ask that you didn't punish Tressel or any of the stable lads. They were only following my orders." He looked her in the eyes. "If you will excuse me, I've a few personal items I'd like to collect from the office and, with your permission, I'll be off the estate by morning."

"No," Claire said more calmly. She studied the disappointment in his eyes and said the word again. "No. Let this be a lesson learned—for both of us. You are correct. I never asked about the horse. But you need to trust me more, despite my inexperience, and I need to ask more questions of you—even if that means you're telling me what questions I should be asking. I don't want to be a harsh mistress, but mistress here I will be. I expect you to remember that. Now, shall we be off? It's looking like rain and I want to see this ditch scheme you've been so excited about."

"Yes, miss," Carey replied smartly. "And if I may so bold?"

She arched an eyebrow. "Already, Mr. Carey?"

"Yes. It's about the horse, ma'am, Dickon?"

"Go on."

"He is an extremely valuable animal—" he held up a cautioning hand. "Please, wait before you say anything! What I'm about to say is no less than I said half-a-dozen times to Mr. Carter."

She waited. "Say what you have to say, Mr. Carey."

He noted the restoration of the honorific with some relief.

"It's only that while he needs regular exercise, he shouldn't be your everyday horse," Carey said. "Anything can happen in these country lanes..."

"Keep him for my Sunday best?" she asked with a slight smile.

"Well, something like that. But 'never' would be better—for the estate. Miss."

"I will take that under advisement," Claire replied.

"That's what he said, Miss Burton," Carey muttered as he walked off to collect his own, more sedate mount. She pretended not to hear.

Claire was yawning discreetly behind her kid-gloved hand by the time they had finished inspecting what seemed to her several miles of narrow ditches crisscrossing the fields, some with cast iron pipes lying in the tall grass next to mounds of mud.

Dickon was a smooth ride, but he required a deal more attention than Toddy or the demure mare she rode back in Surrey. He tended to get restive and pull if they stood in one place for too long, and her shoulders were going to ache in the morning.

"... and if we divert the runoff toward the wood hard by Copperton Spinney," Carey was saying as her thoughts drifted off toward hot tea, fresh buttered scones and a steaming bath.

She was watching Dickon's forefeet as he high-stepped gingerly through the muck when she heard someone speak to her and Carey.

"Lord Montfort!" Carey pulled up and saluted the viscount with a touch to the brim of his hat.

"Miss Burton, Carey." He bowed slightly from the waist toward her, unable to keep the surprise off his face, but immediately turned his conversation to the steward.

"I've been studying this project with interest, Carey, and I have a proposal. If we extended the ditchwork beyond that field just there and onto my estate, the result will be much more effective for both of us and less expensive besides, since the work is already under way. I understand you're planning to use the reclaimed land for horse pasture." He glanced over at Dickon.

"I'm thinking of putting more acreage into barley," he continued. "Cider may be the lifeblood of Herefordshire, but to my mind, the country could use more decent beer."

"It's an interesting proposal, Lord Montfort," Claire said. "Have your property man draw up some figures and Mr. Carey and I will look them over before giving you an answer."

"At your command," Montfort said. "May I enquire as to how the school is progressing?"

"It is very satisfactory, Lord Montfort. If you'd like, I will ask the teacher to arrange a visit for you. The pupils would be thrilled..."

"And," he cut her off. "Parents would be more comfortable with their offsprings' attendance, if you will. You see, Carey, I know how Miss Burton thinks. I may not be useful in and of myself, but my title has intrinsic value not to be wasted."

Carey seemed mildly embarrassed at Montfort's comments, but Claire was unfazed.

"I was going to say," she went on, "that the pupils would be thrilled if you could share with them some of the true history of this area, from the viewpoint of the family that helped shape it, in place of the romantic tales they pick up at home. Some of the less violent parts, that is."

It was Montfort's turn to be nonplussed.

"Indeed?" he said. "You would turn me pedagogue? I think not, Miss Burton. That kind of truth should come from gentler lips than mine."

He touched his hat to her. "I'll be on my way, before you

entangle me in your academic snares. Carey, you'll have those numbers day after tomorrow."

He paused before riding off, though, for one more comment to Claire.

"I see you discovered Dickon at last. Did she read you the Riot Act, Carey?"

"You knew?" Claire exclaimed.

"My dear Miss Burton, everyone in the county knew. Handled right, this horse will be as famous one day as the Godolphin Arabian. If I were you, I wouldn't have him out in the wet and mud like this."

"Oh, not you, too."

"Ah, I should have known Carey would have been fussing at you already." A smile lit up his face. "I see it didn't do any good."

He spurred his horse and leapt out of earshot before Claire could sputter a reply.

Chapter 12

WHILE CLAIRE BURNED the scholar's lamp, the school fell into Simmie's capable hands. It was Simmie who saw that it was properly furnished and prevailed on Mrs. Hanniman and the rector to speak to the parents of promising students.

Simmie engaged Evangelina Gilbert to teach the handful of boys, while Simmie took on the two girls whose parents permitted them to attend. The more difficult task lay in explaining to families that a scholarship stipend was not charity, though the unspoken intent was to replace the income lost because the pupils toiled at books rather than at farm or shop chores. It was Claire's hope that eventually at least one or two would allow her to send them to university, even a girl now that Girton and Newnham colleges were taking hold.

Annie Parsons arrived at the beginning of July ready to work at Oak Grove and was dismayed at first when she understood that Claire expected her schooling to be first among her duties.

"But Miss," she exclaimed, holding back tears, "my aunt said I was to train for being a lady's maid. Whatever will I do with book learning?"

"You will do both," Claire responded. "How can a lady's maid do her job properly if she can't read instructions for cleaning preparations, for example, or notes left for her by her mistress?"

Parsons soon became a star pupil. Her gratitude fairly burst from her when she was with Claire, and her praise for Beatrice Simms knew no bounds. Claire looked forward to the evenings, when Annie came to her room to help her prepare for bed; the girl always had some tidbit of wonderment to share.

"Pardon me, miss, but did you know...? she invariably began, and Claire would relax as Annie brushed her hair and wait for the flood of excited words to begin. It could be anything from an historic fact to a line of poetry or a bit of arithmetic—Annie once labored with paper and pencil to show Claire how to add fractions. The girl absorbed everything that came her way and thirsted for more.

Meanwhile, Claire's respect for Latimer grew. She looked up to him and envied his erudition. And, she acknowledged, he was pleasant to look at. Leaning on his arm when they took a turn about the garden gave her a heightened appreciation for the male physique in the flesh. She was certain he could have taken his place with honor among the athletes of the ancient Olympiad and convinced herself her admiration was purely aesthetic.

Beside him, though, she frequently felt clumsy and unfeminine. She was a little too tall, a little too plump, her hair definitely too ruddy. Under the Herefordshire sun, a decided bronzing had warmed her milk-white London complexion. And no one would call her nose Grecian.

Josiah Carter's letters became less abstruse as the author's fame enlarged. It was evident, Latimer noted, that these were written with an eye toward publication. Claire still had not let him see the diaries, however, and he had stopped pressing her.

She sometimes read straight into the night, alone in her room, puzzling over the strange life Josiah Carter led as he pursued fame and fortune. He seemed to be two men, the romantic Josiah who teased, made her laugh and brought a glow to her cheeks—and the cynical man about town who kept late hours and low company. How could they possibly be the same person?

As high summer approached, she found herself riding out more in the afternoons, sometimes with Carey and sometimes not, but always on Dickon, much to the steward's disapproval.

"It's not your skills as a horsewoman I worry about," he would say to her at least once a week. "I just worry. He's a once-in-a-lifetime animal."

"Everything living is 'once in a lifetime,'" Claire would reply. It became a ritual with them. "We can't all wrap ourselves up in cotton wool, Mr. Carey. What's the point to being alive if we're afraid to live?" Every time the words left her lips, Claire marveled that she could think, much less express, such an idea. It was as though she absorbed her new knowledge of life from the very air she breathed in this place.

If Claire knew she was being observed in her travels, she gave no sign. Occasionally she would glimpse Rhys Fitzgordon on his big black stallion riding the valley ridge or their paths would cross among the fields and hedgerows. They would exchange pleasantries and go on their way. He hadn't called at Oak Grove since the morning after the fire.

But one day in late July, after he presented his compliments, instead of riding on he circled round to pace beside her. Her pulse quickened.

"I never thanked you for deciding to expand the drainage project," he said in the same bored drawing-room tone he had used to enquire after her health. "It appears to be a great success."

"It made good business sense," she replied in the same noncommittal tone.

"I don't suppose you'd sell me that horse?" he then asked.

She pulled up in astonishment. "Really, Lord Montfort! What do you take me for! Even if I hadn't grown quite fond of him, every man on the estate would have my head if I let him go!"

"He was born and bred on Montfort land, you know."

"So it's not enough now that you want my house, and my woods, and my fields, and my foxes and birds and trout," she said, emphasizing each "my." "Now you want my best horse! By what right, may I ask?"

"Because I want him," Montfort shot back. "There's no harm in asking, I always say."

"Ask," she snorted. "Since when do you ask for anything? And what do you mean, he was born and bred on your land?"

"My late father spent every penny he had trying to produce a champion stallion that would found a line," Montfort said. "My Brenin here," he said as he patted the big black on the neck, "is very fine horseflesh, but Dickon was the prize. My brother didn't really care about horses, though, so when Joss asked, George sold him. A thousand pounds can buy more than enough fine port, claret and brandy. Or an hour at the tables in George's club."

They rode on.

Then he said, more seriously, "I'm surprised you care to ride him."

"Because of what happened?" Claire would have shrugged, had her habit and corset permitted the gesture. "From everything I've been told, it wasn't the horse's fault. Josiah..." To her dismay, her voice caught. "Josiah fell badly, nobody knows why, and hit his head on a stone. Accidents happen. Trains crash, carriages run down pedestrians, riders fall. Unless the horse is unmanageable, why hold a dumb beast responsible..."

"For being an instrument of God's will?"

"Don't attempt to be blasphemous, Lord Montfort. That comment is tasteless, not shocking. I'd be amazed if I had reason to think you really believed that."

"What about the devil, then? Do you believe he aids the wicked?"

"Of course not. Signing pacts in blood with Lucifer is so, so medieval. We live in a scientific age now."

"Yet the people hereabouts will tell you 'accidents,' or the devil's luck, help me to my ends all the time."

"Then those people don't have enough to do or are woefully backward. There are other explanations." She caught herself and changed the subject. "Did Josiah really pay a thousand pounds for Dickon, or is that just more local exaggeration?"

"Oh, no. Joss paid. In a way, it was his final revenge on the high and mighty Fitzgordons."

"I don't understand," Claire said. "You all were boyhood friends. Why did Josiah become so bitter?"

"Edward Latimer tells me you've been reading his diaries, so you tell me."

"Josiah was ambitious. People were jealous of his success." Her words sounded flat.

"Joss was ambitious, yes. He didn't want to spend his life as a country solicitor like his father, and there's nothing wrong with that. England is great because she rewards talent and brains. But Joss cheapened his gifts for easy money and traded the regard of his friends for the flattery of strangers who will forget him in another year."

"You said revenge. I still don't see."

"It's not unusual for the dog with a thorn in its paw to blame the thorn bush rather than his own blundering. Joss blindly chose to profit by hurting the people who loved him, then he was angry when they turned their backs on him." Montfort touched the brim of his hat. "Good day, Miss Burton."

And with that, he rode off.

He was back the next day, though, clearly waiting for her where she usually left Oak Grove's acres and turned onto the public road.

They rode in silence for almost a mile before she said, "I'm not selling you this horse."

"I'm not asking," he replied. "I seldom ask for what I want more than once. It just seemed like a pleasant day for a ride and you seem to be going my way."

She laughed. "It seems more that you are going my way, milord."

"So it seems," he said, and gave his horse the spur.

Dickon matched his horse stride for stride as they cantered down the leafy lane. For Claire's part, she could have gone on like that for hours, he was such a fine horseman and Dickon was so splendid, but Montfort soon pulled up and brought his horse back to a walk.

"I've been thinking about your school," he said. "My mother and sisters will be arriving soon, and I may commend your enterprise to them. A school would be much more in their line, at least in theory."

"Indeed?"

"All the ladies in our circle in London have some pet charity at home to brute over tea, but the far reaches of Herefordshire haven't given my sisters much scope. Everything is too perfectly bucolic and prosperous. In fact, my sister Gladys will be chagrined that she did not think of a school herself."

"Lord Montfort, you aren't saying you want to introduce me to your sisters? You mustn't. I refuse to be snubbed."

"My sisters will do what I tell them to."

"Then you don't know ladies very well, Lord Montfort. There are a hundred different ways to put someone her in her place that gentlemen won't notice. I forbid you to even mention my name to them. If they want to be introduced, they will let you know."

"Is it so bad for you here, then?" he asked. "I would never have guessed. You seem so—content." He was groping for words. "Thriving. Healthy. If I had known you before you came here, I'd even presume to say rustication becomes you."

"You do presume," she said. "Shall we ride on?"

She was relieved when they came to a crossroads and he said, "Business takes me this way, Miss Burton. I'll presume you intend to continue on that way and bid you good day."

Yet the next day he was back, waiting for her without comment. And the next and the next. She started to expect him, and when he didn't come, her disappointment was palpable. Though she became more comfortable conversing with him, she could never quite relax. The air seemed to fizz about them—or was it just the bees in the summer hedgerows?—and his moods kept her guessing from one minute to the next.

Some days they said little and rode together for a mile or less. Other days, she talked more about her family and restricted life in Surrey, while he talked about the old days in and around Abbot Pyon, retelling stories handed down by his grandfather and the older servants, before the railway came and the faery folk still dwelled in the orchards.

They also talked farming and agricultural innovation. On those days, they walked as much as rode. He would help her to dismount so they could walk into a field to examine some fence work, a crop or a new breed of sheep he was trying out and then lift her up into the saddle again without effort.

The casual contact as his powerful hands encircled her waist and sometimes slipped down to support her buttocks never failed to give her a jolt. He always did it without ceremony, and sometimes without even looking at her, and she appreciated that he didn't treat her like a breakable object the way Edward Latimer did or those forgotten boys with whom she had danced at arm's length in London.

A gentleman, she knew, would have merely cupped his hands for her to step up to the saddle, but it never crossed her mind to remonstrate with him. The summer heat and haze, combined with a sense of isolation in the narrow lanes, created a cocoon in which familiarity between them seemed right. Little by little, though she wasn't aware, he and nature were conspiring to strip away her defenses.

The way he handled her made her feel real and solid, but the memory of that pressure on her body sometimes kept her awake at night and her mind would fly back to that unaccountable kiss in the cottage. She tasted again his lips and felt his hot tongue thrusting into her mouth, followed by the surge of heat down below. She would toss restlessly in bed and touch herself until she couldn't stand it, then throw the sheets back in frustration and stand at the window gazing at the moon until her racing heart and ragged breathing returned to normal.

Somewhere out there on the dark lawns, invisible to her, his mastiffs would be patrolling. It was almost as though he were watching her, could reach into the room and touch her through her thin nightgown. She shivered as the sweat chilled her body, and she ached for relief but couldn't say what it would be.

By day, she would shake those fancies off, and they would ride, two landowners casting proprietary eyes on their holdings, strengthening the bonds of mutual interest forged by their status as gentry. And something else. Try as she would to tell herself she imagined it, she would catch him studying her, much the way he did the first day they met in the lane. His measuring eye should have been offensive, but it wasn't.

It simply made her conscious of the mystery her body refused to yield to her understanding. It made her want to reach out and touch him, to stroke his cheek where the faint burn scar ran from eyebrow to lip, to stroke her fingers across his firm lips, to know again what it felt like to press close against the length of his body, to feel his breath tease her throat and face and ears.

It was very confusing—and intoxicating. Colors were brighter, bird song louder, when she was with him. She was sure she could hear his heart beating even though he stood apart from her. Yet all their talk was commonplace and neither reached to bridge the physical distance between them.

For a dissolute lord, she mused, he displayed an unusual depth of knowledge and interest in land improvement and animal husbandry. On both, he talked as though she were an equal—that is, a man—and she hoped he never noticed how she reddened and grew silent when he discussed the more intimate activities of the breeding shed. He was a great advocate of using scientific methods to improve livestock, and while he could illustrate his points in the pastures around them, she kept up with his train of thought through her once-forbidden reading of Mr. Charles Darwin's works, which she had found in Josiah's library.

Montfort was also steeped in the lore of the land and seemed to take it as seriously as he did current agricultural science. They were walking through a small orchard rustling with sound as the breeze agitated the leaves overhead and stocky, cream-colored Ryeland sheep cropped the grass below.

"But surely these are just old wives' tales now!" she laughed as Montfort finished describing how young girls thereabouts used apples to identify their future husbands.

He reached up and plucked a green apple.

"Try it." He held the apple out to her at arm's length, but as she reached to take it, he crooked his elbow, making her step closer, and closer again as he raised it just out of her reach. The corners of his eyes crinkled and a grin split his face as she hesitated.

In an instant, getting the apple away from him became of paramount importance, and she knew he could read it in her face.

Claire lunged and snatched at the fruit with both hands before he could dance away, and their bodies collided solidly. Their eyes met and for an instant Claire thought he was going to kiss her again. Instead, he stepped back and tossed the apple to her.

She examined the small greenish-pink apple critically. "Surely it needs to be ripe?"

"Now who's taking a silly folk tale seriously?" Drawing a sharp knife from his boot, he handed it to her. "Make the longest peel you can and then throw it over your shoulder."

She labored over the task for a full minute. When finished, she triumphantly raised a strip nearly four inches long and waved it at him. "Which shoulder?"

"Left? Right? Does it matter?"

"If I'm going to do this, I should do it properly."

"Left, then."

She tossed the peel and spun around to see where it landed. Before either of them could make out whether it formed a letter— the initial of her future husband—a sheep intruded and the peel dangled from its mouth as the animal chewed contentedly.

Claire laughed. "I think I should stick to science—or accept the fact that I'm not meant to see into the future. Three months ago, I could have told you what the next three years of my life would bring. Or even the next thirty." She sighed and switched her crop through the ankle-high grass. "Now I'm not sure about the next three days. Or hours."

"Best never to know," he said. "Expect the worst and not be disappointed."

Claire had no response to that. She stepped closer to the apple tree and touched a bright green bushy branch that sprouted downward from the trunk.

"What's wrong with this tree?" she asked, intending to change the subject.

Montfort barely glanced at the tree before answering. "That's mistletoe. It's considered good luck hereabouts, and a lot of the farmers will even try to gather the berries for the seeds to see if they can get it to grow. It does better if it's left to itself, though."

"But surely it kills the tree?"

"On the contrary. Where there's mistletoe, the trees bear better and live longer." He warmed to his subject. "Look around you and what do you see?

Claire considered, knowing the obvious answer wouldn't satisfy.

"Trees. Grass. Sheep. Mistletoe, of course." She looked up. "Birds, but I don't know what kind. And I can hear bees, or insects of some sort."

He took her by the arm and drew her closer to the tree, then pulled a low-hanging branch close to her face. "Turn the leaf over."

She revealed a bright green caterpillar. "Oh!"

"The caterpillar lives on the apple tree," he said, stating the obvious. "The moth it becomes—and it's unique to these orchards—helps the tree bear fruit. It's a drab thing, but beauty is as beauty does, my nanny used to say. It's called the mistletoe moth. That bird you see up there"—he pointed high in the tree—"that's a mistle thrush. It lives on the berries that bear the seeds that grow more mistletoe on more trees and bring more moths. They all live on one another. They can't live without one another, in fact. Even the trees, Miss Burton. Every orchard has mixed varieties, with hardier types planted on the windward side of a field to protect the tender ones."

"Everything working in harmony, nothing standing alone—that's fascinating! I've not come across anything like that in my reading."

"You won't find most of what's worth knowing in books, Miss Burton. Haven't you sensed that yet? The physical world is the best teacher, but men and women disregard the lesson."

The pressure of his hand on her arm compelled her to look up into his face. His eyes, dark amber pools, searched her face and for a moment again, she hoped he would kiss her. Then he blinked and pivoted, breaking the spell.

"I have business to attend to," he said hoarsely. "I trust you won't be offended if I leave you here?"

A sudden chill washed over Claire as she watched him ride away and, hugging herself for warmth, she turned her back abruptly and studied the trees before her. Where did she fit in?

As the days passed, Claire became more educated in the ways of nature and more like a true countrywoman, though she unconsciously shied away from making any connection between what she observed in the fields and what men and women did together to procreate. She also caught herself puzzling more often on what, in nature or the physical world, had created a man as mercurial as Rhys Fitzgordon.

In conversations with Carey, she found herself dropping a comment here and there that Montfort had made, just to see whether the steward thought they made sense. They always did, and finally she had to confess where the clever ideas were coming from.

"How would you feel, ma'am," Carey said to her after one of these discussions, "if you and I and Lord Montfort and his steward, Mr. Grindle, had a meeting of sorts, to see if we could do more together? The drainage down by the spinney wouldn't have worked half so well if only one or the other of us had done it. I know it's a sore subject, but the two estates were managed as one for centuries before Oak Grove was divided off."

"Yes, I see," Claire said slowly. "I will suggest it to Lord Montfort the next time I see him."

Carey walked away pleased, for he was a traditional man as well as an engineer at heart. He was troubled, though, by the viscount's sudden amiability where Oak Grove was concerned. But he didn't know how to put Claire on her guard, so he said nothing.

Edward Latimer had no such compunction, however.

"People in the village are talking about you, Miss Burton!" He fairly hissed. He had ridden over on a Wednesday evening, thus underlining the seriousness of his purpose. Claire and Simmie had finished tea and Claire was alone with him in the drawing room.

"They say you're seen riding all over the countryside with him, alone," he continued. "Don't you understand what they're thinking or don't you care?"

"I appreciate your concern, Mr. Latimer, but Lord Montfort is a perfect gentleman toward me. And as the two biggest landholders in this part of the county, we have many practical interests in common. We're talking business, not love. He's never so much as made an improper comment to me."

"Leave business to your men of business. It's not ladylike, this riding around that you're doing. With him. You must be aware of his reputation. And how being seen with him is confirming society in their worst beliefs about you! 'Love!' I can assure you 'love' is not the word being bandied about."

"What people? That's so vague. Tell me who is saying such things."

"That does not signify. Even if they aren't saying it openly yet, they will be if you don't stop. I've told you what the man is like! He is just out to use you, and he'll cast you aside when he has what he wants."

Unable to sit still under his harangue, Claire began to pace about the room. "I should point out, Mr. Latimer, that I spend a great deal of time alone, unobserved, with you. At least with Lord Montfort, I'm under the public eye. Are 'people' gossiping about us?" she asked with heat.

"That's different." He looked at her hungrily. "Besides, I care about your welfare. Probably more than I should."

"Whatever do you mean, 'more than I should?" she asked, although she could have supplied the beginnings of an answer from the green fire she saw in his eyes.

"Miss Burton, this is hardly the way to spring a declaration on a lady, but surely you must know by now that I am fond of you, that I could wish someday to put you under my protection, if circumstances allow."

"I see," Claire said. "Fond. Someday. If circumstances allow." This was not how she imagined a love scene between them would play out.

"Yes."

"Mr. Latimer. I can scarcely form an appropriate response. I thank you for your concern. I thank you for your interest in me, and your—your patience. But I think we'd better drop this subject, both subjects, that is, for the time being. You already know my views on marrying..."

Latimer made as though to reach for her hand and she eluded him with as much grace as she could manage.

"I had hoped," he said, his gaze boring down on her, "that you could overcome your feelings for a thoroughly unworthy man, a man who wouldn't even marry you when he should have, and let me save you from a lifetime of loneliness and scorn."

"Mr. Latimer," she said sternly, "I sincerely hope this regrettable scene will not undermine our friendship and that in a day or two we'll return to cooler heads. In the meantime, I will try my best to receive your harsh words in the spirit which you intended them."

She rang the bell, and Noonan appeared almost too promptly.

"Mr. Latimer finds he must leave already," she said. "Please show him out. I have another matter to attend to."

Latimer paused by her side as he left the room and spoke low so that only she could hear.

"I will persist," he said. "I cannot stand by and watch the ruin of another woman I care about."

"Oh, Simmie," Claire moaned as she sprawled across the chaise in Beatrice Simms's sitting room. "He all but said to my face that I was a fallen woman. What am I to do? I don't know whether to laugh or cry."

"He may have been tactless, but he does have a point, dear."

"And that is?"

"I fear we both sometimes forget how restricting country life can be, how unforgiving of the unconventional. If we were in town, there would probably much less remark about your free behavior and the company you keep. Not so many people would know you."

"Free?" Claire sat up abruptly. "Is that what you think, too, that I am 'free?'"

"Don't, Claire. I know better than anyone that you're not bad or wild, but you have to admit you can be impulsive. And now that you are independent..."

"This is your roundabout way of saying 'yes' to my question."

"Yes—and no. I'm trying to step outside myself and see how others who don't know you might assume, based on the little they see and hear."

"And the verdict?"

"Not what you would wish, I'm afraid. Not that either of us would wish."

"But pupils still come to the school, shopkeepers don't turn away my custom."

"Ah," Simmie said. "That's the money. They don't necessarily care for Lord Montfort either, but they love his power and his money. I've heard enough chatter since we've been here to also know that Mr. Carter was more tolerated than loved."

Claire looked thoughtful.

"Power," she repeated. "I've always looked at my money as giving me the ability to do good, to make the lives of others better or easier, if they'd let me. I hadn't thought about power. How some of them must loathe me, if they smile when they'd rather snub me when I walk into their shops and hand over my filthy money. Simmie, how awful! Do I have no friends in this place but you?"

It was Simmie's turn to ponder.

"Edward Latimer came as a friend today, Claire. How do you feel about that?"

"That he was cruel and said hurtful things and confessed— very unwillingly! -- that he was 'fond' of me. Fond! Is that the way a man talks to a woman he all but proposes to? I'm 'fond' of Kip and Dickon, and of this place"

"Don't be angry with me for what I'm about to ask, Claire," Simmie said hesitantly, watching her friend's face closely. "I used to be able to say anything to you, but you've changed."

"Never to you, Simmie. You know that."

"Well then." She took a deep breath. "Are you angry with Mr. Latimer because he criticized you—most harshly, we'll agree—or because he expressed his feelings toward you rather—let's say, tepidly."

"You're saying he hurt my pride in more ways than one," Claire said flatly.

"And?"

"I don't know." She got up and walked to the window, where darkness was falling across the garden. Annie would be looking for her soon, since the household was in the habit of retiring early. Not this night, Claire thought absently.

She turned and rushed to Simmie, sinking awkwardly to her knees before her friend and taking both of Simmie's hands in hers. Searching her face anxiously, she said again, "I don't know, Simmie. He's a fine man and I admit that I can't help but admire his face and figure, his learning and his good character. Everyone in the parish respects him. But he frightens me sometimes, Simmie. He is so certain about right and wrong, and so often he makes me feel like a naughty child."

She sighed and turned her gaze toward the bright coals burning in the fireplace, resting her head on Simmie's lap while the older woman placed her arm around Claire's shoulder.

"I can't help wondering how much longer I can manage on my own. The world is hard, Simmie, and it's particularly hard on women. How much more could I do, how much safer would I be, if I were married?"

"No one can answer that question, Claire, not even you. The world may be hard but it's also uncertain. What seems a blessing one day can turn to ashes the next, yet the most beautiful flowers can bloom on stony soil. You take a leap a faith and hope your heart steers you true.

"Mr. Latimer must see life the way he does," Simmie added. "He wouldn't be able to teach others and offer guidance if he had doubts. And he can't be entirely hard. Have you forgotten about Lucy?"

"No, I haven't forgotten that poor girl. He can't hide how it pains him whenever her name is mentioned," Claire rose. "I'm sorry to be weeping on your dress like I was a little girl again. It's time for bed, don't you think? I don't know about you, but I have to be out early tomorrow to inspect the new barn."

"You go to bed," Simmie said. "I'm going to stay up a while longer and finish next week's lesson for my girls."

Claire dropped a kiss on Simmie's forehead. "Good night. You are such a true friend."

At the door, though, she stopped and turned around. "Simmie?"

"Yes, dear?"

"Everyone loved Lucy Latimer. Yet she ran away." She spoke the last sentence half as a question.

"Unless she comes back, we may never know why," Simmie said. "The human heart is mystery. We sometimes have difficulty understanding ourselves, much less other people. She must have had her reasons, even if they were poor ones."

"It was a terrible thing to do, to leave behind everyone who loves you without a word. No explanation"

Simmie's gaze fell on Claire's hand and watched her absently twisting the heavy gold ring.

"Yes," she replied.

As the night deepened over Abbot Pyon and its environs, the two men on Claire's mind were thinking of her as well.

Edward Latimer, still seething, sat late in his study lighted only by the fire, drinking a mediocre brandy and wishing it was Montfort's whiskey. But he hadn't visited Montfort Abbey since he and Rhys had clashed on Oak Grove's front steps nearly two months ago.

Latimer was angry at himself for the clumsy way he had handled Claire. He had gone to Oak Grove intending to exhibit a concern that would gradually lead to the revelation of tenderer feelings for the woman. Instead, he had lashed out at her and exposed his intentions in the grossest manner possible. It would take him weeks to undo the damage, assuming she would ever admit him to her home again. She had thrown his words back in his teeth without hesitation.

Women were a snare and a stumbling stone. He had failed with Lucy, and now Claire Burton had turned him into a fool as well. If he couldn't get a grip on himself, he would never win her over.

He was just as angry at Rhys, however. He had warned the man off, yet the man defied him, just as the woman did. Already he could hear them laughing at him, as she was sure to recount every detail of his failed proposal as they sported together next.

The glass in his hand cracked as he imagined Rhys's hands on Claire's body, his lips sucking and licking her tenderest, secret places, her moans of pain and rapture as the pair rolled together in some deep covert away from prying eyes. As he pictured his enemy's climactic thrust between her writhing hips, however, he was the man looking down into Claire's tear-filled eyes as she gasped and begged for release.

Latimer lunged to his feet with a low cry as bile rose in his throat. He pushed the ugly images out of his mind. He had no reason to think Rhys had come anywhere near Claire in that way yet, and he believed the woman when she said Rhys had made no improper advances. But she was too trusting about men. If Rhys wanted her, he was more than capable of taking advantage of her. And then it would be too late. She would have passed from one wicked man's use to another's like a common street harlot, until all decent options were closed to her and she ended in perdition.

What had not occurred could be prevented, however. He'd start in the morning with a note of apology, he decided as he lurched off to bed.

Montfort wasn't having a much better evening. As he gripped the mantel in his study with one hand and jabbed a poker into the burning logs with the other, he told himself he could—and should—halt his nearly daily meetings with Claire Burton. But he was stimulated by the attraction she clearly felt for him. She tried to hide it, but he could feel the tension of anticipation rolling off her and see it in her eyes.

He felt it, too. He was drawn to touch her like iron to a magnet and it was merely a question of which would spring to the other first.

He had tried once or twice to stay away, but even in those short intervals, he missed her laughter, her quizzical looks when he uttered a double entendre she didn't quite comprehend, her serious application to the actual business of estate management. She made him see just how empty his life was.

But he didn't trust himself to marry again, and any other arrangement was out of the question, unless he could persuade her to go abroad with him. The idea of dragging her down like that was repellent, though. So whatever it was between them had to stop before they were both irretrievably damaged. Calling it lust wasn't wholly honest, but he rejected the alternative.

Not tomorrow, though. Tomorrow he had promised to go over the new building they had undertaken between the estates to house the overflow harvest they expected in coming years now that the drainage project was completed.

After that, he would go away for a while, maybe to Scotland or even Russia. He had always had a hankering to see wild places. If he could pull himself out of her orbit, she had a better chance of creating a respectable life for herself. She had had a lucky escape from Joss Carter and she deserved better than to fall in with another bad lot like him.

Chapter 13

CLOUDS THREATENED THE next morning, but Claire rode out to meet Rhys Fitzgordon at the appointed time. To let the weather affect plans in England was to sit indoors perpetually and do nothing.

He was waiting for her.

"Riding the prize stallion again, I see," he commented. "Shame on Carey for not stopping you today. Dickon might get wet."

"What about me, Lord Montfort? Don't I matter?"

"Not compared to the thousand-pound horse," he groused.

"I'll race you to the lane," she teased.

"Not on your life! If anything happens to that horse when I'm around, I'll hang myself. But first I'll drown you."

"That drowning may come sooner than later," Claire said with dismay as a few drops began to fall. The drizzle was no worse than any other summer shower, so they continued. High dark clouds soon filled the upper sky, however, and the rising heat became oppressive. Montfort suggested they turn back.

She was sorry for it, though. Montfort seemed different toward her today. More solicitous, more attuned to her somehow, though those were not exactly the words she sought. As it was, she attended to him more closely than usual herself, and that made all the difference between them.

The wind rose in a sudden gust and a crack of lightening set the horses dancing. Claire looked to Montfort since they were closer at this point to Montfort Abbey than Oak Grove.

"We'll never make it," he said, divining her thoughts. "We're close to the oast house, though. Follow me."

They raced for shelter as the rain pelted down and reached it just as the clouds burst.

Though she'd passed it many times, Claire hadn't seen the inside of the peculiar-looking structure tucked away at the edge of the hop field. Oast houses were used to dry and roast the harvested hops, or sometimes barley, before brewing. The twin kilns themselves were brick cylinders crowned with cocked pyramids topped by white sail-like peaks. Attached to the kilns was a low rectangular building.

Montfort twitched a key from the ring on his pocket chain and jabbed it into the lock. Swinging the door open, he pushed her inside. Then he returned with the horses and shut them in the adjoining room directly under the kilns.

Claire shook droplets from her skirts and brushed at her sleeves as Montfort surveyed the half-empty space.

"A storm this violent should blow over quickly," he said. "I'd invite you to make yourself comfortable, but as you see..." He indicated low stacks of filled burlap sacks along the wall and shrugged. The room was otherwise empty. "If it were later in the year, there would barely be room for us to stand."

Claire navigated the perimeter of the small space and inhaled deeply. The pungent dusty smell of dried hops permeated the room and rose in dizzying swells as her skirts disturbed the air near the floor. Splats of rain pulsed against the small windows and she waved a gloved hand before her face, hoping to stir a breeze in the increasingly close, uncomfortable room.

She loosened her stock, though barely a finger's width, and then unbuttoned her gloves.

"Oh, for Heaven's sake, take them off," Montfort said half-laughing. "I won't tell anyone."

IIe had already shcd hat and gloves and was peeling off his

long coat. He shook the water off and spread it, damp side down, on a pile of the hops sacks near the corner. "It's not luxurious, but it will do," he said, indicating that she should sit.

The sky overhead boomed and crackled and the roof thrummed with the force of the rain. At least, Claire thought it was the rain. Their eyes met in the diminished light and he abandoned his resolve of the night before.

Rhys pulled her into his arms and drew her into a long slow kiss. When she responded in kind, he broke off.

"Don't move from that spot," he said. Then, with a loud snap of the key, he locked the door.

As they stood together in the center of the room, he slowly peeled off her right glove and drew the tip of his tongue across her upraised palm. She shivered.

Dropping the glove to the floor, he dealt with her left glove with the same deliberation and lifted her fingers halfway to his lips. His eyes narrowed as he took in the row of amethysts and the black enamel of the ring she wore.

"I'm going to make you forget that," he said, and began to kiss her mouth again, more slowly this time. He stopped long enough to gently remove her hat and toss it aside. Then he reached out and swept his hand lightly across the hair above her ear.

"Take it down," he said.

Mutely, her eyes locked on his, she began removing hairpins and slipping them into her jacket pocket. Her hair stayed in place almost until the last one was out, when it suddenly tumbled down her back and over her breast. She stood abashedly, her hands toying with the ends of a strawberry-tinged tress that cascaded nearly to her waist, waiting for him to say something.

He began kissing her again, slowly but urgently, his hands buried in her hair at the back of her head, pulling the strands backward from the roots as he steered her toward the soft place where his coat lay. She wrapped her hands around the back of his head, burying her fingers in the dark curls, and clung to him as he eased her onto her back, kissing her mouth all the while.

She floated, breathing deeply to savor his musky scent, now mingled with the strong aroma of the hops that wafted up as she sank back and crushed them.

On his firm lips she tasted salt and also, faintly, on his skin, where moisture beaded on the fine hairs. She ran the tip of her tongue across his cheek to enjoy the comingled flavors of warm sweat and clean rain.

Lying beside her, his arm across her chest, he started a chain of kisses and rapid flicks of his tongue running from her hairline, then down, over and across her ear, pausing to explore the delicate curves. He gently probed the small central whorl, sending a light shudder the length of her frame. Satisfied with her response, he murmured nonsense sounds deep in his throat that vibrated on her skin as much as she heard them.

He continued down to her neck, going only as far as her high collar permitted. He paused to remove her starched linen stock, then repeated the performance on the other side. His gentle breath on her neck relaxed her body yet stirred her blood as it rushed to warm the places he touched.

When his short stiff moustache brushed across her cheek and approached her lips again, she moved impatiently to meet him. She sighed, mingling her warm breath with his, as his tongue entered her mouth. She closed her eyes to concentrate as he excited the tender nerves that connected her mouth to the secret throbbing place between her legs. She felt a flood of warmth there, that hot sensation of opening to him that she had dreamed of alone in the night.

She tightened her arms around him and returned the kiss almost savagely. Their tongues met and jousted, his thrusting and hers pushing it aside likewise to enter him. She spurred him to crush her tighter to him and tasted blood on her lips. The coppery taste excited her and she insinuated her body further under him to feel his strength press down on her as it had in her midnight longings.

She uttered a little cry of surprised disappointment when he finally broke the kiss off.

"Rhys?"

Wordlessly, he lifted himself from her and adjusted his trousers as though they were too tight. She struggled to catch her breath as her chest rose and fell in long, deep rounds of inhalation and exhalation. His eyes were wide, dark pools, the gold flecks like distant suns, as he started to unbutton her bodice, pausing only to press another hungry kiss on her lips before turning his attention to the tiny fastenings.

She lay still, afraid to move, afraid to think, until he finished.

He peeled open her lapels, then untied the ribbon that closed her chemise, gently pushing aside the sheer muslin to reveal the treasures beneath. He ran the backs of his fingers gently across her exposed throat and she drew her head back like a contented cat, inviting him to continue.

She gasped and clutched at his broad shoulders when he ran his tongue along the yielding flesh swelling above the hard edge of her corset. The sensation was exquisite.

He circled his thumbs over the tops of her breasts, massaged them gently and moved down over the sides and into her cleavage. He worked his fingers into the small space and under her left breast, carefully lifting it free so he could suckle the rosy nipple. The sensation was so intense she tried to wiggle out from under him, but he grabbed her wrists. With one strong motion he brought them together in his vise-like grip, lifted her arms above her head and held them there.

"Relax," he murmured into her ear. "If you struggle, you won't enjoy it as much. Hold tight to the sacks if you must."

The movement strained her other breast against the confines of the corset and, as she closed her fists on burlap, he freed it as well. She nearly swooned as he alternately sucked, licked and nuzzled first one breast and then the other. When she thought she couldn't bear any more, he raised his head and began rubbing her erect, eager nipples with the palm of his hand and rolled them both between his thumbs and forefingers.

When he stopped, she was giggling in semi-hysterical gulps as tears streamed from the far corners of her eyes into her hair. Her hands clutched the rough burlap as though she were afraid she would float away. Her lips and breasts felt swollen, and she stretched more deeply into the moment.

While she languished before him, a lazy smile lighting her face, he took in the situation and considered. The rain fell in sheets against the small panes of the building and the distant rumble of thunder followed on the heels of a flash of lightening. Now was the time to stop, he warned himself.

The air fairly crackled around them as, in a decisive gesture, he reached up and pulled his shirt over his head.

"Claire," he said softly as he gently lay down beside her on his back. "Darling, pleasure me now."

Eyes shining in the dim light, she rolled onto her side, rutched her skirts up and straddled his body. Carefully measuring her length atop his, she stretched out, her full breasts pressed against his naked chest, and began to kiss him the way he had delighted her. First the little thrill of kisses from the hairline, down and into his ear and then along his jaw line onto the neck. She was an apt pupil and she went slowly, showing her teacher she had followed his lesson well. His low groans as she reached the vulnerable spot at the base of his throat excited her. Twice she did this on each side and then kissed him long and hard on the mouth. Once more their tongues tangled in mock battle before she pulled away and slid lower down on his body.

Once settled in her new position, she brought her sharp little teeth to bear gently on his flat nipples, then ran her nails lightly down the faint line of dark, curling hairs that ran from his broad chest to his waistline. Then she started at the beginning again, this time kissing and nibbling until he writhed beneath her and his hips bucked gently. He clutched at his crotch and groaned again.

She looked up to see him watching her through slitted eyes, the tip of his red tongue just visible between his lips. She crept up his length again to kiss him deeply on the mouth, then slid further down to sweep her tongue across his taut belly.

Just as she approached his waistband again, he locked her in his arms and abruptly swung them both over so that she was supine beneath him once more. He sat erect, his knees pressing in on her sides, and through half-closed eyes she watched the muscles of his thighs flex beneath his tight breeches. He reached beneath her and untied the ribbons of her corset, loosening the laces just enough to create a space between the fabric and her skin. Then he untied the bands that fastened her petticoats to the bottom of the corset and, with his weight on his hands and his head at her waist, he blew softly and steadily up under her garments. Her stomach contracted and her back arched involuntarily.

She wanted more. But when she fumbled to reach her corset laces, he gently pulled her hands away.

"Leave it," he murmured as she protested faintly. "We don't need to take it off to satisfy ourselves."

With that, he reached back and raised up her heavy serge skirt, shoving as much of it as he could over her left shoulder get it out of his way. Her face partially covered and unable to see him, she suddenly felt out of her depth and afraid.

In a flash, she was back in her parents' drawing room two years before, with Josiah pressing her back on the sofa, fumbling under her skirts and jabbing at her as she fought to keep her composure. "I want you, Claire," he kept panting. "Let me show you I love you."

She had already agreed to their engagement, so his ragged pleadings bewildered her. It would have been comical, except for those dark bruises he left on her thighs and the beastly look he shot her when she heard Mama's carriage and pushed him to the floor. "You shouldn't have taken so long," he all but snarled.

The passage from his journal about that encounter flashed through her mind and she gagged.

Rhys found the bare flesh of her thigh between stocking and garter, and Claire struggled harder. His fingers kept going until they found the gap they sought in her pantelettes. Fire shot up through Claire's belly and she fell still, mute and helpless.

Rhys shifted on top of her and began tugging at the half-undone waistband of her petticoat. Her riding skirt slipped down and she felt welcome air on her face.

"Rhys, no," she gasped. "What are you doing?"

Instead of answering her, he shoved her petticoats up around her waist. He insinuated a powerful arm under her hips, lifting her slightly, and immobilized her.

"I won't hurt you, love," he said. "I promise—this time will make you forget any disappointments with Joss."

She felt him yank at her nether garments and heard the soft rip of linen.

She flinched when his fingers touched her again—and then again and again. She succumbed to building waves of bliss. They started in hot bursts where he stroked her, then shot swiftly out to the crown of her head and the tips of toes, which curled in her boots each time. She thrashed from side to side, as far as his tight grip allowed, and her hips began rising rhythmically in anticipation as she pressed harder against the source of her ecstasy. The world around her shrank, and her body became less than nothing, except for the tiny, blazing hot sun between her legs. She cried out incoherently each time he lashed her desire, until a fiery blossom of light engulfed her and she dissolved.

The heavy scent of hops assailed Claire's nostrils when the world rushed back in on her. Dreamily she called out for Rhys, but only a sigh escaped her lips. Course cloth met her fingers as she groped blindly for him.

She thought she'd never have the strength to move again. Her skin tingled like she had been rubbed all over with nettles, but the sensation was beyond delightful. She wanted to hum in tune with her thrumming body. The rain pounded on the windows and the ground outside, but all she heard was the blood singing in her ears.

From a far distant place, she felt him shift her body to elevate her hips on the edge of a thick hops sack. She waited, half-sick with anticipation, legs splayed on either side of his thighs. Then she felt his fingers part her folds and smear the sweet hot honey they found there. Something hard and slick pressed against, then into her.

"Claire," he said in her ear, his voice a register deeper than normal. "Do you want me to stop?"

"No," she moaned. "No, don't stop! I feel like I'll die if you stop!" She pushed up against him, and in a swift heartbeat, he thrust his full length inside her. The world stopped as he and she sucked in the hot air of the close room. She thought she heard a muffled, "Damn," but her startled yelp of pain overrode whatever it was he had said.

Then, teetering at the cliff edge of passion, they tumbled over the precipice. Her cries came too rapidly to distinguish any beginning or end. She dug her nails into his hard back for purchase as the fury of his coitus drove her against the stone wall behind them. His sharp grunts matched the storm of his rutting.

She arched her back and clung tighter as he grabbed her buttocks in the final frenzy of their coupling. Deep in her center, she felt heat explode and fell limp, her body convulsed in rapture.

The emptiness he left when he abruptly pulled away from her brought a sob to her dry lips.

When he didn't return to her immediately, she forced herself to lift her head and look for him.

He sat less than a foot away from her, staring out at the rain.

"Rhys? What's wrong?"

"You lied to me," he said through clenched teeth. "You're a virgin. Or were." He wiped the back of his hand across his mouth as though he had tasted something foul.

"I don't understand." She sat bolt upright now. "I never said—

I never said anything that—"

He stood and glared down at her where she lay, the marks of passion easy to read in her eyes and on her rosy flesh.

"Christ almighty, Claire, I think you know by now what kind of man Joss was. And you can't deny what's been on both our minds every day we rode out together. What was I supposed to think?" His mouth crooked in a sardonic smile. "You certainly seemed to know what you were about here."

Claire felt herself flame from the bottoms of her feet to the roots of her hair. Wordlessly, she scrambled awkwardly to her feet and glared at him.

He snorted. "You've nothing to say to that, do you? You may lack experience, but Joss had a real knack for spotting the ones who'd tumble, I'll give him that."

"Why are you so angry with me?" Claire said at last. "You got what you wanted. So did I."

"You don't know what you want," he said with exasperation. "Have you thought about this at all, where it could end up? Where it won't? I won't marry you, if that's what you're after. It's nothing personal. I won't marry any woman again."

His stony look frightened her.

"I killed my wife," he said at last. "I murdered her just as surely as though I had pushed her down those stairs or shot her with a pistol. I knew she loved another man and I knew I didn't love her. But we married anyway, and it nearly killed both of us in the end. I wish to God it had been me instead. Don't you see, Claire?"

"Then..." Words died on her lips.

"Why bother at all?

"Yes."

"I'm no coward. And day still follows night." He reached for her hand but halted when he saw her begin to draw back.

"Claire, we're two adults who obviously take pleasure in each other's bodies. There's no harm in that, as long as we agree that's all it is. I've seen you at your window at night. Joss has been gone for two years, and I'm guessing that was a pretty lonely time for a woman like you. I'm saying forget that and live life however you can."

"What do you mean, you've seen me?" she stammered. "Have

you been spying on me? What," she licked her lips, "what did you see?"

"I've seen evidence of a lonely woman, Claire," he said softly. "That's all. There's always a light late at night, either in the library or one of the bedrooms. I suspect it's yours, because it's always just the one. That has to be you."

She let him take her hand. "You're too hungry for life to turn your back on it and follow a ghost, Claire. Ghosts can't touch you—like I can." He drew closer and leaned in to kiss her.

She snatched her hand back and tried to cover her exposed chest.

"Isn't it a little late to be discussing terms, like we're negotiating a contract? Are you expecting me to be your mistress now?"

"Lovers, Claire. We'd be lovers. You hardly need my financial support or protection," he pointed out.

She grimaced. "So precise you are, Lord Montfort. You—you seduce me and now I'm supposed to pretend it was nothing but a pleasant way to pass a rainy morning."

"Well, it was, wasn't it?" he barked. "But don't go making it into a grand seduction scene. We had some nice sport, but I left the final choice up to you."

"Sport!" she shouted. "You call fornication 'sport?'"

"Fornication?" He laughed and drew his shirt over his head. "My dear Miss Burton," he said, as he began fastening its buttons. "You sound like my esteemed friend, the rector. I was going to suggest you give up your fantasies about Joss Carter once and for all and come away with me. I like your company and clearly we have other things in common. Italy, perhaps? You can't imagine what a Herefordshire winter is like."

He looked up to see a welter of emotions flit across her face, beginning with anger, racing through astonishment and revulsion and ending in the neighborhood of bravado.

What a beautiful mess she was! Dust streaked her dark skirts and the deep lace hem of her half-attached petticoat trailed on the floor, threatening to trip her if she moved carelessly. Her long, tousled hair concealed most of one naked breast, but the other peeped out from her bodice, a pink ribbon trailing across its alabaster expanse. Her lips, still crimson from kissing, were slack. Her eyes, in the too-white face, were as dark and stormy with passion as the sky outside.

Under his gaze, bravado crumbled into shame and she looked away.

"How dare you!" She cast about for her scattered garments. "How dare you! Think of the scandal."

"Claire, you need to understand something," he said quietly, all laughter gone from his eyes. "You are already beyond the pale. Joss Carter was a cad. He used women for his pleasure—all kinds of women—until he tired of them and then moved on. And he was a man who bored quickly. A parade of them came through Oak Grove when he wasn't romancing someone's wife in London or visiting his lady of the moment in a rural bower in the Cotswolds. All his servants knew to stay away from the summerhouse when he had ladies as guests. The only puzzle in these parts is why he chose you in the first place. Of course, everyone assumed—"

"I hate that word! Whatever happened to 'judge not, lest ye be judged?' You and Edward Latimer, too. Well, I've got a surprise for you. I am a lady, despite what any of you think. So pretend to be a gentleman—get out and leave me to pull myself together. I never want to see you again."

"If that's what you want, fine. But let me tell you something first. Joss was worse than a cad where you're concerned. He played with your inexperience and your romantic notions until you can't see the truth. He's ruined you, all right, but not in the way society means when it uses that word.

"He's chained you to a lie, and you can't see it, you're so wedded to that dream he conjured of what might have been—that never was going to be. You dress like an old Quaker woman, you moon around the countryside spouting your pieties of 'Josiah said this' and "Josiah said that.' I'll wager you never take that ring off. It's sickening. Virginity! You may have been 'intact' before the law and the church, but Joss stole your soul as surely as he ruined your reputation.

"Josiah loved me!"

"What kind of love is it that doesn't fight for itself? You say you loved each other, but at the first sign of trouble, you retreated to your books and he ran away."

"Are you finished, Lord Montfort?"

"With you? Yes. I can't stomach humbug."

Rhys snatched his hat up from the floor, stalked into the next room and returned leading his horse. Claire, her back to him, heard him swear as he fumbled with the key in the door lock. Then a strong hand on her shoulder spun her around and inches separated their faces. She bit back a yelp, and he snatched up her left hand.

Glaring at Josiah's ring, he snapped, "You are a fool, Miss Claire Burton." He flung her hand down and stalked out into the light drizzle that lingered after the storm.

Off to the west, a pale rainbow shimmered above the horizon. He made a rude gesture at the sky, swung up into the saddle and gave his horse a savage kick.

Claire watched Montfort until he was out of sight, then studied her pallid reflection in the wet pane. Her hair was wild, her face unrecognizable. Groping for a word, the best she could come up with was "womanly." Her eyes looked like the eyes of those girls from her ill-fated season who had found husbands.

When they came back from their honeymoons, they carried themselves differently and looked out at the world with a new, more confident expression. At social events, they sat apart from the unmarried girls, whispered behind gloved hands and glanced at them with pity.

But, young or old, only the married ladies in her circle exhibited that change. A spinster of any age could be spotted immediately, because she walked and talked and hesitated like a girl. So what did that make her?

Claire touched her cheek, traced the line of her lips, ran her fingers up through her hair, let her hand come to rest at the base of her throat. She knew what it made her. Montfort and Latimer were right. She had eaten of the tree of knowledge. She knew now what it was she yearned for in the night.

The word she sought to describe that pale, languid-eyed reflection was wanton. She burned with lust, she admitted, forcing herself to confront the word. She was lustful and unable to control herself. Instead of disciplining her flesh, she yielded to it. The sore ache between her legs removed any doubt. For part of her regretted only that Rhys had gone when they could have, she assumed, repeated their "sport."

Montfort's words stung, but not the way he intended. He shocked her into recognizing her carnal nature. Like a serpent in her heart, lust deceived her into thinking she understood love.

She groaned and covered her face, blotting out the image that wavered and japed before her as fresh rain ran down the glass.

Her anger extinguished by this appalling new understanding, Claire's only thought now was to get back to Oak Grove as quickly as possible without being noticed.

Pinning her hair up under her hat was no problem, especially since the loosened corset allowed her to raise her arms more easily. But the corset presented a different challenge. With no one to help her, she couldn't lace it tightly enough to close her riding jacket over it. Try as she might, couldn't pull the laces tight enough.

In desperation, she undid the buttons on the jacket's long cuffs and slipped the garment off so she could shed the corset entirely. But that left her with no way to hold up her petticoat, so that had to go as well.

She settled the jacket on her torso as best she could. Without the foundation garment, it still didn't fit properly. Her breasts felt odd squashed against her body rather than supported high on her chest and the compression felt—well, she pushed that thought out of her mind as soon as it came. The jacket was buttoned and that was all that mattered.

Her stock lay on the floor in the corner where she and Rhys had "sported"—she said the word aloud this time—and she discovered that tying a tidy neck knot backwards was next to impossible. She began to wish she had been soaked in the storm. Explaining her disheveled appearance would be easier when she got home.

Finding both gloves took several minutes. One had landed behind a hops sack.

Wrapping the petticoats around the corset, she stuffed the large bundle under her arm and retrieved Dickon from his shelter. The small room reeked of steaming manure. He shied repeatedly when she grabbed at his bridle, and her boots were soiled before she caught him and led him out.

Mounting the uncooperative horse one-handed proved to be impossible. Had her legs been steadier, she might have managed it, but Rhys had loved her too well. Her flesh quivered like Dickon's in the rain and she longed to lie down and sleep.

She tried standing Dickon next to a pile of sacks and climbing up on it to reach his back, but it was like trying to ascend dry sand.

The soft, rustling crunch as the hops shifted under her feet gave Dickon a further excuse to pirouette away from her.

Extending her left arm and leaning as far as she could without dropping Dickon's bridle, she stuffed the bundle of cloth behind the sacks closest to the wall, then scrambled onto the horse's back. Ducking her head, she rode out into the wet air but got only a few feet before she pulled up, jumped to the ground, tied the reins to a bush and ran back inside to retrieve her undergarments, which she just remembered were monogrammed.

Resigned to walking, Claire led Dickon onto a narrow track across the fields that she hoped led toward home. She tramped nearly a mile, grateful for the high hedgerows, before she stopped at a small pond. Walking so close to the edge that ooze seeped into her boots and wet her hem, she pitched the clothing as far as she could over the water and watched it sink. It took forever, the petticoat unfurling across the surface like a monstrous waterlily. She thought she'd scream with impatience before it finally went under.

Disburdened, she easily mounted Dickon from a slope in the lane—the horse now placid as a lamb—and set his head toward home. Though it felt like a lifetime had flown by since she'd left the house that morning, it was barely noon, and it seemed to Claire that every tree sheltered a farm laborer pausing for his bread, cheese and beer.

The ones who saw her merely touched their caps and carried on with their meals, but at the turning in the lane between Oak Grove and Oakley Court, she thought she heard her name, followed by a burst of laughter.

"Oh, aye, that Burton woman's a sly one all right," she heard through the hedge. "But his lordship'll get what he wants in the end, one way or another, mark my words. He's not up at the crack o' dawn every day for the pleasure of her company."

Claire tugged back gently on the reins and strained to hear more.

"Now there you're wrong, Alf," a second man said. "I think there's a deal o' pleasure in it. These 'projects' between the two of them, the money's no skin off his nose. He'll knows it'll all come back to him when he gets his hands on Oak Grove." More laughter.

"And call her a sly 'un?" the man continued. "What about him? I'd be up at dawn as well as him, if meant a good roll in the hay with that 'un. She's uppity, but fills the hands above and behind, know what I mean?”

“My missus’ brother’s lad works in his lordship’s stables,” the man called Alf said, “and he says that for being out ridd all day, his lordship’s horse is pretty fresh when he comes home at night.”

“I’ll wager there’s some hard riding goin’ on, but it don’t involve the horse,” the first man chimed in. “If his lordship can’t sweet talk Miss Burton into sellin’ up, he’ll no doubt get it out of her on her back.”

Claire flinched at the way he uttered “miss.”

“It’s how she got in the first place, so ‘twould serve her right!” Gales of guffaws followed Alf’s comment.

Claire spurred Dickon so hard she drew blood from his flanks. In a clap of thunder, rain began to fall hard again and she barely managed to control the frenzied horse as they galloped down the dark, overgrown lane. Dickon put a foot wrong on the sodden, uneven ground, and down they both went.

Stunned but unhurt, she fumbled to her knees and half-crawled to where the horse lay groaning, unable to rise. Her sure touch and gentle words were of no use now. After a moment, she stood and begun trudging back to where the men had laughed and joked at her expense. One, she remembered, had had a gun.

The men were gathered around the stable yard when Claire returned, but she managed to flee to the house unseen. She couldn’t look Tressel in the eye and was in no state to tell him what had happened to his prize horse. He and the others would find out soon enough they’d been right to doubt her, if they hadn’t already.

Claire was unable to concentrate. She transcribed a few lines from Josiah’s diary, then wandered down to the library in search of a better pen nib. From there, she wandered vacantly onto the terrace, to find the sky had cleared. She lingered among the rose beds in the garden until the afternoon heat and humidity drove her into the summerhouse.

What had Montfort said? “A parade” of Joss’s women. Claire eyed the opulent silken cushions, the shuttered windows, the winking golden birds. “More comfortable than hops sacks,” she muttered under her breath as she slammed the door behind her and went back to the house.

A note from Edward Latimer waited on the hall table. She

carried it up to her room and threw it on the desk unopened. If it was another lecture on her behavior, she wasn't in the mood. Nothing he could say would top the lesson she'd gotten from Montfort that morning.

She drank tea alone in her room, sent a message to Mrs. White that she would skip dinner, then left a message for Simmie saying she had a headache and had retired. She claimed the headache as an excuse to send Annie away early as well.

Exchanging her robe for a lighter nightgown, she sat at the dressing table mirror to stare again at the stranger who had usurped her familiar reflection.

She leaned in for a closer look.

Faint bite marks showed crimson against the whiteness of her breasts. So intense had been her pleasure in Rhys Fitzgordon's lovemaking that she hadn't noticed the pain he must have inflicted in the throes of their passion. Now, though, her flesh all but shouted witness to their *sport*.

It was the last straw.

Snatching up a heavy silver hair brush, she hurled it into the mirror. A thousand tiny shards flew out in all directions, spangling her gown, the carpet and the embroidered cloth covering the table. All around her the room shimmered in the flickering reflected lamplight.

She flecked away the bits that fell on her nightgown but trod heedlessly on others. Her bare feet bleeding, she crept into bed and cried herself into exhaustion.

Chapter 14

MONTFORT SWORE UNDER his breath as he cantered away from the oast house, his horse's hooves kicking up clots of mud. He had called Claire Burton a fool, but he was the bigger one. What had he been thinking?

He liked Claire. He liked her so much, in fact, that she had melted his resolve to keep away from her. Her first kiss should have told him everything he had learned about her in the last hour, but he was too infatuated to heed the warning signs. A virgin! What the hell was Joss doing messing about with an inexperienced girl of good family still under the protection of a father and a brother? Was it possible he really had intended to marry her? A connection with the Burtons would have done nothing to advance Joss's career, social standing or wealth. It didn't make any sense.

Except that there was something about Claire Burton that turned a man's head. Despite her occasional awkwardness, she engaged with life with an optimism that was infectious. If he felt it, it could be that the libertine Joss had fallen under her spell as well.

The fire at Oak Grove ignited emotions in him he never thought to experience again. He worried about her, alone but for Miss Simms and friendless in unwelcoming country. By day, he rode the fields, keeping a distant eye on her travels. Until he'd given himself away today, she never knew he patrolled her grounds at night. Judicious bribes kept her servants mum, though the lowering expression on his face would have been enough.

It was that single lamp burning in the darkness that drew him in, and their daily meetings began. If things had been different—if he were different—he'd be proud to present Claire to the world as Lady Montfort. But Isabel finished him. Their quarrels grew increasingly violent as they fueled their mutual hatred with whiskey and wine. The servants became accustomed to cleaning up broken glass and righting the furniture while their master and mistress slept off their fury late into the day.

Montfort hurled names at Isabel he never expected in his life to use to a woman—any woman—and she taunted him mercilessly about the night George died. And then she had died.

Both times, his memory failed when he strained to piece together what had happened. His mind drew a thick black curtain across the fatal hours. One accident he could accept, but two stretched into improbability.

Only Edward Latimer knew of the fears that jolted Montfort awake in the night and haunted too many waking hours. Latimer's occasional barbed remarks rankled, but they served to remind Montfort he couldn't trust himself. The only good to come from his marriage to Isabel was their honeymoon—it meant he was in Italy when Lucy disappeared. She, at least, wasn't on his conscience.

Well, he thought grimly, Claire was safe. His brutal words guaranteed that even should he weaken again and attempt to woo her, she would have nothing to do with him. So let her go back to mooning over Joss. Joss had given her land, money, freedom and a memory to cherish however she saw fit. It wasn't lost on him that she wore Joss's heavy ring where a wedding band should be.

His mind on that ring, Montfort hesitated a moment, then turned his horse toward Abbot Pyon.

As he approached the rectory, a bevy of ladies walking in the opposite direction scurried onto the grassy edge of the road and averted their faces under their bonnets. His salute was everything politeness and rank required, but his scowl, had they been looking, betrayed his contempt. He knew what they were thinking. Silly rabbits, all of them—except for one, Mrs. Talwell, who drew herself up as they passed and gave him a defiant glare.

As he dismounted and tied his reins to the iron fence, he heard them twittering as they continued on into the village. His lot today, it seemed, was to give priggish ladies empty thrills.

Latimer was standing in the doorway. "You passed the delegation, I see," he said as Montfort walked in. "You should have been here, though I'm sure they would have lost their courage if you had. It was delicious, watching them hemming and hawing."

"Delegation? Something amiss with the choirmaster again, or is some farm lad balking after putting his lass in the club?"

"My life should be so simple. No, my friend, they were here out of concern for *me*."

Montfort cocked an eyebrow.

"They are confused, the poor dears. 'What should they do,' they wondered. Do about what, I asked. 'Well,' they said, 'if there should be a certain lady in the parish, who seems to be a good Christian in all she does, goes to church and so on, but who they know isn't....' I let the silence draw out, for I knew where they were going."

"You make it sound like a Greek chorus. Did they speak in unison?" Montfort said.

"It's mainly that officious Charlotte Talwell. The other three sat and looked at their hands in their laps. Just because her husband paid to put the new roof on St. Michael's last year—something you should have seen to, I might add—she sets herself up as distaff rector of the parish."

"It was very amusing, I'm sure, but I came to talk to you about something and I'd rather not delay."

"Oh, very well. You never had much of a sense of humor, and it's gotten worse."

"They wanted to discuss Miss Burton," Montfort prompted him, "and get your opinion on whether they should be more accepting of her, no doubt."

"Very perceptive of you, but then—no doubt," he hit the words hard, "you've got the buxom Miss Burton on your mind these days. I know you ride out with her frequently. We quarreled about you, in fact. I made it clear I did not approve. But I can assure you, Montfort, you're not going to catch her. You should see how she watches me now when she thinks I don't notice. She was fussed when I criticized her behavior with you simply because she is not used to correction, not because she cares about you."

Latimer noted Montfort's reddening face with satisfaction.

"But I digress," Latimer continued. "Mrs. Talwell and her minions put on their Sunday finery to call and express their deep worry about my behavior. It has been noted in the village, you see, that I spend a great deal of time at Oak Grove. My actions—above reproach per se, they assure me—is being misconstrued. Their daughters, you know. So impressionable. That woman, so dubious. My example. Very bad."

"Have you no sympathy for their perspective, Edward? Their lives are so narrow and they must love their daughters. It can't have been easy, coming here."

"Oh, I do sympathize. Daughters are a care and a worry. You can't relax your vigilance for a moment." He frowned and paused. "But like most women, they enjoy running down other women, and their thinking is painfully scattered.

Montfort pursed his lips slightly as Latimer continued.

"Then as they're leaving, they encounter the wicked Lord Montfort on his way here. The next thing you know, they'll be importuning the bishop to rescue them from their scarlet rector."

"Not funny, Latimer. Imagine the trouble there would have been—could still be, if Joss had managed to finished that wretched novel before he died and it turns up. You'd be smeared in the public's eye much the way I've been."

Latimer slammed his fist down on the desk between them.

"Not like you, Rhys," he hissed. "I've done nothing to make them believe any ill of me that Joss could spread. Not like you. Now what did you want?"

Montfort grimaced, dropped his head and passed his hand over his face. "Ring for something," he said. "I've not eaten since dawn and it's been a rough morning."

Latimer squeezed Montfort's shoulder hard as he stepped past him to the bell. "I'm sorry. Those blasted women cut close to the bone sometimes, with their holier-than-thou maternal cant. Where were they when Lucy's mother died? She needed a caring woman's guidance then, but they had their own daughters to think about. They were jealous of Lucy's beauty and sweetness. I still find it hard to forgive their coldness to her."

"You did the best you could," Montfort said.

"Don't," Latimer snapped. "I know you mean well, but don't. If I did the best I could, then why is Lucy gone from us?"

"I can't answer that. You know I never as much as spoke to

her again after she rejected me. We all failed her in one way or another—you, me, Joss, even George. Let's just hope she's found some happiness wherever she went. To think otherwise is too terrible."

As men of the world, Latimer and Montfort both knew what happened to young women who, for whatever reason, left their homes and tried to make their own way in life. Most ended up on the streets, condemned to degradation, disease and early deaths from sickness or violence. Some 55,000 prostitutes could be found in London alone, but every town had its ladybirds, dollymops and bobtails, terms that made light of their trade in flesh.

To picture Lucy lying dead in a ditch was preferable.

So heavy was the thought of Lucy that when Montfort spoke the name of Mary Collins, the turn in the conversation seemed to follow naturally.

"I think I know why Mary Collins came to Abbot Pyon," Montfort said without preamble. "She was looking for Joss."

Latimer's reply shocked him.

"I wondered how long it would take you to arrive there."

"You knew?"

"There was enough information to patch together," he shrugged. "They said at The Dragon that she spoke oddly. An examination of her clothing indicated it hadn't been made here in Britain. She was traveling alone and from all accounts, didn't seem bothered by that—again, gossip at The Dragon. Ergo, she was American. It was too much of a coincidence, what with Joss returning from the States not two months before."

Montfort poured himself a glass of ale from the pitcher on the table.

He chose his words slowly. "When I found her, Mary Collins was wearing a ring on her left hand. It was fairly wide, and molded into the gold were leaf shapes and vines. I thought it was a mourning ring, because there were rows of black enamel, two, I think, and it was set with three stones, rubies maybe, or garnets. I didn't look that closely."

Latimer raised his glass to his lips and looked narrowly at Montfort over the rim, then lowered it. "And you've seen this ring before, have you?" he said casually.

"Dammit, Latimer, you have, too. Claire Burton wears one like it all the time. Only the stones are purple."

"I won't ask you how you know that, since an equestrienne wears gloves and I don't think you've called formally for tea, " Latimer said. "I know because I work closely with her and see that ring every day. I ask myself how many Joss had made and whether more of his castoffs are going to turn up in Abbot Pyon looking for him."

"You can be so thick at times," Montfort spat. "Doesn't it worry you? First this Collins woman is murdered, and then someone sets fire to Oak Grove."

"Frankly, I assumed you had more to tell than you wished about that fire. And then there's the matter of those exotic leaves in Mary Collins's hair."

His words hung thick in the air. Then Latimer cracked a smile, his teeth gleaming white though the expression on his face changed little.

"Don't fret, Rhys. I believe you are guilty of nothing in either of those quarters. I merely wanted to point out how it could look to anyone who doesn't know you. The police, for instance."

"You're unbelievable."

"Yes, well. Actually, there is something we should discuss about Mary Collins, since you've come this far in unraveling the puzzle. Her name wasn't Collins."

"And how in blazes do you know that?"

"I know because I spoke with the woman. She said her name was Marguerite Carter. She claimed to be Joss's wife."

Montfort fell back into his chair like a marionette whose strings had just been cut.

"You spoke to her."

"Yes. She was hanging around the cemetery like a lost cat. And be glad I found her there before she attracted anyone's attention. She was watering Joss's grave with tears like a heroine out of one of his novels."

"My god, what if Claire had seen her?"

"Exactly. That would have been a fine mess. Joss's estate in chancery! There would have been nothing left for anybody."

"I was thinking more of Miss Burton's sensibilities. That would have been a devastating blow in so many ways—to learn you had thrown over friends and family to claim a property in error, to be so woefully wrong about the circumstances..."

"To give up your virtue for nothing? Your tendresse for Miss Burton is quite a change, Rhys."

"I think she's a decent girl," Montfort said flatly. "In fact, I've sworn off her. She's too good for me and she deserves better than you, with your cynicism and low opinion of women."

"Ho, then! What's brought the proud lord low?"

"Think what you like. Yes, I've been riding out nearly every day trying to get into her good graces, hoping she'd sell Oak Grove to me in the end, but she doesn't even understand what I'm about, unless it's marriage, straight and proper. That's too high a price for me. I'm surprised you haven't cried off as well, knowing about this American woman."

"Mary Collins is dead and buried, and she took Marguerite Carter with her. I think that's the end of the matter."

"Did she have proof, Edward? How do you know a relative won't turn up looking for her?"

"And how do we know she wasn't just some tramp he took up with in America? We don't. But I think it's unlikely. If Mary Collins has any family, they'd have wondered long ago why they hadn't heard from her since she set out. But knowing Joss, she was probably just another stray he picked up along his way. America is full of them, I've read."

"What do you suppose happened to her?"

"I don't speculate. What could any woman expect, wandering around the country alone like that? She's fortunate nothing worse happened to her. Some vagrant probably attacked her."

"You sound so certain. And so pitiless. No wonder humanity is turning away from the Church, with clergy like you to shepherd them."

Montfort rose to go. "There's one more thing. I've decided to go abroad, I don't know for how long. My estate manager can handle any business matters that arise, should you need him. And you can have use of a hunter when the season starts, as usual."

"I wish you good travels, then, " Latimer replied. "Will I see you before you go?"

"No, Edward. The sight of you is getting to be more than I can stomach."

"The world is a mean place, Rhys. Just remember, when Oak Grove is in your hands again, how families like yours climbed to the lofty positions you hold today. It wasn't by feeling pity. For anyone."

Montfort was scarcely out the door before Latimer settled himself at his desk. Taking out a fresh sheet of fine cream paper, he immediately began writing, *"My dearest Miss Burton..."* If all went as he wished, he wouldn't need to take up Montfort's offer of horses.

Claire suffered through only a few fitful hours of sleep before she dragged herself out of bed the next morning. Flinging the drapes open, she surveyed the damage to the room without emotion. Someone would have to clean it up. She would apologize, but she wouldn't—she couldn't—explain what had come over her.

She waited an hour, then rang for Annie, asking her to bring warm water, salve and bandages for her feet.

"I had a nightmare," Claire said before Annie, eyes wide, could speak. The tiny, shallow cuts stung as Annie dressed them.

Prompted by the worried maid, Simmie was in next.

"I had a fever in the night, and it gave me bad dreams. I must have sleepwalked," Claire told her. "I'm fine now. Inform Mr. Carey and Tressel I won't be going out today." Then she crawled back into bed.

Simmie felt Claire's warm forehead. "I knew the moment I saw those storm clouds, there'd be trouble."

"Yes," Claire said distantly. Simmie ordered Mrs. White to send up a tisane of mint, fennel and chamomile to bring down Claire's fever. By noon, she was able to take a light broth, lovingly spooned into her mouth by the vigilant Simmie, and the sleep that followed was quieter and more restful.

By nightfall, Claire was awake again and more alert. Simmie smiled with relief as she tried to tuck the blankets more closely around Claire.

"I was sure you were going to be really ill," she said, unable to conceal the worry in her eyes as Claire pushed the coverings back impatiently.

"I need to get up. As you can see, I am not ill, but lying in bed needlessly will make me so. And I need nourishment. I'm famished!" She stepped out of bed and winced.

"Perhaps a tray...?"

"Oh, Simmie, I'm so sorry to snap at you. Yesterday—is it only yesterday? -- was so terrible. But it doesn't signify. I got a little wet in the rain and had to make the best of it until I could come home."

"I heard about Dickon," Simmie said, then hesitated.

"Don't spare me, Simmie."

"They say Tressel threatened to quit, but Mrs. White assures me he won't. I'm afraid Mr. Carey is looking quite grim."

Claire winced. "I don't suppose anybody had a word of concern for me, not that I deserve it. Why do I never listen to anyone?" She rang impatiently for Annie. "I deserve everything Mr. Carey and the rest of them must be saying about me right now. And Mr. Latimer no doubt will use it as another reason to chide me."

"He called while you were asleep," Simmie said. "I told him you'd caught a chill."

"There was a note from him yesterday," Claire said. "I didn't open it. He's been so short with me lately. He was so kind in the beginning and now he acts as though he just wants to get the work on Josiah's papers done so he can be shut of me."

"He seemed eager to see you today," Simmie remarked. "He said he'd be waiting to hear from you."

Annie alone seemed oblivious to the cloud hovering over her mistress. The dressing table had been restored to its normal state and a mirror brought in from another bedchamber, and as Annie happily brushed the tangles out of Claire's hair, she burbled about a Scott poem involving knights and fair ladies. While Annie extolled Lochinvar and histed over the treachery of his lady's family, Claire absently opened Latimer's note and began to skim.

She got only a few lines past "*My dearest Miss Burton,*" when she asked Annie to leave. Still seated at the dressing table, she forced herself to read slowly, from the beginning.

My dearest Miss Burton,

I sincerely hope that when we parted last, the impatience I expressed did not seem to be directed at you. Impatience, it indeed was, but merely because of the inability of myself to find the proper time, place and words to explain my feelings for you. I fear you see in me a harsh man only interested in correcting and chastising you. Believe me, my concern stems wholly from my regard.

These past weeks laboring at your side in our work of mutual interest has revealed to me your bright intelligence, spirit of loving kindness and soul of purity. Day by day, my feeling for you has traveled further from friendly interest in your welfare to a keen desire to make that welfare the most solemn duty in my life, after my obligations to my calling. In short, it is my deepest wish to unite my life with yours and, as your husband, have the right to call myself your friend, supporter, companion and protector.

Miss Burton, I request that you make me the happiest of men by bestowing upon me your hand in marriage. From that day forward, we will put the past behind us and together build a future as if it never were.

Realizing that this proposal may take you completely unawares, I apologize sincerely for startling you with such a declaration. I will understand if you wish to take some time to consider your answer, and, should you decline, will continue ever to be

Your most sincere friend,

Edward R. Latimer, CE

Claire carefully folded the letter. Her hands were shaking, so it took her several tries before it slipped back into its envelope. Curling in on herself and clutching the small cream packet to her chest, she rocked back and forth on the small slipper chair.

Marriage!

She sprang up, only to be hobbled by the stinging in her feet. She hopped over to the chaise near the window, settled herself and gazed out at the bright crescent moon hanging like a spangle in the deepening twilit sky.

To be married to Edward Latimer, she told herself, would mean safety. She would no longer have to fight every day for acceptance nor battle temptations she knew now she was too weak to resist.

As Mrs. Latimer, she would be secure from the insults of men like Rhys Fitzgordon. And she would have the influence she longed for. With the sanction of the Rev. Edward R. Latimer, rector of St. Michael the Archangel, the people of Abbot Pyon would embrace rather than reject the good things she wanted to do for them. But to be married to him would mean exchanging freedom for obedience—a state she was more accustomed to, except for these recent exciting, dangerous, lonely months.

Put the past behind them. She understood now what Edward meant, and why Rhys was so angry despite his offer. That knowledge would make her decision easier.

The sky was dark when Simmie came back with a tray of food.

"Oh, not dressed yet—did you change your mind after all? Well, never mind. I'll bring a chair over and I can pass you things as you want them."

Claire slipped Latimer's letter under a cushion.

Simmie handed her a small plate of roasted chicken with some lettuces, then reached out to feel her forehead. "You look feverish again. Are you feeling ill?"

"I want to ask you a question," Claire said. "But I'm not sure how. It's, well, delicate."

"If I can't give you a satisfactory answer, I'll say so."

Claire took a deep breath. "What is it men want? From women, I mean."

Simmie looked down at her lap and took what seemed to Claire like hours to reply.

"What do you think, Claire?"

"Men want to be admired, but not the way we women do. They want to be seen as powerful and in control of life," Claire said slowly, measuring her words. "They want their own way in all things—"

"Like we women do?"

"Yes and no. We want our homes, the things around us, the particular way that suits our taste. Men need to be right all the time."

"And we don't?"

"Not in the same way. Women are used to bending, keeping silent, snatching their happy moments from behind men's backs. When I think of Papa, I marvel at how little he really knows about what goes on in his own home. And I don't mean to criticize Papa! I suspect it's that way in every home. The women lead the men to believe they are in charge, but they aren't really."

"So what you are saying is that women trick men into thinking they are right and pretend to obey when it suits them?"

Claire nodded uncomfortably.

"And what did the men do to deserve such treatment? Surely, if their wives and daughters loved them, they would be happy to obey and ashamed to deceive them?"

"That's what I trying to get at," Claire said wearily. "Why do men and women marry—apart from the obvious?"

Simmie shifted in her chair.

"The obvious?"

"Yes. Women need a home and someone to support them. Apart from children and someone to keep house for them, what do men get?"

"Oh dear, Claire. You've gone from a girlish romantic to a cynic in less than a day! Where is all this coming from so suddenly?"

Claire averted her face. "I can't say, at least not yet. But I used to be so sure of what life was about and now I don't know what to believe. I know there's more. Men have needs, physical needs. Isn't that what I'm reading about in Josiah's diaries? But they don't need wives for that."

Simmie got up and lit the lamp beside Claire's chair. She revived the fire in the cooling grate, then pulled the heavy velvet drapes across the tall windows.

"You aren't retiring already?" Claire asked, disappointment evident in her voice despite her weariness.

"No," Simmie replied, settling again in the chair next to Claire. "I think we're going to be up talking for some time. I'm going to tell you a story that I hope will help. You're leaving out the most important part of why men and women marry—or not—as the case may be. Love."

"But what is that? I don't know anymore!"

"How could you, if you've never been in love?" Simmie held her hand up to silence Claire's startled protest. "Here me out and then you can talk."

"I was married once. John Simms was the most wonderful man I've ever known. Kind, generous, funny. Oh, how he could make me laugh! Sometimes I think that's what I miss most about him."

The lamplight illuminated Simmie's face in the shadowy room. It could have been simply the soft light, but the power of memory transformed it. She looked like the young woman who first came to Thurn Hall 10 years before, when Claire was just 16 and Simmie was Claire's age now.

No, Claire corrected herself, Simmie looked like that grave young woman, only happier. With a pang, Claire realized that in the youthful preoccupation of those days, she had never seen that Simmie was unhappy.

She became a new person to Claire now, seen for the first time as separate, with a personality, a history and thoughts of her own. Claire waited, afraid to disturb her. Simmie sighed and continued.

"I met John when I was governess in the home of a wealthy corn merchant near Oxford. He came into the parish a month after I did as the new curate. The children loved him—he always had some surprise in his pockets and was ready for a game or a story.

"He came from a large family of younger brothers and sisters, so he still saw the world through their eyes, I think.

"I missed my family and he saw that, too. It wasn't long before his pockets included some small thing for me—an extra sweet, an unusual plant specimen he'd found on one of his walks, one of Mr. Arnold's poems he'd copied out. It was simple kindness at first, but before we knew it, our regard had deepened and we were courting—discreetly, of course. The master and mistress of that home never would have tolerated it if they'd suspected.

"When John and I decided to marry, though, they let me stay on through the weeks while the banns were read, even though they disapproved. But I was so happy I didn't care. Not only was I going to make a home of my own with a fine man who shared my interests, we were in love and had such dreams together!

"I'm sure every bride feels the same way, but the heavens smiled down on our wedding day. There is so much joy in those early weeks, Claire! We couldn't afford a wedding trip, of course—we went straight from the church to our new home. But to share our first meals together, to say goodnight and not have to part! Each day, we discovered more to love in each other and more ways to show our regard.

"I learned the secret then—if each of you puts the other first in his thoughts and actions, love and happiness increase day by day! And John proved to be such a tender lover, always considerate of my feelings, that it wasn't long until we were truly one and I treasured every minute of the day and night. There was no happier wife in the county than me, I was certain.

"We shared a year of bliss together. We didn't have much in the way of money, but we were better off than many a poor curate. John had a small allowance from his family that just saw us through. Then our son was born. I thought I could never be happier. But within a month, everything I lived for was gone.

"John called on a poor family on the edge of town one wet night and came down with a fever the next day. I nursed him as best I could and summoned the doctor to our home more than once—for by the second day, our baby was ill as well.

"My husband died in my arms on the fourth day, believing he left me secure and with our baby to comfort me. I couldn't tell him little John had gone ahead to greet his papa in heaven.

"I don't know how I got through the next days and weeks. I was ill myself, but to my sorrow, I recovered. I soon had no money, for the income from John's living ended immediately, as did the small allotment from his family, who chose not to continue it since our boy was gone. I was alone.

"How could they be so cruel?"

"It's the way of the world, Claire. They did not know me and their other children naturally would come first. I had earned my own bread before, and if John had not provided for me, that was not their concern."

"But Simmie!"

"No, dear, let me finish. There's not much left to tell. Just as I was preparing to leave our house and move to lodgings, one of my former master's business acquaintances called. He was direct. As a widower of some months' standing, his children needed care and he wanted a wife. A former governess fit the bill nicely on both points and he remembered me as quiet, ladylike and not unattractive—would I marry him?

"I'm sorry to say, Claire, that I seriously considered his offer for two days before I declined."

Claire couldn't stop herself. "But how could you?"

"How could I accept—or how could I say no?" She smiled sadly. "I know which you mean—but many of my acquaintance were astonished that I turned down a grand home, higher social standing, the chance to wear fine clothes and ride in my own carriage. But the thought of sharing the bed of a man I did not love repulsed me. He was a perfectly fine gentleman in every way but one, Claire. There was no love between us."

"Mama says love come afterward."

"No, Claire. She is correct that income and connections can't be ignored entirely, but if those are the only reasons a woman marries, well—unless she is very fortunate in her husband, she faces trials she cannot imagine. In the place of love there will be only duty or even dread. Marriage is such an intimate state, you cannot imagine!"

Claire flushed.

"Just as it's a sin to marry a woman only because she is rich or beautiful?"

"Yes. Without the sweetness of love to sanctify their union, neither a man nor a woman is any better than the beasts in the field.

"Yet society approves such marriages."

"Such marriages often lead into secret sins," Simmie said. "Men and women need to love and be loved, and if the choice is between a cold home..."

"... and a warm bed?"

Simmie looked at Claire sharply.

The silence lengthened between them, and Simmie took Claire's hands in hers. "Now tell me what it is you really want to know. Has something happened?"

Claire handed her Latimer's letter, the amethysts on her hand glinting in the lamplight. She watched anxiously as Simmie read.

"What are you going to do?" she said as she returned the letter to Claire.

"I don't know, Simmie. I only answered to say I would consider his offer." Simmie sat up, brows raised, mouth open to speak, though she said nothing. "You don't approve?"

"I'm just surprised, Claire. You've been so firm about Mr. Carter. And this is so sudden, don't you think?"

"I was wrong about Josiah's character, I know that now, and I think my inexperience made me rather foolish. I tell myself that if I truly loved him before, I would still love him. But I must not have. I barely mourn him."

She looked away into the fire and Simmie could barely catch what she said next. "And there's more. I don't want to speak about it, I'm so ashamed, but Lord Montfort, he, well, I..."

Simmie gave Claire's hand an encouraging squeeze.

"Lord Montfort kissed me, and instead of showing him I was insulted, I let him see I liked it. And I did," she blurted. "I hardly knew what I was doing. We were in the oast house during the storm, and it was so exciting. I know it was wrong, but I let him do it again. And more. And he laughed at me when he realized—oh, Simmie!" Claire cried hoarsely. "Please say you didn't know what everyone here thinks about me and Josiah! I've been such a fool!"

"I've had a suspicion," Simmie said quietly.

"Do you see my problem?" Claire said urgently. "How can I accept Mr. Latimer with that standing between us?"

"Oh, Claire, think! Of all people, Mr. Latimer would know—and obviously he's decided otherwise. He alludes to it in his letter. The real question is whether you love him. And whether he'd make you happy."

"Happy," Claire said. "Do love and happiness go together, Simmie? Or is that a romantic dream?"

Simmie rose and pressed her lips against Claire's forehead. Brushing her hair back the way she used to when Claire was still a girl, she looked at her sadly and pulled her shawl close around her shoulders.

"All I know is that it's difficult to have one without the other," she said and left Claire to her thoughts.

Chapter 15

"TO LOVE" WAS the first duty Edward Latimer promised his bride as he spoke his vows on their wedding day. She, too, pledged to love, after first swearing before God to obey and serve her new husband.

With mixed feelings, the bishop had traveled from Hereford to Abbot Pyon to perform the ceremony on this hot August day. Claire Burton and the Rev. Edward Latimer were marrying in the least time the church permitted—the banns had been read four successive Sundays immediately after they agreed to marry, so barely seven weeks had gone by since she had accepted him. Had it been any other man, the bishop would expect a christening before Lent.

It scarcely left time for Latimer to find a suitable curate for St. Michael's and get him installed. As it was, the new man found himself lodged at The Dragon. Most of Latimer's possessions sat in crates at Oak Grove, to be unpacked and arranged in the master's bedroom while he honeymooned in the Lakes with his new wife, but the rector wanted no company under his roof before then.

The bishop stayed at Oak Grove rather than at the rectory, however, and that laid his doubts to rest. Like its mistress, he observed, the estate was handsome without too much of the vulgarity of new money. The rector of St. Michael's showed acumen in bringing both under his purview, he concluded, and the income at least would go a long way toward promoting Latimer's career on a broader stage, out of the diocese.

The bishop acknowledged Latimer's many personal gifts, but he didn't care for the man.

After receiving Latimer's proposal, Claire spent a restless day sandwiched between two sleepless nights before inviting her suitor to Oak Grove to receive her answer.

He made her wait most of the day before calling. In one sweeping glance as he entered the drawing room, he took in her somber expression and dark gray gown. Any other girl would have spent the time fussing over her hair and costume, he reflected, eager to be at her best for the most momentous day of her life. This evident lack of care braced him for a denial only half-expected until then.

"You do me a great honor, Mr. Latimer," she said when he stood before her. "I didn't understand until recently how I was regarded in the parish—"

"Stop. If that is your only reason for rejecting my offer, I reject it!"

"Yes."

"Yes, that is your only reason? It's not that you're still loyal to Joss or—you don't care for me?"

"No, I mean yes. Yes, I accept your offer. Here is my hand—Edward."

He noticed then that Carter's heavy ring no longer encircled her finger. As he clasped her hand in his, she stepped closer, raised her face to his and closed her eyes. After a long moment, she felt his warm lips press against hers long enough for his whiskers to tickle her ears and then he released her.

"You make me the happiest of men," was all he said.

They stood awkwardly, looking at each other. "Would you like to sit down? Perhaps I should ring for some refreshment?"

"Don't ring. Let's be just we two for a while, may we?"

Claire found his evident discomfort endearing—so different from the exuberant Josiah, who never stopped talking even when he was kissing, and definitely not like Montfort. Montfort bullied people to get what he wanted. If that didn't work, he gulled them into believing they wanted the same things.

Latimer seated himself beside her on the sofa, close but not too close, and took her hand lightly in his. She let her breath out with a sigh.

"I'm so happy, Edward," she said. "Your letter was a shock, but the more I thought about it, thought about how well we work together and the way I've been living—well, it just seemed right."

"That is how I see it, too," he said. "When a man and a woman are attracted to one another, they should be joined in matrimony. I'm sure you're familiar with St. Paul's admonition—"Better to marry than burn...""

Claire blinked.

He continued. "I admit, when you first came into the neighborhood, I concerned myself more with how wrong it was for a young woman like yourself to be on her own, and where my duty might lie in saving you from a life of waste and loneliness."

He moved closer and slipped his arm lightly around her waist. "You are headstrong, my dear, but I gradually found that I loved you. And suddenly the path of duty became sweet!"

Claire squirmed in his light embrace so she could face him, and a wave of astonished delight swept over her. Edward's face shone as he gazed down on hers, his green eyes wide. Her eyes widened in response as he bent his head to kiss her again.

This time, the contact stirred her and she dismissed her disappointment at his odd way of speaking his love. This she understood, as the kiss, soft and leisurely, ended with their breath mingling in a long sigh.

"I love you, too," she said as he held her closer. She relaxed in his arms, soothed by the steady pounding of his heart against her ear, and let her mind drift to their wedding night—and all the nights to come

Now here she was, joining her life to his permanently. Streaks of sun broke through the clouds on what promised to be a sweltering day, mottling the white walls and the pale stone floor of the church. The breeze through the trees in the churchyard splashed wavering pools onto every surface as light and shadow melded and flickered. Despite the rising heat outdoors, a damp chill seeped from the ancient walls.

The gathering to witness them solemnize their union was

small, since neither of them wanted a show—on the bride's side, Mrs. Hanniman, the Gilberts, Simmie. Supporting the groom were Mr. Talwell and, as his best man, an old schoolfellow clergyman whose name Claire had forgotten already.

The best man should have been Josiah, she thought with a start, then recollected that if Josiah were alive, she wouldn't be standing here now next to Edward Latimer. Montfort, then. But Carey had let slip the morning of the day she decided to accept Edward that his lordship had left the county unexpectedly, giving no date of return. Finding out so casually, without a word from him, stung.

A bird in the churchyard sang madly, recalling Claire to the business at hand. Once committed to marrying Edward, her road ahead in life seemed as straight and clear as life could be in England's green, wet climate. But the first cloud on the horizon appeared almost immediately.

"Forsaking all others," the bishop intoned. Alas, Simmie was forsaking her.

The two of them were driving home from church the Sunday of the banns' first reading when Simmie broached her plans.

"Mrs. Gilbert and Evangelina have invited me to make my home with them," Simmie said in the same offhand tone she used to remark on the weather on an average day.

Claire pulled back on the reins and brought the curricle to a halt in the middle of the lane.

"Simmie, no! You mustn't leave me. Who will I talk to?"

"You'll have a new husband to look after and get used to. I don't want to be in the way."

"But you'd never be in the way," Claire felt a lump form in her throat and nearly choked. "I need you! You're my best friend."

"I'll always be your friend, Claire, but once you and Mr. Latimer are settled in at Oak Grove, you won't really want me around all the time. You'll see. And I don't want to tiptoe around the house fearful of surprising you in an intimate moment." To Clair's astonishment, her friend almost simpered.

"But how will you live?"

"I've some money put by, and Lina and I are thinking of starting a small boarding school for girls. It's a new idea we have, to prepare girls for university. There are two colleges at Cambridge now, and it's only a matter of time until Oxford comes up to the times."

"You feel qualified?"

"Lina learned so much from her father in the classics, and she is teaching me. We think parents will feel more comfortable with their daughters being tutored by women."

"It sounds so exciting!" Claire paused. "I thought we'd spend all our days in pretty much the same way we had, except for the turn of the seasons. And now everything is changing."

"For the better, Claire, for the better. Nothing can stay the same forever. I'll be helping others in addition to myself, and you—you'll be an excellent wife and mother, I'm sure!"

"But where will I find a governess as good as you?"

"You'll always know where to find me."

"Edward," Claire ventured the next evening, when Latimer had ridden out to Oak Grove to discuss their wedding trip.

"Yes, my dear?"

"Let's go for a stroll in the garden. There's something I want to discuss."

"Is this always the way with the ladies?" he jested. "What do they do when there's no lovely walk to soften the blow when they want to raise a difficult subject with their spouses? Claire, I hope you will never be afraid to open your mind to he whose dearest wish is to guide and advise you."

"Very well, then. Simmie told me yesterday she intends to move into the village with the Gilberts."

"I approve. Where is the difficulty?"

"Well, I don't approve, but her mind is made up. The difficulty is that she's always had to work for her living, so you can see that her life will be harder than it's been when she's responsible for everything."

"Can't she just go back into service?"

"Of course," Claire said impatiently, "but that's not the point. She's my dearest friend, and it's my fault she's here at all instead of safe at home with my mother and sisters. It's a great relief, though, that if she must leave Oak Grove, she'll be nearby in Abbot Pyon. She and Evangelina Gilbert plan to start a school.'

Latimer arched an eyebrow. "Another one. Bless us, we'll be a veritable Alexandria on the Wye at this rate."

"It's a boarding school for young ladies intending to go to university. I want to help them with it."

"That's commendable, my dear, but once we're married, you won't have time for schools, students, preparing lessons and the like. I will need you here by me, at home."

"That's not what I mean, Edward. I'm going to invest in the school." She held up a hand in his direction. "I know the settlement papers are signed. I'll do it out of my pin money. You know I'm careful about dress and my personal needs are modest. I'll have more than enough and they won't need much. Maybe fifty pounds or so a year. I just didn't want my contributions to look underhanded by not telling you."

"That's nearly a tenth of your annual allowance, as I'm sure you're aware, dearest. But your money will be to do with as you please," Latimer said blandly. "This proposed school will permit your friends to put a good face on accepting your charity. Just don't come to me asking for more money if you find you've run short."

"Yes, Edward." There was too much truth in his words. She did intend to help Simmie, school or no, and the new school was the perfect excuse. The discussion pained her, though, because of their heated dispute only a few days before. He was so tight-fisted it made her ache to admonish him about his own need to be more charitable.

"... with my Body I thee worship, and with all my worldly Goods I thee endow," Edward intoned in his rich baritone as the ceremony progressed, his eyes locked on hers. Their green fire burned through the fine lace that veiled her face and trailed to the floor behind her.

The Anglican marriage service didn't require the same pledge from brides, since, even if they were rich in worldly goods, their wealth by law automatically became their husband's, apart from anything set aside beforehand in the marriage settlements.

Those legal documents occasioned their first serious argument.

"But Edward," she exclaimed two days into their engagement. "I promised Oak Grove to my brother. I told him it would be his after me and that he could draw on it any time he needed funds. I said I'd pay his boys' school fees."

"Your circumstances are different now," Latimer said, slowly setting his coffee cup into his saucer. They were breakfasting on the terrace at Oak Grove, free to speak since it was just the two of them until she rang for the maid. Already, Edward looked quite at home, she observed.

"Write to your brother," he said. "He'll understand. Marriage changes everything."

"I refuse. I gave my word. Besides, it's in my will."

"Offer him a cash sum he can invest. Our marriage will cancel out any dispositions you've made as a spinster, and the smallest gift from you would be more than he should expect. I can't believe you'd selfishly put a brother and his children ahead of our own."

At that, Claire gave in, of course. He was thinking of their future family. Mr. Chamberlain made another hurried trip to Oak Grove, and when the paperwork was complete, Cameron Burton came into possession of £2,000 with which to educate his three sons and launch them in life when the time came.

"Tell him," Claire whispered to the dapper lawyer as he climbed into his gig to return to the Hereford rail station, "tell him that if he's ever in need, I'll do whatever I can to help. Mr. Latimer is a good man. He won't want to see anyone, especially family, suffer."

Cameron accepted Claire's present with good grace and it was he who gave Claire away when they reached that point in the ceremony. No one else from Thurn Hall attended and even Aunt Manwaring sent her regrets, along with a dozen silver fish forks.

"Father is angry as the devil," Cameron explained to Claire when he arrived the night before. "No, not about the marriage—as far as he's concerned, you've done a smart thing, catching a clergyman, all things considered. But you've put him in the wrong."

"I? I put Papa in the wrong how?"

"He expected you to be begging his forgiveness by now, Claire, didn't you know? Now it is he who must be forgiven."

"I see," Claire said sharply. "I was afraid it was about losing my fortune."

"There was that as well," Cameron conceded. "But his pride matters to him more."

Fathers, Claire thought. Were all fathers like hers? How would Edward treat their daughters, should they be so blessed?

"... In the Name of the Father, and of the Son, and of the Holy Ghost. Amen."

Edward gripped her left hand in his as though he half-expected Claire to snatch it away. He slipped the heavy gold band on her third finger. The heat from his palm radiated up onto hers and it was a relief when he released it and they turned back to the bishop to kneel for his blessing.

Edward's physicality, so near, simultaneously reassured and agitated her. The time for turning back had passed. This man was part of her now, soon to be one flesh, and Claire struggled to push out of her mind the images that distracted her.

Could God read her thoughts? Could Edward? The blood rushed to her center and she felt faint.

Until this moment, she hadn't thought to wonder about Edward's state of mind. Men, of course, even decent men like Edward, surely brought more knowledge, even if theoretical, to the marriage bed than women. Would he know?

Claire closed her eyes, forcing herself to focus on the bishop's prayer, and Montfort appeared unbidden in the darkness, the way he looked that last day, passionate and disheveled, before he grabbed up his things and left her in cold fury.

Cold rose from the stone floor, reaching under the fine silk of her wedding dress to touch her skin. Montfort stroked her naked body and she shivered—then snapped her eyes open. The colors and sounds of here and now blotted out the image.

In that blink of an eye, the bishop had pronounced them man and wife.

Yet nearly an hour remained to the ceremony before they could leave the sacred space and re-enter the world as that new being, a couple. There were prayers, admonitions, the sharing of the Lord's table—an act so intimate, and so declarative of their new state, that Claire thought she spied a tear in Edward's eye.

Once again, he and she both were admonished to love one another. A final time, she was reminded of her promise to submit. Feeling queasy, Claire swore a silent vow in her heart to be a good wife to Edward, rather than a disappointment. For that was her real fear, that he expected too much of her and she would fail.

Much had been said that morning about mystery, comfort and honor, but the word "happiness" never entered into it, she considered as she took the pen and carefully to wrote her name in the church registry.

But how could they help being happy, she reminded herself, blessed as they were with health, wealth, mutual sympathies and attraction?

She wrote her old name—Claire Elizabeth Burton—for the last time, handed the pen to the verger and slipped her hand into the crook of Edward's welcoming arm. As they stepped into the sunlight, he smiled at last and warmed her heart. She drew closer to him and hoped for a private moment soon in which they could steal a kiss.

And so it was, the moment she became Mrs. Edward Latimer, that Oak Grove, its furniture, farms and livestock, its orchards and trout stream, even Josiah's prudent investments and bank account, passed into the hands of Mr. Edward Latimer. He received all that in return for a ring worth a few pounds at best. No wonder neither the church nor the world expected her to place a ring on his finger as well.

Claire felt this change keenly, for she had secretly enjoyed her short season as a woman of means. But she trusted to a generosity and fairness she assumed were intrinsic to her husband's character and let the feeling pass. Since they were one now, she reasoned, which of them held legal title to their property was insignificant. Money and what to do with it were never issues in her father's home.

As for Edward, she had wanted to read his mind. Given that double-edged ability, she would have learned that he was totally focused on his wife.

In the church, he drank in the breathy way she hesitantly spoke her vows, the way she pursed her lips as she signed her name in the vestry, the way she clutched his arm as she walked at his side. He watched avidly as his wife gazed shyly up at him as they left the churchyard, her head turned resolutely way from the grave under the willow tree. He noted the sunlight flashing on his wife's strawberry-tinged hair and her cheeks freshening pinkly in the hot breeze. He reveled as his wife's ruby lips spoke his name, her voice low with love and promise. His wife. His.

❦

The new Mr. and Mrs. Latimer tarried long enough at the rectory to take tea and cakes with the wedding party and a few more prominent parishioners. Then in late afternoon, the groom whisked his bride away in an Oak Grove carriage to Hereford for the night.

Annie, deemed ready to execute all the duties of a lady's maid at last, could barely suppress her excitement as the footman loaded her small trunk onto the carriage. When she caught Edward Latimer's eye, however, she stopped bouncing from foot to foot and stood aside to let him hand Claire into the conveyance.

Pressed into a corner, she broke into a wide grin when Claire caught her eye. "Did you see, miss—I mean ma'am, Mrs. Latimer—"the girl stammered, holding a book out to Claire. "Miss Simms gave me a volume of Mr. Wordsworth's poems."

"Yes, Annie, and Mr. Latimer and I have his 'Guide to the Lake District.' Our journey will be not just pleasure but education, don't you agree, Edward?"

Latimer held out his hand and Annie yielded the book with reluctance. After examining the tooled leather binding and gold leaf stamped on the spine, he returned it to her eager hands. "Miss Simms gilded the lily. A plain volume would have done as well. See that you take care of it, Parsons. And see that you take even better care of Mrs. Latimer. No neglecting your duties."

"Yes, sir," Annie said meekly.

"Since you intend some rather strenuous hikes during our stay at Windermere," Claire remarked, "Annie and I intend to make good use of our days. Annie is proving to have a fine taste for poetry."

"Parsons is a fortunate young woman to have such an interested mistress. It's not every servant who is permitted the leisure to read," Latimer said, and the use of Annie's surname wasn't lost on Claire.

Before long they were winding through the narrow medieval streets of Hereford. Edward had declined the bishop's invitation to stay at the palace and took them instead to a small hotel. The spick-and-span Victoria Hotel faced busy Widemarsh Street, away from the dirt and noise of the train station, but Latimer knew from past stays it provided quiet for travelers after the day's commerce subsided.

Claire allowed Edward to settle her in the lobby while he signed the register and instructed the clerk. He returned with two keys and they followed a porter up the stairs.

At the landing, Edward touched her elbow and drew her aside, letting the porter and Annie go on ahead.

"I've arranged for Annie to sleep in your room tonight," he said, looking past her shoulder. Claire stifled a protest.

He peered into her face. "I expect you are tired and rather—" he hesitated. "Rather anxious, considering. I want our marriage to be happy—"

"Edward..." She reached up and gently placed her gloved hand on his cheek.

"Please, Claire, remember where we are and let me finish." She withdrew her hand and let her arm drift to her side. "I know you will do your best to be a loving and dutiful wife, dearest. I think it's best, therefore, that we take some time to get used to each other before you fulfill that part of your wifely obligation which is liable to be most distasteful."

"I see." Her lip quivered and she turned her head away.

His brow darkened. "I was correct. You are over-tired and consequently fretful. I'll have our dinner sent up to your room as early as possible and, perhaps, if you feel up to it after, we can read aloud for a time before retiring."

"Yes, Edward."

"Come, my love, try to smile for me. This is a happy day for us. We can read some of your favorite Mr. Wordsworth, if you'd like."

Claire feigned a smile and took his arm. "I'd like that, if you aren't too tired as well. I mustn't always be thinking about myself now."

He gave her hand a pat. "That's the spirit, dear."

Claire had never traveled north. Once settled in their first-class carriage, she found the clackety-clack rocking of the car soothing despite her aching head, for she had slept badly and been ill at breakfast. As they journeyed through the Severn Valley and over the Malvern Hills, she took as much pleasure from watching Annie trying to spy famous landmarks as she did from seeing the landscape flow by their window.

More than once, she caught Edward watching her over the Bradshaw's he professed to be studying.

"What is it?" she asked after the third or fourth time.

"I am marveling at how God has blessed me," he said matter-of-factly. "Only a few months ago, I was a lonely bachelor and then you came to Abbot Pyon and bewitched me."

"Oh, Edward, that hardly seems the right word. It makes me sound like the Witch of Endor or something. She didn't end well."

"Charmed, then. Stole into my heart, like a fairy invading my dreams." He nodded toward Annie, practically perched on the windowsill. Claire caught the hint.

"Annie, that is, Parsons," she said in a low voice in Annie's ear. "Please change places with Mr. Latimer." The girl grinned from ear to ear as she scrambled to the other side of the carriage and Latimer moved over to sit next to Claire. He took her hand and went back to his reading while Claire resumed alternately watching her maid and the ribbon of green unspooling outside the window.

They smelled Birmingham, shut the window and exclaimed over the blackened sky long before the train pulled into the station there. Steam powered the many industries of the midland city, with "scarcely a street being without its manufactory and steam engine," Bradshaw's proclaimed. The guide neglected to mention, however, the tons of coal that powered the steam and the resultant soot. The cloud seemed to follow them all the way to Manchester, for "Cottonopolis," like its sister city to the south, ran on steam.

They arrived at Windermere, tired and begrimed, in time for another spectacular sunset. They could see the vast placid lake from the station, and so excited was Annie to drink in the sight that Claire practically had to restrain her. Fortunately, Edward was busy marshaling their baggage and transport to the small private hotel he had booked and didn't notice Annie's agitation. Claire knew already that he wouldn't approve.

The Swan, a whitewashed cottage nestled among a stand of trees near the lakeside, was small compared to the hotels in Windermere proper, but Claire thought it just right for a honeymoon stay. They'd be sharing the premises with a pair of student hikers and an older married couple from Ely. Edward had taken a suite of rooms for them, however, so they'd have all the privacy they wanted.

Every room provided an unbroken view of water and mountains. It was a view Claire would be thoroughly weary of by the time they returned to Oak Grove.

"Edward?" Claire said more sharply than she intended when she saw her husband directing the porter to take Annie's bag into Claire's room. Claire closed the door on Annie and stood with her hand on the knob behind her, effectively trapping the girl on the other side. "Edward, why doesn't Parsons have her own room downstairs with the other servants?"

"I didn't want you to be alone at night, dearest."

"But Edward! I hardly know what to say." Claire bit her lip and gazed out at the blue water. "This is our honeymoon. Won't it be awkward...?"

Latimer stood close to her and placed his hands on her shoulders so that she was forced to meet his eyes.

"Surely you aren't expecting us to begin our conjugal life together in a public hotel?" His evident shock flustered her.

"No, no, of course not, if that's how you feel." She was stammering now. "I don't know what you expect, how I should, what..."

"I'll tell you when it's time, Claire. You don't have to worry yourself."

If that weren't bad enough, nearly every fine day, Latimer set out early to hike, sometimes not returning until night had fallen. A woman can read only so much poetry in a day, Claire thought to herself, slamming the volume of Wordsworth down on the fourth day.

"Annie!" she called, going to fetch her hat. "Annie, we're going for a walk. And bring my sketching things."

When Latimer returned that evening, Claire was giving Annie a drawing lesson, going over the girl's tentative pencil marks with a black crayon, showing her how to strengthen some lines and reposition others for a more effective rendering. Annie jumped up and took his hat away while he settled into the chair the girl had vacated.

"You're asking for trouble there," he remarked without preamble. "You're filling her head with ideas and you'll make her dissatisfied."

"She's so bright, Edward! She'll go back to her regular schooling once we're home and I wouldn't be sad to give her up if she qualified to enroll in Simmie's school."

"And then what? She won't fit in anywhere and no local lad will want to marry her. I wish you to remember yourself. You're my wife now and shouldn't be so familiar with your inferiors." He put his arm around her waist and pulled her closer for a kiss.

Another two days had passed before Claire realized Edward seemed to be waiting for something. They toured Lake Windermere on one of the steam-powered pleasure boats that plied its waters, picnicked on the shore, visited a few shops in the town center. He paid her every attention a new bride could wish. But every time they returned to the Swan, he went immediately to the desk and asked for their mail. There was nothing until the start of their second week, when Latimer received a letter.

He tore it open, scanned it quickly, then folded it deliberately and placed it in his coat pocket. His lips were white.

"Is something wrong?" Claire asked.

"An ill friend. I'm afraid I must go away tomorrow and I'll be gone overnight. In Carlisle," he said before she could ask.

"I'm so sorry. Can I help? Would you like me to come? Is there a woman there?"

"There's no need. He's the crotchety scholar type who can't abide a woman in his house - except for his cook, his housekeeper and the maid. Come, let's take a stroll by the lake before tea. The light this time of day is so fine, and it won't long before we're back in Oak Grove."

Latimer left before dawn, so Claire again was alone with Annie when nausea overtook her shortly after breakfast. It was happening more frequently, but since it subsided as the day wore on, Claire ignored it as best she could.

"I think I'm going to be glad to be home," she said to the girl, sipping cautiously at a glass of water. "I'm never ill. It must be something in this place that doesn't agree with me, the food or—"

She eyed the glass dubiously and set it down. "Or the water.

"Beggin' your pardon, miss," Annie said, not noticing her slip. "There's a herb my ma and sisters use to make a tea that settles their stummachs when they're feelin' poorly. I could ask at the chemists in town."

"An herb?"

Annie twisted her hands into her apron. "Well, it's mostly dried mint, with some rosehips and strawberry leaf mixed in. They say it's a good idea to eat some dry toast before you get out of bed, too, and to not let your stummach get too empty. And it passes after the first few weeks..."

Claire peered suspiciously at Annie. "What are you trying to say?"

"If you haven't told Mr. Latimer yet, I can keep the secret, miss," Annie said. The corners of her mouth quivered as she tried to hold back a smile. "You'll be looking forward to a little stranger in the house, am I right?"

"Annie, you mustn't say that! It's not possible. It's impossible!" Claire went white as a sheet and almost missed the sofa when she sank back to sit.

"It's all right, miss. The banns was read proper and you're a married lady. That's all that counts. Anyone could see Mr. Latimer was right fond of you almost from the first week, and lots of people in the village figured you'd end up at the altar sooner or later, what with all the time he spent with you."

"Stop, Annie!" Claire shouted. "Just stop. Not another word!" She started giggling and hiccupping so violently she frightened Annie and the girl grabbed up the glass Claire had been sipping from and threw the water on her mistress. It did the trick.

"Come here, Annie," a dripping, calmer Claire said, holding out her arms. "I'm sorry. It's just the shock. I didn't realize. How stupid I've been."

Annie averted her eyes and smoothed her hands down her apron. "I'd best get you dry, Missus Latimer. I doan know what I was thinkin', ta douse you like that."

Claire followed Annie into the bedroom, her lips pressed together to hold back the words ready to burst forth. *If only Simmie were here,* Claire thought. *But what could I tell her? What could she do?*

She numbly cooperated as the girl unfastened her bodice and helped her into a dry one. She stared into the mirror without seeing as the abnormally silent Annie redid her hair.

"Annie?" she said as the girl carefully placed the last hairpin. Claire raised her head and two pairs of worried eyes met in the mirror. "Mr. Latimer..."

"I'll be careful not to say nothin' until you say, Miss. I'll do whatever you want. Always."

Annie's fierce emphasis on the "always" tugged at Claire's heart. Her marriage was ruined before it started, she realized, and while she appreciated Annie's loyalty, it was unlikely she could repay it. A dark road lay before her and she had no right to ask this innocent girl—or anyone—to travel it with her.

Chapter 16

EDWARD LATIMER BARELY made the train to Liverpool—for despite what he had told Claire, he was bound for that busy port city. With most mid-week travelers heading away from the sooty industrial towns to begin long-anticipated holidays in clean light and air, he had a compartment to himself. Secure in his privacy, he surrendered himself to thoughts kept at bay since their arrival in Windermere.

He had spent as much time as possible away from Claire, but the punishing effort he put into his rugged marches over the fells distracted him only during the day. Sheer physical exhaustion helped him control his urges at night, but sleep brought evil visions rather than the oblivion he prayed for.

Simply being near Claire aroused him. The light touch of her hand on his, the tender way she spoke his name, stirred his desire. More than once at nightfall, he had been on the brink of sending Annie down to the servants' area to sleep. But Claire was his wife now, sealed to him with God's and the bishop's blessing, not a common street trollop to be used when convenient. He was determined to keep their marriage bed pure and defile neither it, nor her, until he could control his lust.

But she was becoming restless, pale and nervy. Her appetite was off. Her health suffered from his abstinence. He knew he was wrong to deprive her of her conjugal rights—she was already well into her childbearing years and it was a wonder she was still so robust and blooming. Unsatisfied, her maternal drive would damage her womb and make it more difficult for her to conceive and remain healthy.

As the train rattled on toward the west, he stared out the window and brooded, the book on his lap untouched. The marriage had seemed beneficial for them both, but now the hint of a doubt nagged at him. The married lifestyle suited him, to be sure. To be master of a household with all that comprised— dependents, servants, responsibility—conferred gravitas on a man. A bachelor, no matter what his position in life, always struck others as somehow insubstantial and pitiable, if not peculiar, as he aged.

But to be married was another matter entirely. To have a woman a constant presence in his life until death could undo him. Especially if he was not indifferent to the woman. If he were to drop his guard, Claire would insinuate herself his deepest secrets.

As he did every day, he thought of Lucy with a pang. If only she had obeyed, so many other things in his life would remain unaltered. Dear Lucy had been content to build her world around him, as he did around her. After their parents' deaths, the two of them took care of one another. With Lucy's steadying hand in his, he wouldn't have fallen to the temptation of Claire or her wealth. Montfort would still be his friend. Montfort's brother, George, would still be alive. Carter, too. So much heartache, so much catastrophe, caused by one frail woman!

The braking train lurched as it approached the descent to the station, jolting him back into the present. He swung his Gladstone down from the shelf overhead, tucked his book inside, then reached into his pocket. The letter was gone -- but to forget its contents was impossible.

Come if you can. She was here but someone got here before me. The Ship and Mitre, King's Road.

Ordinarily, Latimer would have walked the two miles to the pub, but after depositing his bag at the station hotel, he hailed a cab. Tapping his fingers against the window ledge as the cabbie navigated the bustling noonday streets, he vacillated between impatience and anxiety. What if his hired agent was wrong? What if this were another wild goose chase?

A man resembling an ordinary dockworker waited for him outside the small pub.

"No, I don't want to go in." Latimer waved him away as he turned toward the entrance. "Take me to the place."

The man's accent was local but not rough. "There's a boarding house in Balliol Road. The landlady is expecting you."

"You told her my name?"

"Do you take me for stupid? I know what you're paying me for. She expects to speak with a man seeking a lost relation. That's all she knows and all she wants to know."

They walked away from the pub and started up the street away from the docks.

"Did she leave anything behind, anything at all?"

"She claims the other gentleman took the lady's things away with him."

"When?"

"A month or two ago, she says."

"Did he give a name?"

"Yeah. He said his name was Carter."

Latimer stopped dead in the street.

"He claimed he was Josiah Carter?"

"Didn't give a first name. Just said his name was Carter and the lady sent him. Since nobody else'ed been asking, he looked all right, and the lady said she'd be sending for her trunk and all, the landlady gave them up."

"Blast! What a blithering fool!"

The landlady looked sharp enough, though, and she answered his questions without wasting words. She stood squarely in the doorway of her nondescript establishment, a substantial figure in faded black bombazine and a grease-spotted apron, as if she expected the two men to shove past her and steal the meat right out of the pot in the kitchen. She eyed Latimer's black coat and white cravat and the lines around her mouth relaxed only slightly.

No, the gentleman hadn't sent the trunk on to another address, he'd taken it with him. It was small. Of course she'd never looked in it! No, the lady hadn't mentioned any names or where she was going when she left. 'Bout Whitsun, that was. The lady kept to herself. She didn't talk much, but anyone could tell she were from somewheres else. But she weren't Irish. From the south, mebbe. Yes, she'd recognize the man again if she saw him. He was quality, had a thin red scar running across his cheek. He'd given her a quid "for her trouble."

She pocketed the shilling Latimer gave her and shut the door on them with a solid thud.

""I'll send a cheque to settle my account," he said tersely to the man as he hailed a passing cab. "I won't be needing your services any further."

He directed the cab to take him back to his hotel, but instead of going inside, he paid his fare and began to walk. He could be back in Windermere with Claire by nightfall, but he needed to think. He had given no sign to his agent that he recognized the man the landlady described, but there was no question it was Rhys. Damn the man for not leaving well enough alone. Latimer had the power to destroy him and thought he'd made that message clear. Why else would Montfort have gone abroad? Now here he was, interfering. Where was he now? What had he learned? What was in that trunk?

He stalked through the streets of Liverpool for hours sunk in a black reverie, the scowl on his face repelling any pedestrians who, in deference to his garb, ventured to nod politely or touch their caps. By late afternoon, the sunlight slanted through tall trees across dusty grass and he found himself beside a pond, the iron of the park bench chill through his trouser seat.

He hadn't eaten since breakfast, but he knew it was late only because starched nurses were gathering up their charges and heading for the gates, pushing prams and towing reluctant toddlers in their wakes. Latimer watched them impassively. He scarcely remembered being a child, since his mother had died early and life with his lonely father in the aftermath of her loss was a bleak landscape punctuated by paternal crimination and rebuke.

He was in upper form at boarding school when his father married Lucy's mother. A baby's birth at that stage in his life caused scarcely a ripple in his awareness, since he was away at school, then university, and the baby was a girl. When he was home, he was scarcely expected to spend time in the schoolroom. Everything changed when his father died suddenly while Latimer was at university. Under the guardianship of Montfort's father until he came of age, he had even less reason to spend time at home.

By the time Lucy caught his attention and wound the first

tendrils of affection around his heart, she was trotting around Abbot Pyon on her pony and he had returned to the village as rector. She danced through her days with gaiety and enthusiasm, charming everyone she met, simultaneously enchanting and alarming him.

Then, just after Lucy turned 15, her mother died, too. The burden of controlling and protecting such an impulsive, passionate creature nearly drove him mad. In the end, he had failed.

Watching the last of the children leave the park, Latimer wondered how, if he and Claire had children, he would bear the responsibility. When he had proposed marriage, he was focused on possessing her and Oak Grove, glossing over the primacy of marriage stated so plainly in the service. Procreation. The act itself and how to subordinate it to his will so absorbed his mind that the idea of children appeared distant and unreal.

He dug his heel viciously into the soft grass and pounded a fist on the hard arm of the bench. There was a sudden movement a few feet in front him, and his head jerked up. A child who had ventured too close to the silent man in black jumped back with a yelp and ran to join the other children lollygagging after their harried nurse.

Latimer waited until they were gone and walked slowly back to his hotel. Deeply disappointing as the day was, it nevertheless had given him considerable food for thought. Almost against his volition, plans were forming in his brain.

Claire was sitting in her robe by the window in the sitting room, listlessly staring out at the lake when Latimer returned to the Swan barely a day after his departure. Annie had run down to the servants' hall for her dinner, leaving Claire free to give way to the feelings she tried to suppress around the girl.

A steady drizzle ruffled the water's surface, keeping most visitors indoors. She had been ill again at breakfast and the probable cause was settling on her mind like a stone. The herbal tea Annie recommended helped to calm her stomach, but she feared there was no remedy for the sick feeling in her heart. She pressed her head against the cool glass and sighed.

She lifted her face when she heard the door open. "Edward! I didn't expect you back so soon."

Her paleness startled him. The dark circles under her

reddened eyes betrayed that she had been crying. Then he saw the missing letter lying, unfolded and face down, on the table beside her.

"You read that?" he demanded.

"Yes, Edward, I'm sorry. I found it on the floor in your room and didn't realize what it was until I had looked at it."

"You had no right. What were you doing in my room anyway?"

She sighed. "I missed you. We've been married for nearly a fortnight and I feel sometimes I see less of you than before. To sit in your chair, to touch the things on your washstand—it made me feel closer to you." She didn't mention how she had buried her face in his shirts to inhale the faint, clean scent of him. She sensed he would be shocked.

She looked up into his angry face. "Why didn't you tell me the truth? I would have understood."

He drew a breath before speaking, then said carefully, "Understood what?"

"I know how much it must mean to you to find your sister." She stood and came over to him where he hovered by the mantel, torn between anger and remorse. Her touch on his face was like a moth's wing. "And I can see you were disappointed."

He hesitated, then enveloped her in his arms, all but crushing her cheek against his breast so she couldn't see the look of relief on his face. "Yes, I was disappointed."

She slipped her arms around his waist and listened to the agitated beating of his heart. He held her that way in one strong arm, his left hand tight on her waist, while with the right he began to gently work the pins out of her hair. She hardly dared to breath as, one by one, they dropped soundlessly to the carpet.

When he had removed a sufficient number, he worked his fingers into the thick coil at her neck until the tresses tumbled down her back. Then he shifted his weight so he could turn her to face him and, tilting her chin up, kissed her full on the mouth.

His kiss was deep and voracious, sending thrills down her spine and into her limbs. Her knees melted as she hungrily kissed him back. He shifted his hold, clutching her derriere with one strong hand and pushing her hips forward as though he intended to literally sweep her off her feet and carry her away. She leaned back into his embrace, ready to abandon herself to him. The rush of pleasure from knowing her husband wanted her at last quelled the melancholy voice in her head that mechanically reiterated the growing list of lies already corrupting their marriage.

She luxuriated in the feel of his powerful shoulders and arms as he shoved the door open with a kick and carried her into her bedroom, where he carefully placed her on the bed. Her happiness ended abruptly when he turned up the lamp and rang for Annie.

With effort, she sat up. While she scanned his face for an answer to his sudden shift in mood, he studied her avidly in the lamplight.

She could read his desire easily. His dark pupils expanded so wide that the irises shrank to narrow rims of brilliant green. In the blackness were bright vertical splinters—the reflection of the lamp at her elbow.

His nostrils flared and his breath came in shallow, rapid pants. The bulge in his well-tailored trousers was unmistakable. He stared at her—and if she could have seen herself as he did at that moment, her joy would have shriveled to horror.

He saw swollen lips and smudged eyes stark in a white face, tousled hair seeming to writhe in the light and shadow cast on her, the bed and walls by the wavering flame. To his eyes, she swam in a torrent of fire but did not burn. Not the frail daughter of Eve, but the demonic Lilith waiting to carry him to Hell.

He gripped the foot of the iron bedstead and tore his eyes away from hers.

"I can see you're not well," he said. "I noticed the moment I saw you. We will go home tomorrow."

Annie knocked on the open door, hesitant to enter. He turned to her. "See that your mistress's things are packed and ready for the porter in the morning. For now, make sure she has a light supper and an early night. We'll take the 10 o'clock train."

"Yessir," the girl replied meekly.

He raised his voice. "Surely you realized she was unwell! What's wrong with you, girl?"

When Annie had scurried off to change the order for Claire's dinner, Latimer turned back to Claire, now sunk back against the pillows, her arm flung across her forehead as if she truly were ill. "I'm sorry," he said. "I'm sorry for... I'm just, sorry."

She closed her eyes and he left. His footsteps crossed the sitting room and faded into his bedroom. The door clicked shut. She buried her face in the pillow and, her emotions a tangle of disappointment, frustration and fear, she waited for tears that refused to come.

Only Annie was sorry to leave the Swan and return to the station in Windermere town for the long journey home. As soon as she left the small inn, she would be a mere lady's maid once again rather than pupil or—she would dare to think it—a friend, and she suspected her merry evenings in her mistress's boudoir also would be over. That her schooling might end as well added to her silent misery. Life at Oak Grove would be different with a master in charge.

Everything would be different going forward and she sensed calamity on the horizon. In many ways, the young girl knew more about life and sex than Claire. In her world, a pregnant bride had no reason for shame. Many farm couples, pledged to one another, waited until a child was on the way before walking to the church together. Given that a farm took many hands to run, proof of fecundity was prudent.

But sharp-eyed Annie knew Latimer had yet to bed his wife, before or after the ceremony. She could read it on his face each evening when it came time to turn the lamps down, bank the fire and retire. Whether he wouldn't or couldn't was immaterial to Annie. She saw him avoid meeting Claire's eyes and the way he barely touched her before sending her off to bed alone. And Claire—the brave way she pretended nothing was amiss made Annie want to kick the reverend rector in the shins.

So next Annie pondered whether Latimer had married Claire out of pity or, worse—had he used her predicament to coerce her into a marriage of convenience to take her money and land?

But Claire hadn't kenned to her condition until after they arrived at Windermere. If it hadn't been for herself, Annie thought, Claire still may not know. The way the quality raised their daughters made no sense.

It wasn't long until the penny dropped. The lost corset, the missing petticoat—Annie was responsible for these things and noticed their absence immediately, yet nary a word was said to her by anyone. Then there was the gossip below stairs and in the village shops. Viscount Montfort's reputation, the way he was seen hanging about Claire.

Excellent at her sums, thanks to Miss Simms, Annie quickly worked forward from that day to this. The realization cost Annie hours of lost sleep as she played out what could happen when Claire's secret was out.

Annie reckoned Mr. Latimer was too much the gentleman to beat his wife. But she'd steel herself to step between them in case she was wrong. A man could get carried away, only to be sorry later, if seriously vexed. She'd seen it with her own eyes, with her sister Bess and her man.

What if the reverend would demand a separation and send Claire away? She knew of a snug little cottage on her da's farm. For her sake, Annie thought, he might let them have it—at a reasonable rent, of course.

But even if they had to wander the world, Annie vowed, she'd stick by Claire and look after her. If she had to, she'd even stand up to the Lord High-and-Mighty who did this to her mistress.

Annie pictured herself standing in the doorway of the cottage, ordering the proud lord off her da's freehold. Claire would be ever so grateful. That is, assuming Claire didn't want to see his lordship again. That gave Annie more food for thought. Getting a farm girl to agree to a slap and tickle in the hay was one thing. How did a man get a lady out of a corset if she weren't willing?

But never mind. That was her mistress's business, Annie decided. Keeping her safe would be Annie's.

Clutching her new drawing portfolio and pencil box—purchased with her own money but with Claire's guidance—Annie blinked away a tear, lifted her chin and followed her employers down the platform to the waiting train.

It was barely dusk when they drew up to Oak Grove's entrance. Claire watched the swifts darting about the chimney tops as the footman unloaded their luggage, then, seeing Latimer was halfway to the door, followed slowly behind.

"Where is Kip? Why isn't he here to greet me?" she asked Mrs. White as Annie collected her wraps at the foot of the stairs. "Kip's all right, isn't he?"

"Master's orders, ma'am," Mrs. White said gruffly with a slight nod in Latimer's direction. "He said the dog should stay below stairs when he's not wanted for a run in the garden or such."

"Edward?"

"I don't fancy mud and hair on the furniture and carpets, my dear. Besides," he said, looking directly at Mrs. White, "any one of the servants will tell you how much extra work a dog in the house makes for them. It's not their place to complain, but ours to show consideration. And Mrs. White is very fond of Kip. She told me so."

"Quite right," Mrs. White all but mumbled. "If you'll excuse me, I'll see to dinner. Half an hour, sir?"

"That should be plenty of time, Mrs. White."

Claire said nothing until they were up the stairs and out of earshot of even Annie.

"Edward," she said with asperity. "How is a dog in the kitchens any less of a problem than he is in my sitting room? And why is it now that Mrs. White is taking orders from you? As your wife, I should be running the household."

"Forgive me, dearest, but I told Mrs. White before we returned that you weren't well and that we should all do our outmost to spare you any bother. Just until you're feeling stronger, of course."

"I'm not an invalid, Edward, just tired from the journey."

"You're overestimating your powers, my dear. Everyone around you can see how pale you've become, how—forgive me!— how peevish. Better to nip this in the bud rather than see you seriously damage your health. You're my responsibility now, after all."

"But Edward—!"

"Nay, my dear. Go and freshen up." He lightly touched his lips to her forehead. "When you're ready, I'll take you down to dinner."

Days passed in which Edward Latimer fetched and carried for Claire, seeing she had the softest cushions at her back, the choicest cuts from the meat platter at table, that her glass was filled with fortifying sherry several times a day and that her tea remained hot. At the same time, he kept her away from the stable, as well as Carey or anyone involved with the business of Oak Grove.

When the weather was fair, he walked her once around the garden in the morning and at dusk, but within days of their return, the skies turned foul and so much rain fell that the trout stream at the bottom of the front lawn rose halfway to the gravel drive.

Each morning after breakfast, Edward went into the library and firmly shut the door, leaving her to wander the rooms of Oak Grove like a haunting spirit. Once she had tried joining him, only to discover he kept the stout double doors locked, even when he was inside.

"I don't like being disturbed when I'm working" was all he said when she asked.

His nearness continued to torment her, especially in the evenings, but her ache for him grew less sharp as her body adjusted to new demands. But her puzzlement continued unabated. Clearly, he cared for her. That was evident from his solicitude. Yet he kept his distance, as though she were some dangerous creature apt to strike if he relaxed his guard. He circled her, tormenting them both, like a hawk lured by a captive hare, fearing ensnarement yet longing for the prize.

Her nausea tended to come very early in the morning and subside quickly, so by the time she sat down to breakfast at 9, she could eat if she went slowly and stayed away from richer foods like the kedgeree Mrs. White had added to the sideboard since Edward had taken up residence at Oak Grove.

"Perhaps," she ventured that morning at breakfast, "perhaps you were right. I am feeling so much better now." She watched warily as he spread a warm slice of toast with gooseberry jam and placed it on her plate.

"I'm glad you agree with me, Claire. You had me more worried than I cared to say. I didn't want to alarm you. But it looks like you might even be putting on a little flesh. It becomes you."

She took a tiny bite of toast, chewed slowly and swallowed.

"I was hoping…" she began.

"It's too soon for you to be riding, Claire. I expect you to stay in the house unless you go out for a stroll with me. Or if you must go out, take the footman with you. You shouldn't be alone."

"I was going to say, Edward, I was hoping we could return to our work on Josiah's papers. Truth be told, I miss the mental exercise." She hesitated and touched the back of his hand lightly. "I miss working with you."

"I would like that. Truly," he said, slowly withdrawing his hand. "Not today or tomorrow, but the day after that?"

She snatched her hand back as her face fell. "Why not now, today, Edward? I want to be useful, I want to have purpose. You're leaving me with nothing to do!"

"Don't be petulant, Claire. I have business in the parish today." He pushed back his chair and stood abruptly. "And tomorrow you may not feel like it."

Latimer stayed out for the better part of the day, and in her loneliness, Claire turned to Annie. Leaving the door to her rooms open slightly, she gave the girl another drawing lesson and the afternoon passed more quickly than she expected. She liked teaching, and she enjoyed the girl's hunger for learning.

As Annie concentrated on sketching a bowl of fruit Claire placed for her on the tea table, Claire's thoughts strayed involuntarily to motherhood. Her own mother had left the actual raising of her children to nurses and governesses. In these modern times, would she be expected to turn her children over to servants? Edward was so traditional, she feared he would insist.

She passed her hand over her eyes with a sigh. Edward. Would she even be at Oak Grove by year's end and able to provide for a child decently? Thank God the law had changed, so that if he did turn her out, he couldn't punish her further by claiming the child and raising it as he wished.

Hearing her husband's tread on the stairs snapped her out of her reverie. "Hurry, Annie," she whispered as she shoved paper, pencils and charcoals into the girl's hands and sent her into the adjacent dressing room.

Claire was washing charcoal dust off her hands when Edward knocked and entered on her reply.

He took the room in at a glance. "I'd rather you'd called for the carriage and gone to visit your friends in the village than put more notions into Parsons's head," he remarked. "You haven't seen your Miss Simms since we've been back."

"But you said you didn't want me to go out without you! And it's not wasted time. It's a shame to waste any person's abilities." Claire dried her hands on the linen towel hanging on the washstand. "At any rate, Simmie is away visiting the parents of some prospective students near Bristol. I couldn't have."

"But you would have, knowing my wishes?"

"No, Edward. Please don't put words in my mouth." She approached him and made as if to straighten his cravat, but he grasped her wrist and stopped her.

Startled, lips half-parted, Claire forgot what she had planned to say. His grip was light but firm and she was afraid to move. Her pulse accelerated as he looked at her face curiously.

"Claire," he said softly, "do you love me? Do you trust that I would never do anything intentionally to hurt you if I could avoid it?"

"Edward, of course! I wouldn't have married you if I didn't!"

He embraced her, planting a series of kisses on her hair.

"It's all right then, it's all right," he murmured.

Hair brushed and Annie sent off to her room, Claire climbed into bed more weary than she ever had been after a long day out on horseback. She extinguished the lamp on the night table, pulled the bed clothes up to her chin and lay on her back watching shadows cast from the fireplace chase across the ceiling as she waited for sleep to come.

A weight on the bed roused her from a light slumber, and she sensed more than saw in the dim light a dark solid bulk on the bed beside her. She struggled to free her arms from the heavy quilt.

"Don't be alarmed, dearest." Edward's voice. He had come at last.

"Edward," she sighed.

"Hush. Don't say anything. Lie still." His voice in the darkness, so close in her ear now that he loomed over her, sounded thick and alien. She felt his warm breath against the skin of her face as he pulled the bedclothes back and exposed her nightgown-clad form supine on the canopied bed. The sudden chill brought gooseflesh up on her body and, less sleepy now, she raised her arms to embrace him.

Gently, he pushed her arms back to her sides. "Be still." His voice dropped a register. "I will hurt you as little as possible. "

He pushed her nightdress up around her waist, exposing her nakedness, and slipped his left hand between the deep pillow where her head rested and her nape. Burying his fingers in her silky hair, he turned her head up slightly and began kissing her urgently. She tried to respond, but his kisses were sloppy and aimless as he alternately pressed his lips against her mouth and bit at her lips.

With his other hand, he squeezed and rubbed her right breast hard through the thin fabric until she wanted to push him away. Pinioned under his weight now, she squirmed ever so slightly. He shifted his weight over her and pushed his knee between her legs until she made space for him. He moved his hand from her breast and reached down to clutch his penis. She felt him fumbling between her legs and then a pressure against her closed softness.

His first thrust caught her by surprise and she cried out in pain as he forced himself up into her against her dryness. He grunted and paused.

"Oh, my darling, oh, my darling," he said raggedly.

He drew a breath deep into his chest and began grinding his hips against her slowly. Once, twice, three times, then a final deep push that Claire feared tore her flesh. Their mutual cries at that climax—his of release, hers of pain—were a cruel counterfeit of a passion neither had enjoyed.

Claire stifled another cry as he pulled out of her abruptly. They lay silently together in the darkness, and for no reason she could explain to herself afterward, she reached up and placed a hand on his cheek. It was wet with tears. A moment later, he stood, pulled her nightdress down over her legs, drew the coverlet back over her, and left the room.

Chapter 17

HER HUSBAND WAS finishing his coffee when Claire came into the breakfast room the next morning.

"I hope you slept well," was his greeting to her.

"Yes," she said tersely as she seated herself and he poured her a cup of tea.

Coming around the table, he placed the steaming cup by her hand, slid the cream pitcher closer and helped her arrange her serviette. Leaning over the back of her chair, he spoke low into her ear.

"My darling, I want you to know from the bottom of my heart that if I could have spared you last night's experience, I would have."

She spun around, forcing him to step back and meet her eyes. He pulled out the chair next to her at the table and turned it so her could sit facing her.

"My dear," he began, taking her hands in his. "My dearest Claire, my wife, marriage is the greatest glory in a woman's life, next to motherhood, and a man is not a true man in the single state. But marriage is also duty and for a woman especially, it necessitates some obligations that are unpleasant and that she would avoid if possible. Our conjoining last night is one of those things. I know I hurt you, and I am sorry."

She flushed and averted her head. Predisposed for such a response and not understanding its origins, he continued more earnestly.

"I am pledging to you, here and now, my dear, that I will not importune you in that way more than necessary. I pray to God daily for the strength to control myself, so that the animal aspects of our relationship do not coarsen our spiritual bond—"

"You aren't making any sense, Edward," Claire managed to interrupt. "Stop preaching and talk to me like an actual human being. Last night..." She floundered for a word. "We, last night... kissing. Kissing is nice. Surely God wouldn't have created us to kiss if it weren't to be pleasurable? We show our love for one another in kissing."

"Don't be coarse. Like all pleasures in life, kissing in the right circumstances is enjoyable but should be moderated. Men and women are not beasts, we have souls and, as such, are called to subdue the flesh, not indulge it. The procreative act—you understand that is what we did last night? "

Claire felt bile rising in her throat.

"—the procreative act above all is one of those behaviors. It has a specific ordained purpose, but wicked men and women pervert it, and degrade themselves by it. It may seem unfortunate that the Creator fashioned men differently, so that they find more physical pleasure in the act than women, but I sometimes think if God had not been so wise, decent men who respect their wives would find it difficult—"

Edward stammered to a halt. In the awkward silence, Claire observed, he was blushing hotly. A surge of spite prompted her to say with as much sweetness as she could put into her voice, "Would find it difficult to do what, Edward?"

"Not to do what we did last night more frequently." The words tumbled out. "Again, I apologize, but it had to be. You can't deny I delayed for as long as possible. Too many husbands ravish their unsuspecting brides on their wedding nights and use them with abandon thereafter. They have only themselves to blame if their wives later become unbalanced from the strain of it."

He bowed his head so low it was nearly in her lap. She stared into the thick blond waves and compared their boyish softness to the man's hard eyes and expression. "I would not let myself be one of those brutes, because I love you!"

"It's all right, my darling," Claire said after a moment, stroking his head the way she would a child's. "You think too much of it. If this is the worst marriage has to offer, I will count myself fortunate indeed."

Claire calculated that she had a perfect opportunity now to visit Simmie in Abbot Pyon without strong objection from her husband. After breakfast, Latimer, as usual, had retreated to the library, leaving Claire to occupy herself until late afternoon. The curricle was waiting in the drive and she was in her bonnet and cloak when she tapped at the library door.

"Edward," she called softly.

She heard the key turn in the lock. He stood in the half-open door, his hand braced on the broad vertical edge, blocking her view of the interior while she told him of her plans.

"You're taking a boy with you?"

"Yes, since you wish it."

"You'll not tire yourself?"

"No, Edward."

"Very well. My regards to Miss Simms." As he stepped back to shut the door, he tripped and caught himself on the door. His weight swung it wide, giving Claire an unobstructed view of the vast room.

"Oh, Edward," she gasped. "Whatever are you doing?"

Books lay in uneven piles all around the room, on the floor, on chairs, some even stacked crookedly on their sides on the mostly bare shelves. A stray volume on the floor by the door had caused Latimer's near fall. A light patch on the paneling shown where Josiah's portrait once hung.

"Surely you're not still looking for that manuscript?" she added. "I thought it was clear from Josiah's papers that it doesn't exist?"

"It's none of your business what I do in the privacy of my study," Edward snapped. He passed his hand over his eyes. "Forgive me. That was uncalled for. I'm taking an inventory, and the books were never properly shelved after the fire."

He shut the door so abruptly it would have caught her skirts if she hadn't reacted quickly. The lock snapped to like a slap in the face.

Claire gave the reins an emphatic slap and the horse leapt against the harness. The tug of the leather in her hands, the vibration of wheels on gravel and the animal's lively motion felt right. To be in control of something again was a fine thing. It wasn't as good as being up on a spirited mount galloping across the fields, but it was as close as she would be for some time to come. She would miss the hunt season for the first time since she was 10, she realized with regret.

The horse gradually slowed as the full force of her predicament descended and her hold on the reins slackened. She wanted nothing more, short of being free of her troubles entirely, than to unburden herself to Simmie.

Claire wasn't showing yet. Annie assured her it would be well after Michaelmas and the apple harvest before she would. Her breasts were swelling, though, and Annie couldn't lace her corset as tight as she could have even a week ago. Already the girl was spending her afternoons letting the seams out on Claire's bodices.

At some point, Latimer would notice her changing body. She needed Simmie's advice, if not collusion, on when she could reasonably tell her husband she was pregnant and how best to approach the subject.

But how would Simmie react to her news? Her friend had been tolerant of Claire's willful flouting of convention so far—too tolerant?—but she had put herself beyond the pale this time. In fact, Beatrice Simms would be more than justified in cutting herself off from any association with Claire, for the sake of her fledgling school.

Claire urged the horse back to a brisk trot, and the village soon sprang into view around a curve in the road. While the boy (another Tressel lad) secured the horse, she drew her wraps around her and tried to quell the fluttering in her stomach. She hadn't seen Simmie since her wedding day and feared, against reason, that she would be different somehow. Yet it was she who had changed.

Claire lifted the heavy doorknocker, and a small girl led Claire to a sitting room at the back of the house. "Mrs. Latimer, miss," the girl announced barely above a whisper, standing aside to let Claire pass.

"Just a moment, Lane!" Simmie said brusquely as she rose

and enfolded Claire in her arms. "Claire, dear, how good to see you!" She released her and turned to the maid. "Now, Lane, what did I tell you?"

"To speak up, miss."

"And what else?"

"If you please, miss, to announce visitors in the room, not from the hall."

"And what else?" There was a pause. The girl's hand flew to her mouth.

"Oh, miss!" She turned to Claire and curtsied. "Pardon, missus. May I take your cloak, missus?"

Claire handed over her things and followed Simmie toward the small settee by the bright fire. The day outside was warm, but because the houses in town were built wall to wall, practically supporting each other, no sunlight penetrated to the back rooms to warm them.

A young man rose as Claire approached.

"Oh," Claire said without inflection. "I'm sorry, Simmie. I should have sent a note ahead to see if you were free."

"This is Mr. Morton, Claire." Seeing the blank look on Claire's face, she added, "Mr. Latimer's curate."

He bowed. "I hope you are well, Mrs. Latimer. My best wishes on your recent marriage."

"Thank you. I do hope I'm not interrupting."

"I was just leaving," he said, then broke into a smile that made his plain face handsome. "Really, Mrs. Latimer. I'm not just being polite. Miss Simms and I were discussing Latin texts that would be suitable for young ladies. And there's my sermon for Sunday still only half-written."

"Mr. Morton is a Cambridge man," Simmie broke in. "So you see, he is up on the latest teaching practices at the women's colleges."

Claire raised an eyebrow.

"Both of my sisters are at Girton," he explained. "I will write directly and ask for their recommendations, Miss Simms." He retrieved his hat from the sofa. "Thank you for the excellent tea— and don't bother poor Lane." He smiled again. "I'm sure she's had enough sorrow for one day, forgetting to ask for my hat and then Mrs. Latimer's cloak.

When the door had closed behind him, Claire sank with a sigh onto the chair he had vacated and peeled off her gloves. "Do you mind ringing for more tea? And is this a good time for me to call, really?"

"It is, but even if it weren't, I would make it so. I've longed to see you and, frankly, I've been a little worried."

"But Simmie! Why didn't you call at Oak Grove? I've missed you so much and the days are so tedious. Edward won't let me do anything."

"I thought you knew," Simmie said. "The day you returned, your husband wrote asking me not to call. He said you were unwell in Cumberland and that you preferred not to be disturbed for the time being. He hinted—well, he left me with the impression that you didn't want anyone intruding on the two of you. He wrote, he said, because you were too shy about it to make your feelings known to even such an old friend."

Lane brought in a laden tea tray, and Claire reached eagerly for the cup Simmie handed her. It rattled so loudly in its saucer she had to set it down. Her words burst forth.

"Not want to be disturbed! Intrude!"

"It made sense to me, Claire. When a man and a woman love each other and want to be together, a honeymoon away from their friends is usually when they have the opportunity to explore themselves and each other in their new relationship. Yours was cut short—"

Now Claire couldn't sit still.

"He cut it short, Simmie. He couldn't stand being there alone with me. He made Annie sleep in my room every night. He didn't— we didn't even—" She clutched at her skirt, the dampness of her hands creasing the fine silk "He didn't even come to me until last night. And it was horrible. This morning he apologized so much it made me sick."

She covered her face and wailed. "I'm lost, Simmie! I never should have married him. I don't know what I'm going to do!"

Simmie threw her arms around Claire in an effort to calm her.

"The wedding night can be a terrible shock," she said. "It will get better with time, I promise you. Few men are absolute brutes. As you get to know each other, he'll learn to be more tender. You'll teach him."

"No, no, no!" Claire sobbed as she pulled away. "You don't

understand. I'm going to have a baby!"

"Claire, that's impossible. Even if you had had relations on your wedding night, you'd have no way of telling this soon. You've been listening to old wives' tales if you think so."

Claire clasped Simmie's head in her hands and forced her to look at her. One clipped word at a time, she repeated, "I'm going to have a baby." She released her and fell back on her heels. "About Lady Day, Annie says."

"But—" Simmie did a silent calculation. "That's March. Oh, Claire."

Claire pushed a strand of hair out of her eyes. "Yes. I've been a fool, insisting on my own way and not taking anyone's advice, and now I'm going to pay for it. The only question is how dearly."

"Did you know—well, of course you couldn't have known when you accepted Mr. Latimer's offer."

"No. I've only just known myself for about two weeks. Annie recognized my symptoms. I was sick every morning at breakfast."

"I see."

"It's humiliating to be so ignorant." Claire sniffed and Simmie pulled a handkerchief out of her pocket.

"Let's sit down—over here I mean—and discuss this rationally," Simmie said, rising and offering Claire her hand. "We'll figure something out. Pour out your tea and I'll give you a fresh cup."

Claire wiped her eyes. "I should never have married him," she said again. "He'll turn me out of the house without a penny, and I can't blame him. If I hadn't lost my head after Dickon, at least I'd still be able to support my child and have a roof over my head. I've lost everything—my self-respect, Oak Grove, any reputation I had left. There's no chance Papa will ever reconcile with me now." She took a gulped of tea. "I won't be able to help you anymore."

"Love can forgive many things, Claire. You can't assume Edward will be so cruel."

"That's just it, Simmie. I don't think he loves me. I'm not sure why he married me. He is solicitous, but he hardly spends any time with me. Even as he sees how it pains me, he cuts me off from every pursuit that ever gave me enjoyment. He frowns when I wish to ride, he discourages me from calling on my friends, he's taken management of the household out of my hands. And he so obviously avoids touching me that I must repel him. If he wanted to drive me mad, he's on the right path!"

"How can I help you?

"You can't, Simmie. You have the school to think about now, and your partnership with Lina. I don't think we should even call on one another now. The scandal will be horrendous when it comes out."

"I still think you are misjudging your husband, Claire. He is a proud man. If anything, scandal will be the one thing he'll want to avoid. Perhaps you could go abroad for a while. Together, I mean. Until after the baby is born."

"Oh, Simmie. You don't understand. I don't want to stay with him. He is hard. He preaches at me constantly and he treats me like a child. My own Papa was never so condescending. To live with him after he learns this will be to have no will of my own ever again."

Her voice dropped so low Simmie barely caught her next words.

"I've done a terrible thing, Simmie, the one thing I said I'd never do. I married a man I don't love."

They sat silent for many moments before Claire began to speak again.

"I admired Edward, but I know now that wasn't love. It was Josiah all over again. His behavior these past weeks wouldn't upset me so much if I loved him. It would make me sad, not angry and afraid. How could I have gotten it so wrong twice?"

"Claire," Simmie said firmly. "I think it's time you told me what happened the day Mr. Latimer proposed to you. Or did it start before then?"

"It?" Claire laughed hollowly. "What is 'it?' My inability to control myself? Josiah saw it the moment he laid eyes on me. *He* saw it, too. Is my wickedness written on my face, Simmie? Is that why Edward shuns me?"

"Let's leave your husband out of this for the moment, Claire. 'He?'"

"You'll force me speak his name? Surely you can guess. There could be no one else." A piece of wood popped in the fireplace as Simmie waited.

"I won't lie, Simmie. It was Lord Montfort. It stormed and we took shelter in the oast house." She griped Simmie's hand fiercely.

"I knew what I was doing. I wanted to. I used to lie awake night after night thinking about what it would be like. My imagination was a feeble thing, as you can imagine. He was—"

Without meaning to, she dug her nails into Simmie's hand. "The making of this child was the most glorious thing I've ever known! I never wanted it to end. And I want this child now with every fiber of my being, even as it means my ruin forever."

Claire withdrew her hand and folded herself into her arms. "Afterward, we quarreled. We said terrible things to each other and he left me there. On the way home I overheard some farm hands sniggering about how he planned to seduce me to get Oak Grove back—their language was coarse and degrading! Then I killed Dickon. The next day Carey said Rhys had gone abroad. I felt such a fool. And there was Edward. Courteous. Strong. Speaking the words I needed to hear."

She laughed. "Shall I tell you what we quarreled about? He wanted me to go abroad with him, to be his mistress. I was too high and mighty—too proper—to realize what he was offering me.

"I wish now I had said yes—not because of the baby. He may not have wanted being saddled with a squalling bastard—but I would have had a few months more of happiness to look back on before slinking into oblivion."

Simmie went to a cabinet on the far side of the room and returned with a small bottle. Taking Claire's cup she poured a jot into the cooling tea and handed it to Claire.

"Brandy," she said. "Drink a good swallow and come and sit down. Let's get past the drama and start sifting through the practicalities. This is life, Claire, not a melodramatic novel. You've made some dreadful mistakes, I'll give you that. But it's not the end of the world. We just need to examine your options and decide the best way for you to get on with your life."

The dusky colors of an early-fall sunset painted the sky as Claire drove back to Oak Grove. She'd left three letters with Simmie—for she knew sending and receiving this correspondence from Oak Grove would be fatal to her plans. Her husband exercised his right to supervise every parcel, every note, every caller, that came to his door, and she hoped to keep her flight secret until the last possible moment. For that was the course she was determined to follow.

One letter went to Mr. Chambers to see what recourse she might have in obtaining a maintenance income from the estate, with or without her husband's cooperation—a slim chance at best. One letter went to her mother, informing Lady Henry of her daughter's irretrievably broken marriage and begging her to speak with her father. The third letter, to be delivered a few days after her mother's, was a request to Sir Henry for Claire's £5,000, the sum that had seemed so magnificent once and now was likely her only feeble hope of escape and a new life with her child.

Claire was later than she wanted to be. She stood in the brightly lit hall expecting a dressing-down from an irate husband.

Instead, he approached almost placatingly.

"We have visitors," he said. "It's a business matter, however, so if you'd like to go up to your room rather than join us at dinner, you may do so. In fact, I'd prefer it."

Through the drawing room door on the left, Claire spied two figures clutching crystal glasses that rang as they toasted one another with vigor. Josiah's claret was of the best and these men—from the city, judging by their dress—were enjoying it heartily.

"I should be introduced, Edward," Claire said. "If you told them I'm indisposed—as you seem to have been telling my friends in the village—it will be clear now that you fibbed. And they must be important or you wouldn't be serving them our finest wine in our best glasses."

He bristled at her sharp tone. "You will take a tray in your room. After I introduce you, you will excuse yourself."

Claire handed her wraps to the waiting Noonan and checked her hair in the large pier glass beside the door. Taking Edward's arm, she formed a proper hostess's smile and let him escort her into the room.

"Gentlemen," he said as the two men stopped speaking and turned to bow to Claire. "May I present Mrs. Latimer. My dear, this is Mr. Scott"—he nodded—"and this other gentleman is Mr. Hodgeson." The man raised his glass to her in salute.

"Scott and Hodgeson, that's us," the first man said with forced bonhomie. "Estate agents par excellence, if you'll pardon my French." He laughed loudly. "That was a joke, that. French, wot?"

"Very pleased to meet you, ma'am," the man indicated as Hodgson said. "I hope Mr. Latimer conveyed our apologies for our mistake in arriving a day early."

"Claire?" Edwards said sotto voce.

"Welcome to Oak Grove, gentleman," Claire said. "I hope your stay will be comfortable. If you will excuse me, though, I've had a long day, and I'm told you plan to discuss business at the dinner table."

She tugged on Edward's arm as she turned toward the door. "My dear. Since I've been out, please give me a moment of your time to go over the arrangements you've made for our guests. I want to be sure nothing was overlooked."

Edward carefully shut the door behind them as they left the dining room.

"Edward," Claire hissed, dropping his arm as soon as they were alone in the hall. "Why have you brought estate agents here? And where is Mr. Carey? He knows Oak Grove better than anyone. If you're thinking of making changes or—God forbid—raising a mortgage, you'd be wise to leave the arrangements to him."

"Yes," Edward responded. "I've noticed you rely on Carey to an unseemly degree. But no matter. I've decided to sell, and what happens to Carey after that will be up to the new owners."

"Sell!" Claire all but shouted. "Oak Grove generates a fine income. Why would you need to sell any of it off?"

"I no longer fancy living in Herefordshire, if you must know. I'd like to see a bit of the Continent again and, come spring, I'll purchase a villa suitable for a small household. France, perhaps. Normandy is cheap."

"We don't need cheap. We have everything we need here!"

"An estate like this eats up coin at an alarming rate. You've plowed nearly its entire income for the year into these so-called 'improvements' Montfort cozened you into. You're a poor manager, my dear, as evidenced by the way you conduct yourself with your inferiors. It's one more item for the tittle-tattle that fuels what passes for society around here, and I'll not have my wife laughed at."

"And when were you going to tell me?"

"When you needed to know. It's your own fault, Claire. Consider that when you go running back to your governess to cry on her shoulder like a child. I should forbid you visiting in that quarter, but since we'll be leaving this place soon, it hardly signifies. Now go to your room. Mr. Scott and Mr. Hodgeson will be wondering what's keeping me."

Claire climbed the stairs slowly, wondering what she had to be angry about. This development would simplify her plans. She could say nothing to Edward—until he needed to know, she thought, wrinkling her nose. She'd play the obedient wife and they could go their separate ways with few in Abbot Pyon the wiser. All she had to do was be patient for once.

To tell oneself to be patient and to actually be patient are incompatible, Claire acknowledged to herself as she paced down the hallway from her room to the top of the stairs for the fourth time. Edward and the estate agents were still shut in the dining room. She wanted to talk to her husband again before he retired, partly to learn what had transpired and partly to assure him that she would not be difficult after all.

By 9 o'clock she had forced herself to sit and read. She chose the dullest book she had at hand—Josiah's abandoned copy of *L'Île mystérieuse*, retrieved from the library when she still answered to Miss Burton and since forgotten. Settling uneasily by the fire, she left her door open a few inches the better to hear Edward when he came up. She was confident there would be no repeat of last night's conjugal performance.

Claire picked up her paper knife, opened the first few pages and started reading. Following the technical French Mr. Verne used to describe the scientific processes employed by the castaways helped her to focus her attention. If she were to live abroad—though "cheap" Normandy would be out of the question for her, she supposed—brushing up her French would be a good idea.

To her surprise, the story engaged her. How fortunate those men were, free to build a new world and write their own rules. And the dog Top was so amusing and heroic. Claire pictured Kip, snug in the kitchen with Mrs. White. How he would love bounding through the virgin forests of Mr. Verne's Lincoln Island.

Giving him up turned out now to be another helpful step toward her departure. The page before her blurred momentarily as she thought of Kip, Toddy, the suffering Dickon, and then mentally strayed across the fields and orchards of Oak Grove. Leaving them should be easier than the tug in her heart suggested.

She blinked and sliced a few more pages, not wanting to hurry the tale. Of course, there would be no women on the mysterious island. The novel was written by a man, after all. Men all seemed to think women spoiled their fun. So she tried to imagine herself in the role of the young boy, Herbert, and how differently she would approach the problems the struggling band faced—assuming she had a similar degree of scientific education, that is. Could she be that self-reliant and resourceful when she arrived on her own spiritual island in an exile she had engineered?

The loneliness of the men's situation struck her as pitiable. Women crave society. Not tea trays, gossip and diversions, but the mutual sympathy that comes with sharing their daily trials and triumphs. Claire lifted up a silent prayer of thanks for Simmie. Without a caring friend to help carry the burdens of her heart, Claire would be worse off than Mr. Verne's stranded heroes.

But soon Simmie and everything familiar would be as lost to her as the homeland of the island heroes. From the shores of her distant island, Claire told herself, she would have a choice—to gaze across a sea of time longing for the past or to turn her hand to the hard labor of building a new life, even a new identity.

The thought opened an unsuspected world of possibility that slapped down the self-pity rising in her heart. Once free of Edward, she could make a new beginning and put her mistakes behind her. It would be a new life. Two new lives...

Shouting on the ground floor jerked her back to the present. She made out Edward's carrying voice above the din, trained as it was for the pulpit. The voices of the two London men, unfamiliar, blended together. And there was another voice, one she was sure she recognized.

L'Île mystérieuse fell from her fingers, its pages splaying face down on the floor. Claire flew to the hallway and listened again. The roar continued, and one voice rose above it, clear and commanding. She rushed to the top of the stairs.

There, in the hallway, Edward remonstrated with Lord Montfort, while the two strangers milled about, appealing first to one combatant and then the other to come back to the dining room. Edward grabbed Montfort by his coat lapels and attempted to drag him toward the partially open door, while Noonan hovered nearby, clearly uncertain whether to pull the door back or shut it. Claire shouted, too, but no one heard her.

Then, with a mighty shove, Montfort pushed Edward to the floor. "I'm warning you, Latimer," he said loud enough for everyone to hear. "What I said just now is God's own truth. I'll come back tomorrow, when you're willing to see reason." He tossed a packet of papers onto Latimer sprawled on the cold marble. "Take a good look. And lest you think you can just throw those deeds on the fire, know they are copies.

He picked up his hat from the floor, dusted it off and set it on his head.

"Gentlemen," he said to Scott and Hodgeson, "I recommend you return to London first thing in the morning. I guarantee you'll have no business here." Pausing at the door, he spun back on his heel and looked up Claire. "Good evening to you. Mrs. Latimer." Then he disappeared into the night.

Claire considered going down to her husband, but only for a moment. "Noonan," she called out to the butler just shutting the door behind his lordship. "I think our visitors are ready to retire. Please show them to their rooms." In a twirl of heavy skirts, without waiting to see whether Noonan obeyed her as before, she returned to her room, breathless with excitement.

She closed her door this time and walked toward the fire, her thoughts racing. She stumbled over the damaged book lying on the floor and a cream-colored piece of paper slipped from between two partially cut pages well toward the back of the volume. Pulling it out, she saw it was part of a letter.

The handwriting was feminine and well formed. Josiah's name leaped out. A billet doux from another of his many lady friends, no doubt. She crumpled it and prepared to throw it into the fire, then paused. Josiah had never cut any of the other pages of the novel. He had died before he had the chance. The volume was otherwise untouched until she began to read it tonight. Why cut one page and insert this letter?

She flattened it out and saw it was signed "L." Then she noticed Edward's name. Was the letter from Lucy? She read the letter in its entirety, then got up and locked her door, horrified. The first page was missing.

... on your mercy. (This page began.) *He punishes me. He comes to my room at night and does terrible things to me, things I hardly know how to describe. He hurts me and says it will teach me to keep away from men. I hate myself and the things he makes me do. He tells me it's all my fault and then says I can't help it I was made the way I am. A snare to tempt men, he calls me, but only in the night when I'm forced to listen to his whisperings and can't hide from his cruel judgment. During the day he is all loving kindness, just what a brother should be.*

Claire blinked tears away, though one fell on the page and blurred the ink. "Snare" became "snow"

I used to be so happy, Josiah! Now my health is giving way—I can't keep food down in the morning and I'm weary all the time. He looks at me in the morning as if nothing has happened in the darkness. Then he prays with me for hours asking God to chastise my heart and make me obedient. Who will chastise him for his wickedness? I know he must be wicked for all that he weeps and begs my forgiveness after he hurts me.

I am tainted now and hardly dare show my face in decent society. George, my dearest friend in the world, abandoned me when Edward told him what I was. Please, please, Josiah, don't abandon me, too! I have nowhere else to turn. He's cut me off from everyone I loved. I must get away from here. Please help me.

L.

Scrawled at the bottom of the page in Josiah's broad hand were the words, *"Too late!"*

The page drifted to the floor as Claire rushed to the wash basin and retched. Her stomach heaved until nothing more came up, but the dry gasping continued. No wonder Lucy had run away. Lucy couldn't explain what was happening to her—the poor girl. But Claire—how could she not recognize the brutality, the tears, the apologies, she'd witnessed in her husband?

Where was Lucy now? Had her child—for Claire had no doubt what Lucy's sickness meant—survived, or were both mother and babe resting somewhere in an unmarked grave? Did Edward even know the extent of what he had done to his half-sister?

Claire picked up the letter and read it again, hoping she had somehow misunderstood. A troubled, motherless girl, trusting for love from a rigidly moral man like Edward, how bleak her life must have been! But there was no mistaking it. *He comes to my room at night... He hurts me. During the day he is all loving kindness... can't keep food down...*

She was packing a small valise when Latimer walked in from the dressing room without knocking.

"What are you doing?"

"I'm leaving, Edward. I can't stay under the same roof with you another night."

"You'll abandon your marriage promise because I made a business decision without consulting you? I think not, Claire. Or is it because of last night? I assure you, other wives get used to it in time."

"Neither reason. It's because you are a monster."

"I see. I see all too clearly." He grabbed her hard by the shoulder and forced her to look at him. "Montfort shows his face once in my house and you no longer want your lawful husband. I suspected there was more between you than he would admit, but I conquered my jealousy and gave you the benefit of the doubt."

She twisted out of his grip and lashed out, missing him by inches as he evaded her blow. Turning back to the valise, she picked up Lucy's letter and placed it on top of her clothing.

Latimer pushed her aside and seized it.

"Is this from him?" She reached for the letter but swiped at air as he held it out of her reach.

"You're my wife now and you will honor your vows," he said coldly. "Perhaps I've been too gentle with you."

"So you will hurt me, too—like you hurt her?" Claire gestured toward the letter he held between thumb and forefinger. "I know what you did to Lucy, Edward. I'll leave this house tonight if I have to walk to Abbot Pyon!"

Wordlessly, before Claire could react, he locked the dressing room door and pocketed the key. It took her a moment to register he had come with it, prepared.

Secure from intrusion, he read the letter. Then he casually crushed it between his hands and threw it in the fire.

"Thank you, my dear. Josiah told me had a damning letter from Lucy that he hadn't received before he left for America. I've been looking for it since he died. It's why I killed him."

Chapter 18

Claire thought she must have misheard him.

"Josiah fell from his horse," she said, trying to sound dismissive.

"Don't be stupid." Edward picked up a poker and prodded the burning letter further into the flames. "I met him in the lane that day. We quarreled because I kept my sister from running away to America with him and he was still angry. He always fancied Lucy—you've read his disgusting journals, how he lusted after women. I couldn't let that happen."

He waved the poker aimlessly. "She sent the letter too late and he only found it when he returned from America. He threatened to spread these vile lies about me around the world. So I knocked him down and crushed his skull with a stone." He thrust the poker hard into the grate and sparks flew up, along with bits of glowing paper.

Claire stepped back warily, placing the chaise between them. "That's why you wanted to find the manuscript, why you've torn the library apart! You were afraid he had written about you. You — and what you'd done."

"Afraid? No. He made sure I knew his intentions to destroy me. The letter was his insurance, to prevent a libel suit. I'd all but decided he'd lied about it, the way he misled me about so many things. And now here it is." He jabbed the last black fragment into ash. "Or was."

"Is that why you married me?"

"Regardless of what you may think at this moment, I did love you. Marrying you, however, was a mistake. You make me forget myself."

He studied her, the poker dangling by his side. "You needn't be afraid of me, my dear. " He raised the poker and examined its length. "As if a stick of furniture would protect you, though" He swung the iron down with a thwack on the upholstered arm of the chaise. The cracking of the wood beneath the padded fabric startled both of them for an instant.

Claire scrambled for the bell pull beside the bed, hoping to cross the short space before he could react. The poker barred her way before she'd gone two steps. He pressed it against her bodice and forced her to retreat a step. A long horizontal line of soot smeared the silk.

"I meant to tell you earlier, but I didn't have the opportunity. I dismissed Parsons this afternoon."

"What! Why?"

"I said you were finding her too familiar and were too embarrassed to say so. Don't worry. I sent her off with a train ticket, a month's wages and a reference, which, I must add, she did not deserve. You ruined that girl with your attentions."

"But I don't understand! If we're going abroad, I'll need a maid more than I do here at home."

He sat splay legged on the end of the chaise, twisting the poker between his knees. "I don't like my wife relying so much on other people. I'm glad we're leaving this place. It will force you to give all your attention to me."

Claire placed her hand on her belly protectively. She tried to keep her face smooth as her mind raced for something to say that wouldn't provoke him.

"I'm tired, Edward," was the best she could do. "Could we discuss this in the morning?"

"I am tired, too, my dear, but I'm afraid I can't accommodate you." He stood and took her arm, all but dragging her to a chair by the fire. "Please. Sit." He gave her a shove and she obeyed.

He replaced the poker in the rack by the fireplace—well out of her reach—and sat again on the chaise, with his hands on his knees, leaning in toward her. "You haven't asked why Lord Montfort called this evening."

"It was no business of mine," Claire said shortly.

"Even though he threatened me, knocked me down? Claire, where is your wifely concern?"

"It was no business of mine," she said again.

"It is, though, my dear." He straightened his back. "Prepare yourself for a shock."

Before she could stop it, a laugh erupted from her throat. What could be more shocking than what she had just read and heard? She masked it well enough with a cough that Latimer rose and poured a glass of water from the pitcher on the night table. He handed it to her and sat impassively as she drank. When she set the glass down, willing her hand to be steady, he resumed.

"Do you remember the woman who was found murdered by the churchyard?"

She nodded once.

"That woman claimed to be Josiah Carter's wife."

Claire felt the shock write itself on her face. "But that's—"

"Impossible, you were going to say? Do you really believe that? Or that he wouldn't abandoned her in America?"

"No," she said more calmly. "No, that doesn't surprise me, if it's true. But he really did marry her?"

"Montfort claims to have discovered the place in the States where they were married. He says he's spoken to the witnesses and the parson who performed the ceremony. He's met her parents. He says he even employed a man to make a photographic plate of the church register."

"How can he be so sure it's the same woman?"

"Her family recognized her from her effects. Why does it matter? Montfort found a legal wife. Dead or alive, it comes to the same thing in the end."

Claire shuddered, then frowned. "Josiah's will! He left Oak Grove to me in—how was it put?"

"In absence of the superseding claims of spouse or issue," Latimer supplied. "Yes. Oak Grove never was yours, thus now is not mine. I had hoped to sell and be gone long before any of this was known, much less settled. We could have lived in comfort for many years while claimants squabbled in Chancery Court. A sale would have tied it up that much longer. The case could have run until every farthing was exhausted."

"But that's wrong, Edward! And what if this woman's family demands restitution for all I've spent, for what I've done with Josiah's papers, the biography? We could be ruined by going through court!"

"That's where you can be invaluable, my dear wife." Latimer leaned so close she could see her reflection in his narrow pupils. "The clever Lord Montfort holds the deed to Oak Grove now. Why do you think he went haring off to America? He's got what he wanted. But you are going to help persuade him to sign that deed over to me. Then all can go on as before."

"He'll never do that."

"Oh, but he will. Much as he struts about and moans like the gloomy Dane, he still values his life. I will dictate a letter to you and have it taken over to Oakley Court tonight. This will all be ended tomorrow morning and I'll be on the Dover packet by evening."

"And if I refuse?"

"What would the point be in that? Montfort is free to decline your request for a tete-a-tete—but if you won't help me arrange a meeting, I can always send one of the servants in your name."

"Then that's what you will have to do, Edward. You seem to excel in putting other people's words in your mouth."

"So be it. It's better, in fact. No incriminating letter to worry me this time." He picked up the poker again, and Claire quailed. "If you move an inch, I shall strike you down."

He disappeared into the dressing room, where Claire could hear him opening and closing drawers. He returned with a handful of her stockings and tossed them on the foot of the bed.

Without preamble, he reached for her and grasped her arm. Half out of the chair, she grabbed the heavy tumbler at her side and struck him on the side of his head as hard as she could. He staggered back and dropped her, but before she could get her legs under her and run, he lashed out and threw her back. He wrapped his arms around her and squeezed so hard her lungs emptied explosively and spots swam before her eyes.

When he tossed her on the bed, she tried to kick him, but her heavy skirts got in the way. She flailed wildly at his face, making contact once or twice before he slapped her so hard her head snapped back against the headboard with a crack. She stopped hitting out at him when he grabbed a feather pillow and pressed it over her face. She struggled to push it away until her strength failed her, she ceased kicking and her arms fell limp on the bed.

Despite the warm night, chill seeped through the walls and along the dark silent corridors of Oakley Court. The house was all but empty. In years past, when Montfort's father was alive, the house would buzz at all hours as friends, political allies and place-seekers caballed on the fate of the empire while their wives, sisters and daughters formed alliances equally as powerful in their own way.

But after the death of her favorite son, the dowager Lady Montfort preferred anyone else's country home to her own, and her second son's absence provided the excuse she wanted to take her daughters anywhere else at the close of the London season. If he wouldn't persist in burying himself there, the house could be shut up permanently, as far as she was concerned.

To Rhys Montfort, too, the house was filled with ghosts, but tonight he was impervious to both the cold and the memories. His blood still roared after the fight at Oak Grove, and the ring of his boots on the polished ebony boards of the gallery above the great hall echoed his satisfaction. The faces lining the long wall looked down proudly; if he were an imaginative man, he told himself, he would read approval in his ancestors' eyes.

He'd gotten what he wanted, or nearly so. For once, he had Edward Latimer off balance. Only the sight of Claire watching, impassive, from the top of stairs had tamped his gloating mood. She hadn't even cried out when he struck Latimer down.

He'd been back for only two days, but already he'd heard the rumors—the honeymoon cut short, the apparent estrangement between the couple, the bride's ill health. It was Carey who had let slip that Mrs. Latimer no longer rode out or visited in the village.

It was Carey, in fact, who had ridden over to Oakley Court that afternoon to tell Montfort about Latimer's London guests. Carey was a dark one, Montfort decided, and probably not even sure himself whether he was looking out for his own interests, Oak Grove or its erstwhile mistress.

"What do you expect me to do?" Montfort had asked the man curtly.

"Nothing, I suppose," Carey had replied. "I just thought you should know. This could affect everything you've been working on with our people, if someone who doesn't understand or care about the farms comes in." He paused, then plunged on. "And I don't think Mrs. Latimer knows. She won't be happy."

"Marriage changes people, Carey. For all we know, Mrs. Latimer has been chivvying her husband to get rid of the place and trade up for something in a more fashionable county."

"She's not like that, sir. If she's not well—"

"Who says that?"

"Anyone can see it, my lord. She scarcely goes out of the house since they've been back from the Lakes."

"There's your answer then. They may intend to travel for Mrs. Latimer's health." Montfort all but dismissed the man, then recovered himself. "I do thank you for this information, however. I will call on Mr. Latimer immediately."

Carey allowed himself a smile. "It would be a grand thing if you could be the buyer, my lord."

"Indeed."

Now, as the clock ticked on the mantle, the coals shifted with a sigh in the library grate and the fire warmed his whiskey, Montfort was unable to tear his thoughts away from Claire.

Humiliating her hadn't been his intention, though once he'd done it, he wasn't sorry. Over the long days and weeks since that day in the oast house, though, he'd had plenty of time to dissect his own motivations. It came down to fear. Fear of needing her love. Fear of opening the door to pain and loss again. Fear of bringing her harm or even death.

He splashed more whiskey into the glass. The one thing he hadn't been afraid of was rejection by her. Deep down, he'd known since that kiss in the cottage—maybe even from the day they'd met. If he were honest with her, she would respond with honesty. She couldn't be any other way. But fool that he was, he had pretended to trick her, and ended up tricking himself.

And now Latimer—for a second time, Latimer divided him from the woman he loved. He barred the way, implacable, like the angel with the flaming sword at the entrance to the Garden of Eden. Only for this exiled Adam, Eve remained forever on the other side of the gate.

Well, Oak Grove was no Eden, and he now held the keys to its gates.

"Pardon me, my lord." He hadn't heard the valet's knock on the door.

"Yes?"

"There's a boy here with a message from the New House. Shall I bring him in?"

Montfort set down his glass, rose and nodded. After hearing what the boy had to say, he went up to his rooms and rifled through the bag he'd brought back from America. He shoved a small pistol in his coat pocket and a few moments later was striding across the windblown lawn.

A cold breeze touched Claire's face and she opened her eyes to darkness. She tried to sit up but rocked helplessly like a turtle on its back. Her arms were bound painfully underneath her body and her legs were tied together. Trying to move set her head to throbbing, and her wrists and ankles were restrained so tightly her limbs ached. She lay still and tried to think.

The fire had died down, so it must be late, she reasoned. The house was silent.

Tensing her muscles, she managed to flop onto her right side, facing the fireplace. Edward had tied her ankles beneath her skirts, so if she could come to a sitting position on the edge of the bed, she might be able to hop across the room. The paper knife should still be on the table by her reading chair, if it hadn't gone flying in her struggle with Edward.

She inched her hips to the right and gingerly swung her feet out into space and down with enough momentum to carry her legs forward off the high bed.

A rattle behind her broke her concentration and she fell to the floor. Fire shot up her arm when her elbow struck the bare boards at the edge of the carpet and she bit back a cry. Heart thundering, she strained to locate the sound. The knob to the dressing room door vibrated roughly and she scrambled crabwise under the bed.

The clatter stopped and the door swung open. Slow footfalls approached the bed, stopped, shushed across the carpet toward the fireplace. There was a muted grunt as a body collided with something heavy. Silence. Soft irregular breathing. Movement toward the bed. Claire held her breath.

"Miss? Miss? Are you in here, miss?"

Annie!

"I'm under the bed," Claire said as loudly as she dared. "Where is my husband?"

"He's gone out, miss. I saw him from the window, hurrying across the lawn toward the wood. Are you hurt?"

"No, Annie. Can you see to pull the curtains tight and light a lamp? Then you can help me get out from under here."

Claire heard a rattle of curtain rings and a moment later a light flared. Annie found the paper knife and cut through the stockings Latimer used to bind Claire.

"Oh, Annie," Claire exclaimed, giving the girl a hug. "I've never been so happy to see anyone in my whole life! But what are you doing here?"

"I couldn't believe you'd send me away like that, without a word direct," the girl said simply. "So after he sent me to the station in Hereford, I turned around and walked back. I slipped up the back stairs and hid in the dressing room, then I fell asleep. It was the row that woke me. And the good Lord must have been watching over me, 'cause if I hadn't, the mister would'a caught me out. I climbed in the wardrobe and waited. Then I heard him leave.
"

Annie sniffed. "I'm so sorry, miss!"

"What could you possibly be sorry for?"

"I wanted terribly to come in and see you was all right, but I was afraid he'd come back. Then I saw him in the garden and I still waited. If I'd a known he'd tied you up like that, I would'a risked it!"

"How did you get in?"

"Mr. Latimer forget to ask for my keys."

Claire gave Annie another hug. "Quick, find my cloak and bonnet. I was just about packed to leave when all this started, so I just need to see where my case ended up. You've already got your train ticket, yes? And I have enough money for mine." She rummaged through a drawer in her dressing table and produced a slim pocketbook.

"Where are we going, miss?"

"We'll go to London. My aunt won't leave us standing in the street, no matter what she thinks of me. At least not for a night.

But first we must hurry to Oakley Court."

Latimer hadn't bothered with a lantern. He knew the way to the abbey ruins so well he could have found his way in total darkness.

Calculating he had nearly an hour to wait, he sat on a half-wall of the wrecked chapel, well concealed but situated to detect Montfort's approach. If the moon slipped behind the clouds, he'd still hear him moving through the tall weeds.

"Meet me at the royal tower," Latimer had told the boy to say. "I have something important to tell you."

"Be sure to add that she seemed worried and had been crying," Latimer had added.

He leaned back against a broken buttress and watched an owl sail across the clearing. Montfort would come alone, of course, though Latimer hoped he wouldn't bring one of his infernal hounds along.

His thoughts wandered to Lucy. Despite all his threats and pleas, she had told on him. First to George, then to Josiah. "Told on." The phrase was childish, he admitted, but when she was a child, the worst thing anyone could call her was tattletale. She quickly learned to keep her complaints to herself, necessary for a little girl if she wanted to play with the boys.

He raised his eyes to Montfort Abbey's broken tower, discernable only because it was a darker black against the sky. One of Lucy's favorite games was to play queen and knights. George once stole an embroidered velvet table covering from his mother's boudoir and used it to make a throne at the base of the bloody tower where the infamous Jacinta had met her end. The boys crowned her with wildflowers, and it was only when they paraded her back to the house that Lady Montfort discovered the theft, for at that point Caesar wore a splendid velvet saddlecloth.

How Lucy had cried! Not because the game ended so abruptly, but because she didn't want to see George punished.

Lucy's tears. He wished he could get the sound out of her weeping out his head.

He wrapped his fingers around the short iron bar in his pocket. What was he doing out here? He should have just gone to Oakley Court and had it out. As long as his secrets were safe, he had enough power over Montfort to get the deed to Oak Grove, and even if Claire managed to tell someone, she had no proof.

From her first day in Herefordshire, her behavior was irregular and it was a known fact that already-unstable women could be unhinged by the initial shock of the marital obligation. Finding two doctors to certify her and lock her away in a private asylum wouldn't be difficult. He had money enough.

Or would, once Montfort was persuaded.

He heard a rustling too measured and too low to the ground to be wind and stood, ready to face his adversary.

The wind was rising when Annie and Claire slipped out the back door into the service area of the house. Though it was barely autumn, dry leaves skittered across the stones and made Claire jump. She skirted the house, staying as close to the walls as possible lest the light from the house cast their shadows across the broad lawn and reveal their presence. Edward had left the first floor ablaze with light, and the urns and topiary on the terrace cast long, distorted shapes beyond the bright rectangles of light from the windows. They rippled on the ground like dark water.

Annie stayed so close behind Claire she collided with her when Claire stopped suddenly. But when Claire grasped Annie's hand and tugged her toward the garden, Annie tugged back.

"No, miss! That's the way he went!"

Claire hoped she sounded more confident than she felt. "I'm certain Mr. Latimer's errand will take some time. But we need a lantern from the stable. We can't afford to get lost in the dark."

Annie trailed Claire reluctantly around the perimeter of the stable yard and halted.

"You'd best let me go in, miss, in case there's anybody about. I doubt word's gotten over from the house that I lost my place and I can say you was wanting me to take a message to Miss Simms or somethin'. If he's there, I can just run."

"I'll wait by the summer house. Be careful." Annie set Claire's valise down and, chin high, set off at a brisk walk toward the stable. She was back at Claire's side in no time, though to both women it seemed like hours. She held up a small bull's-eye lantern.

"I was lucky. Bill Tressel was beddin' down the horses tonight. He's sweet on me and dropped what he was doin' in a flash to help me out. Thank goodness he had just started his work, otherwise he would' a come with me!"

They covered the mile to Oakley Court in less than a half-hour. Claire stumbled to a halt when they rounded a curve in the drive and saw the massive, crenelated front of Oakley Court looming against the sky. A flag on the tall central tower whipped and snapped, signifying that the viscount was in residence.

Approaching was now the difficulty. Intermittent moonlight reflected off the gravel drive, but apart from a pair of torches flaring on either side of the archway that pierced the main tower, no lights showed. Just off to their right, though, about twenty feet away, two red sparks gleamed. Over the wind, Claire heard a growl.

"Annie," Claire said. "One of Lord Montfort's mastiffs sees us. His keeper should be nearby, but if he isn't, you run for the house. Head for the light and when you get to the doorway, make as much noise as you can."

Claire took the valise from Annie and lifted it in both hands, intending to throw it if necessary, and started walking slowly toward the dog. She put as much distance between her and Annie as she dared, hoping the animal would keep its eyes on her yet not be provoked to attack.

"Hello? Is anyone about?" she called. "Hello!" Only wind and a rumble from deep in the dog's chest. It had come closer, even as she had, so that they stood barely ten feet apart. It would have her in its jaws in an instant, regardless of whether she ran or waited. She could see it now, poised to spring.

The phrase Montfort had taught her and Carey, the one to control the mastiffs he'd given her after the fire—would he train all his dogs to the same command? It was her only hope.

Before she could speak, a deep male voice called out from beyond the crouching canine. The dog sank to the grass and whined.

"You there, halt!" the man shouted at her now. He snapped a stout chain to the dog's collar and raised his lantern to inspect her and Annie, who now stood close beside her.

"Ladies!"

"Please," said Claire, shielding her eyes from the glare. "I have urgent business with Lord Montfort. Can you take me to him?"

"His Lordship went off toward the New House less'n an hour ago," the man said, a question in his voice. "That girl behind you, isn't she the lady's maid there? She can take you if it can't wait."

Annie spoke up. "We just came from there and didn't see anyone."

"His Lordship took the shortcut through the woods..."

"Annie," Claire said, thrusting the valise at the girl. "Wait for me. I'm sure his Lordship's man here will see you safe and dry in the kitchen. I'll be back as soon as I can."

Claire took off running before Annie could protest.

Montfort had no trouble finding his way in the night. As boys, he and George often went out with the keepers or to fish. They'd spent one entire summer in pursuit of a prize barbel rumored to lurk in the swift-running waters of the river. When Rhys had landed it at last, his older brother had been as proud as if he himself had been the victor.

The white moon was riding high now, bathing the land in liquid silver, and the night was alive with unseen creatures. Crickets and other night insects droned steadily, and far off a tawny owl scree'd to its mate. As he followed the path through the wood and onto the verge of the meadow, he wasn't surprised to see a fox slip into the underbrush, a limp hare dangling from its jaws.

Nor was he surprised to find Latimer in the chapel ruins.

"Come out now, Latimer," he called as he approached. "No need to make a game of this."

Latimer stepped out of the shadows and waited.

"God, man," Montfort said as he closed the distance between them. "You look like Varney the Vampire, skulking there. May I assume Mrs. Latimer is not with you?"

"My wife's whereabouts are no concern of yours."

"I daresay not. Do you care to explain this ridiculous charade or do I have to guess? If you wanted to meet, you could have just said so. We're not sworn enemies."

"No? Then what was your purpose in buying Oak Grove out from under me?"

"It simplifies things, Latimer. A number of things, in fact. You don't have to worry about a protracted lawsuit—you can just pay me rent and live there as long as you wish. You and your wife."

"And in return?

"In return, you will stop threatening me. We both know you had something more to do with Marguerite Carter's death than anyone suspects."

"No one would believe you—you, of all people," Latimer sneered. "The man who let his brother die and murdered his faithless wife?"

"Nevertheless, I think both of us would like this matter dropped. Police methods have improved, Latimer. They're much more scientific now. My name may be black as pitch hereabouts, but I still have enough pull to get the right people asking questions. Do you want to risk that?"

"I've already warned you—they'll be asking just as many questions about you. I had no motive to murder the woman. It's clear now you had all the motive in the world. A jury would just need to see that deed you were waving at me this evening to hang you."

Montfort stood so close to Latimer he could see the moonlight reflected in his eyes.

"You haven't asked how I found her family. Don't you wonder what led me to them so easily? Aren't you afraid of what else I know?"

Latimer retreated a step. "I suppose you are going to tell me."

"Joss came to see me a few days before he died. Don't look so startled. He was worried about Lucy. When he got back, no one could tell him where she was."

"What else did he say?"

"I really wasn't interested in listening to him. We'd hardly been friends since that damn book of his. He seemed sorry enough, but the damage can't be undone. When I saw that ring, though, the ring your wife wore and the dead woman, too, I remembered a remark he made—something about a friend coming over to join him, and then they'd be traveling."

"And? That was hardly enough information."

"I'd assumed he meant a man, but here we were, faced with a woman, clearly foreign and clearly with a connection to Joss. He always used the White Star line, and that means Liverpool. If she was the one Joss was expecting, there had to be more baggage, so I went to Liverpool."

"How one earth did you run her to ground at that lodging house?"

Montfort raised an eyebrow. "So. You went looking to?"

"Yes."

"Obviously, you were too late." Montfort sat down on a block of stone and tried to make out the expression on the silent Latimer's face. "And if you must know, it wasn't so hard. Joss used to stay there."

"What were you hoping to find?"

"The same as you, of course. Proof—or not—the woman was who she said."

"Nothing else?"

"What else could there be?"

"Joss didn't tell you anything else?"

Montfort cocked back his hat and looked up from under the brim. He hadn't felt this confident around Latimer in years. "About a manuscript, say? A diary? Or a letter?"

He leapt back as Latimer pulled his hand out of his pocket and lunged. Out of Latimer's reach, he pointed the small pistol he'd brought.

"Let's not get silly, Latimer," he said. "You can't fight me—I proved that earlier this evening. Let's just go back to settling rents and terms and forget all this, shall we? I apologize for taunting you. It was childish of me. There is no unfinished 'Rector,' Mrs. Carter had no diary, there are no incriminating letters about anything. What could Joss have had on you anyway? You're the decent one among us—in deed, if not in thought."

The two men eyed at one another warily.

"How can I be sure you're telling the truth?" Latimer said at last.

Montfort laughed softly. "You act like you do have something to hide. It was only a cheap novel, Latimer. Your reputation would stand against anything Joss could have written. You were right. People already thought badly of me, so they were ready to believe worse. Come. Let's go back to the house and come to an arrangement, like civilized men."

He held out his hand, but Latimer averted his head. He was returning the cosh to his pocket when a cry startled them. Montfort turned in the direction of the sound, which came from the far side of the ruins. Latimer brought the bar down hard on the back of Montfort's head.

As Montfort dropped to his knees, he thought he heard an

unearthly shriek, as though the hounds of hell pursued someone through the abbey ruins. He fell to the ground and the shriek echoed in his skull again. All was silent for a moment before the night chorus resumed its manic chatter.

Chapter 19

CLAIRE WAS NO sooner out of sight of the house and into a stand of trees before she wished she had asked for the night watchman or even some boy from the house to come with her. She hesitated, then ran on. Unless Josiah had been inaccurate about geography as well as history, the ruins would to be just beyond a rise to the west of the house and less than a quarter-mile away.

Within a hundred yards, she felt a path under her feet. She picked up her pace and followed it until she all but collided with a stone wall—a remnant of the outer castle defenses. She opened the lantern eye and spun slowly in a semicircle, shining the beam left, up and right. The barrier stretched out of the light in both directions, but the path hugged it as far as she could see. The wall was too high to climb, but she wouldn't have in any case. She'd do no one any good if she plunged into the darkness on the other side and broke her neck.

She turned left. Oak Grove should be due south, so this path should take her away from the precipitous drop into the dungeons.

As she followed the track along the wall, she thought she heard voices carried faintly on the wind. After a few minutes, she rounded a curve in the wall and plainly heard men talking. She stopped, faintly relieved. They weren't shouting. They didn't even sound angry.

She felt vaguely foolish. Surely Edward wouldn't harm one of his oldest friends. He was angry with her, upset by this news Montfort had brought about the property. Could it be that he had said those horrible things about Josiah and the dead woman simply to frighten her? Murder happened in sensation novels, not in real life. And respectable men didn't go around murdering people. It was absurd. Crime was a lower-class phenomenon. Wasn't it?

She remembered Lucy's note, now less than ashes. She hadn't imagined that, nor Edward's violent reaction. She refused to think about what he planned to do to her when he came back to the house, expecting to find her helpless on the bed.

A rustling behind her in the underbrush sent her heart racing and she swung the lantern abruptly. In the narrow beam stood a fox, a bloody hare clutched between its teeth. Its amber eyes met hers briefly before it calmly trotted off into the night.

The sound of the men's voices caromed oddly amid the trees and stones. She needed to reach them and warn Montfort. But where were they?

The moon, behind her when she'd left the house, now was high and to her right. The track wound among the tall grass and turned abruptly into the trees. She listened hard, then retraced her steps as the wind shifted and took the voices with it.

Her chest grew tight and her breath quickened as she realized she was lost. A wrong turn could take her away from Edward and Montfort. A false step could be her death.

Brambles caught at her skirts, and mud oozed up over her boots as the path petered out. Sucking sounds accompanied every step as she inched forward on ground soft as dough after the steady days of rain. Here and there on the path ahead, puddles sullenly reflected the light.

On a drier path again, Claire followed a low line of stones, the remains of another wall, she thought, or part of the old chapel. The voices grew louder and she hurried recklessly on the uneven ground.

Between one step and the next, the earth gave way beneath her feet. She tumbled back hard enough to knock the breath out her lungs in a loud cry and slid down a steep embankment.

A shower of dirt, small stones and dead leaves rained on her at the bottom of a narrow roofless passage. She righted herself and brushed debris off her face with muddy hands. Cold moonlight poured in like icy water from above and she saw she was in what once were the castle's cellars. At intervals along the steep wall opposite, dark openings indicated entrances to corridors or chambers. She gulped and pushed away visions of must have occurred in those dark places in the dark past.

She assumed the lantern was lost and groped along the wall. The voices floated above her now. She tripped and her outstretched hands plunged into a fall of mud close to the wall. She sank up to her elbows into the muck, where one hand struck something smooth and hard. She pulled back and rubbed her hands on her skirt, trying to get free of a tangle of dead vegetation or rotted fibers that clung to her fingers.

After a few halting steps, her foot struck hollow metal. Kneeling cautiously, she waved her hand in the air just above the ground until she felt warmth and retrieved the lantern. By some miracle, it had not gone out.

With relief, she opened the lantern shutter. And saw, clinging to her skirt, a hank of something long and trailing. A jeweled comb enmeshed in the reddish strands winked dully in the lantern light.

Claire shrieked and dropped the lantern, slapping frantically at her skirt, then shrieked again.

Latimer hit Montfort off balance and the glancing force of the blow sent a surge of pain up his arm. He dropped the cosh, abandoned it in the grass and picked up a fist-sized stone. What had worked for him once would work again.

He watched Montfort impassively as the stricken man groaned and raised himself on his forearms, forehead nearly touching the ground. Montfort crawled slowly away from him, dragging his legs along with the strength of his upper body. As he labored to put distance between them, Latimer wondered whether a second blow would be necessary.

Nevertheless, in two strides he caught up and poised himself to smash Montfort's skull. At the zenith of his swing, he hesitated.

"Edward, for the love of God!" Montfort struggled for breath. "Help me up. I'll give you what you want."

Latimer lowered his arms and stepped closer. "What do you have I would want now?"

Montfort drew a wheezing breath and choked. "The land, I'll

give you the land." He collapsed onto the muddy ground and moaned. His body curled in on itself, fists close to his chest.

Latimer stood close enough to kick him now if he wanted to. He bent to hear Montfort gasp, "Shouldn't have tried to fool you... of all people... I..." More words were lost in a fit of racking coughs. "The manuscript... yes..."

Latimer's heart thudded. He threw the rock aside and reached down to push Montfort over onto his back and assess his injury. Too late he saw Montfort's eyes fly open as the man's hands shot out to grasp his ankle. Latimer flailed and went down.

The soft earth cushioned this fall but he barely had time to recover before Montfort was on him.

Claire's mind shut down and she ran through the narrow passage, stumbling over the uneven stones and crashing off the rough, turfy walls. She gulped in cold, damp air as she fought to suppress the bile surging into her throat. She didn't notice the gradual rise of the ground until she shot into the clearing.

The night was deathly quiet except for her harsh pants. The silence was the silence of alarm, the wild things of the land quivering in dread as they waited, hidden, for the hunter to pass. It was the hour when the world teetered between death and birth. She remembered the hare and shuddered.

To her right stood the dense crepitate curtain of the wood. To her left, ragged spikes of absolute black thrust upward—the fractured walls of the chapel. Farther left she sensed more than saw the ruined tower. Her flight had brought her around to her goal.

The blank dome of the sky pressed down on the edges of the earth, trapping Claire and every other living thing like specimens in a bell jar. She gasped for breath and prayed for strength as even the stars seemed to be dying.

But as a cool breeze freshened from the east and plucked at her hem, Claire spirits rose irrationally. The stars would not go out. The night would not win. Sunrise was creeping closer, and at the edges of the world, the first tinge of dawn bled into the sky, flattening the deep obsidian into a thousand variants of raven, jet, sable and deepest indigo.

Like a match flaring in the darkness, Claire's heart revealed its secret at last. Finding Montfort safe and alive mattered more than anything ever would in her life. She would be allowed to atone for her mistakes. The future beckoned with a stingy hand. But what happened now would determine the difference between a life merely bleak or entirely without joy. The world without Montfort in it somewhere would be a world with no light for her.

Gathering her skirts, ready to spring across the sodden meadow, she heard a faint shout and recognized Montfort's voice. Ragged grunts and oaths led her directly to the place where two men struggled. Both were on their feet, wrenching and grappling at something. She attempted to thrust herself between them and stop them, only to find herself rudely shoved onto the stony ground.

She heard a shout of triumph and the fight abruptly ended. A shadow loomed over her, blocking out the moon, then a hand reached down and pulled her to her feet. She knew him instantly, the feel of him and his scent.

"Thank God, you're not hurt!" Clutching Montfort's sleeve, she turned to face her husband, so relieved that she didn't notice how still both men were. "I've left you, Edward," she said, embarrassed at how feeble she sounded. "I think you'll agree your behavior in all respects has been abominable and I expect no interference from you. Let me go and no more will be said."

She felt Montfort shift his weight from one foot to the other as he cleared his throat.

"Mrs. Latimer," he said dryly. "You probably can't see it, but I happen to know that, thanks to your interference, your husband now has my pistol in his hand and is pointing it toward us."

A ghost of a laugh came from Latimer's direction. He stood about five feet away but stepped closer so Claire could see the small weapon he held.

"I have no desire to use this," he said, "except to persuade you. A bullet hole in a corpse shouts murder, although I suppose if I had more time, I could make your deaths look like a crime of passion."

Claire moved fractionally closer to Montfort.

"For the sake of argument, though, I'd like your opinion," Latimer continued. "Is it more likely, Montfort, that you would kill my bride and then yourself or vice versa?" He didn't wait for an answer. "No, no one would believe you'd destroy yourself simply because you committed a crime. She, deranged by jealousy and shame, would have to shoot you."

He paused, as though playing out the scenario in his mind. "A pity," he said at last. "It could be perfect. My masterpiece."

"Your masterpiece!" Montfort asked.

"He says he murdered Josiah," Claire said. "With a stone."

"Josiah, yes," Latimer said, his voice so soft they could barely hear him. "No one questioned it. Accidents happen. Life goes on."

"And his wife?"

"She persisted in lying to me. I tried to make her tell the truth and suddenly she was dead."

"But why did you tell me so much?" Montfort asked.

"I needed your complicity. No, I needed your fear to bind you to me. I could never depend on love to hold anyone close. Even God requires his creatures to fear him. We don't obey his commandments because we love him, we seek to avoid punishment. Ecclesiastes. Fear is the fountain of life. Praise spoils the child but the rod, the rod. You must learn to love the rod, my father always said."

Latimer choked back a sob.

Claire released Montfort's sleeve and gripped his arm, digging her fingers into the hard muscle to hold him still. Pitching her voice so that Latimer could hear her clearly, she said, "Edward punished Lucy, Rhys. He loved Lucy, so he punished her. Is that what you mean, Edward?"

"She was too trusting. I had to protect her."

"How did you do that, Latimer?" Montfort said through clenched teeth. "What did you do to Lucy?"

"Don't you dare speak her name, Rhys! It's because of men like you that Lucy suffered. You, and Joss, and your preening brother George. She didn't know how men use girls like her and throw them away. Leaving him in the cider house was the hardest thing I've ever done, but I had to protect my lamb!"

"What did you say?"

Claire wrapped both hands around Montfort's arm as tightly as she could and pulled him back. "No, please. He'll shoot you."

"I should have let the flames take both of you, Rhys. As it was, I barely got you out of there after the roof collapsed. You were so drunk you didn't remember going back for him, and that was the blank slate I needed. I was in complete control—until *she,* this woman who is now of my flesh, came along." He spat on the ground.

"Where is Lucy, Latimer? Do you know?"

Latimer laughed like a drunken man. "Do I know? Is she in Heaven? In Hell?"

"I know," Claire said, her clear tones ringing on the night air. "She ran away, didn't she, Edward? She couldn't wait to get away from you, because of the way you hurt her."

"Stop!" Rage made Latimer's command more a roar than human speech. "Not another word. This whore lies, Rhys, did you know that? My wife is a liar. She lied to me about her virtue, she lied about loving me. She'll tell any lie now to save herself."

"I think it's too late for that," Montfort said sharply. "What were you about to say, Mrs. Latimer?"

Even the night seemed to hold its breath as Claire gathered the courage to speak aloud the horror.

"Lucy was carrying his child. She tried to run away, but I think Edward killed her, too. There's something—something horrible down there in the ruins, half buried in the mud. I think it's Lucy."

With a low howl, Montfort wrenched free from Claire and lunged low. Latimer stumbled back when Montfort's head connected with his solar plexus and a sharp crack split the air. Claire threw herself to the ground and waited, eyes squeezed shut, digging her nails into the earth.

The struggle ended almost as soon as it began. Afraid of what she would see in the pale, creeping dawn, she raised her head. Two men were on the ground, one kneeling over the other, but she couldn't distinguish them.

"Come here quickly!"

"Rhys!"

Claire scrambled to her feet and stumbled over to find Montfort holding Latimer awkwardly. Her husband's legs were bent sharply at the knees and his upper body lay limply across Montfort's thighs and chest, cradled in his arms. She knelt beside them.

"He's shot himself," Montfort said. "It must have been an accident. He was aiming at me when I took him by surprise."

"I'll run to the house for help," Claire said.

"No, stay. It's a belly wound and it's bad. The pain should

have knocked him out, but the loss of blood will do for him in short order in any case."

Latimer was trying to speak. "Lucy," he said weakly. "Lucy. You lie. I couldn't kill her. I did everything for her. Where you found her—she fell. She was going to Joss, to meet him at her tower, to run away. I waited there. We argued." He grimaced.

"Oh, Lucy," he wailed. "Your tears. I never stop hearing your tears! She cried all night and begged me to fetch help, to take her home. It was a night just like this one. The sun was just rising when her tears stopped."

"For the love of God, Edward! Say you didn't let her die here!"

"... in my arms. My angel died in my arms."

Claire reached out and tentatively touched Edward Latimer's hair, gently stroking it away from his face. She closed his staring eyes.

"I found a letter Lucy wrote," she said levelly. "Josiah had hidden it in a book. It was terrible, what she wrote. Edward burned it so nobody would know. No one would believe me, he said."

"Nobody will know, now." Montfort eased Latimer' to the ground. "I want you to go back to the house and summon my butler. Tell him there's been an accident and don't say anything else. But first, take me to what you found."

Claire took Montfort's hand and led him down into the yawning passage as the first rays of morning tipped the topmost stones with gold and left him beside Lucy Latimer's shallow grave.

Montfort returned to Oakley Court to find Claire in the library where he and Latimer had shared so many conversations, liberally aided by cigars and fine malt whiskey. Already those times seemed like a dream of another life.

Claire was huddled under a wool throw on one end of a small leather sofa, Annie at her feet staring into the fire. Tea sat on a table within reach, untouched and stone cold. Neither spoke or looked up when he entered the room.

"Annie, is it?" he said softly. The girl stood and faced him, her eyes dark against her pale face.

"You'll be wanting to speak to miss," she said. "I'll wait outside until she calls me back. She'll be needing me."

He nodded, but as he stood aside to let her pass, he took her arm. "Not a word to anyone."

"I'm no fool," the girl said, raising her eyes to meet his.

Once the door had closed behind her, he sat beside Claire and took her hand. It was stiff and icy.

"Claire," he said. "I know you're exhausted, but we must talk."

"So much waste," she said without looking at him. "Why? And for what?"

"Edward Latimer said it himself. Fear. He was so possessed by his own fear he couldn't see what was real anymore."

"But to destroy the very people he loved!" She shifted in the chair and drew the wrap more closely around her. "He was going to kill you tonight. Then he was going to come back to Oak Grove and kill me."

"I wouldn't have let that happen. I knew that message couldn't have been from you. He said to meet at the queen's tower. Only Lucy called it that.

Claire plucked at the loose weave of the wrap. "Lucy. What—?"

Montfort rose abruptly and went to the sideboard, where he poured a pale amber liquid into a stemmed glass. He knocked back half of it in a gulp and refilled the glass before seating himself on the sofa opposite her. Hunched forward, twisting the stem before him in both hands, he looked down into the bright liquid glowing in the firelight, but what he saw was mud and cowed men with shovels and rakes. Lanterns that burned feebly in the harsh daylight. Rotting cloth and stained bones. A small glittering comb with the entwined initials "LL" picked out in garnets and pearls, its twin revealed as the diggers gently pared the earth away from Lucy's remains.

"There's no doubt it was Lucy." He grimaced. "Two years! It's horrible to think of. Two years out there alone in the cold and rain. While we all thought of her, talked of her, worried about her, hoping she was well."

He took another gulp, then set the glass aside as if repudiating it. "It seems so obvious now, the way he used to prowl those ruins at night. God! How much other peculiar behavior do we humor in our neighbors, laughing it off as harmless eccentricity! He was mad!"

He shot her a glance.

"I'm sorry," he said. "He was your husband. You must have seen good in him or you wouldn't have married him."

"Edward." She pronounced the name as though it were from alien tongue. "Edward didn't know how to love. He wanted to, I could see that—he could be kind and thoughtful. But in the end he just didn't know how. He saw life as though he were looking at it through a dirty windowpane. "

She looked at him finally, her face a mask of questioning pain. "Nothing was clear or clean to him. I think he hated himself and that loathing blackened everything else."

"What you said about Lucy..."

"Yes. He didn't deny it when I confronted him, but I don't think he knew the worst of it. All these months, he'd been searching for anything—a journal entry, a note, a scrap of paper—that would give him away. He talked of how he tried to burn the house down as though it were the most rational idea in the world."

"'The Rector.' He was hardly rational if he thought any publisher would have printed a story like that. It's abominable. And I can't believe Joss ever intended to expose him at the risk of hurting Lucy."

"Whatever Josiah was planning, it cost him his life."

"Joss wasn't all bad, Claire."

She looked up in surprise and watched as Montfort went to the desk and came back with a large softbound book.

"Joss did leave a manuscript," he said before proffering the book to her.

She took it gingerly and, opening to the first page, the title written with Josiah's unmistakable flourish. She brought it closer to the light and read, "Clarissa Barton; or, The Noble Heart."

"Did you read it?" she asked softly.

"I did. You should, too. It will answer one question, at any rate—why Joss left you behind."

She stroked her hand across the smooth page. "It hardly matters now. Mr. Carter and Miss Burton—neither of them was real. They were characters in the kind of story we like to tell to children. 'And they lived happily ever after.'"

Claire slowly unwound herself from the sofa and gestured toward Montfort's glass.

"Do you think I might have some?" While he busied himself

with decanter and glass, she hugged herself, the plush Persian rug soft under her feet. He handed her a glass and drank deeply. Fire fizzed down her throat and warmed her from her belly to the crown of her head.

"What is this?" she asked, looking into the depths of the glass, grateful for a distraction.

Montfort held his glass up to the light. "Cider. Our best. My mother often serves it here instead of champagne. In a good year, it's difficult to tell the difference."

Claire held her glass up next to his and examined the delicate pattern etched on the bowl. Moths dancing through a riot of apple blossoms. Tiny bubbles flew up in columns behind the figures and vanished when they reached the surface. She drank again.

"You can't," she said finally. "You can't tell the difference about anything here until it's too late. I thought Herefordshire would be like Surrey, only more picturesque. It tricks you, though. The same sun, the same rain, the same people, you think. Oh, the foods and the way people talk is a little strange at first. But it turns out everything is strange." She emptied the glass and set it down carefully. "Did I say strange? Incomprehensible. Fey. I never should have come here. I don't belong and I never will."

"Don't say that. None of this was your fault. The seeds were planted long before you'd ever heard of Josiah Carter or known there was such a place as this."

"You're saying it was fate, then? Destiny?"

"I don't know what to call it. Is anything inevitable? Can we go back and put a finger on the place where, if we'd known, we'd make a different decision, take a different course, and alter the outcome? Do we even know the outcome would be better? We're still alive, after all."

He shook his head. "I don't know, Claire. I ask myself constantly what I could have changed, could still change, about myself. If you'd known everything in the beginning, what would you have done differently? Refused Josiah? Given up on him? Listened to your father and sold Oak Grove?"

Her answer pierced his heart.

"I never would have let you walk out of the oast house alone." She turned so that he couldn't see her flaming cheeks.

"If Edward had come back to Oak Grove with your blood on his hands, I wouldn't have cared what he did with me," she said so softly he barely caught her words. But he did, and without asking himself if he had misunderstood, he drew her gently into his arms and kissed the top of her head. She leaned forward and rested against him for a dozen heartbeats, neither of them speaking. Then she faced him, her eyes asking for a kiss.

Slowly, he touched his lips to hers. This kiss spoke of weariness and a bottomless yearning for ease. Instead of stirring passion, it offered comfort. She stepped away first, leaving him optimistic for more, on a better day and in a better place.

"You said we needed to talk," she said, pushing away from him gently. "We'd best do that now. Constable Reid and Dr. Bevans are sure to hurry, if they know it's Edward who's dead. We probably don't have much time."

"I'd keep you out of this if I could."

"I'm the one person who must be involved. I don't want anyone to think Edward killed himself, and if you are the only witness—" She broke off.

"I can say it for you. There is ample reason to assume I murdered the man I quarreled with just hours before. Be thankful now you're in the wilds of Herefordshire and not in London. As it is, the papers are going to be vicious, especially when this about Lucy becomes public."

For the first time, Claire felt faint and she knew it wasn't the cider or the lack of sleep. Montfort snatched the glass before it tumbled from her fingers and half-guided, half-pushed her onto the sofa.

Claire braced herself when Montfort's butler ushered Dr. Bevans and Constable Reid into the room, but the men all but ignored her.

After conferring in hushed voices in a far corner of the room, Bevans broke from the group and came over to her.

"My deepest condolences, Mrs. Latimer," he said solicitously. "Lord Montfort explained how he and your husband met to confront some poachers. It was doubly tragic you had to witness the unfortunate accident with the pistol. We have no need to further distress you now, but the coroner will want to meet with you before the inquest, of course, and take your testimony. If you'll permit me, I can take you back to Oak Grove. You'll feel better, no doubt, once you are home and among familiar things

Claire thought she must be dreaming after all. The lord of the manor spoke and that was enough?

She looked for Montfort, hoping to catch his eye, but with a curt nod in her direction, he turned his back. Willing for once to play the helpless female, she turned what she hoped was a limpid gaze on the doctor and accepted his help rising from the chair.

"Yes, thank you," she murmured. "You are too kind."

Home, Claire brooded as Bevans's carriage rolled away from the grand entrance of Oakley Court. *I have no home.* Thurn Hall was barred to her; in fact, her father most likely would strike her name from the family Bible when the scandal broke. She had been a trespasser at Oak Grove from the very beginning and now it belonged to Montfort. Simmie would take her in, but Claire would never ask her to make such a ruinous sacrifice.

She nearly offended Mrs. White when the doughty housekeeper met her in the hall with a warmer-than-usual welcome and expressed her readiness to inundate her with the only remedy for sorrow she knew—hot drinks and comfort foods.

"Thank you," Claire said curtly to the woman's greeting. "I want nothing more than my bed at the moment. Annie will see to my needs.

At a word from Carey, the London men hastened back to town without troubling Claire further. In fact, she had forgotten they were in the house. The inquest came and went in a blur. The verdict was a foregone conclusion—death by misadventure.

She spent the intervening days taking stock, both of her goods and her options. The small valise carried away from Oak Grove the night she was widowed was carefully repacked. Items went discreetly into Hereford for sale. Claire was scrupulous about raising cash only from items she had either brought with her from Surrey or that Edward Latimer had given her during their betrothal and brief, miserable marriage, so her takings were small.

She kept apart from Montfort even after the inquest, and she answered the short formal notes he sent inquiring after her health with the simple repeated message, that she was indisposed.

When a thick packet of papers arrived for her from Oakley Court, she set it aside unopened, knowing full well that a simple "yes" would make Oak Grove hers again, with or without the man.

The manuscript Montfort sent her sat on her bedside table

night after night, unopened as well.

The night came in late October that Claire took a lingering turn around the stable, savoring the sweet scent of hay and the warm, strong odors of horseflesh and well-oiled leathers. Her eyes were dry as she visited each horse with a word and an apple from the big barrel by the door. Giving the last horse a final pat, she walked briskly to the house, Kip trotting at her heels. She didn't see the horseman looking down from the ridge into the shadows of Oak Grove's gardens and lawns, hoping for a glimpse of the woman he loved.

Back in her room, she picked up "Clarissa Barton" at last and read only as far as the dedication page before carefully shelving it with Josiah's other volumes in the library.

"*To CB________,*" he had written. "*To a woman I could never deserve, I dedicate this poor endeavor and with it renounce my claims forever, knowing brief pain will spare for her a happier life.*"

In the dark morning, Claire left the packet of papers for Carey with instructions that they be returned to the master of Oakley Court and, with Annie, she climbed into an Oak Grove carriage for the last time. They arrived in Hereford just as the red sun glinted on the eastern horizon and boarded the train for London, two unremarkable women among the many unremarkable passengers who embarked from the station that day.

Epilogue

Two years later

THE EARLY MORNING sun had burned away the dew already, and thin lines of heat rose in the middle distance, casting a wavering haze over the hills that flowed in soft golden waves to the horizon. Ranks of olive trees followed the contours of the hill up from the valley floor nearly to the place he stood, and the sirocco stirred the leaves so that they darted and shimmered like schools of silvery fish.

Overhead, a swift climbed and plunged soundlessly in the clear sky. He was aware of the earthy bleat of goats nearby. The unseen goatherd's plaintive song mingled with the trill of warblers and the dull clank of a cowbell as another boy, dallying on the road below, half-heartedly prodded a lanky heifer forward.

All his attention, however, focused on his destination, hidden amid jagged rows of cypress. But for those dark sentries, the low villa's stone walls and terra cotta roof would blend into the dun and sepia landscape. A thin wisp of smoke rose from one of the chimneys. Someone moved about in the walled garden that encircled the house, glimpsed and lost again among verdant shrubbery. A servant girl drew water from a well in a small courtyard and vanished through a side door.

His horse danced beneath him, but he watched and waited as the sun rose higher. What had she said about destiny? After months of searching and an eternity of longing, his destiny awaited in that modest villa.

Steeling himself for disappointment, Montfort held back a moment longer, then spurred the eager horse onto the narrow path that wound down the steep hillside and through the olive groves. He had been invited, he reminded himself. He just wasn't sure by whom.

"*Ti sei perso, signore?*" a small boy asked, running up and stroking Montfort's horse with a practiced hand as he dismounted near the iron gate in the garden wall. For a moment he thought he was looking at one of Tressel's whelps, but that was impossible.

"Are you lost, sir?" the boy asked again in the northern Tuscan dialect canonized by the Florentine poets.

"No," Montfort replied. "*Sei di questa casa? Desidero vedere la padrona di questa casa.*"

"Sì, signore," the boy said, bobbing his head rapidly. He belonged to the house. He widened his eyes and flapped his hands in the direction Montfort had come from. "*Oh, scappare, signore! Lei è un drago!*"

"Tonio!" an imperious female voice called from the low portico of the villa. "*Arrestare il nonsense!* Stop your nonsense and bring the gentleman to me!"

Montfort found himself under the cool tiles facing an old woman half his size, swathed in black despite the heat.

"You are Viscount Montfort, I presume?"

"Yes, madam."

"It took you long enough to get here. Don't make me linger any longer than I have to in this infernal heat. I suppose you'd like a drink—of water, I mean. I don't hold with anything stronger in these foreign climes. It's enervating. Though we can offer you fruit juice if you'd like something with more substance. How far did you ride today?"

"Just from the village."

"Whom are you speaking to, aunt?" a light voice said from the inside the house. "I thought we'd agreed we'd use only Italian so we could perfect our skills." And before he had time to prepare himself, the speaker stepped out and joined them.

"You!" they exclaimed together.

Claire's face flamed as her hand flew to her mouth, that flush and her russet hair the only color amid the uniform black she wore as well. Her attire reflected the conventions of second mourning, from her dull black gown, the black lace mitts on her hands and the heavy jet earrings that swayed at her ears. He had hoped she would have moved on by now to the purples and grays of half mourning—the final six months of the two-year period observed for the death of a husband.

He felt his countenance redden as well. Clearly, she was not expecting him. Now what?

"Who is this dragon?" he demanded, for want of anything better to say. He caught her suppressing a smile.

"Aunt," she said solemnly. "May I present Lord Montfort?" The old lady nodded in his direction. "And, my lord, may I present Mrs. Manwaring?"

"Your servant, madam."

"Pfhh!" Claire's Aunt Maud responded. "Claire, I suggest you see to an extra plate at breakfast. I'll show his lordship where he may refresh himself. It's a lovely day for a turn in the garden. Perhaps his lordship would like to see some of the more exotic botanicals we have here."

The old lady looked up at him with sharp eyes. "You are interested in horticulture, Lord Montfort? I understand you are quite the farmer in Herefordshire."

"As a matter of fact, I am, Mrs. Manwaring."

Claire vanished without a word, and he followed her aunt into the house, made his ablutions and waited in the comfortable salone she had indicated. It was plain they had been in residence for some time. The room lacked the impersonal feel of a temporary home, and many items of furniture and ornaments reflected the taste of at least one of the current inhabitants.

A small pianoforte stood in a corner of the room, and a fine equine bronze stood on the mantel amid a pack of china dogs. Thrown over the arm of a chair he found a toy velvet fox, and a small wooden rocking horse occupied the hearthrug

The room took up one long side of the villa, allowing a view of the courtyard he had seen from the hill as well as a portion of the garden that was sheltered from the worst of the sun by shade trees.

He peered through the half-open slats of the shutters and watched a girl playing peek-a-boo with a chortling toddler in the garden. Several moments passed before he recognized the girl as Annie Parsons.

He was on his second glass of fruit punch and pondering this discovery when Mrs. Manwaring returned.

"Do you like children, Lord Montfort?" she snapped.

"I've never thought about it, ma'am," he replied. He glanced out toward the garden again. "They seem pleasant enough at this distance."

"Well, never mind. I need to talk to you before I send you out into the garden with my niece. I suppose you know why I had Miss Simms write to you?"

"You," he said, failing to conceal the disappointment in his voice.

"You didn't think it was she, did you? Poor boy." Claire's Aunt Maud seemed human all at once. "You'll have your work cut out for you, but since you're here, I presume you mean to try?"

Montfort waited for her to continue.

"If this were all left to Claire, she'd live out the rest of her life a guilt-ridden widow, and I have no intention of spending the rest of my days in purdah with her, much as I care for the girl. It won't be good for the child either. Or you."

She raised a quizzing glass that she wore on an ornate chain and studied him. "Look at you. You're in the prime of life and you look like a vagabond. You should have at least two or three children by now—legitimate ones—and have taken up your seat in Parliament. You're not going to do anything useful until you sort things out with my niece."

"Un drago," he muttered under his breath. Then, to her, "How do you presume to know all this?"

"My niece has made a fair mess out her life for one so young," Mrs. Manwaring said with deliberation. "Between her impulsiveness and her stubbornness, which she gets from her father, more's the pity, she is about to make the most monstrous mistake of all."

Still he waited.

"She loves you, and she will never lift a finger to do anything about it." Mrs. Manwaring's eyes flashed, full of intelligence and zeal. "I know what you're thinking. An old woman like me, what do I know? Believe me, she loves you. It's all in what she avoids saying, day after day, and then gives away the moment she does."

"What are you trying to tell me, really?" he asked, looking toward the garden rather than his interlocutor.

"Claire is an ardent soul, Lord Montfort, but she doesn't trust herself anymore. She is so determined not to repeat the mistakes of the past that she would rather ruin her life by denying herself the thing she wants most. You."

"Mrs. Manwaring," he said slowly. "I am flattered, but you must be aware of what the world says about me. What it continues to say, since the events of two years ago."

"Do you love my niece?"

"With all my heart."

"That is enough for me. You have my blessing—now go out to the garden and persuade her."

Anger and panic battled with a feeling Claire failed to recognize as the first stirrings of joy as she sat in her room wondering why Rhys had come, how he had found her, what she should do.

Rather than wait for him in the garden, as her aunt bid her, she met him on the veranda when he emerged from the house.

"It is quite a surprise to see you, Lord Montfort," she said in her best drawing room manner. "How are those I left behind in Abbot Pyon?"

She flinched when he scowled at her. "I didn't travel more than a thousand miles to engage in pointless chit chat with you. I want you."

Claire felt the blood rush from her face. "That's impossible," she said, looking off into the garden, anywhere but at him.

"Dammit, Claire, why are you being so willful? I understand why you refused the deed to Oak Grove, why you went away, though you could have done me the kindness of a farewell instead of running off without a word." Like Joss did to you, and like I did, too, he thought without speaking the words.

He stood before her now, blocking her view of the garden, and it took all her will to keep her eyes down. "This is my home now, Lord Montfort," she said. "Or wherever my aunt chooses, since I am dependent on her generosity. And I cannot ask you to give up yours. We may go back to England some day, but to Herefordshire? Never!"

Her heart sank as he turned abruptly. She gripped her wrists as she listened to footsteps, hard on the tiles of the veranda. *Leave,* she whispered to herself. *Leave, before I change my mind.*

The footsteps stopped. "Claire," he said, "I'd have Oak Grove torn down tomorrow if I thought that would make a difference. But that's not what this is about. I ask you straight—do you love me?"

Her heart began to beat as though it would burst from her breast. Like a sleepwalker, she came to the edge of the veranda to stand beside to him, still not looking at him.

"Yes," she said to the air, the trees, the sky.

"Do you believe me when I say I love you."

The word burst from her lips without hesitation. "Yes."

"Then it doesn't matter where we live. Perhaps, someday, when our children are older—"

She blinked awake, the spell of the past broken at last, and faced him, eyes wide.

"Don't look so startled," he said, taking her hand. "You've given me time to think, to dream, my love. And I see us growing old and fat together, terrorizing our servants, spoiling our children, frowning at our neighbors as we parade our brood into church on Sunday. Don't you see? I want to marry you, as soon as you put off all that black stuff, and start building a future with you."

"But I've been wrong twice! How can I be sure this time?"

The sound of laughter bubbled up from the garden. Annie and her charge had disappeared into the orchard and their voices drifted back on the warm air as though they had risen into the trees like birds. Claire felt Rhys squeeze her hand gently.

"Your little girl, too, Claire. You needn't worry about her."

"You could look at a child of Edward's and not see his evil in her? Not be reminded of those terrible days?"

"She is your child, Claire. That is enough for me."

Stepping around to face her, he extended his hand in invitation. "Come, introduce us," he coaxed.

Hugging herself tightly, she let him lead her with his eyes, matching him step for step as he walked backwards onto the gravel path into the shrubbery. They'd gone only a short distance when the ones they sought emerged, Annie with the child hoisted on her shoulder. Boldly she approached them, laughing, as the wriggling child gently pommeled the young woman's beaming face and tugged at her apron straps.

Hearing them, Montfort swung round and halted.

Claire placed herself between them. "This is Alice, Lord Montfort," she said with mock formality.

Her eyes moistened as the child reached forward eagerly and offered her father a spray of deep red pomegranate blossoms freshly plucked from the trees where she'd been playing. The rich spicy scent floated around them.

As Montfort bent to accept the gift, Alice's bonnet fell back, exposing a cloud of dark, hyacinthine curls and bright, dark eyes that mirrored his own.

Barely suppressing a gasp, Montfort reached for Claire's hand and firmly entwined his fingers with hers.

They stood that way for a moment, and by mutual assent, they walked without speaking into the garden and disappeared under the sheltering trees. Safe in each other's arms at last, they lost themselves in a kiss.

<<<<>>>>

Acknowledgments

To have my first completed novel, "Daughter of Eve,'" honored as a Daphne du Maurier finalist in the unpublished historical category in 2015 was both encouraging and humbling. It showed me I hadn't wasted my time researching and writing it— and how much reworking needed to be done. I received valuable feedback from the judges for the Kiss of Death chapter, which runs the contest, as well as editors and agents at RWA 2015 in New York and after. As a consequence, the book has received a significant overhaul and a new title, "Memory's Bride."

But it was the day-to-day encouragement from friends and fellow writers that kept me going and finally led me to revisit the novel this year and decide it was worth publishing. Thank you from the bottom of my heart to my fellow members of our writing "Quad"—Heather Heyford, Heidi Hormel and Geri Krotow...

... and to poet/writer/mentor/journalist extraordinaire/friend Tom Squitieri, for reminding me so eloquently of why we write in the first place.

Deepest thanks also to DeLynn Royer for reading a draft of the novel back in its beginnings and asking good questions; to my long-time friend, encourager, book-sharer and travel buddy, Elizabeth Bechtel; and to Barbara Phillips Long, who never tires of discussing the minutiae of history—and historical accuracy—in "historical" novels. I did my best to avoid anachronism in "Memory's Bride," Barbara, but if there's something wrong, I know you'll find it first and tell me gently.

And thank you to book designer Merry Banerji and graphic artist Anjali Banerji for bringing "Memory's Bride" to fruition so beautifully.

I would be remiss if I did not explain how my fascination with Herefordshire, England, came about. Author Phil Rickman's Merrily Watkins series gripped me from the very first volume I happened upon, "The Wine of Angels," several years ago. The novels seamlessly blend crime, folklore, history, contemporary issues and mystical experience with memorable characters, chief among them Herefordshire itself.

The first chance I got, I went to Herefordshire, a place still so remote despite its short train distance from London you can feel like you stepped back centuries. Ancient spirits abide despite motorways, modern housing schemes and 5G.

Though I will never do it the justice that Rickman does, I had to write about Herefordshire at least once. I hope I captured some of its spell for you. And if you like contemporary mystery with an evocative setting and a generous helping of the supernatural, go read Phil Rickman.

And finally, I salute you, Anthony Trollope. Charles Dickens is justly renowned for his indelible, colorful characters and stories that pluck at the heartstrings. Trollope wrote in that great and prolific vein of Victorian realism, with stories just as engrossing but created around complex characters you could imagine taking tea with or see stalking the halls of Parliament. "Memory's Bride" owes no small debt to two Trollope novels: "Miss McKenzie," in which a plain spinster comes into an unexpected inheritance and discovers who her true friends are; and "The Prime Minister," in which the often tedious Miss Emily Wharton pines for a man (over her father's objections) and learns too late he's a cad. Claire Burton was a little luckier on both counts.

About the Author

An award-winning journalist, Decca Price lives in the foothills of Pennsylvania's Allegheny Mountains. Among her passions are Victorian England, travel and cats—especially her two Siamese rascals—and mysteries of all kinds, especially the mysteries that lurk inside every human heart.

The Nancy Drew novel her Great-Aunt Ada sent all the way from California one Christmas ("The Mystery of the Old Clock") put her on the path of other classic mystery writers--Agatha Christie, Dorothy Sayers, Margery Allingham, Daphne DuMaurier, Victoria Holt, Mary Stewart and Pennsylvania's own Margaret Sutton among others. More modern favorites include P.D. James, Ruth Rendell, Barbara Michaels, Minette Walters, Anne Perry, Peter Robinson and Kate Atkinson.

She is a member of Romance Writers of America, Sisters in Crime and Pennwriters. She is available for workshops on craft, writing and productivity. See more at www.deccaprice.com/workshops.

Want to connect with Decca? Sign up for her monthly newsletter to get first looks at upcoming books, free short stories, articles about life in Victorian England, even the occasional recipe! Your email address will never be sold, shared or used for anything else, and you can easily opt out at any time.

Website: https://deccaprice.com/
Facebook: https://www.facebook.com/DeccaPriceBooks
Twitter: https://twitter.com/DeccaPrice
Instagram: https://www.instagram.com/deccaprice/

www.ingramcontent.com/pod-product-compliance
Lightning Source LLC
Chambersburg PA
CBHW060248100726
47907CB00003B/810